THE SEA DEVILS

A Novel By

JIM JOWERS

To: Ens Jon Baron

Best Wishes,

Jim Jowers

10-11-2000

THE UNTOLD STORY OF HEROIC HELO COMBAT SEARCH
AND RESCUE MISSIONS BY U. S. NAVAL AVIATORS

THE

SEA

DEVILS

A Novel By

JIM JOWERS

Publisher
CJH ENTERPRISES
Milton, Florida

Library of Congress Cataloging-in-Publication Data number: 99-072508

1. Novel. CDR. Tom Colby is tasked to lead the Navy helicopter rescue squadron into combat against overwhelming enemy forces and fire-power. Through CDR Colby's leadership and training, the Sea Devil pilots rise to meet the challenge.

Cover and design: "picture this," by Lee & Harriet Tuck

Editors: Stacie Toups and Staff of CJH ENTERPRISES

ISBN 1-890683-03-5

Bulk sales for fund raising activities are available at discount prices
Contact: DRS II ENTERPRISES
6301 Wisteria Drive
Milton, Florida 32570
Telephone (850) 623-2876

Publisher
CJH ENTERPRISES
6064 Mayberry Lane
Milton, Florida 32570

First Printing
April 1999
by
Pace Printing
Pensacola, Florida

Printed in the United States of America

This book is dedicated with deepest love and affection
to my soul mate and wife, Dr. Catherine Jowers.
Her love and faith saw me through the
long months of combat flying.

Also to my brother,
Dr. Will Jowers, who flew Air Force combat
missions in the F-105G Wild Weasel,

and finally to

My brother Sea Devils
and the memory
of
Commander Clyde Lassen, USN
Congressional Medal of Honor winner,
Friend, squadron mate and
One heck of a Hukie Two pilot

PROLOGUE

The Death Angel

NAS Ream Field
Special Ops Area
Imperial Beach, California

Commander Charlie Wiseman sat in the copilot's seat of the Navy SH-3A helicopter and watched Lieutenant (junior grade) Jack Hatchet perform the various maneuvers of his flight check. *The kid's good*, Charlie thought, *he'll make a good plane commander*. Charlie Wiseman's greatest love was flying. He knew without a doubt that he was the best pilot in the squadron. A graduate of the Navy elite test pilot school, he had over 300 flight hours of flight time in the SH-3A helicopter and would soon be flying combat rescue missions. Charlie hated war with as much passion as he loved flying. The Vietnam conflict was not the war his country should jump into with the pretext of stopping the spread of Communism. His Jewish ancestors had been fighting wars for the past six thousand years.

Brushing the thoughts from his mind, Charlie reviewed the notes on his knee pad. Servo failure was the one remaining item for review. The SH-3A was equipped with two hydraulic servo flight control systems, primary and auxiliary. The helicopter could fly with either system disabled, but if both systems failed flight control would be lost.

Jack Hatchet hated servo-off flight with the increased cyclic stick pressure that was required to control flight. Glancing at the control panel he confirmed altitude of 200 feet and speed of 120 knots. For the past few

1

minutes he had smelled the stench of hydraulic fluid. *Probably the sonar winch*, he thought, *it was always leaking*. Then the feedback pressure in the cyclic stick became stronger. He keyed the intercom mike and said, "Commander, I smell hydraulic fluid, and we're getting a strong chatter in the cyclic. Wanna check it out?"

"I got the aircraft," Charlie said and placed his right hand on the cyclic stick. His left hand grabbed the collective lever. The stick tried to jump out of his hand. *Damn, the primary servo's going out*, he thought and turned the aircraft toward NAS Ream Field. He glanced at the instrument panel. The Tacan window showed 24 miles. *We'll never make it to home base. Gotta try for a water landing.*

The helicopter was in a thirty degree left bank when he keyed the mike and said, "Jack, it feels like the primary's going out. I'm gonna try to land on the water. Turn off the primary."

"Primary off," Jack said and pushed the servo switch forward. At that moment the hydraulic fluid level in the servo became too low to control the piston. The forces in the cyclic stick increased a hundredfold and the helicopter continued the roll to the left. Upon reaching the inverted position, the nose fell through and they began to plunge toward the water.

Charlie knew there was only seconds left before the crash. He keyed the radio switch and yelled, "**MAYDAY! MAYDAY! MAYDAY!** Sea Devil Seven-Six on two-seven-zero radial at twenty-four. Lost servos and can't . . . " The radio transmission ended abruptly as the helicopter smashed into the ocean. He felt himself thrown forward as his seat ripped from the cockpit deck and smashed through the windshield. There was a crushing pain, then darkness.

*   *   *

Two airplanes circled the crash scene of Sea Devil 76, a Cessna 310H and a yellow bi-wing Jenny. The death angel, Ensign Michael Colby, USN (deceased), flew the Jenny. Michael knew that the pilot in the Cessna could not see his beautiful airplane. The Jenny was invisible to most earth people. His mission was to pickup up Charlie Wiseman. He glanced down at the ocean and saw Charlie sitting in the white life raft. *Charlie can wait a few minutes*, Michael thought and flew formation on the Cessna. *Just like the Blue Angels,* he smiled. He overlapped wings and moved within six feet of the sleek Cessna.

Michael saw the drop tank that was tucked under the left wing. Pressing a switch on the computer console, he read the display:

ONE HUNDRED POUNDS OF COLUMBIAN COCAINE

Another smile crossed his face as he pushed the laser arm switch on the instrument panel. He aligned the cross-hair sight on the tank and pressed the fire button. A green beam of light flashed from the Jenny and illuminated the tank. It began to glow, then dropped away from the wing of the Cessna. Like a bomb, the tank plunged toward the ocean and splashed into the waves. *Commander Bob's boss is gonna be mighty mad when the plane lands,* Michael thought and continued to fly a tight formation.

Lieutenant Commander Bob Wilson, USNR, was pilot of the Cessna 310H. Circling the crash scene at two-hundred-feet, he switched the radio to Ream Field tower and reported the helicopter crash. He continued to circle until a Kaman H-2 Sea Sprite helicopter approached the area. Then he climbed the Cessna to 2,000 feet and flew east toward the beach.

Michael Colby banked the Jenny away from the Cessna and dove toward the ocean. *Time to pickup Charlie,* he thought and pushed another button on the console. Pontoons began to inflate, and the Jenny became a seaplane. Skimming the top of the waves, he brought the airplane to an abrupt stop beside the pilot in the life raft. Charlie Wiseman waved then climbed up the side of the Jenny and sat in the rear seat.

Michael pushed the throttle to the fire-wall and the little Jenny leaped into the air. He pointed the nose toward Bonita, California. *A quick stop to see brother Tom,* he thought, *gotta warn him about Linda's accident.*

ONE

The Magic White Scarf

Colby Residence
Bonita, California

Lieutenant Commander Tom Colby slept beside the pool in the warm afternoon sun, dreaming about the war. The nightmare details of Lieutenant Don Becker's briefing flooded his mind. A tear trickled down his cheek. Within the next ninety days he knew that he would either be a POW or dead.

A bright, yellow airplane suddenly appeared beside the pool. Large black letters on the fuselage read, **NAVY-ONE**. Tom remembered his father's stories about the bi-wing Jenny, the World War II Navy training airplane, often referred to as the yellow peril. The plane stopped five feet above the apron of the pool and hovered like a helicopter. No sound came from the engine as the long wood propeller sucked water droplets from the air and blew them back across the fabric wings. The plane slowly settled down on the pool apron, and the engine stopped. The pilot climbed from the open cockpit and walked toward Tom. He wore a white flight suit, brown leather flight jacket and a leather helmet with plastic goggles. One end of a white silk scarf was twisted around his neck and tucked inside the flight jacket. The other end fluttered in the Southern California wind.

The passenger in the rear cockpit wore a white flight suit and a white flight helmet. His name was Commander Charles Wiseman, the executive officer of the Sea Devils. He waved at Tom, but something was

4

terribly wrong. Charlie's nose was missing. The pilot removed the leather helmet and ran his hand through the long blonde hair. Tom realized that the pilot was a ghost - his younger brother, Mike. Ensign Michael Colby had been lost at sea 10 years ago during night flight operations from the carrier *Lexington*.

"*Hello, Tommy,*" Michael said.

"Can you hear me, Mike?" Tom asked.

"*I read you five by five, big brother. I'm on a real tight flight plan, so I can only stay for a minute. Had to come by and pick up Charlie. My next passenger is on the USS Concord, in the west Pacific.*"

"Why's Commander Wiseman in your plane?"

"*He's dead, Tommy. I have to stop by Doctor Luke's hospital for a nose job. Then Charlie will be good as new.*"

"Will I be killed in the war, Mike?"

"*Not as long as you wear this,*" Michael said and threw the white scarf in Tom's lap. "*Enjoy Linda, Tommy. The time is short.*"

"**HEY, WAIT A MINUTE!**" Tom yelled as Michael climbed back into the open cockpit of the Jenny. "**IS SOMETHING GONNA HAPPEN TO MY WIFE?**"

"*Some events can be altered, others cannot. That scarf is your connection to the Force. Remember to wear it at all times while you're in Vietnam. Keep the faith, big brother,*" Michael said and pushed the throttle forward. Without making a sound, the yellow airplane streaked into the sky and zoomed toward the west at the speed of light.

*　　*　　*

Jackie Anderson unlatched the gate and walked to the pool carrying two glasses of wine. The squeaking gate woke Tom from his dream. He sat up and clutched the white scarf, then searched the sky for the yellow airplane.

"Hey, Tom!" Jackie said. "Looked out the window and saw you soaking up the sun. So, I thought you would enjoy a glass of wine and some company."

Tom gazed admiringly at his beautiful blonde neighbor in the revealing bikini bathing suit. Taking the glass of wine, he said, "I really do need a glass of wine. I was dreaming about the ghost of my dead brother."

5

"You're too old to believe in ghosts, Tom."

"It was so real, Jackie," Tom said as he rubbed a hand through his black hair. "Maybe I'm getting too old to be thinking about flying combat missions." At thirty-five, he was just entering the prime time for naval aviators. Within two years, he would have command of the Sea Devils. He handed Jackie the white scarf. "Mike brought me this scarf. He said that it would protect me when I'm flying combat missions. He also said something about Linda. God, I hope she's safe from harm in Pensacola."

Jackie draped the white scarf across her lap. "How's Linda's father?" She asked trying to change the subject from ghosts and war.

"He's still in intensive care recovering from the heart attack and a triple by-pass operation. Sure hope he makes a quick recovery so Linda can come home before my ship sails for Vietnam."

"Me too," Jackie said. "How's bachelor life?"

"Really depressing. My squadron leaves for Vietnam in less than a month. We'll be flying combat search and rescue missions. Lieutenant Don Becker's squadron is returning from six months of combat SAR operations. He briefed our pilots this afternoon. They lost thirteen helicopters and forty-nine crewmen in combat. Unless we develop some new tactics, I know that I will be killed or captured in the next three months."

"My God, you're morbid today," Jackie said as she sipped the wine. "What happened to Don's squadron?"

"It was terrible," Tom said as he recalled the scene in the squadron ready room. "Skipper Blackwell rules the Sea Devils with an iron hand. He should've previewed Becker's briefing prior to the meeting. As Becker announced the shocking news of their combat losses I noticed that he was wearing the Purple Heart and Distinguished Flying Cross ribbons, but his gold wings were missing. It was the worst possible thing he could've said to our pilots who're trying to prepare for combat. I stopped Don, and had Bull Walker present the sacred Sea Devil hymn."

"What's the Sea Devil hymn?" Jackie asked.

Tom smiled as he remembered the shocked look on Becker's face. "It's a stupid hymn that never fails to shatter the inflated ego of a naval aviator. Ensign Walker is the senior ensign in our squadron. We call him the Bull Ensign. I made a big production of calling Bull forward and ordering him to bestow the Sea Devil hymn on any officer who visited our

6

squadron wearing the Purple Heart or the Distinguished Flying Cross. Bull ordered the officers to stand and honor Lieutenant Becker as they all sang together: HYMNNNN! HYMNNNN! HYMNNNN! FUCK HIM!"

"That is gross," Jackie smiled and sipped the wine. "I came over to invite you to dinner Friday night to celebrate your birthday. I made reservations at the Hotel Del Coronado. Please say that you'll go," she begged.

"I'd love to, Jackie. However, I promised Tommy that I'd watch his football team clobber the Chula Vista Spartans. The game starts at seven. Will you go with me, and then we'll make it a late dinner?"

Hiding her disappointment, Jackie replied, "I'd love to see Tommy play football. Yes, a late dinner will be fine. I'll change the reservation to ten-thirty. Judy will be out on her date until midnight. Does Tommy have a date for the dance after the game?"

"He probably does," Tom answered, as he sipped the cold wine and relaxed. *Damn, Jackie's a beautiful, sensuous lady,* he thought. The silk scarf was draped across her lap. He bent over and kissed her lips.

Jackie captured his head with her hands and looked into his brown eyes. "Please take me to the spa and make love to me, right now."

Rising, Tom took her hand and walked to the spa. Without a word being spoken they stepped down into the bubbling water. As her hands caressed him, Tom forgot about the war and his fear of dying. He leaned his head against the top of the spa and closed his eyes as the beautiful blonde made love to him. *To the Force, Mike,* he thought as he visualized Michael landing the ancient Jenny on the *USS Concord* to pickup his next passenger. The white scarf was already bringing him good luck.

The Anderson Residence
Bonita, California

Judy Anderson unlocked the front door and called, "Mother, I'm home!" Receiving no response, she quickly walked upstairs and looked out the master bedroom window that overlooked the Colby's backyard and pool. She stood awestruck as she saw her mother making love to Commander Colby. Smiling, she ran and grabbed the camera then began snapping pictures of the sex scenes in the spa.

7

"Tommy will never believe this," Judy said aloud to herself. The film lever would not advance. She realized that she had completed the roll of film. Quickly, she removed the film from the camera and left the house. Closing the front door softly, she released the hand brake and let the Volkswagen roll down the hill. Shifting to second gear she eased out the clutch, just like Tommy had taught her. The powerful little forty horsepower engine roared to life. Well, tonight she was going to teach Tommy something beautiful.

Judy drove to the Telegraph Canyon Shopping Mall and left the film. She thought about Tommy Colby as she walked into the mall. *Would the pictures shock him?* She didn't think so. She hoped that he would be just as turned on as she was while she snapped the pictures. If he would just stop treating her like a sister. She had been in love with him since they moved next door, four years ago. Now, she must find some way to arouse his interest in her. Maybe making love to him was the answer.

19th Hole Club House
Navy Pensacola Golf Course
NAS, Pensacola, Florida

Dr. Paul Thompson, LT, USNR, sat at a table in the 19th Hole Snack Bar and watched Linda Colby in the phone booth. They had played 18 holes of golf, and she won by four strokes. Linda was thirty-five years of age, short and slender with auburn red hair and gray-green eyes. She wore white golf shorts with a matching knit top that revealed firm breasts, pointed and without a hint of sag. Paul liked what he saw.

Linda finished talking to her mother and returned to the table. Paul stood as she reached the table and held her chair. "How's the Admiral feeling this afternoon?" He asked. Paul had performed the triple by-pass surgery on Admiral Bush.

"Just great, Paul!" She said excitedly. "Mother said he was moved from intensive care this afternoon. Isn't that fantastic?"

"Yes, it's a big step. I was kinda expecting it today or I would not have left the hospital."

"Oh Paul, thank you so much for saving Father's life. Mother believes it was an act of God, but I know it was your skilled surgeon's hands. What can I ever do to repay you?"

8

"Linda, you don't owe me anything," he answered looking at his hands. "Maybe it was the surgeon's hands, but I also believe that God had something to do with it. When Penny died from leukemia last year, I lost faith in both God and the surgeon."

"Paul, you should've told me," she said and took his hand. "Penny was your wife, right?"

"Yes, Linda. Penny had beautiful red hair like yours. She was almost as pretty as you are, and she loved life so very much. In fact, you two even smell alike. What's that tantalizing perfume?"

"Opium, my dear," she answered. "Please tell me about Penny."

"She was so very special," Paul answered. He told Linda about the life he had enjoyed with Penny and her love for the Navy. "Penny shared my love for flying and secretly enrolled in a flight school out at the Pensacola Municipal Airport. She soloed before she was hospitalized with leukemia."

"Thanks, Paul," Linda said and squeezed his hand. "I know that Penny was very special to you. Did you worry when she was flying?"

"No, not really," he answered quickly. "I felt that she was capable of doing anything she decided to do. I never thought about her falling out of the sky, or crashing."

"Oh, I wish I had your faith," Linda sighed. "Tom's an experienced aviator, but I'm still anxious when he flies. His squadron's going to Vietnam this month, and I just know that he'll be flying combat missions."

"Hey, take it easy!" Paul said as Linda clutched his hand. "The Tonkin Gulf Incident will probably be resolved before his squadron gets there. President Johnson's campaign promise was not to involve the United States in a land war in South East Asia."

"Oh Paul, do you really think so?"

"Yes, I believe the President will keep his word to the American people," he replied. "Also, my dear, I would really enjoy cooking a special dinner for you tonight at my humble shack on the bay. You can call your mother from my place and tell her that your doctor is taking you out to dinner."

"Thanks, Paul. I'd love to have dinner with you," Linda said. The sun was setting as they walked from the restaurant toward the white Corvette.

9

Lieutenant Paul Thompson's "shack" was a two story, four-bedroom brick house on Pensacola Bay. During dinner of rare steaks, baked potatoes and tossed salad, Linda discovered that Paul was a native Californian. He graduated from Stanford Medical University and accepted a commission in the United States Navy, specializing as a Flight Surgeon.

"What do you miss most about California?" Linda asked as she sipped the wine.

"My hot tub and the nice cool ocean breeze," he replied immediately. "Pensacola's nice, but it's so darn hot and humid in the summer and freezing cold in the winter. Do you miss Florida?"

"Oh, yes! I really missed my parents and hometown friends at first," she murmured, "but after living in San Diego these past four years, I've grown to love California, and I also miss our hot tub. Wish I could get in it now and soak this stiff golf shoulder."

"Do I have a surprise for you, beautiful lady," Paul said as he took her hand and walked across the room to the screened patio. "This is called the Florida room. My first addition to this beautiful home was this genuine California hot tub. The screen cage keeps out the giant mosquitoes."

"Oh Paul, you have so many pleasant surprises! Would you please refill my glass and join me in the tub?"

Paul refilled the glasses and stepped into the tub. "How's the water? Too hot?"

"No, just right," she answered. Time stood still for Linda. The silence in the room was broken only by the sighs of the lovers as their embrace reached the peak of ecstasy. Suddenly the peak was reached and passed.

Two

Death At Sea

Otay High School
Bonita, California

Tommy Colby perspired freely in the 102 degree Santa Ana heat as he threw passes to the crossing ends and running backs. "Okay, Wiseman, relieve Colby and try to get on target," Coach Wallace yelled at his number two quarterback. "That's enough for today, Tommy. Hit the showers and take the afternoon off to rest up for Friday night's game."

"Thanks a lot, Coach," Tommy said.

"If this heatwave doesn't break, our main attack will be the pass with just enough running plays to keep their defense honest," Wallace continued and drank from a can of Coke. "How does the arm feel, Tommy?"

"Feels great, Coach," Tommy answered as he jogged toward the locker room. He was elated to finish football practice early. The hot Santa Ana wind that blew in from the desert was stifling. After his shower, he dressed and drove the Mustang to the mall. He saw Judy's pink Volkswagen pull away from the One-Hour Photo drive-by window. Honking the horn he pulled in beside her, "Hi, Judy! I'm going out to Brown Field to take up Dad's one-seventy-two. Want to ride copilot?"

"Oh, yes! I'd love to," Judy answered as she parked the Volkswagen and got in the Mustang. "Are you ditching football practice, Tommy?"

"Heck no! Coach Wallace wanted to give David Wiseman some practice time," Tommy said as he drove to Brown Field airport. He parked next to a white Cadillac in front of the operations building. "That's

11

Commander Bob Wilson's new Cadillac," he said to Judy. "He must have a charter for the three-ten today."

Lieutenant Commander Robert Wilson, USNR, leaned against the flight counter talking to John Harding, flight clearance official. "Hello, Tommy," he said. "Ditching football practice for a little flight time in the one-seventy-two?"

"No, sir, Commander Bob," Tommy answered. "Coach Wallace gave me the afternoon off. Oh, by the way, this is Judy Anderson. Judy, meet Commander Bob Wilson, the world famous Naval aviator and charter pilot for whale watching."

Wilson reached for Judy's hand and said, "It's always my pleasure to meet a beautiful lady. Please don't tell me that you are flying with this juvenile football star?"

"Good afternoon, Commander Bob," Judy smiled as she gripped his hand. "Yes, Tommy's teaching me how to fly. He's also my best friend."

"Well, little lady, you learn how to fly that little Cessna one-seventy-two, and I'll let you fly a real airplane, my twin-engine Cessna three-ten," Wilson said as he released her hand.

"Oh, I'd love too!" she exclaimed. "I'll be back just as soon as I solo and hold you to that promise." Then she walked into the pilot lounge to wait for Tommy to file the local flight plan.

"Tommy, is Judy your girlfriend?" Wilson asked.

"No, sir! She's just a good friend and next door neighbor. More like the sister I never had," Tommy answered.

"Those are the kind of ladies you have to watch out for, Tommy. We aviators call them the marrying kind. Have you two made love?"

"Jesus Christ, No! Be quiet or Judy will hear you. We haven't even kissed, and besides that, she has a boyfriend."

Wilson unbuttoned his shirt pocket and removed a small package containing a miniature pair of naval aviator gold wings. Placing the wings in Tommy's hand, he said, "These are often called the golden leg-spreaders. If you pin these on Judy, you're guaranteed to get laid. Have a nice flight."

Wilson started toward the flight line, then paused and returned to the flight clearance office. "Oh, by the way, Tommy, I had a telephone installed in my three-ten." He handed Tommy a card with the telephone number. "If you ever need to reach me in the air, don't hesitate to call." Waving to Judy, Wilson turned and walked to the flight line.

Tommy completed the flight plan. He walked Judy to the flight line and buckled her into the right-hand seat. He climbed in the left seat,

12

started the engine and taxied to the warm-up area near the end of the six-thousand foot runway.

Judy was silent, and he glanced to see if she was frightened. He had given her several flight lessons, but today she looked excited and flushed. "Are you okay?" He asked over the roar of the engine.

She nodded and smiled at him. In the minutes that it took for Tommy to complete the engine check-out, she felt something warm and tingly grow inside her. It had started in her belly and spread rapidly and irresistibly down between her legs. When Tommy advanced the throttle briefly to full power, she was gripped by a powerful orgasm. She leaned forward against the restraining shoulder straps and pressed her legs together with all her strength so Tommy would not notice her quivering legs.

Tommy completed the checklist and held short of the active runway, until Brown Field control tower flashed a steady green light clearing them for takeoff. He advanced the throttle to takeoff power and kept the nose wheel on the runway center line. When the Cessna reached seventy miles per hour, he gently eased back on the control stick and the little aircraft gracefully became airborne. Turning right to avoiding flying over Mexico, they climbed toward the San Diego mountains. "Okay Judy, you have control, " Tommy said as he released the yoke and patted her right shoulder.

"I'll try." She took a deep breath and concentrated on the instrument panel. The glow was still there, and she knew it would take very little to set her off again. Soon she had the aircraft trimmed and climbing toward Julian.

NAS Ream Field
Imperial Beach, California

Bob Wilson flew the Cessna 310H just outside the Special Flight Operations area, west of Ream Field. The ocean area from four to twenty-six miles west of the landing field was a special operating area for Navy helicopters to conduct training flights. Civilian aircraft transiting the restricted area were required to be above two thousand feet altitude and have permission from Navy Ream Tower. Wilson was the pilot and sole person aboard the aircraft. He skimmed the waves, thirty feet above the ocean to avoid the San Diego radar.

Minutes before he had taken off from Ensenda, Mexico with one hundred pounds of pure Columbian cocaine nestled in a drop tank, neatly tucked under the left wing. When he reached the 270 degree radial of

Ream Tacan at twenty-six miles, he planned to do a pop-up maneuver to two thousand feet, simulating a helicopter climbing out of the restricted area. Then he would fly to a private landing strip in La Mesa, California where the cocaine would be delivered. There he would load aboard his charter passenger and return for final landing at Brown Field Airport near the Mexican border. This was his fiftieth smuggling flight. The twenty thousand dollar fee would bring his earnings to one million dollars.

The Cessna 310H is a twin-engine, four passenger aircraft. He had equipped the plane with a UHF radio, and a TACAN receiver that gave the pilot a bearing to the field plus a digital readout in miles. Wilson was monitoring Navy Ream Tower frequency and the emergency Guard channel as he heard, "MAYDAY! MAYDAY! MAYDAY! Sea Devil Seven-Six on two-seven-zero radial at twenty-four! Lost primary servos and can't . . ."

Abruptly, the radio transmission stopped. Sea Devil was the call sign of Navy Helicopter Squadron 24. Glancing out at the three o'clock position, Wilson saw the plume of water where the helicopter plunged into the ocean. Switching the frequency, he broadcast, "Sea Devil Base, this is Cessna Five-One-Three, over."

"Cessna Five-One-Three, this is Base, go ahead with your message," the Squadron Duty Officer said.

"Roger base, request name of SDO, please."

Slightly confused, the Duty Officer answered, "This is Lieutenant junior grade Jackson, sir."

Great news, he remembered Richard Jackson as one of his former squadron mates. Keying the mike again, he said, "Hi, Rick. This is Commander Wilson in the three-ten. I have an urgent need to know the flight crew in Sea Devil Seven-Six, over."

"Good evening, Commander Wilson. Sorry sir, that information is confidential."

"DAMMIT TO HELL, RICK! SHUT UP AND LISTEN TO ME!" He yelled into the microphone. "Give me those pilots names right now, or I'll land this damn airplane at Ream and come down and beat the crap out of you! Do you read me, Lieutenant?"

"Sorry, Commander. The pilot of Seven-Six is the Executive Officer, Commander Wiseman. The copilot is Lieutenant junior grade Jack Hatchet, my roommate," he answered timidly.

"Damn! That's a bummer! But, thank God it's not my buddy, Tom, he thought. Keying the mike again, he said, "Thanks Rick, sorry I got mad at you, but Sea Devil Seven-Six just crashed on Ream radial two-

seven-zero at twenty-four miles. I'm circling the area, and there are no survivors. Now, listen very carefully, I have to switch to Ream Tower and call in the crash. You call Skipper Blackwell and report the accident, then forget that this conversation ever happened. Out."

Circling the crash scene at two hundred feet, Wilson switched to Ream tower radio frequency. He keyed the radio mike and announced, "CRASH! CRASH! CRASH! Ream tower, this is Cessna Five-One-Three reporting a helicopter crash, over."

"Cessna Five-One-Three standby. Break - break! All aircraft maintain radio silence, crash report in progress. Go ahead Five-One-Three, over."

"Roger tower, Five-One-Three on Ream two-seven-zero radial at twenty-four miles. Observed Sea Devil Seven-Six impact water at seventeen-twelve local time. The aircraft disintegrated and sank immediately. No sign of survivors. Five-One-Three is a Cessna three-ten charter out of Brown Field. Request you assign the nearest helicopter to relieve me as the on-scene commander, please."

"Roger, Five-One-Three. Break - break! Any Navy helo in Ream Special Ops Area 303, call Ream tower, over."

"Ream tower, this is Clementine Two-Two on the two-six-five radial at twenty miles. H-2 type aircraft, will assume on scene commander, over."

"Clemetine Two-Two, this is Ream tower. You are assigned on scene commander. Break - break. Cessna Five-One-Three, thanks for your assistance and the crash report. Request pilots name, please, over."

Wilson saw the Kaman H-2 Sea Sprite approach the crash scene. Then keying the mike he said, "Ream tower, Five-One-Three has Clemetine Two-Two in sight. Pilots name is Wilson. I spell Wilco-India-Lima-Sugar-October-November."

"Thank you, Captain Wilson. Sorry about your delay. You may resume your charter. You're cleared this frequency. Have a good day, sir. Out."

The promotion from Lieutenant Commander to Captain sounded great. Then he realized that the tower operator was referring to his charter title. In commercial aviation, and sometimes in general aviation, the pilots in command of the aircraft are referred to as Captain. Wilson rapidly climbed the Cessna 310 to two-thousand feet and flew toward La Mesa, California.

Cessna 172
500 feet above Julian Airport

Judy had completed five perfect touch-and-go landings when Tommy said, "Those were good landings. This time make a full stop."

"Okay, boss," Judy replied and lowered the flaps to fifteen degrees. The airport did not have a control tower, and today it was deserted except for Tommy and Judy. After another perfect landing, Judy gently braked the Cessna to a full stop and glanced questionably at Tommy.

"I have the aircraft, Judy," Tommy said. He advanced the throttle and turned the airplane around to the left and taxied back down the runway. When he reached the end of the runway, he spoke casually. "You're going to experience the greatest thrill of your life. Take her back up, circle the field twice and come back down to get me."

He opened the door, stepped down and walked clear of the airplane. For an instant, Judy sat there watching Tommy walk away. Then she advanced the throttle to full open and raced down the grass runway. Breathing slowly to calm her racing heart, she slowly pulled back on the yoke, and the little airplane leaped gracefully into the sky. This was the moment she had dreamed of so often. To soar all alone like the graceful eagle.

Take her back up, circle the field twice, and come back down and get me. Just who the hell does Tommy Colby think he is to order me around like that? Well, I'll show him! Judy pulled the airplane nose 30 degrees above the horizon and performed a perfect wingover. Pointing the nose of the aircraft at Tommy she dived at full power. Fifty feet above the field, Judy recovered from the dive into a graceful wingover to the left and landed on the first hundred feet of the runway. She taxied back to the spot where Tommy was standing, reduced the throttle to idle, set the parking brake and jumped from the airplane. She ran to Tommy and embraced him with a bear hug. **"Thank you! Thank you! Thank you!** She yelled. "God, that was the most fantastic feeling in the world! I never thought you would ever let me solo," she said and kissed him firmly on the lips.

Breaking the embrace, Tommy said, "You won't ever solo again. Why in the hell did you pull a stunt like that?"

"I'm sorry, Tommy," she whispered in his ear. "You're always treating me like your kid sister, ordering me around. It was just something I had to do. I wanted to show you how good I could fly."

"The wingovers were perfect, Judy. But student pilots do not perform acrobatics on their solo flight," he admonished. "Now, come on and fly us back to Brown Field," he said as they walked arm in arm to the idling airplane.

After takeoff, Judy turned to Tommy and said, "I had the most tremendous orgasm as we were taking off from Brown Field."

"You had a what?" He exclaimed as he turned to look into her flushed face. "How? I didn't even see you touch yourself."

"I know, I know! It's the first time I've ever had one like that, but it was so fantastic. It must have been the vibration of the engine. **Oh God! Do I feel great today**!" She yelled.

Removing the package from his pocket, Tommy pinned the minature gold wings on Judy's blouse, above her left breast. "Judy, you have earned your wings," he said then kissed her lightly on the lips.

"Oh God! Be careful, Tommy, or you will start my fireworks again."

"Sorry, Judy. I had no idea that I could make you feel sexy."

Judy unbuckled her seat belt and climbed onto Tommy's lap. "See how quick these golden leg-spreaders work," she whispered in his left ear. "Now, if you'll climb up to five thousand, two hundred, and eighty feet, we'll officially belong to the mile-high club."

"You were listening to Commander Bob," Tommy laughed as he pulled back on the controls and climbed to five-thousand feet. All was well in Tommy Colby's world as he soared with the winds. This was the greatest day of his life, even better than football.

THREE

Deacon Baker's Trap

Brown Field Airport
San Diego, California

Tommy Colby and Judy Anderson sat in the airport snack bar eating cheeseburgers and french fries. Glancing out the front window, Tommy saw two green and white United States Border Patrol vehicles race toward the control tower. "Looks like the Border Patrol is gonna make a big bust," he said to Judy. "I wonder who they're after this time?"

"They probably have a tip on some pilot who is flying in illegal aliens," Judy replied. Two of the agents rushed from the automobiles into the control tower while the other four walked into the hangar. They were dressed in olive green uniforms and carried shotguns and automatic weapons. After several minutes, one of the agents emerged from the hangar and walked toward the snack bar.

"That's Johnny Morgan," Tommy said. "We played football together last year. He'll tell me if the Border Patrol is planning a big bust. Stay here, Judy. I'll be right back," he said and walked to the counter. "Hi, Johnny!" Tommy said as he gripped Morgan's hand. "What's the Border Patrol expecting to happen here at Brown Field that would require six armed agents?"

"Our Sergeant received a phone tip from Ensenada that a twin Cessna is coming in with a big load of cocaine," Morgan replied. "He feels that this bust will put him over the top for promotion to Lieutenant. Actually, he's one of those religious bastards, and I hate to see him promoted to Lieutenant."

"Well, good luck," Tommy said. "We'll finish our dinner and stay out of your way. How do you like working for the Border Patrol?"

"It's fun," Morgan replied. "I'm sure it will be better after I build up some seniority. Now, I have to run errands for the old-timers." He paid for the four cups of coffee and carried them back to the hangar.

Tommy returned to the table and said, "You were right, Judy. They're expecting a plane to land soon with some wetbacks aboard. Please excuse me a minute while I go to the restroom." Walking to the back of the snack bar, Tommy entered the restroom area and quickly dialed the number that Commander Bob Wilson had given him.

"Cessna Three-Ten," Bob answered.

"Hi, Commander Bob. This is Tommy at the airport. Sergeant Richard Baker and five Border Patrol agents are waiting for a twin-engine Cessna to land at Brown Field. Supposedly, this aircraft has a load of drugs from Ensenada. Will you be returning soon from your charter?"

"Yes, Tommy. We found three gray humpback whales and will be returning in approximately thirty minutes. Thanks for the call. Hang around if you can. I would like to talk to you for a few minutes after I land."

"Will do, good-bye," Tommy said as he replaced the receiver and returned to the snack bar.

Three thousand feet above
Chula Vista, California

Bob Wilson had landed at La Mesa and loaded aboard his whale-watching charter. He was returning to the Brown Field Airport when he received Tommy Colby's call. Turning to his passenger, Glenn Carson, he said, "We have a squealer in the Ensenada operations. Do you have your pistol or anything you don't want the border patrol guys to find?"

"No, I'm clean, Bob," Glenn answered. "I left my three-fifty-seven locked in the trunk of the car at Brown. Do you think the Border Patrol guys will tear this beautiful plane apart looking for drugs?"

"Oh yes, I'm sure they will. When they don't find anything, one of the agents will plant a small package of coke or marijuana in the baggage compartment. That will be enough evidence for them to confiscate my airplane."

"Well, it's time to call in our big gun," Glenn suggested. "The Boss pays Commissioner Harold Hansen a substantial retainer to be available for occasions like this. May I use the phone?"

Bob nodded approval while Glenn dialed the telephone. "Hello, this is an emergency. May I please speak to Commissioner Hansen?"

Turning to Wilson, he said, "Bob, I think we should play this thing out at Brown Field and let the Commissioner rescue us after Sergeant Baker makes his big bust. Can you come up with a game plan?"

"Sure, Glenn. That bastard is a deacon in our church, and he's all set to squash me like a cockroach. Leave the plan to me," Bob replied.

"Hello, Commissioner Hansen, this is the Carson Security Patrol," Glenn said into the telephone, giving the code name for the emergency alert signal. "Please hold for an important message."

Handing the telephone to Wilson, he said, "Watch it, Bob. His phones are probably being monitored by the FBI. Be very careful what you say. Your code name is White Courier."

Nodding to Glenn, Bob took the telephone and said, "Hello, Mister Hansen, this is White Courier with Carson Security Patrol."

"Hello, White Courier. What can I do for you?" Commissioner Hansen said.

"Mr. Hansen, I have a very reliable tip that a plane loaded with cocaine will be landing at the Brown Field airport in approximately twenty-five minutes. Does that give you enough time to get some border patrol agents to the airport?"

"Yes, that's sufficient time to gather a task force," Hansen replied. "In fact, I'll personally lead this group. It would be helpful if your security patrol could meet me at Brown Airport."

"We'll be glad to assist you, sir," Bob assured him. "Tell Sergeant Baker that Bob Wilson and Glenn Carson will meet him at Brown Field as soon as possible. Good-bye."

Bob hung up the phone and turned to Glenn, "Well, I hope that the Commissioner is worth all the money the Boss has invested in him. Play it cool, Glenn. Sometimes those Border Patrol guys get trigger happy, so keep your hands in plain sight after we land."

Mexican Border
San Ysidro, California

Harold Hansen's plush office was on the top floor of the Border Patrol building. The sliding glass door opened onto a small balcony and offered a panoramic view of the Pacific Ocean. Captain Jeff Parsons opened the door and rushed into the office. "I have three squad cars and a hand-picked crew standing by downstairs, Mr. Commissioner," he said, out of breath.

"How long will it take for us to get to the Brown Field airport, Jeff?"

"About ten minutes with flashing lights and sirens."

"Okay to use the lights, but no sirens," Hansen said. "We have about five minutes for you to brief me before we leave. Take a seat and tell me something about Sergeant Richard Baker. Do you have him working a drug bust at Brown Field?"

Captain Parsons sat on the rich black leather couch and quickly recalled the Custom 702 file of Sergeant Richard Baker. "No, sir! He's not on an assignment for me. He has been somewhat of a maverick. During the past five years, he made several big drug busts and was promoted to Sergeant. He's a deacon in some Baptist church in Bonita and is commonly referred to as 'Deacon Baker.' Is he in some kind of trouble?"

"Well, I received a complaint that he's harassing an air charter company operating out of Brown Field. He's up there now, waiting for the aircraft to land. I would like to get there about five minutes after he makes the arrest to check out his method of operations. I've had complaints that he plants a small amount of dope when his search turns out negative. Do you know the troops in his squad? Will they level with you about Sergeant Baker?"

"Yes, sir. Those men will not lie to me. I'm looking forward to this little maneuver. I'd just love to bust his ass if he's double dealing."

"Okay, Jeff, let's go. I want you to get to the bottom of this," Hansen said, as he walked Captain Parsons to the elevator.

Landing Pattern
Brown Field Airport

Bob Wilson saw the three Border Patrol cars racing down the 905 connector road to Brown Field. Turning to Glenn Carson, he said, "They'll be here in about five minutes, and I have a green light from the tower. Stand by my friend, things may get a bit rough after we land. Try not to lose your temper, and we'll have our revenge."

On the downwind leg, Bob lowered the landing gear and positioned the flaps to 20 degrees. When the approach end of the runway was even with his left wing tip, he reduced the throttles to idle and flew the standard Navy approach. He greased the Cessna 310 to a smooth landing on the first 100 feet of runway 27 and turned off at the first taxi intersection. As he taxied to the large ramp area in front of the operations building, a steady red spot light shinning from the control tower focused on the cockpit. He braked the Cessna to an immediate stop and said, "Get ready, Glenn! Here come the Green Berets."

Two green and white Border Patrol automobiles sped from the hangar toward the idling aircraft. Bob cut the ignition to the engines and opened the cabin door as the first car screeched to a stop in front of the airplane while the other circled around to block the rear.

Sergeant Baker opened the passenger door of the automobile in front of the aircraft and spoke through the loud speaker of the radio unit, **"EXIT FROM THE AIRCRAFT WITH YOUR HANDS ON TOP OF YOUR HEAD! COME ON, MOVE IT!"**

Bob walked down the steps of the ramp, followed closely by Glenn. "Good afternoon, Richard, what in the world is wrong?" Bob asked.

"SHUT UP! AND STOP RIGHT THERE. OKAY, MEN, CUFF AND FRISK THEM," Baker ordered.

Tommy and Judy watched from the snack bar as two Border Patrol agents moved in behind Bob and Glenn and quickly snapped on handcuffs and patted them all over. **"Sergeant, they're not armed!"** The agent yelled to Baker.

"Okay, men, search the plane," Baker ordered as he left the patrol car and walked toward Bob.

"What's going on, Richard?" Bob asked. "There's no reason to treat us like criminals."

"Listen, Wilson, I know all about your dope flights from Ensenada. It will save us all a lot of time if you tell us where the cocaine's stashed."

"I can assure you that there has never been any cocaine in my airplane," Bob replied sharply. "I was on a legitimate charter taking Mr. Glenn Carson on a whale-watching flight. Now, I demand that you release us immediately and apologize to my customer."

"You're in no position to demand a damn thing, Wilson. In fact, you make me want to puke," Baker said as he backhanded Bob in the face.

Rolling with the blow, Bob fell to the left and sprawled on his back on the concrete ramp, giving the impression that the blow was more severe than it actually was. **"The plane is clean, Sergeant!"** An agent yelled from the door of the airplane.

"SEARCH IT AGAIN!" Baker yelled at the agent. "And keep searching until you find something." Turning to Bob, he said, "Okay, Wilson, get off your ass and on your feet."

"You can go straight to hell, Baker," Bob replied with a smile as he saw three automobiles approaching with flashing lights. "Here come more reinforcements, Baker. How many planeloads of cocaine are you expecting to land here?"

Sergeant Baker's expression changed to a frown as he saw Captain Jeff Parsons and Commissioner Hansen emerge from the lead patrol car. *How in the hell did they find out about this bust,* he wondered.

"What's the situation, Baker?" Captain Parsons demanded as he approached the group. "Why's this civilian laying on the deck bleeding? Did he resist arrest?"

"No, I did not resist arrest, Captain," Bob answered for Baker as he climbed to his feet. "My name's Captain Bob Wilson, and I was on a perfectly legal whale-watching charter with my customer, Mr. Glenn Carson."

"**SHUT UP, WILSON!**" Baker yelled. "Captain Parsons, I received a tip from my Ensenada source that Wilson left there about an hour ago with one hundred pounds of cocaine."

"That's quite a story, Sergeant," Commissioner Hansen said as he joined the group. "We received a similar tip that a Mr. Williams was flying in a load of cocaine in a Cessna 172. Are you sure your source gave you the right name and type of airplane?"

"Jorge has never been wrong before, Mr. Commissioner," Baker answered. "Anyway, we did find a small bag of cocaine in the plane. That's enough evidence for us to arrest these two and impound the plane."

Hansen looked at Bob and Glenn. "Sergeant, this man is bleeding," he said as he noticed Bob's bloody nose. "Remove those handcuffs immediately and give him first aid." Two agents rushed to remove the handcuffs. Once his hands were free, Bob removed the handkerchief from his back pocket and applied pressure to his nose.

"Sergeant Baker, did you strike Captain Wilson?" Hansen asked.

"Yes sir, but he asked for it, Mr. Commissioner," Baker replied in a low voice.

While Hansen was talking to Sergeant Baker, four of Captain Parsons agents moved in close behind Baker. When Hansen nodded his head, they quickly restrained and handcuffed him. Then removed his revolver and gave it to Captain Parsons.

"What in the hell is going on?" Baker demanded.

"**Sergeant Baker, you're under arrest!**" Hansen yelled. Then, regaining his composure, he turned to Bob and Glenn. "Gentlemen, please accept the apologies of the agency for this incident. Captain Wilson, we'll all turn our backs if you would like to take a swing at Baker's nose." Turning to face the Border Patrol agents, Hansen ordered in a military command voice, "**TROOP DETAIL, ABOUT-FACE!**" All of the agents executed a smart about-face. The two agents holding Baker's arms turned to face to the rear, but still held his arms firmly.

Bob walked forward and stopped two feet from Baker. Resisting the urge to punch his nose flat, instead he said, "Mr. Commissioner and agents please turn back around." After they faced the front, Bob said, "Gentlemen, I'm truly shocked that American citizens can be treated like criminals by the policing force that is suppose to be protecting us." Turning to Hansen, he said, "I'm a Naval aviator and a Commissioned Officer in the United States Navy. I took an oath of office to support and defend the Constitution of the United States of America against all enemies, foreign and domestic, and to obey the orders of the President of the United States and all officers appointed over me. It would be a violation of my oath as an officer and against my ethics as a gentleman to strike an enlisted person of the military service or a Federal Agency. Mr. Carson and I accept your apology. That's all I have to say."

"Well, thank you, Captain Wilson, Mr. Carson," Hansen said as he shook hands with each of them. "Now, would the agent who found the cocaine on the airplane please step forward."

Morgan stepped forward and handed the small bag of cocaine to Hansen. "My name's John Morgan, sir."

"Do you know how cocaine got on the airplane?" Hansen asked.

"Yes, sir! Sergeant Baker gave it to me. He told me to place it under one of the passenger seats if we couldn't find the stuff that was supposed to be on the plane."

"Can any of you troopers verify John's testimony?" Hansen asked.

Three of the agents raised their hands. "Okay, that's all I need to know. I'll expect a full report turned into Captain Parsons as soon as possible."

"Mr. Hansen, are we free to go?" Bob asked. "On the way back from whale-watching we witnessed the crash of one of my squadron helicopters. I'd like to help search for any survivors or try to locate their bodies."

"Oh, my God! I'm sorry that we detained you so long. Yes, you both are free to go. I'll need a statement. Please come by my office later in the week at your convenience," he said and handed them his business card.

"Good night, Commissioner," Bob said as he shook hands again. Turning to Carson, he said, "Come on, Glenn, I'll buy you a quick cup of coffee." As they approached the coffee shop, Bob turned to Carson and asked, "Will you please brief the boss on the Jorge situation?"

24

"After tonight, Jorge will cease to exist," Glenn assured him.

Bob spotted Tommy and Judy in a booth near the front of the coffee shop. "Glenn Carson, meet Tommy Colby and his beautiful girl-friend, Judy Anderson. Tommy and Judy, this is my friend, Glenn."

Glenn shook hands with Judy first and then Tommy. "Pleased to meet you both. Did you enjoy the little show that Captain Wilson orchestrated out on the parking ramp?"

"We were kinda shook up when the fat Sergeant knocked Commander Bob on his butt," Tommy replied. "Did they think you were flying in a load of wetbacks?"

"No, they had us confused with another airplane. Well, I must run. Nice meeting you kids. Good-bye, Captain Wilson. I hope our flight next week is this exciting!" He said as he walked out to his car.

As Glenn left the coffee shop, Judy said, "Commander Bob, I soloed today, and now I'm ready to fly your Cessna three-ten."

"That's fantastic, Judy! I'm proud of you and promise you can fly my plane when we get it all put back together. Those Border Partol agents kinda messed it up a little looking for some non-existent wetbacks."

Turning to Tommy, he said, "On our flight back from whale-watching, I saw a helicopter crash into the ocean. The flight crew was Commander Charlie Wiseman, Lieutenant (junior grade) Jack Hatchet and probably a sonar operator."

"Did anyone get out?" Tommy asked hopefully.

"No way, Tommy. Commander Wiseman got off a radio call about losing servo control, and then I saw the crash. I circled the scene for ten minutes and did not see any survivors. Then Clementine Two-Two took over the search."

"What a bummer!" Tommy said. "This is gonna to be tough on my buddy, David. Do you think they've been notified yet, Commander Bob?"

"Yes, I'm confident that Skipper Blackwell has notified the family by this time. Well, I think I'll drive out to the squadron and see if there's anything I can do to help. Good night, you two."

"Good night, Commander Bob," they said in unison as he walked from the coffee bar.

"Tommy, please drive me back to the mall to get the Volkswagen," Judy said. "Then I think you should go by and visit with David. I'm sure that he needs your support now." Arm in arm, they walked out to his Mustang in the parking lot.

FOUR

Farewell Toast

HS-24 Squadron
NAS, Ream Field
Imperial Beach, California

Lieutenant Commander Bob Wilson parked the Cadillac and walked into the squadron duty office where a crowd of aviators huddled around the radio. Two helicopters were searching the crash area. Lieutenant Commander Tom Colby circled SD-71 in a 200 feet orbit, while Ensign Bill Walker hovered SD-70 over crash debris. Keying the transmit switch, Tom said, "Sea Devil Base, this is Seven-One, over."

"Go ahead, Seven-One," Lieutenant (junior grade) Richard Jackson answered.

"Let me talk to the Skipper."

"Sorry, Commander, the Skipper drove out to the Wiseman residence."

"Okay, maybe it'll work out better this way. Bull just hoisted Commander Wiseman's body aboard Seven-Zero. He's enroute to Ream Field at this time. Call the Skipper and tell him that we've recovered Commander Wiseman's body. Don't speak to anyone but the Skipper. He'll know what to do, over."

"Yes, sir. I have the Skipper on the phone now. Good hunting, out."

Commander Wiseman's residence
Bonita, California

Commander Joseph Blackwell finished talking with the squadron duty officer and replaced the receiver on the telephone. "Good news, Sarah!" He said. "We just recovered Charlie's body."

"Oh, thank God," Sarah whispered. "I was afraid that my Charlie would be in that water grave forever. Joe, I want to go see him now, please."

"That might not be wise, Sarah," he cautioned. "Let me look at his body first, then I promise you can see him, okay?"

"Sure, I understand. This has been such a shock, but I'm relieved that Charlie's body was recovered. Please fix me one of your famous bourbon drinks."

Joe walked to the wet bar and mixed two drinks. He sat beside Sarah on the couch and said, "Sarah, please join me in a toast. To absent friends, and the men who wear the gold wings."

"I'll drink to that," Sarah said. "To the men who wear the wings of gold. May God always protect them and bring them home safely." She took a long drink and sighed, "Oh, I needed that."

The doorbell rang, then Tommy Colby opened the unlocked door and walked inside. "Hello, Mrs. Wiseman. Oh, hi Skipper," Tommy said as he walked into the living room. "Judy Anderson and I went flying in the one-seventy-two out at Brown Field. We saw Commander Bob Wilson. He was flying the three-ten just outside the special ops area and saw Commander Wiseman's crash."

David Wiseman had heard the doorbell and was walking down the stairs just as Tommy entered the living room. "David, please get Tommy and yourself a soft drink from the refrigerator," Sarah said.

"Tommy, what did Bob Wilson say about the crash?" Joe asked.

"Well, Skipper, he heard a mayday broadcast from Sea Devil Seven-Six announcing that they had lost servos and were going in, then he saw the crash."

"That's just like Charlie," Joe said. "To the very end he was trying to tell us what caused the crash."

27

"Yes, Charlie was an exceptional Naval aviator," Sarah said, "but Joe, I thought the helicopter has two servo systems and can fly with either one turned off."

"Yes, the H-3 has a primary and and auxiliary servo that operate the flight controls," Joe said. "Charlie must have lost the primary first, and shortly thereafter lost the auxiliary. Sarah, it has never happened before, but if both servo systems are inoperative, it's impossible to fly the bird." Then, turning to David Wiseman, he said, "David, the squadron just called and said that your father's body was recovered. I need to go back out to the squadron and take care of a few things. You and Tommy keep your mother company until some of the squadron wives get here, please."

"Yes, sir! We'll do that, Skipper," Tommy answered for David. "Commander Bob was going back to the squadron and wanted to talk to you."

"Thanks, Tommy," Joe said. Then turning to Sarah, he asked, "Where do you want me to take Charlie's body?"

"Oh, my God! I just never thought this would happen," she sighed. Then collecting her thoughts she said, "Take Charlie to Goldstein's Mortuary and tell them that I would like the funeral service at the Little Chapel of the Roses and burial at the Glen Abbey cemetery."

"Will do, Sarah. Good night, all."

As he walked to the door he heard Tommy say, "David, after I left football practice today? I took Judy up in Dad's one-seventy-two, and she soloed. She circled the field at Julian once, then dived bombed me!"

"Far out, man! I wish I could've seen that," David laughed.

The next generation of Naval aviators, Joe thought, as he closed the front door and walked to his Cadillac for the drive back to Ream Field. "Charlie, I'm going to miss you," he said aloud. "Now where in the hell am I going to find an executive officer to replace you in the next three weeks?"

Navy Dispensary
NAS, Ream Field
Imperial Beach, California

Night had descended by the time Joe reached the main gate of Ream Field. Instead of turning right to the squadron, he turned left on Kaman Road and drove to the Navy Dispensary. Just as he expected, half of the squadron officers had accompanied the ambulance from the heliport to the dispensary and were milling around the parking lot and waiting room while the doctor completed the examination of Commander Wiseman's body. Joe walked to the nurse's station and spoke to the nurse on duty.

"Oh, good evening, Commander Blackwell. Dr. Cook wants you to join him in the observation room," nurse Trudy Wood said and led him down the passageway.

Commander Cook answered Trudy's knock at the observation room door. "Hi, Joe, come on in," he said to Blackwell. "Thanks, Trudy."

Joe stared at Commander Wiseman's body on the operating table. "Jesus Christ, doc! There's no way in hell that Sarah can see Charlie looking like this."

"I disagree with you, Joe. Sarah needs to see Charlie, to assure herself that it's really him that we're burying. Actually, except for the missing nose, his body is in good shape." Handing Joe a small medicinal bottle of bourbon, he said, "Drink this! It'll make you feel better." As Joe drank the bourbon, there was another knock at the door. Frowning, Dr. Cook opened the door. Standing in the hallway beside Nurse Wood was Sarah Wiseman, Lieutenant Commander Tom Colby and Lieutenant Commander Bob Wilson.

"Sorry for the interruption, Dr. Cook, but Mrs. Wiseman insists that you let her in," Trudy said.

"It's okay, Trudy," he said and stepped aside to usher them into the room. Taking Sarah by the arm, he said, "Come and take a look at Charlie."

Wiseman's body was covered from the neck down with a white sheet. Gazing lovingly at the corpse, Sarah said, "Oh, thank God he's all together. I was so afraid that his body would be torn apart."

"Sarah, the human body is tough, " Dr. Cook said. "It must have been a severe crash because Charlie's seat was ripped from the mountings in the cockpit deck, and he was thrown through the windshield. That must have been when he lost his nose. One side of the Mae West inflated and kept his body afloat until Bull found him. The copilot's and sonarman's bodies are probably still inside the aircraft."

"Could I have a few minutes alone with Charlie?" Sarah asked.

29

"Why, certainly," Dr. Cook replied. "Come, fellows," he said as he ushered them out of the observation room and closed the door.

Sarah placed her hand on his forehead and brushed a strand of Charlie's black hair in place. His body smelled like kerosene. In a soft voice, she spoke to him, "Charlie, it will not be easy to get through the funeral and the readjustment to life without you by my side, but I'll do my best. I have worried about this moment through the past twenty years of your flying career. Now, it's a reality, and I must live through it." Then she pulled the sheet up and covered his head. Confidently, she opened the door and addressed the group of officers in the hallway. Turning to Joe, she said, "Skipper, I'd like to buy the officers a round of drinks at the club, if that's okay with you."

"Sure, Sarah," Joe replied.

Turning to Dr. Cook, she said, "Can you join us?"

"I'd love to Sarah, but the San Diego coroner is due here any minute to issue the death certificate, and I must be here for that. Maybe I can join you all at the club later."

"Thanks, Dr. Cook," she said as she led the group of aviators out of the dispensary and walked across the street to the Officer's Club. Steward Pinky Jardine was surprised when Mrs. Wiseman and thirty-two aviators walked into the bar. Quickly tables were rearranged in a long table and everyone was seated.

Pinky walked to the head of the table where Commander Blackwell sat with Sarah Wiseman. "What would the lady like to drink?" he asked in a soft Creole voice.

"May I order?" Joe asked Sarah.

"Oh yes, please order anything you like," she replied.

"Pinky, bring us pitchers of draft beer, and pour each glass half full," he said.

"Yes sir, you got it," Pinky said as he hurried to fill the order. Several of the junior officers volunteered to help Pinky fill the mugs.

Joe rose from his chair and addressed the group, "Gentlemen, I propose a toast to Commander Charles Wiseman. One hell of an aviator, father and friend. May he rest in peace." As one, the group stood and raised the beer mugs in a salute and drank the beer. Placing the empty mugs on the table, they started to refill them half full again.

Sarah had sat quietly through the ritual not touching the mug of beer in front of her. Then she stood and raised her mug, "Skipper Blackwell, I propose a toast to the Sea Devil Squadron. May you have many victories and always fly home safely." Raising the mug to her lips, she emptied it without stopping. The room erupted in applause, and Pinky reached to refill her mug. "No, no more for me. You gentlemen carry on with the party. It has been a very trying day, and I'm very tired. Please excuse me."

"Take over, Tom," Joe said to Colby as he escorted Sarah from the bar.

Once outside in the fresh air, she turned to Joe and kissed him on the cheek. "Joe, will you please take me by your beach cottage for a few minutes? I just need to walk on the beach and be held for a few minutes."

"Sure thing, Sarah," he answered as he led her toward the Cadillac. He felt a stirring in his groin. Hell, she couldn't be thinking about that, he argued with himself. He started the Cadillac and drove toward his apartment in Imperial Beach.

FIVE

The Flying C Ranch

Pennsylvania Avenue
Washington, D.C.

The black Rolls-Royce moved slowly down Pennsylvania Avenue toward the White House. In addition to the Virginia license plates, a small placard on the front bumper bore two chrome five-pointed stars of a Rear Admiral. The Rolls was the personal automobile of Rear Admiral Thomas Colby, USN. Margaret Colby sat in the front seat beside the uniformed chauffeur, Samuel Watson. She detested riding in the back seat. "We'll be in the White House for a few minutes, Samuel," Margaret said, "then I must go by the hospital to see Doctor Woods."

"Yes, ma'am," Samuel answered. He had been the Colby's butler and chauffeur for thirty-eight years. He had seriously considering retiring until Margaret confided in him that she had cancer. "Will you have to stay at the hospital, ma'am?"

"No, Samuel, at least not for awhile. I'm going to deliver Admiral Colby's latest novel to the President, negotiate with him on some delicate problems, and convince him how nice it would be to fly to California to see a high school football game."

Watson turned into the White House driveway and stopped at the gate as the black Marine sentry saluted. "Good afternoon, ma'am," the sentry said and continued, "That's the most beautiful car I've ever seen. Is it a nineteen sixty-four model?"

"Yes, sentry," Margaret replied. "This is Admiral Colby's motor car, but Samuel and I get to use it occasionally." Margaret handed the sentry a small identification card that bore her picture with two small silver stars in the top right corner.

The sentry recognized the White House pass immediately as he read the name, Margaret Anne Colby. He returned the card to Margaret and saluted as he said, "Welcome to the White House, Mrs. Colby." Then to Samuel, he said, "You may continue, driver."

"Thank you, sir! And you all have a nice day," Samuel said and returned the sentry's salute as he drove down the driveway.

"Samuel, you should not salute the Marine sentry," Margaret said.

"Oh, I know ma'am, but I just wanted to put that uppity nigger in his place. You heard him call this beautiful automobile a car." Stopping the Rolls in front of the White House, Samuel hurried around to open the door for Margaret.

"Samuel, please do not give the Secret Service any trouble," she said, "and please park the motor car where they direct you."

"Good afternoon, Mrs. Colby," the doorman said as he walked out to meet them. "Samuel, the Rolls can stay right where it's parked." Then offering his arm to Margaret, he turned to Watson, "Come on inside, Sammy. We have a cute little maid who might give an old Negro chauffeur a cup of coffee."

The Oval Office
The White House
Washington, D.C.

Lyndon Baines Johnson sat at his desk and thought about his 2 o'clock appointment with Margaret Colby. Margaret was the wife of Rear Admiral Thomas Colby, USN. He had known Thomas and Margaret for twenty years and was an occasional guest at their Flying C Ranch in Fairfax, Virginia. He could not imagine what favor she could want from him. He knew that she was suffering from terminal cancer. Margaret's request had been very simple. This meeting was to be private and was classified top secret. The President's secretary escorted Margaret into the Oval Office then left and quietly closed the door.

"Lyndon, you are so handsome," Margaret said as she walked across the Oval Office and offered her gloved hand. Then, changing her mind, she kissed the President of the United States firmly on his cheek. "You are such a distinguished President, and I can see why the ladies have such a tough time resisting your charms."

"Thanks, Margaret. As always you're like a breath of fresh air to this ancient place." Taking her arm, he walked her to the small couch near his desk. "Would you like a cup of tea?"

"Yes, please."

The President picked up the blue telephone and said, "The usual hot tea for Mrs. Colby," then continued, "I think I'll have the same."

The tea was served by a white uniformed steward. "Good afternoon, Mrs. Colby. We're so pleased to have you as our guest today," the steward said. "I hope the tea meets with your approval."

"You are so gracious as always, Willie," Margaret said. "I am glad the President has finally found a chef that can brew a cup of tea."

Steward Willie Cunningham was a holdover from the Kennedy staff, and he liked the country ways of the new President. However, it was always special to serve an English lady like Mrs. Colby. He remembered that she enjoyed brandy with her tea. He placed a small decanter of brandy on the table and rolled the tea cart from the Oval Office. Margaret reached for the brandy and poured approximately one ounce into each of the steaming cups. "Will one shot be enough, Lyndon?"

"Yes, that's fine. Now what do you need from me?"

"Lyndon, I am truly disappointed in you," she said as she removed a small package from her Gucci bag and handed it to him. "It's not like you at all to act so careless. Promise that you will never let this happen again."

The package contained twenty-four five by seven photographs of the President of the United States and a well-endowed blonde woman. Slowly he looked at each photograph. "How in the hell did you get these, Margaret?" He whispered.

"Now Lyndon, you know that I cannot reveal my sources anymore than I would expect you could," she answered. "I came across these quite by chance. I do not think it was a blackmail scheme; rather a gathering of information that could be used against you at a later time. The photographer assured me that there are no more copies. You will notice that the negatives are in the envelope."

"How much did this cost, Margaret?"

"Lyndon, it's not a matter of cost," she scolded. "I did what was necessary to acquire these. I don't want to hear another word about it." Margaret had paid the photographer five thousand dollars for the photographs and negatives.

"Well, sweetheart, I sure do appreciate your help. If there is anything I can ever do for you, all you have to do is ask."

"I need two small favors," Margaret said. "I'd like for you to consider promoting Thomas to Vice Admiral and give him command of the Seventh Fleet. He wants to get in this little war you and Jack Kennedy started. You know that he would do whatever you and the Joint Chiefs asked of the fleet. Please overlook the fact that he is a Republican."

"Okay, Margaret, I'll talk to the Chief of Naval Operations about it. I don't see any problem with promoting Thomas to Vice Admiral. He's certainly qualified, and I agree with you that he is an excellent choice to command the Seventh Fleet. Now what is the second favor you need?"

"This will be fun, Lyndon. I want you to come to a football game in San Diego, California with Thomas and me this Friday night. My grandson, Tommy, is the star quarterback at his school. This may be the last time I get to see him play."

"Well, I guess we could do that," he said. "Lady Bird and the girls are in Texas on a shopping spree. I just hate to have to drag so dang many people along when I want to go someplace."

"Lyndon, you're a darling," she smiled. "Tom junior has a five bedroom house that will accommodate most of our party. Now for the part you will like best of all. Their next-door neighbor, Jackie Anderson, is a widow. She has a small five acre ranch next to Tom and Linda. By the way, this is a picture of Jackie. If you are real nice to her, she may let you ride one of her horses."

Taking the small picture of Jackie Anderson from Margaret, he said, "She sure is a pretty little filly, Margaret. Okay, we have a deal. I'll call Admiral Colby and invite you all to fly out with me on Air Force One."

"Thank you, Lyndon! You have made me so happy," she said and kissed his cheek.

"My thanks to you, Margaret, for getting me out of a messy situation," he said and walked her to the door. "Give my regards to Admiral Woods and come back and have tea with me again, please."

"I almost forgot to tell you, Lyndon. Do you remember Admiral Bush, Tom juniors father-in-law?"

"Yes, Margaret, I've heard a few of his hellfire and damnation sermons," the President replied. "How's he adjusting to retired life? Still preaching?"

"Admiral Bush had a heart attack about a week ago while playing golf at the Navy Pensacola golf course. As you may remember, the golf course borders the Naval Hospital, and his partners rushed him to emergency in the golf cart. The doctors performed a triple by-pass and saved his life. I talked to Linda last night. She thinks her father will be coming out of critical care in a day or two. She plans to fly back to San Diego on Friday if his recovery continues to improve."

"Let me handle it, Margaret," the President insisted. "My aide, Captain John Schmidt, will take care of the details. I feel sure that he can find one of those little Navy T-39's or a Lear Jet that can fly Linda to San Diego. Please call Linda and tell her that she can take two or three of her friends along if she'd like."

"Thank you, Lyndon. You've made me so happy!" Then removing another package from her purse she said, "Thomas asked me to give you a copy of his latest western novel. This is his twenty-third novel about the heroics of Texas Ranger John Rider and his exploits with the southern belles and ruthless outlaws."

"I love to read his books, Margaret. Admiral Colby is an excellent writer," the President said as he accepted the book. "Has he considered retiring from the Navy and writing full time?"

"No Lyndon! Writing is his hobby, but the Navy is his life. Enjoy the book. We'll be ready to fly to San Diego on Thursday," she said and walked out of the Oval Office.

Margaret Colby sat on the couch in Admiral Arthur Woods' office and sipped a cup of tea. For the past hour, doctors and medical technicians had drawn blood and conducted a series of x-rays. As Margaret patiently waited for the report from Doctor Woods, she remembered the day five years ago when her best friend, Bonnie Woods, was killed in an accident on the Beltway. After six months of mourning, Arthur had confided in her that he was impotent. His dinner with a two-time divorcee had ended in disaster when he allowed her to lure him into the bedroom. Despite all her attempts, his manhood remained limp. Finally, Arthur had dressed and fled to the sanctuary of his Washington townhouse.

Two weeks later Captain Thomas Colby had received orders as Commanding Officer of the aircraft carrier *USS Forrestal*, home ported in Norfolk, Virginia. Margaret felt this was her opportunity to help her dear friend. She invited Arthur out to dinner at the Flying C and remembered the conversation almost as if it were yesterday.

"Arthur, I loved Bonnie like a sister. We sometimes talked about situations like this," she lied. "Bonnie made me promise that I would take care of you if this ever happened."

"That sounds like something Bonnie would try to get you to do," he answered. "I've been so worried about your life-threatening cancer, and dear Bonnie's life was snuffed out by that drunk bastard! It's so difficult to accept."

"Oh, you Yanks! You make it sound like something distasteful to me. Actually, I've had a crush on you for years, and I fully intend to keep my promise to dear Bonnie," she said firmly. Then she smiled as she said, "Arthur, this is going to be fun. We have a role reversal where I will play doctor, and you will be my patient. Will you be a good boy and obey the doctor's orders?"

"Yes, Margaret. I'll try, and I hope you are a better doctor to me than I've been to you," he answered sadly. Margaret had hired the best sex therapist available to instruct her on the techniques and treatment that she applied to Arthur. At first it was just touching, stroking, talking and sleeping together without threat of performance on Arthur's part. She worried about Arthur as she softly stroked his manhood, and there was no response.

It was the black garter belt and lacy French panties that finally aroused Arthur's manhood Margaret remembered and smiled. That beautiful erection that she held and kissed. Then straddling Arthur, she brought him to an exploding climax.

"Well, I see you're in a cheerful mood," Arthur said and walked into the room.

"I was just remembering the magic in that black garter belt and fancy lace panties," Margaret said as she rose and kissed his cheek.

"You know that's a lot of bull," he snorted. "The magic was in the sexy wench wearing the fancy panties and black garter belt."

"So, how is the medical condition of this sexy wench?" She asked as they sat together on the couch.

"Not good, my dear. Your white blood cell count is beginning to rise. That's one sign that you may be coming out of remission."

"As my grandson, Tommy, would say 'what a bummer!' Oh Arthur, I do want so much to get well. Please tell me how much longer I have to live," she begged.

"Margaret, I've never lied to you," he answered. "If you come out of full remission, we could have six months, maybe less."

"Would it be okay if I flew to San Diego this weekend? I talked the President into flying us to San Diego on Air Force One this weekend to watch Tommy play football."

"Margaret, you never cease to amaze me," he answered. "Yes, you may fly anywhere you wish. May be good therapy for you seeing your grandson play football. Does he still plan to be a doctor, or has he changed his goal to pro football?"

"No, Tommy has not changed his mind. He loves football, but he still wants to go to Stanford and be a doctor. I established a trust that will pay for all his expenses."

"Now that does not surprise me a bit, but how in the hell did you get Lyndon interested in flying to San Diego to see a football game?"

"Oh, I arranged a blind date for him with a cute little blonde widow."

38

"I might've known," he said. "I'm worried though. Your influence with the Commander-in-Chief will probably get Thomas promoted to Vice Admiral, and then he'll be senior to me."

"My darling, I assure you that I have very little influence with the President about military matters. But if I can get Thomas three stars, then I promise to get you three also," she said and kissed him. "Now, I must find Samuel and get back to the ranch. I would love to have dinner with you after we return from San Diego."

"It's a date," Arthur said as he walked her to the door. "Have a nice trip and remember to get your rest. You're a very special lady, Margaret Colby."

The Colby Residence
Flying C Ranch
Fairfax County, Virginia

Margaret loved the Flying C Ranch. It was their home when Thomas was stationed in the Washington area. She often elected to live there while he was on sea duty tours. The ranch had been in the Colby family for three generations. Admiral Colby's Texas father had purchased several adjoining foreclosed farms in Fairfax County while he was stationed at the Washington Naval Yard in 1931 during the Great Depression. Lieutenant Colby had combined the acreage and named it The Colby Ranch.

Admiral Colby's father had retired from the Navy in 1951 with the rank of Rear Admiral and moved back to his native Texas after deeding the ranch to Thomas and Margaret. Thomas had added a landing strip with a hangar and changed the name to the Flying C Ranch. There were twelve rooms in the ranch house and eight in the guest house. There was also a bunkhouse for the ranch foreman and the cowboys who rode herd on the Black Angus cows.

Margaret settled herself on the couch in front of the fireplace and sipped the Jack Daniel's whiskey that Samuel had brought her as soon as they had returned from the hospital. It was chilly, and the fire was a great comfort. She struggled to compose herself before Thomas came home from the Pentagon. She had decided not to tell Thomas that Dr. Woods felt her cancer was coming out of remission until after their San Diego trip.

Hearing the car turn into the driveway, she rose and went to meet her husband. She opened the door and waved as Admiral Colby, wearing a civilian suit, emerged from the back seat of the white U. S. Navy sedan.

"I won't need the wheels tonight, Jones," he said to the driver. "I have to go up to the Hill early in the morning. Please pick me up at five." Clutching his briefcase in his left hand, he walked toward the ranch house as Seaman Jones backed the Chevrolet down the driveway for the return trip to the Pentagon. "Good evening, darling," he kissed Margaret. "Is there time for a martini before dinner?"

"Yes, Thomas," she answered and rang a tiny silver bell as a signal to Samuel. "Come sit by the fireplace with me." Samuel arrived with the martini for Admiral Colby and a fresh whiskey for Margaret.

"Good evening, Admiral," Samuel said as he placed the drinks on the coffee table.

"Thank you, Samuel," Colby said. "Tell me, did Margaret keep her appointment with the doctor today?"

"Yes sir, and in addition we visited the White House," Samuel bragged as he walked back to the kitchen.

"So that explains the call from the White House Chief of Staff," Thomas said as he sipped the martini. "Margaret, it seems that the Commander-in-Chief has invited us to fly to San Diego this Thursday on Air Force One. Do you know anything about that, my darling?"

"I just dropped by to give the President a copy of your novel. Being a southern gentleman, Lyndon invited me to stay for tea. We were discussing Tommy's football talents, and Lyndon said he would like to fly out and see Tommy play. Can you take a few days off from your busy schedule?"

"Oh yes, sweetheart. An invitation from the Commander-in-Chief is treated as a command. I will be on temporary duty, TDY to the White House, at the pleasure of the President. The only thing left on my calendar is appearing before the Armed Services Committee to support the new Navy fighter that will replace the F-4 Phantom."

"Is that Grumman's new proposal, called the Tomcat?" She asked.

"Darling, that's top secret," he scolded. "How did you learn about the Tomcat? Do we have a security leak?"

"Thomas, *Aviation Week* magazine has a lead article on the Navy's new fighter. I read it today at the hospital."

"I don't know how that magazine gets their information so quickly."

"Have you seen the Tomcat, Thomas?" She asked softly.

"Yes, my dear. Last month when I visited the factory in Long Island, I got a flight with the factory test pilot. It's a beautiful jet, Margaret. I wish Tom Junior had stayed in jets instead of specializing in those damn helicopters," he complained bitterly.

"You miss flying, don't you Thomas?"

"Yes, very much. But I admit that the Tomcat is too hot for an old fart like me. You need the reflexes of a twenty-year-old to wring out that baby."

"I will buy you a Lear Jet. Would you like to have one, dear?"

"Maybe after we retire," he smiled at her. "I'm glad you talked the President into taking us to San Diego with him. I promise you that this will be a fun weekend." Rising from the couch, he took her hand, "Come, let's go to dinner. I'm famished."

Six

Peeping Tom Photographer

The Colby Residence
Bonita, California

It was a cool night for early fall. The cool breeze was a welcome relief after the hot day caused by the Santa Ana. Tommy Colby and Judy Anderson were busy with homework. Closing the math book, he said, "This has been a very special day for me."

"Thanks Tommy, it was very special for me also. It's not everyday that one gets to solo and join the mile-high club," she smiled.

"Yeah, that was really fantastic!" He said and took her hand in his. "I have something very important to ask you," he said as the telephone rang. Rising to answer the phone, he said, "Hello."

"Hello, Tommy, I'm out at the Ream Officers Club with some of the Sea Devils hoisting a few brews. Any calls?" Tom asked.

"Yes sir, Mother called. She's flying home Thursday. Grandfather Bush is out of critical care. She also said something about Grandfather and Grandmother Colby and the President flying out here for a visit this weekend. She wants you to call her as soon as you get home."

"Damn! That's the last thing we need right now," Tom replied. "Listen son, I'll be leaving here in about fifteen minutes. Is everything okay at home?"

42

"Yes, sir. Judy and I are studying for a math test tomorrow. But I can drive out and pick you up."

"No thanks, Tommy. I've only had two beers, so I'll be okay driving. This has been a most trying day. Sarah Wiseman came out to the Club and bought the squadron a round of drinks. Then she and the Skipper took off for someplace. Probably walking on the beach. She's taking Charlie's death a lot better than I thought. How's David?"

"He's okay, Dad," Tommy answered. "Watch out for those Imperial Beach Cops. They'll use any excuse to stop sailors and then check for DWI."

"You seem to know a lot about that," Tom chuckled. "Bye, I'll be home soon."

"That was Dad," Tommy said to Judy. "He seems to be taking Commander Wiseman's death pretty hard."

"Yes, it's very sad," she said as she took his hand and kissed his fingers. "Now, what's that question you wanted to ask me before the telephone interruption?"

"Judy, this all happened so fast," he answered. "You make me feel so fantastic, and I think that I'm in love with you. I know that you have been dating Danny Goldstein, but I would like for us to go steady, please."

"What about Elizabeth?"

"She's ancient history!" Tommy exclaimed. "Boy, did she ever put a trip on me. She really screwed up my head."

"Okay, we'll give this steady thing a try. Hey, wait a minute," she said as she retrieved the photographs from her purse. "I was going to show these to you this afternoon, but we got sidetracked with all the sex stuff."

"Jesus Christ!" Tommy exclaimed as he looked at the photographs of his father and Jackie Anderson copulating in the spa. "How did you get these pictures?"

"I took them this afternoon with my trusty camera," she smiled. "I looked out the upstairs window and saw Mother making love to your father. That gave me the idea to make love to you in the airplane this afternoon. I know that I still have a lot to learn."

"No way. What you did was so perfect," he sighed. "Oh God, these photographs are turning me on."

43

"When will your father be home?"

"In about half an hour."

"Then we have time to do it again," she smiled and pulled him toward the sofa.

CDR Joseph Blackwell's Residence
Imperial Beach, California

It was nine-thirty when Sarah and Joe Blackwell got out of the Cadillac and walked on the beach. It was a beautiful evening with a full moon. A cool sea breeze was blowing in patches of fog that floated gently around them. They stopped walking to listen to the soothing crash of waves against the beach. Sarah was amazed that the California beaches were free of mosquitoes and nocturnal insects that plagued the eastern shoreline.

"Joe, why do you guys continue to fly when you know that it is so damn dangerous?"

Joe placed his arm around Sarah's shoulder and felt her tremble. Then he said, "Sarah, you know that Naval aviators have the largest egos in the world. We each think we're the best aviator and that we're invincible. But losing someone like Charlie makes you stop and think, because he was one of the best."

"I just cannot imagine what life is going to be like without him by my side," she said. "Oh, we can make it financially. Charlie had ample life insurance and mortgage insurance on the house, and I teach third grade at Park View school. It is going to be so tough on David and Ruth growing up without a father."

"Sarah, you're a beautiful and desirable lady. You're still young enough to marry again, if you wish."

"Did you ever consider marrying again, Joe?"

"No, I never have. Kelly just couldn't adjust to Navy life and all the separations. We've been divorced almost ten years."

"Shush," she placed her hand to his lips. "Joe, there's a person sneaking up to that house," she pointed. "Is that a gun he's holding?"

"No, it looks like a camera. That's Lieutenant Commander Bob Wilson's beach cottage. He always leaves the drapes open so his dates can see the waves break on the beach. I've heard that the ocean is a powerful sexual stimulant to certain females."

Inside Bob Wilson's cozy living room, Sarah saw a beautiful young woman performing the act of fellatio. "Yes, I can see two people in the living room. Who's the lady? One of the squadron wives?"

"Oh hell, she's Petty Officer Tucker's wife. I think her name's Paula," he remembered to whisper. As Sarah and Joe watched the sex scene unfold in Bob Wilson's living room, the peeping tom was rapidly snapping pictures.

Exerting slight pressure to Sarah's shoulder, Joe continued to walk toward the peeping tom. **"HEY FELLOW, I JUST CALLED THE POLICE AND REPORTED A PEEPING TOM,"** Joe yelled.

The man wheeled to look behind him, then ran across the dunes toward the street maintaining his hold on the camera.

"Wonder what that fool wanted with those pictures?" Joe asked. "Probably some blackmail scheme."

"You must have scared him half to death," Sarah laughed and hugged him tightly.

Joe kissed her and turned back toward his beach cottage. "Would you like to watch the waves from my living room?"

"I thought you'd never ask," she teased, "but only if you will let me close the drapes. I don't want anyone to have photographs of me like that."

Imperial Beach, California

Tom Colby left Ream Field and drove down Thirteenth Avenue. He remembered Tommy's warning and kept the speedometer at a steady twenty-five miles per hour. The main avenue to the Naval Air Station was lined with bars, laundromats, fast food restaurants and several apartment buildings. "Damn!" He muttered aloud when he saw the flashing blue and white lights of the police car behind the Jaguar. He slowed to a stop at the curb, rolled down the window and flicked on the emergency blinkers as the police officer approached the Jaguar.

"Good evening, sir. My name's Sergeant Hinson," the policeman said through the window as Tom reached for his drivers license and registration. "I don't need those Commander," Hinson said and looked at

45

the masonic emblem on Tom's academy ring. "I see that you're a traveling man. Where's your home lodge?"

"Navy Lodge Number twenty-four in Pensacola, Florida," Tom answered. "Are you a Mason?"

"Yes sir, "I was raised in Navy Lodge twenty-four in nineteen fifty-three. It's so great to meet a brother from my home lodge," Hinson grinned. "I just stopped you to tell you that your right taillight is not working."

"Thanks," Tom said. "I should've checked it before I left the base. I usually preflight my automobile just as well as I do my aircraft. But this has been one hell of a day. We lost three of our shipmates in a nasty crash earlier this afternoon."

"Sorry to hear that, sir. Has the Navy released the names?"

"No, I don't think so. We recovered Commander Wiseman's body just before dark. The other bodies are probably still strapped to their seats inside the helicopter," Tom answered. "We may never get them out."

"God, what a way to die!" Hinson exclaimed. "I put eight years in the Navy as an air crewman before I decided to get out and work in the safe profession as a police officer," he laughed.

"Have you had to shoot anyone yet, Sarge?" Tom asked.

"No, and I hope I never do, but we're close to the Mexican border and the dope smuggling business gets worse each day. Where there's a lot of money involved, those guys are going to be carrying loaded weapons, and will probably use them if cornered."

"Well, I'm bushed, Sarge. Thanks for the warning about the tail-light. I'll have it repaired first thing tomorrow."

"Good night, Commander. Have a nice evening and come visit our lodge if you have time," Hinson said as he watched the blue Jaguar pull away from the curb and proceed down Thirteenth Avenue toward the freeway. "Should've warned him not to drive through Imperial Beach with alcohol on his breath," he muttered softly to himself. "But I have a feeling that he's gonna be okay."

The Colby Residence
Bonita, California

Tom dialed Admiral Bush's telephone number. He glanced at his watch while he listened to the long distant tingle on the line. It would be a little after eleven in Pensacola. "Hello," Linda answered on the first ring.

"Hello, darling," Tom said. "Tommy gave me the message that you had called and will be home Thursday. Also, I understand that we're having a house full of guests for the weekend. Right?"

"Yes, Tom. Your mother called this afternoon to check on Father's condition. Then she announced that she and Admiral Colby were flying out Thursday afternoon on Air Force One with the President. They want to see Tommy's football game Friday night."

"Yes, that sounds like Mother," he sighed. "Linda, I hate to break the bad news like this, but Charlie Wiseman and his flight crew bought the farm this afternoon. We just recovered Charlie's body, but I'm afraid that the other two bodies are trapped inside the helicopter."

"What happened, Tom?" He heard the alarm in Linda's voice.

"Well, we think the servo systems failed. Bob Wilson was flying through the area and heard a Mayday transmission from Charlie just before the crash."

"Oh, poor Sarah. How's she holding up?"

"Just great, in fact she came out to the dispensary to see Charlie's body. Then she bought the squadron a round at the club. Not one tear in those beautiful blue eyes."

"Please call Sarah and tell her that I will be home Thursday," she said. "Oh yes, Tom. All the bad news almost made me forget to tell you that I'm flying back on a Navy T-39 jet Thursday morning. Do you know a Captain John Schmidt?"

"No, I don't think so."

"Well, this must have been some of Mother Colby's wheeling and dealing. Captain Schmidt called this afternoon and gave me the flight schedule. He said that we would land at North Island around noon. Please ask Tommy to pick me up if you have a busy schedule."

"I'm sure that I can find time to meet you. I've missed you so very much, but I forgot to ask about Admiral Bush. How's your dad?"

47

"He came out of intensive care this morning," she beamed. "Mother and I have been camping at the Navy hospital for the past week. She's out there with him tonight. Do you know Sarah's plans for the burial?"

"The Skipper told us that she wants the funeral at the Little Chapel of the Roses in Bonita with burial at Glen Abbey on Friday."

"How has all this affected Tommy? He and David are best friends."

"I'm real proud of Tommy. He went over this afternoon and visited with David and Ruth while Sarah was at the dispensary and Officer's Club. Then when I came in this evening, he and Judy were sitting on the couch holding hands. Looks like our son has finally discovered the girl next door," he laughed.

"Now Tom, that's nothing to tease about. Judy would be a much better date for Tommy then that floozy Elizabeth. Tommy and Judy often do their home work together, or didn't you know?"

"Hey, sweetheart, that's fine with me. I agree with you that Judy is a nice young lady, and I promise not to tease. Have a safe flight home, and I'll be at North Island to meet you. Good night and pleasant dreams."

"Good night, dear. Please get your rest," she said and place the telephone back on the base. Linda snuggled down under the covers and smiled as she thought about Tommy and Judy. "Wonder what Judy did to finally make him notice her," she murmured to herself as she went to sleep.

SEVEN

Homemade Bomb

Petty Officer Matthew Tucker's residence
Imperial Oak Apartments
Imperial Beach, California

Petty Officer Matthew Tucker, USN, was twenty-three years old. He was five feet, ten inches tall, weighed 162 pounds, and wore his black hair long enough to part. He was assigned to Helicopter Squadron 24 as a sonar operator. He sat at the kitchen table smoking a cigarette and staring at the pictures of his beautiful wife, Paula, and Lieutenant Commander Bob Wilson. "That goddamned son-of-a-bitch!" Tucker swore. Turning to his friend, Steve Jackman, he said, "That bastard has gotta die."

"Wait a minute," Steve said. "I almost got caught taking those pictures for you, and now you're talking about murder. No way, man."

"Someone saw you?" Tucker asked with disgust.

"Matt, it was our Skipper and some blonde dame. Jesus, man, they walked right up behind me while I was snapping these pictures. Paula was all over Commander Bob like a bitch in heat. If there was any seduction going on, Paula was the one doing it."

"Hell, Commander Wilson must have gotten her drunk," Tucker said defensively.

"Not one drink! Paula started the love play. Just look at the pictures. She starts by sucking his nipples and finishes up giving him a blow job."

"That's enough, Steve," Tucker said.

"Okay, man, but I've had enough of this crap. I'm sure that Skipper Blackwell and the lady saw that little sex show over my shoulder. He must've recognized Paula."

"Well, did he recognize you?" Tucker asked.

"Naw, I don't think so. I had on that old ski mask."

"Steve, I want you to make me a bomb," Tucker said.

"Now, wait a damn minute, Matt. I just got through telling you that I'm not going to have any part in murdering Commander Wilson."

"Oh, we're not going to murder the bastard. But after this little bomb, he'll stop and think before he screws another sailor's wife."

Steve Jackman had been in the Navy three years and two months. He had enlisted two weeks after graduation from high school and met Matthew Tucker at Navy boot camp in San Diego. He was almost identical in size with Tucker, except his hair was sandy red. After boot camp, Steve was assigned to Class A Ordnance school while Tucker went to Sonar Technician school. After graduation from ordnance school, he was assigned to Helicopter Squadron 24. A week later, Tucker was assigned to the squadron as a sonar technician, and their friendship continue to grow. Steve had been Tucker's best man when he and Paula were married.

Steve walked across the kitchen to the refrigerator and got two cans of beer. Handing a can to Tucker, he said, "Matt, do you remember Yokosan?"

"Oh, yes," Tucker moaned. "That was some great poontang!"

Jackman and Tucker had shared a room in the Grand Hotel when their squadron flew into the Atsugi Naval Air Station during their first cruise to Japan. Yokosan was a bar hostess who danced and talked with the servicemen. It was common knowledge that the hostess drank tea which was disguised to look like a bourbon and water. She was fascinated with Jackman's red hair. When the bar closed at midnight, Jackman coaxed her back to their room at the Grand and proceeded to seduce her while Tucker snored in the other bed. Yokosan's vocal orgasm woke Tucker

50

who quickly sported an erection. Yokosan whispered in Jackman's ear. After he nodded his head, she rose and walked over to Tucker's bed. Kneeling, she gently engulfed his manhood and performed a very quick act of fellatio.

"Matt, Yokosan was not a hooker," Steve said casually. "She just loved sex. Maybe that's the way it is with Paula. Anyway, I don't think you should preach a double standard. If it's okay for you to screw around, then it should be okay for Paula."

"Well, Yokosan wasn't married," Tucker protested.

"Yes, she was. Her husband was an engineering student at Tokyo University. Yokosan worked as a bar hostess to help with their expenses. We didn't tell you because I knew it would turn you off to bang a married woman."

"Man, she was a great piece of tail," Tucker smiled. "We must have balled her six or seven times that night, and she kept begging for more."

"Okay, so now we can forget about the bomb, right?" Steve said.

"Steve, I told you that we aren't going to kill the bastard, but I do want to scare the hell out of him. Will three sticks of dynamite be enough?"

"That all depends on what you want to blow up; his Cadillac or his beach house," Steve answered.

"Neither one. I want to blow up his office on the base."

"No way, Matt! The Naval Investigative Service and FBI will have us both in jail!" Steve yelled.

"Calm down, buddy. Just make me the bomb, and we'll set it to detonate when no one's within a hundred yards of the building. I want that bastard to know that a Navy man is really pissed at him."

Office of HS-24 Commanding Officer
NAS, Ream Field

Commander Joe Blackwell and Lieutenant Commander Tom Colby sat in the skipper's office discussing the funeral arrangements for Commander Charles Wiseman. After making love to Sarah the previous evening, Joe had finally gotten around to discussing Charlie's funeral. She

51

agreed to a military funeral, but insisted on burial at Glen Abbey cemetery instead of the Roscrans National Cemetery.

"Did Sarah agree to a military funeral?" Tom asked.

"Yes, Tom, you remember that Charlie was Jewish. The Rabbi will have some kind of Jewish service at the mortuary with the immediate family, then we'll conduct the military portion out at Glen Abbey. I have the Master at Arms drilling the honor guard. On the last note of taps, I want you to lead a fly-over of three helicopters with the missing wingman slot. I'd like to lead the flight, but I should be there beside the widow. Don't you think so?"

"Yes, Skipper, you should," Tom agreed, secretly delighted that he would be leading the farewell flight to honor Commander Wiseman.

"Tom, I got a call from the Secret Service about an hour ago. Seems like Admiral Colby and the President are flying to North Island Naval Air Station today. Has your father called about this?"

"No sir, I talked to Linda last night. Her father's out of critical care and she's flying home today from Pensacola. She did say that Mother called to let her know that they were all flying out on Air Force One for Tommy's football game tomorrow night."

"Well, I guess that's what this flap is all about," Blackwell said. "They were planning to land at North Island around sixteen hundred hours today. I told the agent that we had a six-thousand foot runway here at Ream that was perfectly capable of handling the Boeing 707. He said he would check into it and get back to me."

"I wish that Charlie was here to help with all the details," Tom said.

"Me too, Tom, but I know you can handle the job. I called AIRPAC this morning and requested that you be assigned as my Executive Officer until BUPERS gets around to finding a replacement. Now, I want to hear your ideas about this combat search and rescue task. Is there any way in hell that we can keep from getting our ass shot off like that HS-26 bunch?"

"Yes, Skipper, I've been giving it a lot of thought since the debriefing with Lieutenant Becker yesterday," Tom answered. *He recalled the vivid nightmare where his flight crew was attempting to rescue a downed flier near the Vietnam Coast. As he brought the helicopter into a hover over the pilot, the crewman yelled over the intercom that the pilot was tangled in his parachute. Then Petty Officer Steve Jackman leaped from the hovering helicopter and splashed into the ocean near the pilot. The artillery shells from the North Vietnam beach exploded in the water near the hovering helicopter. Tom's only chance of survival was to leave the area. Holding the altitude at one hundred feet and speed of one hundred knots, he flew a racetrack pattern that brought him back over Jackman and the pilot in five minutes. He executed a quick stop maneuver and dropped the helicopter into a steady ten-foot hover over the two men in the water. The five rotor blades of the helicopter created a windstorm of ninety knots on the surface of the ocean and kicked up a whirling storm of saltwater spray that engulfed the helicopter. Tom saw that Jackman's eyes were protected by a scuba mask and that his flight boots had become swim fins. The second crewman operated the rescue hoist. He saw the thumbs up from Jackman, and pitched the hoist cable to him. As Jackman snapped the hook to his torso harness, the shells began to explode once again around the helicopter. Tom pulled the collective up to the maximum limit and jerked Jackman and the pilot out of the water.*

Remembering this vivid dream, Tom said, "Skipper, I'd like to try out some new tactics that will hopefully reduce our exposure time to the North Vietnamese gunners. I'd like to hand-pick a skeleton crew, if it is okay with you."

"You have your pick of the aviators and aircrew," Joe said.

"Thanks, Skipper. I promised Linda that I'd pick her up at North Island at noon. She's flying in on a Navy flight that my mother arranged."

"Hey, Tom, don't knock it. Just think of it as some of the fringe benefits that us poor slobs deserve after months at sea protecting Uncle Sugar's ass. Take Linda to the Mex Village for lunch." The Mexican Village restaurant in Coronado, California was Tom's favorite restaurant and watering hole. The restaurant was also known as the "body exchange" where naval aviators of all ages could meet airline stewardess, college girls, divorcee's, and even Navy cruise wives out for an evening of fun.

"Thanks a lot, Skipper," Tom said as the telephone rang.

Lifting the receiver, Joe said, "Commander Blackwell speaking," then continued, "Good morning, Captain Conrad." Joe listened to the Commanding Officer of the Ream Field Naval Air Station, then said, "Yes, sir, Lieutenant Commander Colby and I will be there." Returning the

53

receiver to its base, he turned to Tom, "That was George Conrad calling to inform me that you and I will meet Air Force One when she lands at Ream Field this afternoon at sixteen hundred hours. The uniform of the day will be tropical white long. So you might as well change uniforms over the lunch hour."

"Will do, Skipper," Tom said as he left the room and walked next door to his new office. He was mentally making a list of aviators and aircrew that would make up the combat rescue team. One of the first tasks of the new team would be to practice the missing wingman formation for Commander Wiseman's funeral tomorrow.

Naval Air Station
North Island, California
Operations Building

Tom parked his Jaguar in the visitors lot behind Building 505, and walked up the stairs to Flight Operations. All aircraft that departed or landed at NAS North Island were controlled by flight operations. The controller on duty was a plump, thirty-six year old Petty Officer First Class who wore the name tag SMITH above the left pocket of his white shirt. He walked over to the counter as Tom entered the room. "May I help you, Commander?" He asked.

"Do you have an inbound on an Air Force or Navy VIP flight out of Pensacola?"

"Yes, sir," the controller replied. "We have a Navy T-39 that left Pensacola this morning." Glancing at the large status board behind the counter, he continued, "Their estimated time of arrival is twelve-oh-five, sir. They should be on the ground in about ten minutes."

"Thank you, Smith," Tom said. "I think my wife's on that flight. Do you know if any Flag officers are onboard?"

"Negative code, sir," Smith replied. "The VIP flights always report any code aboard when they enter the San Diego control area. That gives us time to get the appropriate transportation arranged and notify the Captain. The old man is always down here to meet visiting Admirals."

"That must get to be a bore," Tom replied without thinking.

"I read you, Commander, but he's the boss," Smith said, then continued, "Sir, there's a fresh pot of coffee in the VIP lounge. You're welcome to wait in there, if you wish."

"Thank you kindly, Smith. I believe I will have a cup," Tom said as he walked toward the lounge. The sign on the door of the VIP lounge read "Captains and above," but, what the hell, Tom thought. It would be nice to have a cup of coffee and relax in the plush, overstuffed chairs. The west wall of the lounge had four large windows that overlooked the VIP parking ramp and runway. Tom poured a cup of coffee and settled into one of the comfortable chairs. He picked up a copy of *Time* magazine and glanced at the headlines proclaiming, *NAVY JETS MAKE A TURKEY SHOOT OF NORTH VIETNAMESE PT BOATS.* "Damn war is gonna be over before we get there," he muttered to himself.

Petty Officer Smith opened the door to the VIP lounge and said, "Commander, the T-39 is on final."

"Thank you Smith, and I really appreciate the hospitality," Tom said as he downed the last of the coffee and walked downstairs to meet Linda's flight.

Mexican Village Restaurant
Coronado, California

Tom and Linda sat in one of the booths in the crowded restaurant. He sipped a tall glass of iced tea while Linda enjoyed a frosty margarita. Tom was not on the afternoon flight schedule, but still he refrained from drinking during the day when there was the possibility of being called on to fly. The practice fly-over for Commander Wiseman's funeral had gone well. He thought the Skipper would be impressed when he saw this slightly varied flight of the missing wingman. Tom touched the side of his glass to the rim of Linda's drink, "Welcome home, pretty lady. How'd you like the VIP flight?"

"It's the only way to fly," she laughed. "I tried to get Dr. Thompson to fly out with me. His parents live in the Bay Area. But he wanted to stay at the hospital and make sure that his prize patient has a smooth recovery."

"Thank God he's going to be okay," Tom said. "Now if Mother Bush can just keep him on a diet, he'll live to preach hellfire and damnation and draw his retired pay for a long time."

"I feel very confident that Mother will control his diet," Linda replied. "Dad's heart attack really scared her." Then changing the subject, she said, "You look real nice in your whites."

"Thank you, pretty lady," Tom replied. "The tropical white's are to welcome you home and for a command performance of meeting Air Force One at Ream Field this afternoon with Captain George Conrad."

"Yes, Mother Colby said they would be arriving today. Do you know what the plans are?"

"Not the faintest," he replied. "Air Force One is landing at sixteen hundred hours, and they'll probably drive straight out to the house. Might be a good idea to take a dozen or so steaks out of the freezer, and have Tommy start the grill around seventeen-hundred."

"I wish you'd stop talking in military time," she laughed. "What's seventeen-hundred? Five p.m., right?"

"Yes, darling, have Tommy start the fire at five. Now, let's order lunch. I'm starved," he said and reached for the menu.

The Colby Residence
Bonita, California

Tom placed the thick steaks on the grill. Air Force One had landed at NAS Ream Field at exactly 4 p.m. The Commander-in-Chief walked down the steps followed by Admiral and Mrs. Thomas Colby. The President paused at the bottom of the steps to acknowledge the military salutes from Captain George Conrad, Commander Joseph Blackwell and Lieutenant Commander Tom Colby. He shook hands with the three Naval officers then, turning to Captain Conrad, he said, "Take care of my airplane, Captain. We plan to takeoff at nine o'clock Saturday morning."

The Secret Service agents quickly ushered the presidential party to a waiting limousine, before Captain Conrad could start his "welcome to California" speech. Tom ran to the Jaguar and followed the limousine. He had briefly shaken his father's hand, hugged his mother, then he remembered that his father was wearing the shoulder boards of a Vice-Admiral. *When was he promoted? Why all the secrecy?*

Vice Admiral Colby and President Johnson sat on the patio near the grill sipping glasses of bourbon. Admiral Colby wore his white uniform. The President had removed his coat and necktie. "It's getting a mite chilly, Tom," the President said. "Does it always cool off like this in the evening?"

"Yes, sir. It's our nice sea breeze from the cool Pacific Ocean," Tom said as he went inside and returned with his leather flight jacket. "Try this on, Uncle Lyndon. Do you remember how nice and warm these babies are?"

"Sure do, you young whippersnapper! I wore one of these when you were in diapers," he said, recalling the days when he was a Naval aviator. "Thomas was my flight instructor at Pensacola during the winter of 'forty-three. It was damn cold flying in the Jenny with an open cockpit, right Thomas?"

"Sure was, Chief," Admiral Colby agreed. "You'd better be happy that you were assigned to the Catalina search and rescue seaplanes in nice, warm Key West, Florida. I almost froze my balls off in most of the fighters that I flew over England."

As Tom folded the President's suit coat, he noticed the miniature DFC ribbon that was clipped to the left side of the lapel. "What did Uncle Lyndon do to earn the Distinguished Flying Cross, Dad?"

"That's one of my favorite stories, Tom," Admiral Colby said and continued. "The Chief was a Lieutenant Commander at the time. He was flying the Consolidated PBY-5 Catalina seaplane on patrol along the Florida coast when they accidentally found a German submarine hiding in shallow water recharging her batteries. Chief radioed the Navy destroyer that he had found a U-boat and rolled the clumsy seaplane over into a shallow dive and started a ninety knot bombing run on the submarine. The Catalina was a high wing, twin-engine seaplane with three gun ports. Since there were no bomb bay doors in the sea plane hull, the Catalina carried internal fifty-pound bombs that the crewmen dropped out windows on order of the pilot. Well, after about twenty minutes the Chief's crew had blown up coral all around the sub, and the U-boat Commander surfaced and raised the white flag of surrender."

"It went just like we planned, Tom," the President said. "That damn destroyer rushed in and boarded the submarine and tried to claim all the credit. The Navy should have at least given me the Navy Cross, but I was pleased to get the DFC. It's the aviators medal, and I've worn it proudly all these years."

"Congratulations on your third star, Dad," Tom said to his father. "Was there a special session of the Flag Board?"

"No son, this is some dang fool idea of the Chief," Admiral Colby replied. He always referred to the President as Chief. "He promoted me this afternoon at forty thousand feet, somewhere over the great mid-west, while your mother snapped three or four rolls of pictures. But I just have a feeling that it will have a price tag attached to it, right Chief?" He laughed.

"No, Thomas, I just felt that you deserved it, but I do have a very special job in mind for you. I want you to go out and take command of the Seventh Fleet. Do you want the job?" The President asked.

"**Jesus Christ, yes**!" Admiral Colby yelled. "Thank you, Chief," he gripped the President's hand. "I thought I was doomed to the halls of the Pentagon forever."

Commander Joe Blackwell walked out onto the patio and waved to the group. "Hey, Skipper, come over and join the party," Tom said. "These two old aviators are reliving big Wu-Wu-Two. What're you drinking, scotch or bourbon?"

"Bourbon," Joe said. "Good evening, Mr. President and Admiral Colby."

"Joe, that's enough of the 'Mr. President' crap. You may call me Chief, like Thomas does," Johnson ordered.

"Yes sir, Chief," Joe said as he took the glass from Tom and sat down in a patio chair next to the President.

"Sorry to hear about the accident, Joe," the President said. "Tom tells me that you lost your Executive Officer and two other shipmates."

"That's correct, Chief," Joe replied. "Charlie Wiseman was one of the best aviators in the squadron. I don't know where in hell BUPERS is gonna scrape up an exec for me in three weeks."

"Well, Joe, maybe the Navy squadrons should start promoting from within," the President replied. "When the Army Air Corps lost a squadron commander in Wu-Wu-Two, the next senior pilot in the squadron took command. Remember the twenty-three and twenty-four year old majors that were commanding squadrons?"

"That's a good idea, Chief," Joe said, uncertain what the President meant.

"Hey, Skipper, will you watch the steaks and tend bar while I get some more barbeque sauce?" Tom yelled as he walked toward the kitchen.

"Sure thing, Tom," Joe answered.

"Joe, is Tom qualified to be your Executive Officer?" The President asked after Colby had walked into the kitchen.

"Hell yes, Chief," Joe replied, "but BUPERS would never go along with a Lieutenant Commander taking over the number two slot in the squadron. Next year, when I move on, Tom would be eligible to assume command of the Sea Devils, and Lieutenant Commanders just don't get command of aviation squadrons."

"Let me worry about that, Joe," the President replied. "Now, tell me about Wiseman. Will the funeral be local?"

"Yes, Chief, his funeral is scheduled for ten-hundred-hours tomorrow morning at Glen Abbey cemetery here in Bonita. We're having a military funeral, and Tom's leading the missing wingman fly-over. We'd be honored to have you attend, sir."

"That might be a good idea," the President replied. "Admiral Colby and I would like to visit your squadron in the morning around nine o'clock. I want to address your aviators for a few minutes, and then you can dismiss the squadron to attend the funeral. After taps, I'd like to present the flag to the widow, if that's okay with you?"

"That'll be fine, Chief," Joe answered as he went to refill the glasses. "Gentlemen, I propose a toast," Joe said as he raised his glass. "To absent friends and the men who wear the gold wings!"

"Hear, hear!" The President and Admiral Colby said in unison as they raised their glasses and drank the toast, while behind them on the grill the flames were licking at the steaks.

*   *   *

When Tom went into the kitchen, he continued through to the living room and dialed the Senior Chief at the squadron. "Chief, this is Commander Colby," he said. "I need a real hurry-up favor."

"If we have it in the squadron, it's yours, sir," the Senior Chief said.

59

"Get a flight jacket out of the gear room. I'd guess a forty-four, long. Have the Sea Devil patch sewn on the right side, and on the left side under the gold wings, have duty yeoman letter-in, 'Commander-in-Chief'."

"Yes, sir. It'll be ready by morning muster," the Senior Chief said.

"Thanks a lot, Chief," Tom said. "Oh yes, we'll need a squadron baseball cap also. Get one with some scrambled eggs on the bill like the skipper's, okay?"

"The cap will be ready. Have a good evening, sir," he said.

Returning to the patio, Tom saw the flames licking at the steaks. "Jesus Christ, Skipper! You're letting the damn steaks burn to a crisp," he said as he ran to the grill and doused the flames with water.

EIGHT

Orders to Sea Duty

Petty Officer Steve Jackman's residence
Imperial Oak Apartments
Imperial Beach, California

The rapid increase of personnel at NAS Ream Field had far exceeded the capacity of the barracks. Bachelor petty officer's, Third Class and above, received a housing allowance for quarters off-base. Petty Officer Steve Jackman rented a one-bedroom unit in the Imperial Oak Apartment complex. Matthew Tucker knocked on the door of Unit 206 and yelled, "Come on, Steve! We're gonna be late for muster."

Jackman opened the door and walked out with a small package under his left arm. "There's no rush, Matt. We can make it to the base in four minutes, without speeding."

Ignoring the remark, Tucker asked, "Is that my bomb?"

"Yes, this is your damn bomb, and it may just blow both of us out of the Navy. I really don't want to do this, Matt."

"Well hell, you don't have to," Tucker said. "I'll do it all by myself."

"Yeah, and blow off your dumb ass to boot," Jackman said as they walked downstairs to the parking lot. He place the package on the floor in front of the driver's seat. "Let's just hope the jarheads don't stop us and inspect the car at the main gate," he said as he drove out of the parking lot toward the Naval Air Station.

"I really do appreciate your help, Steve."

"Hell, Matt, I still don't believe blowing up Commander Wilson's office is gonna solve your problem. We just might accidentally kill somebody, then shit will really hit the fan. Can't you accept the fact that Paula just might like making love to him?"

"No, Steve. I still think the son-of-a-bitch got her to go for a ride in his new Cadillac, then seduced her in his beach cottage."

"Matt, this is the last bomb that I'm making for you. I'm not going to make one to frighten off every man that gets into Paula's panties."

"Thanks, buddy," Tucker said. "Now, let's go over the plan one more time before we get to the base."

"Okay, Matt. I wrapped the box in brown paper to make it look like it just came through the mail. I even glued on some old stamps. The return address is his mother's house in Memphis. I'll put the package in Commander Wilson's office before he gets to work, then go on to class. You call the squadron duty officer at eight-fifteen and report a bomb in the building. After they evacuate, I'll detonate the bomb."

"Hey, Steve, what if Commander Wilson opens the package?"

"Man, I hope he does. The bomb doesn't have a trigger. When he sees the dynamite, he'll know that someone is trying to kill him. Maybe that'd be better than blowing up his building."

"Naw, I still want to blow up his building."

"Just don't go anywhere near building twenty-six, Matt," Jackman said as he stopped at the main gate. They breathed a sigh of relief as the Marine sentry glanced at their identification cards and waved them through.

Building 26, NAS Ream Field
Imperial Beach, California

Lieutenant Commander Bob Wilson walked into his office promptly at seven-thirty. He was training officer for the Reassignment Air Group, often called the RAG. He shared an office with Airman Jack Peterson and Petty Officer First Class Ernie Palmer. "Morning, Commander," Palmer said, "Looks like you got a box of cookies from your mother, sir."

"Morning Palmer, morning Peterson," Bob said as he lifted the package and saw his mother's return address when the telephone rang.

"Training department, Airman Peterson speaking, sir," Peterson said, then continued, "Yes sir, he just walked in, hold please, Commander." Turning to Bob, he said, "Lieutenant Commander Colby calling for you, sir."

"Thanks, Peterson," Bob said. He placed the package on top of the file cabinet behind his desk and reached for the telephone. "Good morning, Tom. How's it going?"

"Not good," Tom laughed on the other end of the phone. "Mother, Dad and the President all flew in yesterday. So we had a busy evening. Have you had breakfast?"

"That explains why Air Force One is sitting down by the operations building. No, I haven't had breakfast. I also had a real busy evening with a very good friend."

"Want to meet over at the gedunk in ten minutes?" Tom asked. "We can have some breakfast and have a few minutes to chat."

"Roger that," Bob said as he hung up the telephone. "Any mail, Palmer?"

"We have something that you might be interested in, Commander," Palmer said and placed a large, brown manila envelope on Wilson's desk.

"Jesus Christ! Are those my orders?" He asked as he noticed the BUPERS return address. The detailer in Washington had promised to find him a flying billet on the West Coast. Opening the package, he read:

BUPERS ORDER NR 142516 DTD 41506Z OCT 65.
LCDR ROBERT L. WILSON, 466-51-8127/1310, ON OR BEFORE
30 OCT 65 DETACH DUTY IN A FLYING STATUS INVOLVING
OPERATIONAL OR TRAINING FLIGHTS. PROCEED AND
REPORT TO COMMANDING OFFICER, HELICOPTER COMBAT
SUPPORT SQUADRON TWENTY-ONE FOR DUTY IN A FLYING
STATUS INVOLVING OPERATIONAL OR TRAINING FLIGHTS
NOT LATER THAN 30 NOV 65. ACCT DATA N5F5 1761452.2264
U 000023 AE 5F5466518127.

"This is my ticket back to operational flying, Palmer," Bob said. "Has the Captain seen these?"

"No sir, I don't think so," Palmer replied. "The yeoman brought them over about ten minutes before you got here."

"Well, I suggest you take these back over to admin and have the yeoman route them through Captain Conrad," Bob said.

"Guess you're right, Commander. Hey, Pete, take the Commander's orders back over to admin," Palmer yelled at Peterson.

"Hell, that's okay. I'm going to meet Mr. Colby over at the gedunk for breakfast, so I'll drop them off," Bob said, as he put on his bridge cap and walked out of the office.

Navy Exchange Restaurant
NAS, Ream Field

Tom Colby and Bob Wilson ate breakfast at the Navy Exchange restaurant, often referred to as the gedunk. They had been friends since they first met as roommates at Naval Aviation Flight School in Pensacola. "So tell me, who was the good friend you were busy with last night?" Tom asked. "Did she give you that black eye?"

"Sweet Paula, the cute blonde waitress at the Officer's Club," Bob bragged. "She could teach the Japanese geisha girls a few tricks with her magic tongue. Man, what a nice piece of tail."

"Yes, and she's also married to one of the petty officers in my squadron," Tom lectured. "Bob, you're going to get your ass shot off if you don't stop messing around with married women."

"Your point is duly noted, my friend. Hell, Tom, she nearly raped me in the car before we could get in the beach cottage. The ocean is an aphrodisiac to the beautiful young ladies that visit my beach cottage."

"You still haven't explained the shiner," Tom coaxed.

"This will blow your mind," Bob said. "Tuesday afternoon, I took the three-ten out on a whale-watching charter. We found three beautiful gray humpbacks. Well, when we landed back at Brown Field, we were met by Border Patrol agents who scoured my plane for drugs. This shiner is courtesy of Sergeant Richard Baker."

"Deacon Baker struck you?" Tom asked in awe.

"That fat bastard knocked me flat on my ass, with my hands cuffed behind my back. I'm surprised Tommy didn't tell you. He and Judy were at the airport and witnessed the whole show."

"No, Tommy didn't say anything except that he and Judy had gone flying and that she soloed," Tom said.

"Was Judy wearing the miniature gold wings?"

"Yeah, come to think of it she was," Tom answered. "Oh, come on Bob, you don't think they're messing around, do you?"

"Those kids are a very nice couple," he answered. "Quit acting like a father. What those kids decide to do in an airplane or the privacy of their home is okay with me."

"Jesus Christ, Bob! Do you think they made love in my airplane?"

"You act like it's never been done in an airplane before. Don't tell me that your Cessna's a virgin."

"She is as far as I'm concerned," Tom replied coldly. "Now getting back to your shiner. Are you in trouble with the Border Patrol?"

"No, they had us confused with another plane that was bringing in a load of drugs from Mexico. Commissioner Hansen and another group of agents rushed out to the airport just in time to see fatso Baker punch me in the face. They arrested Baker and carted him off to San Ysidro. I hope they still have the fat bastard locked up."

"I wonder how Baker's gonna explain this to our church," Tom said. Reaching into the pocket of his flight jacket, he extracted a pair of aviator sunglasses and handed them to Wilson. "Bob, you should wear these until some of the swelling goes down."

"Thanks, buddy," Bob said as he slipped the sunglasses into place.

"That looks much better. Now, getting back to the main issue of the day, Dad and the President are visiting the squadron at nine o'clock this morning, and I'd like for you to be my guest. We have an all-pilots meeting scheduled at eight-thirty, and Charlie's funeral at ten. Can you make it down to the squadron before all the big brass arrives?"

"Sure, Tom, thanks for the invitation. I'll be there." Then he said, "Hey, buddy, my orders to sea duty came in this morning. I'm going down the street to HC Twenty-One."

"That's great, so you'll be flying the Hukie-Two again. Think the Skipper will give you a detachment?"

"Yeah, I'll probably beat you to the war zone, my friend," Bob said, then explained his idea of deploying a small combat search and rescue detachment on the guided missile frigates that had a helicopter deck large enough for the Kaman H-2 Sea Sprite.

65

"Well, I wish you a lot of success," Tom said. "It sounds like your plan will work, if you can get the black-shoes to stock enough spare parts onboard for the Hukie-Two." Then, remembering the debriefing from Lieutenant Donald Becker, he asked, "Have you heard the debriefing on HS Twenty-Six?"

"No, I haven't. I know that the squadron should be back in a month or so," Bob said. Quickly Tom explained the debriefing that his squadron had received from Lieutenant Becker. "Thirteen helicopters shot down," Bob questioned. "Jesus Christ! That's just not acceptable."

"I know, I feel the same way," Tom said. "We must develop some new combat tactics, and have more air cover during the rescue attempts. Maybe we can get the Spads to fly wing on us for overland rescues." Spad was the Navy nickname for the Douglas A-1, Skyraider. A single-engine, propeller aircraft that could carry more bombs and ordnance than the B-17.

"I heard that the Air Force has a squadron of Spad's at Da Nang. They call them 'Sandy,' I think," Bob said.

"Well, we should get back to work. See you at eight-thirty," Tom said as they left the restaurant and walked back to their offices.

NINE

Sea Devil Hymn

NAS Ream Field
Main Gate

Brad Bolton was thirty-two years old. He stood six feet tall, weighed one hundred and seventy-six pounds and took his job of guarding the life of the President very seriously. He had not accompanied Jack Kennedy to Dallas, Texas on that fateful November day in 1963. Brad's mother had died in Fulton, Kentucky, and he had gone home on bereavement leave. Brad stood inside the Sentry Station briefing the Sergeant of the Guard. "Sergeant, the President's vehicle will approach the gate at five miles per hour. It will not stop. All military personnel will render the hand salute. No one, repeat no one, will touch their weapon. Is that clear?"

"Yes, Mr. Bolton," the Sergeant said. "If you'll excuse me, I must brief the sentry, sir," he saluted and walked out of the tiny room.

Brad knew that the Marine Sergeant did not like taking orders from a civilian. Well, just too damn bad, Brad thought. He was in charge of security, and by God he was going to see that it was done by the book.

*   *   *

The limousine cruised down Interstate 5 and turned right on the Coronado Avenue off-ramp. The President and Admiral Colby were in the back seat. The driver was Nick Felton and riding shotgun was Don Gossman. Both Secret Service agents were armed with a variety of automatic weapons. Two unmarked automobiles followed closely behind the limousine, each carrying four Secret Service agents. "Did you sleep well, Chief?" Admiral Colby asked.

"Like a newborn baby, Thomas," the President replied. "Miss Jackie mixed up a hot toddy last night that put me right to sleep. Then she woke me this morning at six o'clock to go riding. She's quite a horse-woman."

"Chief, those Bonita folks are almost as crazy about their horses as you Texans."

"Thomas, my secretary called Captain Conrad and informed him that we'd drop by and pick him up at his office this morning on our way down to Tom's squadron," the President said, changing the subject from Jackie Anderson.

"That was mighty thoughtful of you, Chief, but I warn you, George can be a royal pain in the ass."

"Well, Thomas, he's the Commanding Officer of the air station, and to tell you the truth, I kinda wanted him there when I promote Tom to full Commander."

"Chief, I'm only a Vice Admiral and prospective commander of the Seventh Fleet, so I'd be happy for you to take care of all the small details like spot-promoting Lieutenant Commanders," Admiral Colby teased as the limousine approached the main gate.

"That's Brad Bolton on the gate with the Marines. He's a fine agent, Thomas," the President said as the limousine entered the air station. Building One was the office of the Commanding Officer. It was located on Ellyson Road, approximately five hundred yards inside the main gate. Across the street from Building One was a small parade field, bordered on the north by the Chief Petty Officer's Club, and on the south by the Reassignment Air Group buildings and the Base Fire Station. The base was constructed during World War Two as a temporary Army Air Corps Training Field. The buildings were one-story, wood construction. The base had been reopened in 1952 as a Naval Air Station to train Navy helicopter pilots for the Korean Conflict. As the limousine pulled into the parking lot behind Building One, Captain George Conrad stepped out of

68

his office and saluted. Agent Gossman jumped from the limousine and opened the rear door for Captain Conrad.

"Good morning, Captain," the President said as Conrad enter the limousine.

"Good morning, Mr. President. Good morning, Admiral Colby," Conrad said as he struggled to fasten the seat belt.

*   *   *

Steve Jackman sat in the classroom of Building 28 and listened as the instructor explained the warhead of the Mark-46 torpedo. He glanced nervously at his wrist watch. The dial read eight-twenty. Tucker was five minutes late calling in the bomb threat to the Squadron Duty Officer. Jackman made a firm resolution that this would be the last time that he became involved in any scheme with Tucker. The Chief finished his lecture on the Mark-46 torpedo and dismissed the class.

Jackman left the building and walked across the street to a public telephone booth. He dialed the number of the duty office and said, "Listen carefully! There's a bomb in building twenty-six that's set to blow at eight-thirty. You have five minutes to get everyone out." He hung up before the startled clerk could answer and walked down the sidewalk toward the fire station. He didn't want to be herded into a group evacuation of sailors that would be required to muster in the parking lot.

The clerk yelled to the squadron duty officer, **"LIEUTENANT, WE JUST GOT A BOMB THREAT THAT BUILDING TWENTY-SIX IS GONNA BLOW IN FIVE MINUTES! WE GOTTA CLEAR THAT BUILDING, SIR!"**

Seated at one of the picnic tables on the east side of the fire station, Jackman had a commanding view of one third of the small air station. He lit a cigarette and held the small transmitter that would detonate his home-made bomb. The siren on top of the fire station begin to wail. Sailors rushed out of the buildings and ran to the large ramp where the helicopters were parked.

Jackman counted the men that ran from Building 26. He had walked through the building earlier in the morning and counted eight people in the small building. His count reached seven. *Where in the hell is the other person?* His wristwatch ticked off three minutes then he pushed

69

the button on the transmitter. The explosion was muffled by being inside the building. The roof raised three feet straight up in the air. The walls fell outward, and the roof collapsed in a tangle of twisted beams and plywood. Jackman was glad that he had used only two sticks of dynamite. The three sticks that Tucker had recommended would have reduced the building to splinters.

*　　*　　*

Agent Felton heard the explosion as he drove by Building 26. He jammed the accelerator to the floorboard and raced toward the fire station. He turned right on Saufley Road and did not slow down for the speed bumps. The heavy limousine hit the bumps and bounced into the air.

"**Jesus H. Christ**!" The President yelled. "Captain Conrad, I want you to find the stupid engineer who built those damn speed bumps and have him remove them before sundown."

"Yes, sir, Mr. President," Conrad replied, visibly shaken.

Felton screeched the limousine to a halt in front of HS-24 squadron office. He and Gossman jumped from the car to open the rear doors. "Captain Conrad, one of your buildings just exploded," the President said. "Would you like one of these agents to drive you back to your office?"

"No, sir," Conrad said. "The Command Duty Officer is capable of handling any emergency in my absence. He knows how to get in touch if he needs me, sir."

Correct answer for once, Admiral Colby thought as he got out of the limousine and stretched his legs. "Did you break anything, Chief?" he asked.

"Don't think so, Thomas," the President replied. "It was kinda like riding a wild bronco, or a spirited filly," he smiled.

Commander Blackwell and Lieutenant Commander Colby saluted as the presidential party approached the building. "Good morning, gentlemen. Welcome to the home of the Sea Devils," Joe said and ushered them inside the building.

HS-24 Ready Room

Commander Joe Blackwell stood at the podium in front of the packed ready room and prepared to address the group of squadron

70

aviators. Attached to the front of the podium was a three-foot replica of the Sea Devil squadron patch. In the middle of the patch was the three-headed dog, Cerberus. In classical mythology, Cerberus was the dog that guarded the entrance to Hades. "Gentlemen, it gives me great pleasure to welcome these distinguished visitors to the Sea Devil squadron," Joe said and continued, "First, I would like to introduce Commander Colby's father, Vice Admiral Colby. Admiral, please stand."

Vice Admiral Colby stood and the room erupted in applause. He waved to the group and sat down beside the President.

"Now, it's my great pleasure to welcome a man that I'm sure you all recognize. A man who proudly wore the Navy uniform and earned his wings of gold at Pensacola, just like you. Gentlemen, please welcome the President of the United States."

The officers stood and applauded as the President walked to the podium and shook Joe's hand. He turned to face to the group of aviators and said, "Seats, gentlemen."

Tom stood before the President began to speak and said, "Before you make your remarks, Mr. President, the Sea Devils have a small gift that we would like to present to you." Turning to face the room, he ordered, "Bull Ensign, front and center."

Ensign Walker rose and walked to the front of the room with a large package tucked under his left arm. He stopped in front of Commander Colby and handed him the package. Turning to face the President once again, Tom said, "Mr. President, we're honored by your presence with us today. The Sea Devils would like for you to have this small token. When you wear it, you'll be an honorary Sea Devil."

The President accepted the package and ripped off the paper revealing a new Navy flight jacket. Johnson smiled as he held up the jacket and saw that "Commander-In-Chief' had been lettered-in under the gold wings on the left breast above the pocket. On the right side was the Sea Devil patch. "That's the most vicious-looking dog that I've ever seen, Tom," the President said. "That rascal could bite you three ways."

"Bull, will you please hold the President's coat while he tries on his new jacket?" Tom said. The President removed his suit coat and handed it to Ensign Walker and put on the flight jacket.

71

Walker held the President's coat and stared at the miniature ribbon pinned to the lapel. Turning to face the room, he yelled, "**OFFICERS, ATTENTION ON DECK**." Immediately all of the aviators jumped to their feet and stood at attention. "Gentlemen, I have standing orders from Commander Colby to bestow the sacred Sea Devil Hymn on any of our guests who wear the Distinguished Flying Cross."

"**NO, BULL**!" Tom and Joe yelled together.

"Now wait a minute, Tom," the President said. "Did you give such an order to Mr. Bull?"

"Yes sir, I did," Tom replied.

"Well, let's get on with it, Mr. Bull," the President said.

"All together, gentlemen," Walker said and lead the group in the hymn, "**HYMNNNN! HYMNNNN! HYMNNNN! FUCK HIM**!" The group yelled and burst into applause.

The President was stunned momentarily then broke into a laugh. "Joe, you have a real bunch of tigers in this squadron," he said.

"I hope you're not offended, Mr. President," Joe said.

"Not in the least," he answered. Raising his hands to quiet the group, the President continued, "Gentlemen, I flew out here yesterday for a few days vacation and to watch Commander Colby's son play football. I heard about your tragic helicopter accident and the loss of three squadron mates and plan to attend Commander Wiseman's funeral this morning at ten o'clock with you all. Then I want to invite all of you to join me at the football game tonight to see Tommy Colby's team kick some tail. In fact, I think we should all wear our flight jackets."

Captain Conrad said, "You can't do that, Mr. President."

"What the hell do you mean, Captain?" The President demanded.

"Sir, there's a Naval District order that flight gear cannot be worn off-base, and particularly not to sports events."

"Well, I'm not saying if that's a good order or a bad order," the President said, "but Captain, we're gonna wear our flight jackets to the football game tonight. Please call the proper authority and clear this up so the Shore Patrol doesn't try to arrest all of us."

"Yes, sir, I'll take care of it," Conrad said and sat by Admiral Colby.

"Now, where was I?" The President asked, "Oh yes, I have a little surprise of my own for someone in this room. Lieutenant Commander

Colby, front and center." Tom rose and walked to the podium. "Admiral Colby, will you please come up here and help me get this young officer in the proper uniform?"

"Yes, sir," Admiral Colby said and stood beside the President.

The President addressed the group of officers, "Gentlemen, back in the good old days it was Navy policy to frock an officer to the next higher rank when a vacancy needed filling. Well, you all need an executive officer, and I hereby frock Lieutenant Commander Colby to full Commander to perform the duties of executive officer." Turning to Admiral Colby, the President said, "Would you please assist me with the shoulder boards, Admiral?"

"Yes, sir," Admiral Colby said. "These are the shoulder boards that I wore as Commander." He attached the right shoulder board while the President attached the left.

Turning to Admiral Colby, the President asked, "What about the bridge cap with the scrambled eggs?"

"Well, I wasn't about to ask Tom to wear my old bridge cap," he said. Walking back to his chair, he retrieved a new bridge cap from a brown paper bag. "I hope this fits, Tom," he said and placed it on his son's head.

"I must say that he looks mighty fine as a full Commander," the President said. "You're dismissed, young fellow." Tom returned to his seat in a daze. Turning to address the room of aviators, the President said, "Now, gentlemen, we have a comrade to bury. Thank you for the flight jacket. Good luck on your tour to West Pac, and God bless and protect each and every one of you."

The President shook hands with Commander Blackwell and turned to leave the room as the Squadron Duty Officer yelled, "**ATTENTION ON DECK**." The officers stood at attention while the President and Admiral Colby walked out of the room, followed closely by Captain Conrad and Commanders Blackwell and Colby.

TEN

Missing Wingman Flight

Bonita, California

The funeral procession moved slowly along Bonita Road toward the entrance of Glen Abbey Cemetery. The shiny black hearse leading the procession was escorted by two motorcycle policemen. In the limousine immediately behind the hearse, Sarah Wiseman turned to Linda Colby and said, "Thanks for riding with us, Linda. I really do appreciate your support. Is Tom leading the fly-over?"

"Yes, the Skipper asked him to lead the flight," Linda answered.

"I didn't want a military funeral," Sarah sighed, "but Joe talked me into it. He said it was an honor that Charlie deserved."

Linda sat in the limousine's rear-facing seat. She leaned forward and took Sarah's gloved hand, "I should've been here with you the night that Charlie died."

"Joe Blackwell took real good care of me. So sorry about your father's heart attack. Is he out of danger now?" Sarah asked.

"Yes, Dr. Thompson performed a triple by-pass operation, and Father should be able to lead a normal life."

"Did the two weeks put you behind in your college work?"

"No," Linda answered. "Bob Wilson and I are finishing our doctoral dissertation. We'll graduate at the end of this semester."

"I'm so proud of you," Sarah said as she squeezed Linda's hand. "Do you plan to teach after you get your Ph.D.?"

"I had planned to, then Jackie Anderson convinced me that I could have more fun and make more money in real estate. Oh Sarah, I passed the real estate examination and just received my license!"

"That's good news. Tonight, we'll toast your venture into the real estate business," Sarah smiled. "Have you decided on a broker?"

"Oh yes, I'm going to work with Anderson Realty."

"Linda, it's good to have you home. You have the ability to bring a smile to this face no matter how severe my depression gets. I'm glad that I agreed to a military funeral now. Charlie deserves the best. I hope I can get through taps without crying." Sarah wore a black suit and gloves. A black hat covered her blonde curls and provided a veil that shielded her face. Linda glanced at her blue eyes. Sarah was still as beautiful as she was when they first met in Pensacola almost eighteen years ago.

Sarah's fourteen year old daughter, Ruth, sat beside her on the back seat. Ruth also was wearing a black dress, gloves and a hat that was very similar in looks to her mother's. Her blue eyes were puffy. She had sobbed during the private service with the Rabbi at the mortuary. Her head was bowed and her eyes fixed on the small Bible in her hands.

"Are you going to be okay, Ruth?" Linda asked.

Ruth nodded her head, "Yes, Mrs. Colby. We said good-bye to Father at the mortuary. I'll be okay during the funeral." The limousine carrying the President, Admiral and Margaret Colby, Jackie Anderson, and two Secret Service agents followed the family limousine. Tommy Colby, Judy Anderson and David Wiseman followed the presidential limousine in Tommy's Mustang. Behind the Mustang was a line of sixty automobiles carrying squadron officers, their ladies and friends of the Wiseman's.

When they reached the Little Chapel of the Roses, the people left their cars and quickly filled the small chapel. The pallbearers carried the casket to the front of the chapel and placed it on a low table. The senior pallbearer spread the flag over the casket and placed an eight by ten framed photograph of Commander Wiseman and his sword on top of the casket.

Margaret Colby sat between Admiral Colby and the President in the pew behind the family. She was impressed with the beauty and serenity of the small chapel. The Little Chapel of the Roses hosted as many weddings

75

as funerals. The service was very brief. At the end of the service they stood together and sang the Navy hymn. A tear trickled down Margaret's cheek as they sang the last verse that asked the Lord to guard and guide the men "who fly through the great places in the sky". She was determined not to cry and squeezed her eyelids tightly together.

Margaret was most impressed with the chapel and the cemetery. She had immediately decided that she wanted to be buried in the beautiful rolling hills of Glen Abbey where the grass was always green, and the sun shined so beautiful and bright. They had decided long ago that their resting place would be Arlington National Cemetery. Now, she had to find some tactful way to get Thomas to agree with her on Glen Abbey.

At the end of the hymn, the pallbearers carried the casket to the gravesite. Chairs had been arranged on one side of the grave for the family and VIP's. Sarah went forward and sat down. On either side of her sat David and Ruth. Linda sat next to Ruth. President Johnson, Jackie Anderson and the Colby's sat on the row behind the family. The honor guard went through its rifle drill. Three nerve-jarring volleys of rifle fire faded into the mournful notes of taps.

From the west came the screaming roar of four Sikorsky SH-3A helicopters. Commander Tom Colby lead the flight in a right-echelon formation. The flight cruised at two-hundred-feet above the trees and a speed of 120 knots. As they passed over the gravesite, the number-two helicopter pulled up out of formation, leaving the spot open; "the missing wingman" in the formation. The number-two helicopter continued a spiral climb to five hundred feet above the cemetery, as the other helicopters disappeared over the trees.

The aviators among the mourners looked up as Bull climbed the helicopter straight up. Upon reaching five hundred feet, he put the helicopter into auto-rotation and zoomed toward the trees. He leveled the aircraft at two hundred feet above the trees and flew after the other helicopters.

Admiral Colby watched the missing-wingman flight with great interest. He was proud of his son. *Damn, those pilots are good,* he thought. He especially liked the spiral climb of the number-two man. That had to be the Bull Ensign.

Then it was over, and the casket was ready to be lowered into the grave. The honor guard folded the flag and gave it to the President. He walked to Sarah and presented the flag. She sat for a moment clutching it as friends passed by and spoke soft words and touched her hand.

Otay High School
Bonita, California

Sherman Wallace was the head football coach at Otay High School. He was six feet tall and his stomach was enormous, an incongruous attachment to an otherwise well-proportioned body. He had been coaching high school football for twenty-five years, and this was the best football team he had seen to date. Coach Wallace's custom was to gather his team at three o'clock on Friday afternoons for a final pep talk.

Wallace looked at a clipboard while he sucked on a can of Coke. Three universities and the Naval Academy were sending scouts to the game. Wallace had a visit from the Secret Service that morning informing him that the President would be at the game tonight. He decided to withhold the information about the football scouts because players usually screwed up when they tried too hard to make a block or tackle to impress a college scout.

Walking into the locker room, he addressed the team, "Listen up, guys. You all know the Spartans are gonna try to beat our us tonight. Just try your best to execute the game plan that we've worked on. I want to see solid pass protection, and gang tackling if they ever get the ball."

"Hey, Coach, have you heard from any college scouts?" The senior center, Bobby Beecher, asked.

"No, Beecher. I haven't had a call from any of the scouts all week," he lied. "Probably won't know until they meet us at the restaurant after the game, but we do have some VIP fans, right Colby?"

"Yes, Coach," Tommy answered. "My grandfather, Vice Admiral Colby, and President Johnson will be in the bleachers rooting for us."

"You mean to tell us that the President of the United States flew all the way to California just to see us trash the Spartan's," Beecher said.

"Knock-off the bull, Beecher," Wallace ordered. Then addressing the team, he said, "Texans take their football very seriously. Tonight I want you all to show the President how Californian's play football. I want at least fifty points on that scoreboard." The team began to yell and clap their hands to signify their agreement with Coach Wallace's prediction. Raising his hands to restore order in the room, Wallace said, "You are dismissed to go home and rest. Remember, no carbonated drinks, no smoking and absolutely no sex before the game."

"Oh Coach, you take all the fun out of being a football player," Beecher groaned as the team filed out of the locker room.

Wallace touched Tommy on his shoulder and said, "Colby and Wiseman, stop by my office for a few minutes."

"Okay, Coach," Tommy said as he and David Wiseman followed Wallace to his office.

"Have a seat, gentlemen," Wallace said as he walked to the small refrigerator in the corner of his office and grabbed another can of Coke. "That was a very nice military funeral for your father this morning, David. Do you feel like playing tonight?"

"Oh yes, Coach. I've gotta play," David said and continued, "Father would've wanted me to play. He never missed any of my games."

"Well, you know how much I need you to back up Tommy at quarterback," Wallace said, "but I really need you to play defense tonight. Steve Perry sprained an ankle and is just not going to be at full speed. Will you play defensive back tonight?"

"Yes, sir, and I promise you at least two interceptions."

"Okay, David, I'll hold you to that," Wallace smiled. Turning to Tommy, he said, "I'd like for you and David to be co-captains of the game tonight. Is that okay?"

"Sure, Coach, that's great," Tommy answered.

"Okay, guys, let's have a great game," Wallace said dismissing them as he turned his attention to the clipboard and the can of Coke.

"I heard that Coach drinks three six-packs of Coke every day since he stopped smoking," David said as they walked toward the parking lot.

"I wouldn't doubt that. He sure has the potbelly for it. Dad told me that Coach Wallace was All-American at the University of Tennessee during his college days. Come on, I'll give you a ride out to the ranch."

"How's the romance coming along with Judy?" David asked as Tommy turned the Mustang onto Otay Lakes Road.

"For the first time in my life, I'm in love, David."

78

"The love bug has bitten you?"

"David, Judy's the lady I'm going to marry," Tommy stated, then changing the subject said, "Grandmother Colby told me that at least four colleges will have scouts at the game tonight. First and foremost, the Naval Academy, then comes Stanford, USC and the University of Texas."

"Wonder why Coach lied to Bobby Beecher?" David asked.

"Oh, Coach has some dumb fool idea that the seniors will clutch and make mistakes if they know that a scout is watching their every move."

"I sure want to impress the Naval Academy scout," David said.

"Hey, no sweat," Tommy said. "Your father's death on active duty guarantees you a ticket to the Academy. With your great quarterback arm, you can walk-on and probably make starting team your freshman year."

"Sure wish I had some of your optimism. Have you decided on Stanford?"

"Yes, Grandmother Colby established a four-year endowment for me there, but it would be nice to play football for Stanford," Tommy said wishfully.

"Has Judy decided where she's going to college? David asked.

"I'm trying to talk her into coming to Stanford with me, but she keeps saying the tuition is too high."

"Well, heck, ask her to marry you, then you can live in an apartment near the campus."

"David, my friend, you may just have solved my most pressing problem. I'm certain that Grandmother would gladly pay the college tuition of her one and only granddaughter-in-law."

ELEVEN

Tiger Victory

Otay High School
Bonita, California

Tommy Colby sat in the overheated football locker room and waited for Coach Wallace's pep talk. He closed his eyes and sniffed the odors that seemed to deepen in the heat of the room. He could smell the ankle tape, ammonia, unwashed socks and foot powder. It was a locker room smell that an athlete would remember until the day he died. His thoughts wandered to Judy Anderson. *Sweet, beautiful Judy. The new love in my life.* He opened his eyes and leaned toward David Wiseman. "Do you feel up to playing defense?" He asked in a low whisper.

"Yeah, Tommy, I'm really looking forward to it," David said. "I would just love to get three or four interceptions tonight. Sometimes that can be just as rewarding as throwing the long bomb for a touchdown."

"You going to the dance tonight after the game?" Tommy asked.

"Yes, I asked Janine Johnson before Father was killed in the crash. Are you taking Judy?"

"Yes, my man. Let's make it a double date. You and Janine can have the back seat of the Jag. Have you and Janine done it yet?"

"Oh, God no, but I sure want to," David groaned. "She's one of your passionate Protestants who thinks she's going straight to hell if she screws before the sacred marriage vows."

"Well, you Jews started all of that with your laws written on a tablet of stone," Tommy teased.

"Don't lay that on my people. You know that teenage sex is older than any religion or Bible." Then he asked, "What about you and Judy? Have you made out yet?"

"Oh yes, my man," Tommy smiled. "This is strictly in confidence, and I don't want another living soul to know about it, okay?"

"Sure man, scouts honor," David promised.

"Remember the other day when Judy soloed?"

"How can I ever forget that day? That was the day that Dad crashed his helicopter," David answered in a sad voice.

"Damn, I forgot already," Tommy said and then continued. "Well, on takeoff the vibration of the plane made Judy have an orgasm."

"That's the craziest story I've ever heard. You mean she didn't touch herself?"

"No, I swear to God man. She was just sitting there in the seat gasping and moaning. I'd never seen a girl have an orgasm before."

"I think you're pulling my leg."

"I know this sounds unbelievable, but I swear to God it's true," Tommy whispered. "Then Judy removed her shorts and sat on my lap. That was the greatest day of my life."

"Man, I sure wish I could make love to Janine like that," David whispered. "I can't get Janine to take off her panties. Can you give me some pointers on how to get through Janine's strong willpower?"

"Well, try caressing her through the panties," Tommy advised. "Maybe that'll work and she'll get so hot that she will rip them off for you."

"Thanks Tommy, I'll give it a try tonight."

Bobby Joe Beecher pulled the number 50 jersey over his head and sat on the bench beside Tommy and David and started lacing up his shoes. "You going to the dance tonight, Tommy?" Beecher asked.

"I'm not sure, Bobby Joe."

"How many times have you balled Elizabeth?" Beecher asked.

"Just once," Tommy said, "and it wasn't all that good."

"**Not good**!" Beecher yelled. "Bubba, tell our quarterback that there's only two kinds of nookie; good and better," he said to the big, black tackle.

"Bobby Joe's right there," Bubba Jackson mimicked. "Nookie's so good, and it gets better everyday. You ever make love to a nigger, Mister Tommy?"

"God no, Bubba!"

81

"Oh my God, you all don't know whatcha been missing. They say if a white boy makes love to a black girl that he'll never ever be happy with a white woman again."

"Have you ever made love to a white girl, Bubba?" Tommy asked.

"Lord no, Tommy. When I was twelve years old, we were stationed at Pensacola. My pappy told me that if I ever touched a white girl that he'd cut off my pecker with a butcher knife."

"Have you ever made love to a Mexican girl, Bubba?" Bobby Joe asked.

"Yes, suh," Bubba rolled his eyes, "Bout twenty or thirty, as I recollect. Mighty fine nookie, mighty fine nookie."

Bobby Joe Beecher kneeled on the floor in front of Bubba. "Oh, Great Bubba," he said. "Please grant me a great game tonight. I have a date tonight with the cheerleader, Susie Gleason. If I can run back a punt for the winning touchdown, Susie might just give me a glance at her golden nookie."

Coach Wallace was standing in his office looking through the one-way mirror into the locker room watching the antics of Bobby Joe Beecher. Turning to his defense coach, Paul Walker, he said, "If Bobby Joe got just half the nookie he brags about, his pecker would be worn down to a nub."

"Coach, you know that most of it is bragging," Walker answered.

"Yeah, I know Paul. Come on, it's time to start the pep talk," Wallace said as he walked toward the locker room.

Bobby Joe Beecher began to dance around in a little circle chanting, "Nookie, nookie, nookie," as Coach Wallace walked into the locker room.

Tommy saw Coach Wallace standing in the doorway. "Good evening, Coach," Tommy said. Bobby Joe stopped his dance and chant and collapsed on the bench beside Bubba.

"Jesus Christ, it's hot in here!" Wallace yelled completely ignoring the antics of Beecher. Turning to the team manager, Charles Linden, he ordered, "Get some of those windows opened Charlie, and turn on the big floor fans."

"Sure thing, Coach," Charlie rushed to carry out the orders.

Wallace took a long swig on the Coke and turned to address the team. When he spoke, it was in the football jargon of coaches who had once been athletes and played the game in the same arenas they now presided over as adults. "No more chalk talk now, boys. I want you to execute these plays just like we practiced all week. I want us to win this one for David's daddy. **WIN! WIN! WIN!** I want to win this game real big. **MAKE YOUR SCHOOL PROUD**," he roared. "I want you to make your girlfriends proud, your parents proud, your grandparents proud and even make the President of the United States proud. Do you all hear what I'm saying?"

"YES, SIR!" came the thunderous reply from the team.

Coach Wallace raised his eyes and right hand toward the ceiling in an appeal for divine help. "Let us pray," he said and all heads of the players leaned forward, toward the floor. "Our most precious Lord Jesus, we once again come to beg for Your blessings and ask You to forgive us for our many sins against you and our neighbors. Lord, You saw that we had the whole team out at the cemetery this morning to honor David's daddy, may he rest in peace in Heaven tonight. David's gonna play defensive back tonight, and I ask You to help him intercept every pass that their quarterback throws to his side of the field. Lord, You know that the President of these United States will be sitting in our bleachers tonight watching this game. I ask that You continue to bless him and his family, and give him the wisdom to end this little Vietnam War real quick before a lot more of our fine boys get killed in that God forsaken communist land. Lord, this is a very important football game for us tonight against the Chula Vista Spartans, and we want to win so very much. We don't want to ask for anything special, Lord, but help our boys make good clean tackles. Help Bubba and John control their tempers, and please give Tommy good control of his passes. If You see one of my boys make a mistake and commit a clip or a holding penalty, Lord, just blow Your whistle and throw the yellow flag on his head because You're the great umpire of life. Call timeout and give us a fifteen-yard penalty. We promise to play within the rules of the game, but most of all, sweet Jesus, I ask You to help me coach my boys all the way to the championship of life. Amen."

"AMEN," the team yelled in relief.

"Okay boys, follow me," Coach Wallace yelled. He opened the locker room door and jogged toward the north goal post. As co-captains, Tommy and David led the team, bursting through the paper banner that the cheerleaders held under the goal post. Eight thousand, two hundred and sixty-four voices welcomed the team as they ran to the far end of the football field for warm-up practice.

Otay Stadium was unusual in that it was built in a small canyon. The topmost seats were level with the parking lot. Instead of climbing the bleachers for a seat, you walked down. The stadium was six years old and had a capacity of nine thousand.

The presidential party was sequestered in a reserved area immediately in front of the press box. President Johnson was wearing his

Navy flight jacket. He was sitting between Jackie Anderson and Margaret Colby sipping a cup of Margaret's special coffee. He was very pleased to see Navy men throughout the bleachers wearing their flight jackets. Commander Tom Colby sat in the row in front of the President between Linda and Sarah Wiseman. Commander Joe Blackwell sat beside Sarah, and Lieutenant Commander Robert Wilson sat on the other side of Linda Colby. The Sea Devil squadron had commandeered a section of the bleachers in front of the presidential party.

"They sure did build a beautiful stadium in this big gully," the President said to Margaret.

"Lyndon, out here they're called arroyos, not gullies," Margaret corrected him.

"Oh yes, we have a few arroyos down in Texas also," he said. Then he turned to Jackie and asked, "Want to make a friendly wager on the game, Miss Jackie?"

"Yes, I'd love too, Lyndon," she answered. "I'm a loyal fan of the Otay Tigers. Your team will have to be the Chula Vista Spartan's, okay?"

"That's fine with me," the President answered. "Since you have the home field advantage, how many points are you gonna give me?"

"Not one point. This is supposed to be a very close game between two powerhouse football teams. How much do you want to bet?"

"How about ten dollars?"

"Okay, we have a bet," Jackie said as she grasped his right hand and felt a tingling sensation flow through her body.

"I'll bet you a hundred dollars that Tommy's team wins, Lyndon," Margaret said.

"I hate to take your money, Margaret, but we have a bet," he said as he released Jackie's hand and shook with Margaret. "Now, tell me which one is Tommy?"

"My grandson wears number eight," she answered proudly. "Looks like they're about through with warm-up and ready to start the game."

The umpire blew his whistle and each team ran to their side of the field. The co-captains, Tommy wearing jersey number 8 and David wearing jersey number 7, accompanied the umpire and field judge to the center of the football field where they met the referee, line judge and captain of the Chula Vista Spartan's. The umpire introduced the team captains to the officials and instructed the visiting captain to call the coin toss in the air. He flipped the silver dollar high and the captain called, "Tails."

The Spartan's won the coin toss and elected to receive the football. Tommy indicated that the Otay Tigers would defend the north goal. The starting teams lined up for the kickoff. John Conrad was kicker for the Tigers. He sailed the football high in the air to the Spartan's two-yard line. The ball was returned to the twenty-two yard line where the runner was smeared by Bubba Jackson, the Tiger's six feet-four inch, two hundred and fifty-two pound black tackle.

On the first play from the scrimmage line, the Spartan's quarterback dropped back to pass to his left end on David's side of the field. Bubba's big hand just grazed the football as it left the quarterback's hand. David saw the football wobbling in the air behind the intended receiver. He stepped behind the receiver, intercepted the ball and raced toward his end zone, crossing the goal line untouched by a Spartan player. Then he ran to the Tiger's bench where he was congratulated by Coach Wallace and teammates. **"Way to go, David**!" Tommy yelled as John Conrad kicked the extra point.

"Thanks, Tommy," David said, "but a lot of credit should go to Bubba. He got one of his big hands on the football."

Coach Wallace heard the exchange of words between Tommy and David. He had seen Bubba deflect the ball, but it was damn nice of David to give some of the credit to Bubba, damn nice. **"HEY, CHARLIE, BRING ME A COKE,"** he yelled to the team manager.

Wallace chugged on the Coke and watched his team prepare for the second kickoff. Fifty-two seconds had elapsed in the first quarter and the Tiger's led by seven points. Conrad's next kickoff sailed into the end zone where it was caught and downed by the Spartan's. Chula Vista's ball, first and ten on their twenty-yard line. The first down play was to the fullback who was tackled by Bubba Jackson for a one yard loss. The second down play went to the running back trying to sweep around the left end. David Wiseman tackled him at the line of scrimmage. The third down play was an incomplete pass to the right side of the field that sailed over the receiver's head, stopping the clock. On fourth down, the Spartan's kicked the football. The kicker, standing on his own five-yard line, lofted a beautiful spiral kick that was caught by Bobby Beecher on the fifty-yard line. In addition to being center, Bobby was the receiver for punts and kickoffs. He returned the football to the Spartan's thirty-two yard line.

The Tiger's offense rushed onto the field. Tommy called a long pass to Paul Tulley, the right end. He took the snap from Beecher, faked a hand-off to the running back and ran toward the sideline. Spotting Tulley open five yards behind the Spartan's defensive back, Tommy threw the long pass. Tulley caught the football and ran across the goal line untouched by the defensive back. John Conrad kicked the extra point making the score 14 to 0.

"Well, I can see that I've been hustled by two slick chicks," the President said patting Margaret and Jackie on the back.

"It was his idea to bet, right, Jackie?" Margaret said then continued, "Oh, Lyndon, wasn't that a beautiful pass that Tommy threw?"

"Yes, ma'am, right on the money," the President agreed. "Who's Tommy going to play for, the Naval Academy or the University of Texas?"

"Tommy's going to Stanford where he'll be studying medicine," she answered, "but the college scouts should be able to use some of the other excellent players on both of these teams."

"May I have another cup of your delicious coffee, Margaret?" He asked. "Looks like this is gonna be a long, high scoring game."

"I'll let you out of our bet, or we can bet double or nothing, and I'll even give you fourteen points," Jackie said to the President as she passed her coffee cup to Margaret for a refill.

"God, I like Jackie's spirit," he said to Margaret. Then turning to Jackie, he said, "Okay, I accept."

Lieutenant Commander Robert Wilson sat beside Linda Colby and listened to the conversation in the row behind them. His mind was definitely not on the football game. After his morning visit to HS-24, he had returned to find his office blown to bits. He had spent the rest of the day with the Naval Investigative Service. Finally, the FBI had decided to investigate the bombing, claiming federal jurisdiction. Apparently, the bomb was in the box of cookies that had supposedly been mailed from Wilson's mother in Memphis. Petty Officer First Class Ernie Palmer and Airman Peterson had also been questioned by the FBI. Neither remembered much about the package, except that it was wrapped in brown paper and had canceled postage in the upper right-hand corner. The package had been on Wilson's desk when Palmer and Peterson reported for work that morning.

Linda turned to look at Bob. She could see the puffy outline of his black-eye behind the aviator sunglasses. "Did Deacon Baker strike you in the face, Robert?"

"He sure did, pretty lady. It's difficult to duck with your hands cuffed behind your back."

"Well, I think the fat slob should apologize to you and then to our church," she said. "That was not a Christian thing for him to do."

"Don't be too hasty to judge, pretty lady. In his tiny mind, he thought that he was doing his job," Wilson said.

"Well, I certainly want to hear his explanation that would justify such violent action," she insisted.

Changing the subject, he whispered in Linda's ear, "Your mother-in-law seems to be having a good time."

"Oh, yes. It was such a surprise to have them and the President as guests for the weekend. Please come by the ranch after the game and have a drink with us to celebrate Tom's promotion."

"I'd love to," he said as the stadium erupted in a roar. David Wiseman had intercepted another Spartan pass and was running for the end zone. John Conrad kicked his third extra point, and the score was 21 to 0.

Margaret Colby hugged her husband and said, "Congratulations on your third star and your new assignment to the Seventh Fleet."

"Thanks, my love, but it'll be so lonely being away from you. Do you want to stay at the ranch in Virginia or come back out here and stay with Linda while Tom's on the cruise?"

"I'm staying at the Flying C," she said. "But I may come back out this winter and visit with Linda and Tommy if the snow gets too deep." The fans stood as John Conrad prepared for his fourth kickoff. At half time the score was Tigers - 28, Spartans - 0.

Chuck's Steak House
Bonita, California

The jubilant football players sat in the party room of Chuck's Steak House and ate Porterhouse steaks, french fries and beans and relived the highlights of their victory. Final score, Tigers - 42, Spartans - 7. Twenty-one points had been scored by the defense. David had intercepted three passes and returned them for touchdowns.

Tom Warner, from the Naval Academy, had congratulated David on his excellent defense, and expressed his sympathy about his father's fatal accident. Coach Wallace sat at the head table with the college scouts extolling the talents of his senior players and sucked on a can Coke.

John Conrad had kicked six extra points. He turned to Tommy and said, "I was shocked to see my old man wearing his flight jacket to the game. Dad never even wears his flight jacket around the house anymore."

"I think the President had something to do with it, John," Tommy said. "He invited the squadron to come to the game tonight wearing their flight jackets and asked your father to clear it with the Naval District."

87

"Well, I'm glad that Dad got it squared away," John replied. "He seemed to really enjoy the game tonight."

Coach Wallace tapped on his water glass with a spoon to get the players attention. Addressing the players, he said, "You all played a good game tonight, and I'm proud of each and every one of you. This just proves that hard work and practice will pay off when you follow the game plan. We had some mighty good plays on both offense and defense tonight, but I think you'll agree with me that David Wiseman gets the game ball for such outstanding play on defense. David, come up to the head table," Wallace ordered. The players applauded as David rose from his seat beside Tommy and walked to the head table.

"David, it gives me great pleasure to present you with the game ball for your outstanding contribution to the game tonight," Coach Wallace said as he shook Wiseman's hand and gave him the football.

"Speech! Speech!" The team yelled.

"Thanks, Coach," David said as he accepted the game ball. Turning to face the players, he said, "I especially want to thank Bubba for tipping that first pass to me. After the first touchdown, the rest was easy," he grinned then walked back to the table and sat beside Tommy.

"Okay, boys, you played hard tonight and won the game for us," Coach Wallace said. "Go to the dance and have a good time, but remember to be in bed by midnight. We have a big game next week with Sweetwater."

"Coach," Bobby Joe groaned. "You're really a slave driver." His teammates laughed as they walked out to their cars.

Colby Residence
Bonita, California

Tommy Colby drove his Mustang into the driveway and parked beside the Jaguar. The family, along with the President, Jackie Anderson, Sarah Wiseman, Joe Blackwell and Bob Wilson had gathered in the den to celebrate the victory. Tommy walked over and hugged his grandmother. "Did you enjoy the game, Grandma?" He teased.

"Oh yes, and I had a bet that you would win," she answered as she pressed the hundred dollar bill into his palm.

"Thank you Grandma," he said kissing her lightly on the lips. Turning to his father, Tommy asked, "Dad, may I borrow the Jag tonight? David and I'd like to take our dates to the dance, and the Mustang is kinda cramped."

"Sure, Tommy," Tom replied.

"Tommy, you and David may have the limousine," the President said. "The driver will be happy to take you anywhere you want to go."

"Thanks, Uncle Lyndon," Tommy said. "The Jag will be fine, and you might need the limousine for some emergency. Good night all, we gotta run or we'll be late for the dance." As they walked to the Jaguar, Tommy said, "We'll drive next door and get Judy, then drive out and pick up Janine."

"Tommy, I'm not really in the mood to go to the dance," David said. "If it's okay with the girls, let's just go some place quiet where we can relax and talk."

"I know the perfect spot," Tommy answered as he drove the Jaguar into Judy's driveway.

*   *   *

Tommy parked the Jaguar on the back row at the drive-in movie. He and Judy sat in the front seat, while David and Janine sat in the back. The speaker was blaring inside the car, but no one was listening to it. Judy sat astride Tommy's lap. Tommy heard low moaning coming from the back seat. "Can you see what they're doing back there?" He whispered into Judy's ear. He felt her shiver.

"It's too dark," she whispered, "I think she's sitting on David's lap."

"Will you please marry me?" Tommy whispered into her ear.

"**OOH, YES! JESUS CHRIST, YES!**" Judy yelled just as Janine reached her first orgasm and moaned uncontrollably in David's arms.

"You guys okay, up there?" David asked.

"Sorry about screaming, David," Judy said. "This crazy nut just asked me to marry him."

"That's fantastic," David said.

Janine pushed her skirt down and tried to regain control of her senses after the earth-shattering orgasm that she had experienced. "Oh yes, Judy. We're so happy for you two," Janine said in a small, strained voice.

"Well, I've gotta get out of this car and get some fresh air and go to the bathroom," Judy said. "May we bring you all anything from the refreshment stand?"

"A Coke, please," Janine said.

"Make that two Cokes," David said.

"Two Cokes coming up," Tommy answered as he got out of the Jaguar and walked Judy to the refreshment area. Turning to Judy, he asked, "Why were you so anxious to get out of the Jag?"

89

"You big lug," she said as she put her arm around him and hugged him tightly. "Now that they have some privacy, maybe she'll make love to David."

In the back seat of the Jaguar, Janine was all over David. She sat astride his lap kissing him. "David Wiseman, that was the most wonderful feeling in the world," she said. "Now I want you to make love to me." She raised up and slid the panties off her legs and let them drop on the floorboard of the Jaguar. "Do you think Judy knew we were petting?"

"No way, Janine. They were making love up there in the front seat just like we are now and trying to be real quiet about it," David laughed. "Judy probably had an orgasm just about the time David asked her to marry him, and that's why she screamed so loud."

"You men and your big egos," Janine said as she relaxed and sat on his lap. "Oh, I do love you." She kissed him.

"This is the first time for you, right?" He asked.

"Yes," Janine answered.

"First time for me, too, and I know we're gonna love it."

TWELVE

Low Pass By Air Force One

The Anderson Residence
Bonita, California

Admiral Colby and the President were seated in the den of the Anderson's residence drinking coffee. CIA agent, Jack Warner, conducted the intelligence brief in a very low voice. "Jack, the room's clean," the President growled. "The comm boys went all over this place with a fine tooth comb."

"Yes, Mr. President," Warner said and raised his voice to normal volume. "The Soviets dispatched a fifth nuclear submarine to the Sea of Japan. The *USS Yorktown* has been tracking four Russian submarines in that area for the past three weeks. The Air Group lost thirteen helicopters in the Gulf of Tonkin during combat rescue operations. The remaining three helicopters are onboard the *USS Concord*, supporting combat SAR operations. Without ASW helicopter assets, *Yorktown* has advised that she cannot maintain a track and surveillance of the fifth submarine."

"Jesus Christ, Jack!" The President yelled. "If it comes to a shooting war, how in the hell can we cope with three hundred Russian submarines if the carrier can't keep track of more than four?"

"Well, for one thing sir, in a shooting war, the Navy would detect and kill the submarine. Not track them for three weeks."

"What do you recommend, Admiral?" The President asked.

"Chief, the *USS Shiloh* is scheduled to sail to the Gulf of Tonkin in three weeks with Tom's Air Group aboard to relieve *Yorktown*. I'd give her a three day notice to get underway, and keep both carrier's there in the Sea of Japan until the Soviets get tired of playing games," he answered.

"Thank you, Admiral." Turning to Warner, he said, "Jack, get word to CNO that the *Shiloh* will sail within three days to the Sea of Japan for special operations."

"Yes, Mr. President," Warner replied.

"Oh, by the way, Jack, Admiral Colby's going out to take command the Seventh Fleet sometime this month. Anything happening around the Gulf that might be of interest to him?"

"Yes, sir," Warner said. Turning to Admiral Colby, he said, "Most of the news is doom and gloom, sir. The *Concord* lost another H-3 helicopter yesterday. The Commander of Task Force Seventy-Seven point Seven, Admiral Perkins and his Chief of Staff, Captain Stoddard, were returning from the *Concord* to his flagship. The helicopter crashed while landing on the *Turner Joy* and flipped over the side into the water. The crewmen of the helicopter were rescued by the ships, but not a trace was found of Admiral Perkins or Captain Stoddard."

"Damn, that's too bad," Colby muttered. "Jim Perkins was a good friend."

The President turned to Colby and said, "Thomas, I want you to assign a board to look into those helicopter losses as soon as you get there." Turning back to Warner, he said, "Thanks for the brief, Jack. We'll see you out at Ream Field at nine o'clock for our flight back to Washington."

"Good day, gentlemen," Warner said as he gathered the briefing papers and left the room.

"You were kinda hard on him, Chief," Colby said.

"Naw, Thomas. Jack's gonna make a great Director of the CIA some day. Did you notice that he gave me the correct answer, not one he thought that I wanted to hear."

"Yes, he's extremely intelligent. Where did he get his doctorate?"

"University of Texas," the President smiled. "Mmmmm, that bacon smells mighty good. It's seven-thirty on the dot, Thomas. Shall we go to breakfast?"

"Ready, Chief," Colby said as they walked toward the dining room.

Colby Residence
Bonita, California

Tommy placed the steaming cup of hot tea on the silver tray. Then, remembering his grandmother liked her tea spiked, he walked to the bar and grabbed the small bottle of brandy.

"Good morning, Tommy," Margaret said as she walked into the kitchen.

"Morning, Grandma, I was just about to bring your tea upstairs."

"Oh, darling, I'm sorry that I spoiled your surprise. Let's have it in the den so we can relax and talk a few minutes before breakfast."

"Would Grandfather like some coffee?"

"No, dear, he went next door to the Anderson's to talk to the President. They're probably having coffee together. How was the dance last night?"

"Oh, we decided not to go to the dance. David wasn't feeling sociable after his father's funeral, so we took the girls to a movie."

"Drive-in movie?"

"Yes, but it was a double date, remember?"

"Are you in love with Judy?"

"Yes, ma'am, and I have been for a long time, but didn't realize it until last Tuesday when Judy soloed."

"Was that the day you made love to her?"

"Why, yes," he stammered, "but how did you know?"

"A grandmother's intuition," she smiled. "When do you and Judy plan to get married?"

"You mean, you think it's okay," Tommy stammered again. "Gosh, Grandma, you're the best." He hugged her tightly and kissed her cheek.

"You and Judy are a beautiful couple. It's so refreshing to see young people so much in love. I'd just hate to see this marriage interfere with your plans to be a doctor."

"Oh, it won't," he promised. "We want to get married next June. We'll find a small apartment near the campus, and I'll enroll at Stanford in September."

"Will Judy be a student at Stanford?"

"Judy wants to be a lawyer, but I don't know if Mrs. Anderson can afford the tuition at Stanford. We may have to wait until I start practicing medicine, and then Judy can go to college and study law."

"Well, that's too long to wait. You two should enjoy the exciting years of college life together. Would Judy be offended if my wedding present to her was a trust fund to cover her college expenses?"

"Grandma, you're the greatest," he said and was hugging her again when his mother and father walked into the room.

"Good morning, Linda, good morning, Tom," Margaret said. "Tommy was telling me what a great time they had at the school dance last

93

night. Come, let's go to breakfast. Jackie said to be there by seven-thirty sharp or they would start without us."

NAS Ream Field
Imperial Beach, California

Tom Colby returned the Marine sentry's salute and followed the limousine through the main gate. Inside the Jaguar, Linda sat beside Tom. Tommy sat in the back between Judy and Jackie Anderson. Tom automatically slowed for the speed bumps and said, "Now, I truly believe in miracles. Those damn speed bumps just disappeared overnight."

"How long have you been praying for that?" Linda asked.

"Well, for almost two years now," he answered.

"Oh, ye of little faith," Linda laughed. "Remember the Good Book says, 'seek and you shall find, ask and it shall be given unto you, knock and the door will be opened'."

"Linda, you sound more like your father everyday," Tom teased. "I didn't have to seek because I knew the bumps were in the road. I asked the Lord a hundred times to remove the damn things when I should have been pounding on Captain Conrad's door." The limousine stopped at Base Operations. Tom parked the Jaguar near the limousine and said, "Speaking of Captain Conrad, there he is all decked out in his tropical white uniform."

"Maybe you should've worn your uniform instead of those Levi's and your favorite Naval Academy sweatshirt," Linda said.

"Oh, man, Dad! There's Coach Wallace and the football squad all lined up in front of Air Force One like a platoon of Marines," Tommy said. "I didn't know they were coming out to say good-bye to the President."

"Well, gang, let's go say good-bye to my parents and the Commander-in-Chief," Tom said as he stepped out of the Jaguar and opened the back door for Jackie Anderson.

*   *   *

"Looks like you made a big hit with Tommy's football team, Lyndon," Margaret said as she looked out and saw the team lined up by Air Force One. "Now you be real nice to those boys," she ordered.

"Yes ma'am, Mrs. Colby," the President mimicked. *Damn, what a nice gesture. I'll invite them all back to the White House after they win the State Championship.* The President turned and shook hands with Tom. "Thanks for all the hospitality. I've really had a great time. Take care of yourself during the little pleasure cruise to the Tonkin Gulf."

94

"You're welcome, Uncle Lyndon," Tom said. "Come back and see us anytime."

Hugging Linda, the President said, "Come back the White House for a visit when you fly east to visit Margaret."

"I promise I will," she answered and kissed his cheek.

He hugged Jackie and whispered in her ear, "Call me when you get to Washington, and I'll show you my cabin at Camp David."

"I'd love to Lyndon," she whispered, "have a nice flight."

"Thanks for letting me ride your horse," the President said as he shook Judy Anderson's hand.

"You're most welcome, sir. Please come back and visit us again."

"I sure will, sweetheart," he answered as he turned and took Tommy's arm. "Tommy, let's say good-bye to the squad."

Captain Conrad snapped to attention and saluted as the President approached Air Force One. "Mr. President, we're honored by your visit."

"Thank you, Captain," the President said before Conrad could proceed with his speech. "Now, I'd like to say good-bye to the football squad. I understand that your son's on the team. I want to tell these young men how much I enjoyed the game. Will you please accompany us?"

"Yes, sir," Conrad said and got in line behind Tommy Colby. Tommy introduced the President to Coach Wallace, and then to each member of the squad as they walked down the rows of football players. The President shook hands with each of them and made some remark about their contribution during the game.

When they stopped before Bubba Jackson, the President said, "Bubba, you played a great game. Would you consider playing football for the University of Texas?"

"Yes, sir, Mr. President," Bubba smiled. "I talked to the scouts from the Naval Academy, USC and the University of Texas this morning. They all want me," he laughed.

"Well, son, those sure are fine colleges, but I'd like to see you play for the Longhorns," the President said as he gripped Bubba's hand and then moved to the next player. After he had greeted each player, he shook Tommy's hand and walked up the ramp and disappeared inside Air Force One. Admiral Colby and Margaret said their good-byes and climbed the ramp followed closely by the remainder of the Presidential party. The ground crew rolled back the ramp, and the engines of Air Force One roared to life. The pilot taxied to the end of runway 27 and applied take-off power. The Boeing 707 quickly accelerated down the runway becoming airborne at the four-thousand foot marker.

95

"Ream Tower, Air Force One," the pilot said into the microphone.

"Go ahead your message," the tower operator said.

"Roger, tower. The Boss wants to say farewell to some friends. Request permission for low pass at two hundred feet and three hundred knots, over."

"You're cleared for low pass at any altitude and any airspeed. Negative traffic," the tower operator answered.

"Roger, tower. ETA five minutes. Out."

The tower operator saw the crowd of people walking toward the cars in the parking lot. He grabbed the loudspeaker microphone and said, **"Attention in the parking lot. Air Force One will be making a low pass from west to east in four minutes**. Everyone please remain in the ramp area." The crowd on the ramp looked to the west and saw the jet liner dive toward the airfield. Air Force One passed over the group at 100 feet and 320 knots. There was a little wiggle of the wings as the pilot climbed toward the mountains.

"Ream Tower, Air Force One. Thanks for the low pass, and a memorable vacation, over."

"Roger, Air Force One," the tower operator said. "Contact San Diego Departure Control on 327.5. Have a nice flight, sir."

On the ramp, Tom could not believe his eyes. Air Force One never buzzed the tower or made low passes. He wondered who suggested it to the pilot, the President or his father. "It was probably Mother's idea," he said to Linda and Jackie as they walked toward the Jaguar.

Colby Residence
Bonita, California

Tommy looked at the fog as he dressed for church. Fog was an aviator's nightmare. Tommy hated fog. He finished dressing and walked downstairs where his father was reading the Sunday paper and sipping his third cup of coffee. "Morning, Dad," he said. "Think we can convince mother that it's too foggy to drive to church this morning?"

"Not a chance in a million," Tom laughed. "Your mother wants to have a few choice words with Deacon Baker about slugging poor Bob Wilson in the eye."

"I saw the whole thing, Dad. Deacon Baker must really hate Commander Bob's guts to slug him with his hands cuffed behind his back."

"Grab a cup of coffee, if you'd like. I want to talk to you a few minutes before your mother comes down." Tommy poured a half cup of coffee in one of the Sea Devil mugs and walked to the table. He drank the

96

coffee like his father, without cream or sugar. "Before Grandpa Colby left yesterday, he gave me some information about our WesPac cruise. It's probably classified, but let's keep it from your mother as long as we can. No use spoiling her weekend, right?"

"Yes, sir."

"As you know, we're scheduled to leave on the *Shiloh* in three weeks for an eight month cruise to the Tonkin Gulf to relieve the *Yorktown*. Well, Grandpa said that we'd probably get orders to sail within the next three or four days to go out and help the *Yorktown* track some Soviet submarines.

"That's a bummer, Dad."

"I'm afraid that it'll create a lot of hardships for the men, and it's really gonna mess up the transfer of our SAR birds to the *Concord*. The Sea of Japan is a hell of a long way from the Gulf of Tonkin. Much too far for the H-3 to fly without refueling."

"Will you be flying combat missions, Dad?"

"There's a possibility, but I don't know for sure yet," Tom lied. "I just wanted to let you know that the carrier could sail as early as next Thursday."

"Thanks Dad, Mother and I'll really miss you. Can I talk to you a minute about Judy?"

"Sure, son. Is Judy your new girlfriend?"

"It's more than that. I asked Judy to marry me Friday night, and she said yes. So, I guess that makes us engaged," Tommy grinned.

"Have you told your mother yet?"

"No, sir, but I told Grandma Colby yesterday morning, and she thinks it's okay. Is it okay with you, Dad?"

"Are you two in love?"

"Yes, sir."

"Then you have my blessing," Tom said. "When's the wedding?"

"Oh, not until we graduate from high school. Maybe next June when the *Shiloh* gets back from Vietnam."

Tom reached into the right pocket of his suit jacket and removed a pair of blue lace panties. "I found these in the back seat of the Jag. Do they belong to Judy?"

"Oh, no sir!" Tommy gulped. "So old David followed my advice and really did get lucky at the drive-in."

"You were giving David advice on how to seduce his girlfriend?"

97

"Yes, sir. Janine's been a nookie tease for the past few months, and David was really frustrated. So I gave him a few pointers. Looks like it worked."

"Last Friday, David buried his father and played one hell of a football game. Now you're telling me that he made love to his girlfriend in the back seat of my Jaguar?"

"It sure does look like he did, and I think it was the first time for both David and Janine," Tommy said. "Dad, may I return the panties to David?"

"Oh, yes, by all means," Tom handed the panties to Tommy. "Just remember that a gentleman uses discretion about such delicate matters."

"Yes, sir." Tommy tucked the panties into his coat pocket.

Linda clutched a Bible in her right hand and walked down the stairs. She was stunning in a black dress, black gloves and black high heel shoes. "You're beautiful, Mother," Tommy whispered.

"Why, thank you darling," Linda said. "Now, if you gentlemen will finish your coffee, maybe we can get to church before the service starts."

THIRTEEN

Lunch In The Sky Room

HS-24 Ready Room
NAS Ream Field

Commander Joe Blackwell stood at the podium looking out at the packed room of aviators and Chief Petty Officers. He cleared his throat and addressed the group, "Men, I just got back from AIRPAC, and I have bad news on top of bad news. This information is classified confidential and will only be passed to the men in your shops and your family. For God's sake, tell them it's classified, and not to talk to anyone about it. First of all, the aircraft carrier is sailing next Thursday morning at seven-hundred hours."

The group of Navy men groaned as one. Joe heard a few choice cuss words from some of the chiefs. Raising his hands to quiet the group, he said, "I feel just as bad about it as you do, but there's no recourse. We'll fly the aircraft aboard Wednesday afternoon while the carrier's docked at North Island. Then I want all the men aboard the ship by six-hundred hours Thursday morning. The gangway comes up at six-forty-five, and the ship sails at seven-hundred. Remind the men of the severe penalty of missing ship's movement."

The squadron maintenance officer, Lieutenant Commander John Weber said, "That's next to impossible, Skipper. We have two engines and one main transmission change in progress. Why the damn rush?"

"It's classified, John," Joe answered. "CAG said we would be briefed Thursday morning. Now, the other bad news. The *Concord* lost another H-3 SAR bird. The tail rotor failed as they were landing on the flag ship, and she flipped over the side. The crew was recovered, but Rear Admiral Perkins and Captain Stoddard were lost at sea."

"Jesus Christ, those birds should all be grounded," Weber said. "Sure as hell sounds like a maintenance nightmare to me."

"Easy, John," Joe said. "Don't be too hasty to judge." Turning to Commander Colby, he said, "Tom, you have two helicopters left on the *Concord* for combat search and rescue. I want your crew to cover those birds from nose to tail before Sea Devil pilots fly them. Understand?"

"Yes, sir," Tom answered.

"Officers, stand by for the intelligence brief. Chief Petty Officers are dismissed to your shops," Joe said as he walked toward his reserved seat on the front row. The chiefs quickly exited the room while air intelligence officer, Lieutenant Tony Olson, walked to the podium and placed the first vu-graph on the overhead projector.

"This brief is classified secret," Olson said. "The Skipper has covered the major news item. Commander Task Force Seventy-Seven point Seven, Admiral Perkins and his Chief of Staff, Captain Stoddard, were lost at sea yesterday in the helicopter crash. Their bodies were not recovered. The pilot, copilot and two crewmen were recovered without injury. One crewman stated that Admiral Perkins and Captain Stoddard had unbuckled their seat belts prior to the accident. He remembers seeing Admiral Perkins being thrown toward the tail cone when the helicopter begin the rapid clockwise rotation. So remember, guys, keep your passengers strapped to their seats until the aircraft is on deck."

"Tony, I don't want to blow smoke on your Christmas parade," Weber said, "but I'll bet you a case of beer that we don't have an air crewman in the squadron who'll tell an Admiral to sit down and keep his damn seat belt buckled until the helo is on deck."

Commander Blackwell jumped from his seat and turned to face the group. "John, that's a damn good point, and I can see where we need to get some policy clear with our flight crews. These young enlisted men have gotta be briefed to inform all passengers that they're required to have the seat belts securely fastened at all times. I don't care if it's the fucking CNO himself. If any passenger violates this policy, I want his name and rank, and I'll by God take care of it. Subject closed."

Joe returned to his seat and Olson continued the brief. "Loss of the helicopter will severely hamper *Concord's* search and rescue capability until we get on station and transfer our SAR birds over to the carrier. The message traffic reveals that the HS-26 SAR group rescued five downed aviators last week, three Navy and two Air Force."

100

"The carrier *Yorktown* is tracking four Russian nuclear submarines in the Sea of Japan, two Echo's and two November class. A third November sub entered the Sea of Japan last Friday. The Air Group is stretched thin trying to maintain contact with five nuke boats, especially since they don't have helicopters to help the S-2's. The P-3's out of Atsugi are giving some assistance, but they still have the responsibility to fly the Barrier. Gentlemen, that concludes the air brief," Olson said. "Remember, loose lips sink ships."

"Officers, **ATTENTION ON DECK**!" The squadron duty officer ordered. The officers jumped up and snapped to attention.

"SDO, take charge and carry out the flight schedule," Joe ordered as he and Tom walked from the room.

"Aye, aye, sir," the duty officer answered. "Officers dismissed."

El Cortez Hotel
San Diego, California

Linda Colby rode the glass elevator up the side of the El Cortez Hotel to the Sky Room. The hotel sat on a steep hillside overlooking the city of San Diego. The Sky Room was located on the top floor of the hotel and contained a circular bar. The Sky Room was also the best French restaurant in San Diego. Linda had agreed to meet Bob Wilson for lunch in the Sky Room after listening to his urgent plea on the telephone that morning.

Stepping off the elevator into the Sky Room, Linda paused to enjoy the panoramic view of the city and San Diego Bay. The ferry was busy shuttling cars back and forth across the bay to Coronado. The California Department of Transportation was planning to build a bridge across the bay to connect San Diego with the city of Coronado and the Naval Air Station, North Island. Linda did not want a bridge of concrete and steel to mar the serenity and beauty of the bay. Reluctantly, she turned from the panoramic view and approached the maitre d's station.

"Is mademoiselle dining alone?" The maitre d' asked.

"I'm meeting Commander Wilson," she said. "Has he arrived?"

"Yes, mademoiselle. Please follow me."

Bob stood when they reached the table. "Thanks for coming, pretty lady," he took Linda's hand and raised it to his lips. Turning to the maitre d', he said, "Andre, please bring the lady a glass of Chardonnay."

"Right away, Commander Bob," Andre said and held the chair for Linda.

101

"Why does everyone, including Tommy, call you Commander Bob?" She asked as Andre hurried to the bar for the wine.

"I've been called by worse names," he laughed, "but in the Navy most Lieutenant Commanders are called 'Commander'. Were you surprised when Tom was frocked to full Commander?"

"Pleasantly surprised, but Tom was shocked. He was so pleased to have Dad Colby and the President participate in his promotion."

"You should've seen the look on the President's face when the squadron toasted him with the famous Sea Devil hymn," Bob said.

"Oh, no! I can't believe they used such crude vulgarity with the President," Linda exclaimed.

"Skipper Blackwell and Tom both tried to stop Bull from presenting the hymn, but the President jumped in and told them to stop and let the Ensign do his job. The President was very pleased with the flight jacket."

The waiter brought a glass of Chardonnay and took their orders. After he left, Linda asked, "Are you in some kind of trouble, Bob?"

"Oh, God, someone's trying to kill me. Tom saved my life by inviting me down to the squadron last Friday. My office was blown over half of the parade field."

"I heard that a building was bombed, but I had no idea that it was your office. Oh, Bob, I'm so sorry," she said and took his hand. "Maybe some jealous husband is just trying to scare you. If someone was trying to kill you, they would not phone in a bomb threat, would they?"

"Well, I've never looked at it like that," he agreed, "but it sure put the fear of God in me. From this day forward, I firmly resolve to only date single ladies, widow's or divorcee's."

"Robert Wilson, you are full of crock if you think you could ever keep a resolution like that," she laughed.

"Well, I'm sure gonna try, pretty lady. Now, the second thing that I wanted to tell you is that I received my orders to HC-21 there at Ream Field."

"Oh, that is good news. Now we'll have time to complete our dissertation."

"I want us to finish it this month. Next month I'm deploying to the Gulf of Tonkin with a combat search and rescue detachment."

"Do you think the war will be over soon?" She asked.

"Yes, I do. Unless the Pentagon decides to fight a stupid land war like the French tried. It 'll probably be all over within a year."

"Oh, I sure hope and pray that it is," Linda said as the waiter brought their lunch.

"Another glass of wine?" Bob asked.

"Yes, thank you," Linda answered.

After the waiter left the table to get her wine, Linda whispered across the table to Wilson, "Don't get any ideas that this delicious wine is going to make me all mushy and romantic. Remember your resolution, and don't even think about trying to seduce me today, Commander Bob."

"Scouts honor," Bob answered and raised his right hand in a mock boy scout salute. As Linda ate lunch, Bob continued to talk. "Linda, you know that my parents are deceased. You and Tom are the closest thing I have to a real family."

"Thanks, Bob. You're a very special part of our family also."

"Let me finish, while I have this thing all figured out. I have some cash in a safe deposit box, the Cessna 310, my beach cottage and the Cadillac. My will leaves everything to you if some jealous husband succeeds in killing me or if I don't come back from Vietnam."

"God, you're morbid today, Robert! I've never seen you like this."

"Well, my lawyer told me that if I die without a will or relatives that the State will take my estate. I'd damn sure rather you have it than the State of California."

"Thank you, Bob, that's very sweet of you," she said. "I promise to be your beneficiary if you'll promise to stop talking about dying. Deal?"

"Roger, pretty lady. We have a deal," Bob said raising his glass of wine. "Here's to a very long, happy life. Now finish your lunch. I have something to show you at the bank. Just remember, what you see this afternoon, accept on faith. Please don't ask for an explanation or any questions about my estate. Deal?"

"Deal," Linda said as she gripped his hand.

Suite 916
El Cortez Hotel
San Diego, California

After lunch, Linda had accompanied Bob Wilson to the California First Bank. He showed her the safe deposit box that contained the title to his Cessna 310, the Grant Deed to his beach cottage, and one million dollars in one hundred dollar bills. Bob had leased a safe deposit box one row below his for Linda's use. His instructions were simple. If he was reported killed or missing in action, Linda was to transfer everything from his box to her's before the bank sealed his account and safe deposit box.

103

The second shock to Linda was when they returned to the El Cortez and rode the elevator up to Suite 916. Glenn Carson had permanently assigned the suite to Wilson. The two room suite overlooked the Pacific Ocean. Linda sat on the couch drinking her third glass of wine for the day listening to Wilson talk about a power-of-attorney. "Robert, the last thing in the world you want to do is give someone your power-of-attorney. It's like giving a stranger a signed, blank check," she lectured.

"Not if that someone is a person that you trust with all your heart and soul. I've told you that I don't want the damn State of California to get control of my possessions. I want you to have them. That's why I'm giving you my power-of-attorney."

"Okay, Bob, I accept. I know that I promised not to ask any questions, but you just cannot expect me to accept the fact that you have a million dollars cash in your safe deposit box. I must know if the money is stolen or counterfeit."

"I assure you that the money is genuine, and it's not stolen. I earned every dollar of it with my airplane."

"I'll accept that for the time being, but one day you must explain all this to me."

"I will, pretty lady. One last thing," he said as he handed her a key to the suite, "I want you to feel free to use this suite anytime you feel like it. I know how much you love the ocean. If you want to come up here some evening and sit nude on the couch with all the lights out, sip wine and look at the ocean, be my guest."

"I suppose you sit here at night, nude, sipping wine."

"I do sometimes. You should try it. It's very therapeutic and blows off a lot of stress."

"Thanks, Robert," Linda said and kissed his cheek. "When you get back from Vietnam, we will drink wine and enjoy this room together."

"That's a date," Bob said as he locked the door and led Linda toward the elevator. *Yes sir, that's a date that I intend to keep.*

Otay High School
Bonita, California

It was three o'clock in the afternoon when Tommy Colby walked into the locker room. The sky was clear and the temperature a comfortable 73 degrees. A welcome relief after the heat of the Santa Ana winds. The football game Friday night was with the Hilltop Lancer's at their stadium.

David Wiseman sat on the bench near Tommy's locker pulling up his uniform pants. He waved as Tommy walked to his locker. "I really enjoyed meeting your grandparents," David said. "Did you tell your grandmother about being engaged to Judy?"

"Sure did, my man. Grandma thought it was a great idea. She's going to arrange an endowment for Judy's tuition at Stanford."

"All right, man," He stood and gave Tommy a high five.

"Have you decided on a college?" Tommy asked.

"Yeah, I'm going to the Naval Academy and be a flier like my dad."

"Have you discussed this with Janine?"

"Yeah, she's a Navy brat like you and me. Her old man's a Chief, and Janine thinks it would be neat to be an officer's lady."

"Did you make out with Janine after we left the car?"

"Oh yeah, man," David groaned. "It worked just like you said it would. After you guys went to the refreshment stand, Janine sat on my lap and practically raped me. It was the first time for Janine also."

"Next time make sure that you pick up all of the incriminating evidence," Tommy said as he handed the blue panties to David.

"Holy crap! Did Janine drop her panties in the back seat?"

"No harm done," Tommy said, "but I'd have been in trouble if Dad had found them. Are you going to return them to Janine?"

"No way, man," David smiled. "I'll sleep with her panties under my pillow every night."

FOURTEEN

USS Shiloh Sails To War

The Colby Residence
Bonita, California

The three days whizzed by like a whirlwind, and it was time for the carrier to start the long sea voyage to the western pacific. Tommy had helped his father move his personal effects aboard the carrier Wednesday afternoon. His mother and father went to dinner Wednesday night at the Sky Room in the El Cortez hotel while Tommy stayed home and studied Latin with Judy. Thirty minutes after his parents left, they made love. He finally coaxed Judy into giving him the white lace panties. Last night he slept with them under his pillow. Tommy knocked on his parents door, "Hey, Dad, it's five-fifteen. I'm going next door to get Judy, and we'll meet you and mother at the Jag in five minutes."

"Okay," Tom said. "We'll be ready."

Tommy drove the Jaguar up the silver strand toward the Naval Air Station, North Island where the *USS Shiloh* was berthed. Judy sat beside him while his mother and father sat in back. Most of the traffic was headed toward the Air Station where over five thousand Navy men would say good-bye to their wives and girlfriends and leave on the aircraft carrier for the eight month cruise to Vietnam. "Hey, that's Commander Bob's car," Tommy said as he passed the white Cadillac near the Navy Amphibious Base. He pressed the horn. The Cadillac answered with two beeps and followed the Jaguar through the Main Gate of NAS North Island.

"All we need now is a fly-over from Air Force One," Tom said from the back seat.

"Tom, surely you expected Bob Wilson to be here to say good-bye," Linda said.

"Well, I don't want you all to sit out there in the parking lot waiting for the ship to sail," Tom answered. "I'll be busy getting the troops mustered, and the Skipper will probably show up five minutes before we get underway. Ask Bob to join you three for breakfast. You'll have plenty of time to eat before we sail."

"That's an excellent idea," Linda said. The large parking ramp beside the aircraft carrier was packed with automobiles. Tommy stopped the Jaguar by the officer's gangplank and jumped out to open the back door for this father.

"Hey, you can't park in this area," the Shore Patrol sentry growled at Tommy then came to attention and saluted as Tom got out of the car.

"Good morning, sentry," Tom said as he returned the salute. "This is just a quick passenger stop."

"Make it less than five minutes, sir," the sentry said and walked toward the Cadillac parked behind the Jaguar.

Bob was already out of the car. He returned the sentry's salute and said, "I'll be out of your way in three minutes."

"But sir, you don't have any passengers to drop-off," the sentry complained.

"Well, by God, I'm saying good-bye to a shipmate!" Bob said and walked forward to join the group.

Tom kissed Judy on the cheek and shook hands with Tommy. "Good luck in the big game tomorrow night against the Hill Top Lancer's."

"Thanks, Dad, we won last weeks game for David's father," Tommy said. "We'll win this one for you."

Tom was kissing Linda good-bye as Bob joined the group. "Good morning, Bob," Tom said as he gripped Bob's hand. "What brings you to the base before sunrise?"

"Trying to say bye to a friend," Bob said as he hugged Tom in a tight embrace. "Please try not to be a Saturday afternoon hero."

"Will do, Commander Bob," Tom said as he saluted the group. "Good-bye all, see you in about eight months." Turning to Bob, he said, "You'd better move the Cadillac before that sentry scrapes your base sticker." Then he turned and walked up the steps of the gangplank.

"Bob, can you join us for breakfast?" Linda asked as she watched Tom salute the officer of the deck and disappear inside the hangar bay of the carrier.

"Yes, I'd love too," Bob answered. "Come ride with me." Turning to Tommy, he said, "Meet us at the Hotel Del Coronado."

"Roger, Commander Bob," Tommy said and held the door of the Jaguar for Judy.

Bob walked Linda to the Cadillac and held the door as she got into the passenger seat. The sentry stood by the front fender of the Cadillac. Bob saluted and said, "Thanks for not letting anyone steal my car." The startled sentry returned the salute and rushed over to yell at another driver who was trying to park. Bob drove out of the parking lot. "God, you smell good this morning, pretty lady," he said as he sniffed Linda's perfume.

"Thank you, Robert," Linda said and caressed his right leg.

"Oh God, don't do that!" Bob groaned. "I'll have such a hard-on that I won't be able to walk when we get to the restaurant."

"Oh, you aviators are always bragging about your erections," Linda laughed.

"Will breakfast at the Crown Room be satisfactory, mademoiselle?"

"Yes, Robert. The Crown Room will be quite satisfactory," Linda smiled and continued to caress his leg.

HS-24 Ready Room
USS Shiloh, CVS-22

Tom opened the door and walked into the crowded ready room. The squadron duty officer spoke into the telephone. He shook his head as Tom sat in the XO's seat. The duty officer placed the receiver in the cradle and turned to Commander Colby. "There's no answer in the Skipper's quarters, sir."

"Thanks, Rick," Tom said. "His Caddie probably broke down on the Strand. He still has twenty minutes to get aboard before they cast-off lines. Maybe he'll get lucky and make it."

"**NOW HEAR THIS**," the carrier's loud speaker announced. "**SET THE SPECIAL SEA AND ANCHOR DETAIL**."

"The muster reports are ready for your signature, sir," the duty officer said and passed the folder of papers to Tom. "After you sign them, I'll have the yeoman run them down to CAG's office."

"That's okay, Rick," Tom said as he signed the reports. "I'm going by CAG's office. I'll drop them off." Tom walked down the passageway to a door marked, CAG OFFICE. He opened the door and walked inside. CAG was the acronym for the Carrier Air Group Commander, and was pronounced "kag" to rhyme with "rag." He handed the muster reports to the Chief Yeoman and asked, "Is CAG in?"

"Yes, sir, Commander," the Chief answered. "Go right on in."

Tom opened the door and went inside. "Morning, CAG," he said and stood at attention in front of the desk.

"Morning, Tom," Commander Dick Boyd said. "Stand at ease. Did all of the troops get aboard?"

"Skipper Blackwell's not aboard yet, sir."

"That's not like Joe. Let me know when he comes aboard."

"Yes, sir," Tom said and left the office, closing the door behind him.

Crown Room
Hotel Del Coronado

Linda sat in the restaurant of the Crown Room next to Lieutenant Commander Bob Wilson and looked out at the beautiful Pacific Ocean. Across the table from her sat Tommy and Judy. Occasionally, a tear would trickle down Judy's cheek. At six-twenty in the morning the restaurant was almost deserted. Five waiters hovered around the table filling water glasses and coffee cups.

Raising the glass of orange juice, Linda said, "I propose a toast." The other three members at the table stopped eating and raised their glass of orange juice. "To a safe and successful voyage for the *Shiloh* and the Sea Devil squadron. May they have many successes and fly home safely."

The four drank their orange juice and sat the glasses on the table where they were quickly refilled by the waiters. "Now, I want us to enjoy the remainder of this delicious breakfast," Linda said. "If Tom were here he would be telling sea stories with Commander Bob and coaching Tommy on Friday nights football game. So everyone cheer up and we'll go back to see the *Shiloh* sail off to glory."

USS Shiloh
CVS-22

The carrier's speaker announced, **"SHILOH UNDERWAY. SHIFT COLORS TO THE FOCSLE."**

Jesus Christ! The stupid son-of-a-bitching Skipper has missed ship movement, Tom groaned. The ready room was quiet as aviators whispered in hushed tones. Tom stood and addressed the group, "Gentlemen, through some unforeseen event, our Skipper's not aboard. Let's just hope and pray that he has not met with some tragic accident. You're free to go to your staterooms and unpack. There'll be an all-pilots meeting at eight-hundred here in the ready room."

109

Tom turned to the duty officer and said, "Rick, I'll be in CAG's office." He walked out the door and down the passageway. Entering CAG's office again, he walked to the Chief's desk and asked, "Is CAG in?"

"Yes, Commander," Chief Brandon said. "He's expecting you."

Tom followed the routine he had performed thirty minutes ago and stood before CAG's desk. "Have a seat, Tom," CAG Boyd said. "Would you like a cup of coffee?"

"No, thanks, CAG. I don't think I could keep it down," Tom answered.

"Relax Tom, it's not the end of the world. I have no doubt that Black Joe will show up. I'll chew his ass out and throw him in hack for a few days. He'll probably fly out and meet us in Hawaii."

"I sure hope so," Tom replied.

"In the meantime, you're acting Commanding Officer of the squadron. We don't expect to conduct any flight operations between here and Hawaii, since we'll be cruising at most economical speed, about twenty-four knots. There'll be a meeting of the CO's in the Captain's Cabin at oh-nine-hundred. Please be there."

"I will CAG," Tom answered as he stood and walked from the room. *Jesus Christ, going from Operations Officer to Commanding Officer in one short week is just too damn fast,* he thought. *Now, Blackwell's going to screw up my chance to command the combat search and rescue detachment.*

*   *   *

The *Shiloh's* crew stood at flight deck parade as the carrier approached Ballast Point. The famous landmark had received its name during the days of tall sails when the sailing ships would tie up at the point and load aboard large rocks to ballast the ships prior to putting out to sea. A helicopter called the carrier and requested a passenger stop, but had been ordered to stand clear until the carrier was out of the harbor and had secured from flight deck parade.

The Air Boss, Commander Bill Streeper, was talking to the helicopter pilot on the UHF radio and requested the passenger's name. The pilot stated that he had one passenger, a Commander Joe Blackwell. Streeper dialed CAG's number and said, "CAG, we've located your missing Commanding Officer."

"What's the story, Bill?" CAG asked.

"Well, CAG, a helicopter from HS twenty-eight just requested a passenger stop to drop off your Commander Blackwell. I told him to orbit off Point Loma until we cleared the harbor, secured from fight deck parade and have time to set the detail for helicopter recovery."

"Thanks Bill," CAG said. "Land him on Spot Six, and I'll arrange a special welcome committee to greet Commander Blackwell."

"Roger, CAG," Streeper said and replaced the receiver on the overhead hook above his chair. In Pri-Fly there was one barbershop-type chair with a command view of the flight deck. This chair belonged to the Air Boss. All other watch personnel stood during their four hour watch. *I'd sure hate to be in that poor bastard's shoes,* Streeper thought.

"**SECURE FROM FLIGHT DECK PARADE,**" the speaker announced, followed closely by another announcement. "**FLIGHT DECK OPERATIONS FOR HELICOPTER RECOVERY WILL BE SET IN FIFTEEN MINUTES.**" This announcement was hailed with a few choice cuss words from the sailors in dress whites who were also a party of the flight operations detail. The sailors ran down five flights of ladders to their berthing space, changed into dungarees and rushed back up to the flight deck to their duty station as firefighters, corpsmen and aircraft handlers.

CAG Boyd called the bridge and asked to speak to the Captain. Captain Red Roberts was the Commanding Officer of the carrier. He sat in the lone chair on the bridge while the Harbor Pilot navigated the carrier through the narrow channel toward Point Loma. "Good morning, CAG," Roberts said into the telephone.

"Morning, Captain," CAG came straight to the point. "Commander Blackwell's in the helicopter that's orbiting Point Loma. When he lands, will you please have a welcome committee meet him and escort him to my office?"

"It'll be my pleasure, CAG," Roberts said as he motioned to the Officer of the Deck. *Shiloh* cleared the harbor at Point Loma and began to pick up speed as she turned to a course of 270.

The Air Boss reached for his microphone and announced, "**NOW, HEAR THIS. SET THE FLIGHT DECK OPERATIONS FOR HELO RECOVERY.**" Within three minutes, all stations had called in manned and ready for flight operations. The Air Boss picked up the red telephone that connected him with the Commanding Officer.

"Yes, Bill," Captain Roberts answered.

"Captain, we're ready to receive the helicopter."

"Let him wait another five minutes, Bill," Roberts ordered.

"Roger, sir," the Air Boss answered and hooked the red phone back to the ceiling above his chair. When five minutes had passed, he announced over the flight deck speaker, "**STANDBY TO RECEIVE**
111

HELO ON SPOT SIX." Keying the mike, he said, "Navy Helo Five-Four-One, you have a Charlie on spot six. Wind is thirty degrees to port at twenty-six knots." Charlie was the command to land.

"Roger, tower. Gear down and locked."

The helicopter landed on the large circle with a number 6 painted in the middle. Commander Joseph Blackwell jumped down to the flight deck and gave a thumbs-up to the pilot. Blackwell was met by the Chief Master at Arms who escorted him to the door leading to flight deck control and down the series of ladders to CAG's office.

The Air Boss clicked the mike and said, "Five-Four-One, you have a Green Deck." Green Deck was the command to take-off.

"Roger Green Deck," the helicopter pilot gave the pull chock sign. When the chocks and tie down chains had been removed, the helicopter lifted smoothly into a five-foot hover and dove over the left side of the carrier.

"Five-Four-One, you are cleared to North Island frequency, out," the Air Boss said and picked up the speaker microphone. "**SECURE FROM FLIGHT OPERATIONS**." The *USS Shiloh* and her two escorts continued to cruise a course of 270 at a speed of 24 knots. Next stop, Pearl Harbor.

FIFTEEN

Pearl Harbor

Bob Wilson's Beach Cottage
Imperial Beach, California

Linda Colby lay on the canvas chair and listened to the shrieking of the sea gulls as they swooped above the crashing surf. As she baked in the Saturday afternoon sun she thought about going for a swim, then remembered the chilly water. *It must be all of 70 degrees.* She heard the screen door bang close and looked up to see Bob Wilson walking out to the patio with a glass of Chardonnay and a can of Coors beer.

"Hi, beautiful lady," Bob said. "Would you like a glass of wine?"

"Yes, Robert," Linda sat up and took the glass of wine. She looked up into his eyes, sparkling with tiny golden specks. "You look so sexy with one brown eye and one black eye," she teased. "Does it still hurt?"

He gazed hungrily at her oiled, tan body clad in the skimpy black bikini. "Only when I look at you without my sunglasses. God, Linda you're so beautiful."

"Thanks," she sipped the wine. "Were you watching the game?"

"Oh, yes. God, I hate Notre Dame."

"What a terrible thing to say," she scolded. "The Lord will place a little black mark by your name if you hate people or football teams, especially Notre Dame."

"Well, it's just not fair," he fumed. "Notre Dame has the whole damn United States of America from which to recruit the best high school talent."

"The Naval Academy doesn't recruit the whole country?" She asked. "As I remember Senator's and Congressmen have two appointments

113

each, and the President can appoint a hundred candidates. Maybe they're skipping over the football jocks for scholars."

"Oh, Jesus, woman, I can never win an argument with you." He took a drink of the beer and raised his eyes toward the sky in a mock prayer, "Lord, I'm sorry I hate Your team, and I apologize for it. Please erase that little black mark beside my name, and I'll only hate them when they beat Navy. Amen."

"I assume Navy is losing," Linda asked.

"Twenty-eight to seven in the first half," he groaned.

"Thank you for taking me to Tommy's football game last night."

"You're welcome, beautiful lady." He leaned down and kissed her. "It was sure a cliffhanger, with Bobby Beecher kicking the winning field goal with less that a minute left in the game. I bet he was rewarded with some nookie from his girlfriend last night."

"All you men think about is sex," she snorted. "Women don't make love for reward or withhold sex as punishment."

"Oh, no? Tell that to the marriage counselors," he laughed rubbing her stomach. "What's Tommy doing today? Watching the game?"

"No, I don't think so. He and Judy are flying the one-seventy-two this afternoon."

"I promised Judy a ride in my three-ten after she soloed," he said.

"Judy would love to fly your airplane. You're such a good man, Robert Wilson," she smiled, "but what about me? Will you take me for a ride in your beautiful red airplane sometime?"

"Anytime you're ready, beautiful lady," he kissed her again.

"You taste like Coors," she licked her lips. "Coors is Tom's favorite beer."

"Speaking of my buddy, Tom, when will the *Shiloh* get to Hawaii?"

"This afternoon, and Tom's calling tonight."

"I sure hope the squadron has a good cruise and makes a lot of rescues. Tom will probably come back with the Distinguished Flying Cross," Bob said, "but I'll be out there soon with my detachment. Maybe Tom and I can team up on some rescues."

"When are you transferring to HC-21?"

"Next week, I think. The Skipper wants to get me out of his squadron before anymore buildings are blown up," Bob laughed.

"Is the FBI still investigating the bombing?"

"Yes, beautiful lady," Bob said and kissed her again. "NIS and the FBI fought over the case. The FBI finally claimed federal jurisdiction. I think they've questioned everyone on the base by now. In the meantime,

I'm running the training department in one of the classrooms. It will be nice to get back to an operational squadron after two years in the rag."

Linda drank her wine and handed the glass to Bob. "I want to run by the Exchange at Ream on the way home. Do you want to watch the football game or take a shower with me?"

"What football game," he laughed, "lead me to the shower."

Admiral Woods Residence
Bethesda, Maryland

Margaret Colby sat at the dining table sipping a sniffer of brandy. "That was a delicious dinner, Arthur," she said. "The steak was perfect."

"How're you feeling, Margaret? Tired?" Dr. Woods asked.

"Sometimes I get tired, but not tonight. Thomas flew up to Camp David with the President and a group of Navy brass for the weekend. So I invited myself over to have dinner with you."

"So glad you did. You're always welcome, gracious lady."

"Well, I have so much to tell you about our trip to San Diego. Tommy called this morning, and they won their game last night by three points," she beamed. "They're still undefeated."

"I'm glad you got to see Tom before his carrier left for the South China Sea," he said. "Will he fly combat missions in Vietnam?"

"No, I don't think so," she answered. "He's flying the Sikorsky helicopters with the dipping sonar. I guess they'll track the Russian submarines in the Sea of Japan. Oh Arthur, there is just so much to tell. Tom's XO was killed in a helicopter crash, and we went to his funeral in Bonita, California. Glen Abbey is the most beautiful cemetery. I've already told Thomas that's where I want to be buried. Lyndon presented the flag to Mrs. Wiseman, and Tom led the missing-wingman fly-over. Lyndon frocked Tom to full Commander and assigned him as XO of the squadron. Then we all went to Tommy's game and had a great time."

"I can see that you had a busy three days."

"I left out the best part," she said. "Tommy's engaged to a beautiful young lady, Judy Anderson. They plan to get married next June and attend Stanford together."

"Margaret, I think Stanford has a Navy Reserve Officer Training Corps. If you'll encourage Tommy to take the ROTC, I'm very confident that I can arrange to have him assigned to Bethesda Naval Hospital for the internship of his choice after he completes medical school and is commissioned in the Navy."

"That's so sweet of you, Arthur," she said, "but I'm not sure that Tommy and Judy want to have anything to do with a Navy career."

"Will she be studying medicine, also?"

"No, Judy wants to be lawyer. Oh Arthur, I don't want to die now. I want to live to see my great-grandchildren," she begged.

Admiral Woods kissed her. "No more talk about dying," he ordered. "We'll fight this monster one day at a time."

Margaret smiled at him and said, "Linda told me about a bright, young Navy doctor, Lieutenant Paul Thompson, who performed the heart surgery on her father in Pensacola. He lost his wife to leukemia and is devoting every minute of his time studying to conquer cancer."

"The Navy needs more surgeons like that," Woods agreed.

"I think Lieutenant Thompson is a flight surgeon and is due for sea duty soon. Could you arranged to have him assigned to Bethesda, please?"

"Well, I'll certainly talk to BUPERS about it first thing Monday morning. Come, let's take our brandy in and enjoy the fire."

"No, Arthur, let's take our brandy upstairs to your bedroom. I want to make love to you so very much," she whispered as she stood and walked toward the stairs.

Officer's Club
NAS Ream Field

Linda Colby finished shopping at the Exchange and drove to the club for a drink. She walked into the bar and waited until her eyes adjusted to the dim light. A group of aviators sat in the lounge rooting for Navy to come from behind and beat Notre Dame. She walked to the bar and sat on the high stool noticing that her favorite bartender, Pinky Jardine, was tending bar.

"Hey, Miss Linda," Pinky smiled. "What'd you like to drink?"

"Something tall and cool. Fix me a white wine spritzer, Pinky."

"Yes, ma'am. One tall, cool, white wine spritzer coming up."

"Have you been watching the game, Pinky?"

"Yes, ma'am, and I hate Notre Dame," he said as he placed the drink on a napkin in front of Linda.

"That's a terrible thing to say," she scolded. "You sound just like Commander Wilson."

"Yes, ma'am, Commander Bob's the one who taught me to hate Notre Dame," he said.

"Oh, I should've known that Bob Wilson would corrupt you also," she said. "Wait until I get a chance to talk to him."

116

"No, ma'am, you don't understand," Pinky explained. "You see, it's like this. Every year Notre Dame beats up on Navy, and gets these pilots all upset, even the Catholic ones. See Lieutenant Jackson sitting over in the corner? He graduated from Notre Dame. A while ago when Notre Dame scored, he cheered for them, and the group banished him to the corner. If he yells one more time for Notre Dame, they's gonna throw him in the swimming pool."

"Did you see Tommy's game last night at Hilltop?" She asked.

"No, ma'am, I sure did want to, but I had a chance to make two hundred dollars, so I took it."

"Is that a part-time job?"

"Well, Miss Linda, it's kinda like a part-time job. This man offered me two hundred dollars if I'd drive a Mexican couple to Los Angeles. So I took them in my Cadillac. Mighty easy way to make two hundred dollars," he grinned.

"Pinky, that's illegal, and you'll really be in trouble if you get caught," she lectured. "You took a real chance getting through Checkpoint Charlie."

"I didn't go that way, Miss Linda. I went through Camp Pendleton and bypassed the checkpoint," Pinky smiled. "He wants me to do it again next weekend."

The group of aviators watching the football game began to boo and yell when the game ended with the final score, Notre Dame 41 - Navy 14. Linda finished her drink and said good-bye to Pinky. "Have a nice day," she said as she turned and walked from the bar feeling great.

USS Shiloh, CVS-22
Approaching Pearl Harbor

The *USS Shiloh* maintained a speed of 24 knots and reached the Hawaiian Islands in four days. *Shiloh* was an Essex-type aircraft carrier, officially designated the 27 Charlie class. During the Korean War, she saw action as a straight-deck attack carrier. In the last overhaul, the British canted flight deck and steam catapults were added. Air-conditioning had also been installed in the wardroom and the majority of the carrier's office space. The berthing spaces and officer's staterooms were still ventilated with forced air. The *Shiloh* became an anti-submarine warfare carrier to help counter the Soviet submarine force. Her aircraft consisted of four A-4 jet fighters, sixteen H-3 helicopters, twenty-four dual-engine, propeller-driven S-2D's and three E-2's.

As the carrier approached Pearl Harbor, Joe Blackwell and Tom Colby sat in the wardroom sipping black coffee. Joe explained how he had arranged with the Skipper of HS-28 to fly him aboard the *Shiloh* as the carrier left San Diego harbor. "It was a crazy damn stunt, Skipper," Tom said. "You should be glad that CAG didn't give you a letter of reprimand for missing ship's movement."

"Hell, Tom," Joe replied. "I was CAG Boyd's wingman in Korea flying F4U Cosairs. You wouldn't believe some of the crazy damn stunts he pulled, and I was always there to bail his ass out of the fire."

"Well, maybe that's why he let you off so easy, Skipper. You gotta admit that five days in hack while you're at sea is not a very severe punishment."

"Yeah, but that fifth day includes the time we'll be in Hawaii," Joe complained. "We sail for Japan tomorrow, so we'll only be in port tonight. I sure do want to go into Waikiki and meet an old girlfriend."

"Don't even think about it," Tom cautioned. "CAG would put you in the brig if you went AWOL."

"Yeah, you're probably right," Joe agreed, "but that bastard said I was restricted to the base while we're in Pearl. So we'll go to the Pearl Officer's Club tonight. I wonder if they have a Sunday night show?"

"I don't know about the Pearl Club, but I'm sure that the Hickam Officer's Club has a Sunday night show," Tom answered. "Anyway, the club at Pearl will be mobbed with the Air Group."

"You're right," Joe agreed, "but I gave CAG my word that I wouldn't leave the base."

"Skipper, very few people realize that Pearl Harbor Naval Station and Hickam Air Force Base share a common security fence and have a back gate down near the Ship Repair Facility. We can take a taxi and get to the Hickam Club through the back gate."

"Damn, you're a genius!" Joe exclaimed. "That way I can call Shirley and have her meet us at the Hickam Club for dinner. Deal?"

"Yes, I guess so," Tom agreed, "If you're sure that CAG won't get mad and lock both of us in the brig."

"Let me handle CAG," Joe said. "Anyway we need to talk about the SAR detachment."

"I talked with the Chief Brandon in CAG's office, Skipper. He found seats for us on a Navy C-130 out of NAS Barbers Point tomorrow that's going to NAS Cubi Point. Then I guess we'll have to shuttle the crew out to the carrier on the *Concord's* COD."

"It'll be a ball buster riding a C-130 from here to the Philippines," Joe groaned. "Damn! Here comes CAG."

Commander Boyd walked into the wardroom and saw Joe and Tom over in the far corner drinking coffee. He filled a cup from the coffee pot, placed the cup in the saucer and slowly walked toward the two officers being very careful not to spill a drop. "Good afternoon, gentlemen," CAG said as he sat beside Tom.

"Afternoon, CAG," Tom said.

"What time will we dock at Pearl, CAG?" Joe asked.

"I just left the bridge," CAG answered. "The quartermaster's estimating entrance to the harbor at sixteen-hundred hours with the gangway touching the dock at seventeen-hundred hours. Getting anxious for a cold beer, Joe?"

"No, sir," Joe answered. "Tom was just telling me that your office had made arrangement for our SAR detachment to fly out to Cubi Point on a Barber's Point C-130. I wanted to check with the Hickam MAC Terminal for some jet transportation."

"Damn, Chief Brandon must be slipping if that's the best that he could come up with," CAG agreed. Turning to Tom, he said, "I'd like to fly your detachment out on Cat Z, commercial charter, but we don't have enough TDY funds to cover that."

"No sweat, CAG," Tom answered. "We're approximately three weeks ahead of schedule at this point. It's only a twenty-two hour flight with a lay-over in Guam."

Turning to Blackwell, CAG said, "Joe, it would be a good idea to check with Hickam. Those Air Force Generals often fly around with the plane half-empty." Realizing what he had just said, CAG turned to Tom and said, "I sound like the eternal pessimist making that jet liner half-empty. Right, Tom?"

"You're right, CAG," Tom agreed. "Let's be very optimistic and make the jet liner half-full. Then we can get my whole detachment aboard," he laughed.

"Joe, you have a brilliant, young executive officer," CAG said. "Chief Brandon was in the process of cutting orders making Tom the Commanding Officer of the Sea Devils when you finally got aboard. Pull another stunt like that, and I'll bust your ass to Lieutenant Commander and make Tom the CO."

"I read you, CAG," Joe answered. "But I'll gladly take the SAR detachment to the Tonkin Gulf if you want to give the squadron to Tom."

"No way," CAG growled. "You and I earned our Air Medals in Korea. Now it's time for the youngsters to earn some medals." Turning to Tom, CAG said, "We don't know why HS-26 lost thirteen helicopters in the combat zone. I don't want you to try to be a hero like Hiram, the widow's son. If you don't have at least a fifty-fifty chance of survival, I want you to scrub the mission, understand?"

"Yes, sir," Tom answered.

"Well, gentlemen, I have a few things to check before we dock. Please excuse me," CAG said.

Joe and Tom stood as CAG picked up his coffee cup and saucer and took them over to the serving bar. "I didn't know that CAG was a Mason, did you, Skipper?"

"No, I don't know if he's a Mason or not," Joe answered. "I'm a member of the Knights of Columbus, but I don't go to the meetings as often as I should. Anyway, CAG just gave me a perfect excuse to visit Hickam Air Force Base. Now we won't have to sneak in the back gate," Joe laughed. "Let's go up to vulture's row and watch Captain Roberts park this big lady next to the pier."

Vulture's row is the open, narrow passageway just aft of Pri-Fly where aviators often gathered to watch flight operations. As the *Shiloh* slowly cruised passed the Hickam Officer's Club, Tom saw two women playing tennis on the court between the club and the sea wall. The cute blonde in the white shorts reminded him of his high school sweetheart, Ann Curtis. Ann had introduced him to the exotic pleasures of sex. He would never forget Ann.

Tennis Court
Hickam AFB
Honolulu, Hawaii

Ann Cunningham and Kim Ellis were playing tennis on the number two court between the Hickam Officer's Club and the harbor when the *USS Shiloh* entered Pearl Harbor and slowly steamed by the club. Ann had won the first set, 6 to 4 and was leading in the second set, 4 to love. She was thirty-five years old, five-feet eight inches tall and rigidly kept her weight under 120 pounds. She had been married to Major Ted Cunningham, USAF, for ten years and was ready to start divorce proceedings when he was shot down by a MiG over North Vietnam, and declared killed in action. She was pleasantly astonished to learn that his estate was two million dollars. She immediately took a leave of absence from her job as a journalist on the *Washington Post* and flew to Hawaii to visit her parents, Major General Steve and Louise Curtis.

Her short blonde curls were held in place by a pink headband. She stretched to serve when she saw the aircraft carrier. "Jesus Christ! Look at that big Navy carrier," Ann said as she point to the *Shiloh* behind Kim. They walked to the net and stood watching the carrier maneuvered up the narrow channel.

"It amazes me that something that big, made out of steel, will float," Kim said. Kim was a year younger that Ann. She wore her black hair short, was almost the same height, but outweighed Ann by twenty pounds. Her husband was an Air Force Major who was flying the F-100D Super Saber jet fighter out of Bein Hoa Air Base in Vietnam when he was shot down and declared missing in action two months ago.

"My first boyfriend is a Navy flier," Ann said. "Maybe he's on that ship," she said wishfully.

"How did an Air Force brat start out dating a boy who was destined to be a Navy flier?" Kim asked.

"He was not a boy! Even at the tender age of seventeen, he was all man!" Ann remembered fondly. "His father was a Navy Captain on the staff of CINCPACFLEET while we were stationed here at Hickam. Tom and I went to high school together our senior year, then he went to the Naval Academy and promptly forgot all about me."

"Let's go over to the Pearl Club tonight, and see if we can find Tom," Kim suggested.

"No way in hell!" Ann exclaimed. "Have you been to that club when the Air Group's in port? Those fliers turn into animals. Anyway, Dad's leaving for Vietnam tomorrow, and I promised that we'd meet at the Sea Breeze Club tonight at seven for dinner. We just have time to finish this set," she said as she ran back to the service line.

"Thirty serving fifteen," Ann said as she drilled the tennis ball into the net. Reaching into the side pocket of her shorts, she grasped the second ball and pitched it six feet above her head. Her second serve cleared the net but sailed over the fault line.

"Out," Kim called.

Damn, double fault, bringing the score to deuce. "Thirty all," Ann called as she walked to the right side of the court and prepared to serve again. Since the *Shiloh* had passed by she could not concentrate on tennis. Her thoughts were about Tom Colby.

Sixteen

Sea Breeze Club

Hickam Officer's Club
Hickam Air Base, Hawaii

Commanders Joe Blackwell and Tom Colby sat at the bar in the Warriors Lounge of the club drinking Coors beer. "Tommy's football team beat the Hilltop Lancers Friday night in a squeaker, 24 to 21," Tom said as he sipped the cold beer. "Damn, I wish I could've seen that game."

"Hold the fort, I'm going to call Shirley," Joe said. "Do you want Shirley to get you a date?"

"No, thanks, Skipper. I'll have dinner here at the club and go back to the carrier. We have a lot of equipment to get ready to move out tomorrow." Tom sipped the beer and thought about Linda and his sexy next door neighbor, Jackie Anderson. He and Jackie did not keep their Friday dinner date since Linda flew home early and the Presidential party set up headquarters in the Anderson residence.

Tom wondered if Jackie had tried to seduce the President when a pair of soft hands covered his eyes. He felt two large breasts press into his back and a voice whispered in his right ear, "Hi, sailor boy. Do you still remember your first lover?"

God, she smelled good. Tom thought and felt the fingers of her left hand began to caress his left ear lobe the way his first sweetheart would tease him in foreplay. "Is it Ann? Ann Curtis?"

122

"Oh, you big brute! How'd you guess so quickly?" Ann asked as she slid around the side of the bar stool and kissed him, "but it's Cunningham now instead of Curtis. I was married to Ted Cunningham, the great Air Force fighter pilot, until a MiG shot his ass off over Vietnam four months ago."

"So sorry to hear that, Ann," Tom consoled her. "Did he eject?"

"No, he went out in a blaze of glory. His wingman, Fred Ellis saw Ted's jet explode and no chute. Then Fred shot down the MiG with one of his missiles." Ann kissed him again. She broke the kiss saying, "Were you on that big aircraft carrier that sailed by the club this afternoon?"

Joe had finished talking on the telephone and was returning to the bar when he saw the beautiful blonde woman kissing Tom Colby. *Jesus Christ, what a pair of tits,* he thought. Then he heard Tom say, "Yes, Ann, we were up on vulture's row watching as the Captain navigated up the channel. I thought I saw you on the tennis court with a beautiful brunette."

"That brunette is my best friend, Kim Ellis," Ann said as Joe reached the bar.

"Ann, this is my Commanding Officer, Joe Blackwell. Joe, this is my very first girlfriend, Ann Cunningham," Tom said.

Ann took Joe's hand. "So pleased to meet you, Joe. You may be just what the doctor ordered for Kim."

"Kim who?" Joe asked.

"My friend, Kim Ellis, who's sitting over there in the corner," she pointed. "Grab your drinks and come over to our table." She took Tom's hand and led them to the table. "Gentlemen, this is Kim Ellis," Ann announced. "Kim, this is Tom Colby and Joe Blackwell."

Kim stood and shook Tom's hand and then took Joe's hand and said, "Come, sit by me, Joe." She was dressed in a blue silk wrap-around miniskirt and a matching blue silk blouse that clung tightly to her breasts. Her black hair was short and lustrous. "Are you a fighter pilot, Joe?" She asked looking at the gold wings and ribbons on his white uniform.

"I was a fighter pilot in the Korean War, but now I'm just a broken-down old combat rescue helicopter pilot," Joe answered.

"Oh, you don't look so old and broken-down to me," Kim smiled.

"Okay, everyone, drink up," Ann ordered. "Kim and I are going over to the Sea Breeze Club on the beach to a dinner party. Will you gentlemen please be our escorts?"

"I'd love to have dinner with you, Ann," Tom answered. Turning to Joe, he asked, "Are you busy tonight Skipper?"

"No, I don't have a thing planned," he smiled.

Ann stood and took Tom's hand. Addressing Kim, she said, "Tom will ride with me in the T-bird. You can bring Joe in your car. That way we won't have to backtrack for your car later. See you two at the club in ten minutes."

Kim took a sip of wine. "They sure make a cute couple," she said as Tom and Ann walk from the club. "I think Ann still has a crush on him."

Honeymoon Beach
Hickam Air Base, Hawaii

Ann drove the red Thunderbird into the parking lot at Honeymoon Beach and parked on the west end, near the sea wall. The Thunderbird was a rental car she had leased from Hertz. "Do you remember all the beautiful sunsets that we watched from this beach?"

"Yeah," Tom answered, "but all of the sunsets put together are not as beautiful as you."

"There's not many clouds tonight, so we should be able to see the green flash. When the ocean swallows the sun, there'll be a tiny green flash. Tell me when you see the green flash."

Tom watched as the sun became a huge red ball and began to slide into the ocean. The moment it disappeared, he saw a tiny spark of green. "There goes the green flash."

"I told you there was a green flash. Now we must hurry to Father's farewell party." She started the Thunderbird and drove toward the Sea Breeze Club. "Please be nice to the General, Tom."

"Oh, my God! Your father's a General," he remembered. "How many stars?"

"Two stars, Major General," she answered. "How many stars does Dad Colby have?"

"Oh crap, Dad was just promoted to Vice Admiral, three stars," he answered. "But let's not tell General Curtis. Okay?"

"Tom, you worry too much about military protocol," she smiled and rubbed his leg. "Relax and have a good time at the party."

Sea Breeze Club
Hickam Air Base, Hawaii

Major General Steve and Louise Curtis stood at the head of the receiving line as Ann walked into the club with Tom. "Father, this is Tom Colby," Ann said and kissed the General's cheek. She whispered in his ear, "My old boyfriend."

General Curtis shook Tom's hand and said, "Tom Colby, now a full Navy Commander, wearing gold wings. How's the Admiral?"

"Just fine, sir," Tom answered. "He'll be going out to the Seventh Fleet soon." Tom saw one of General Curtis eye brows twitch. *Damn, I shouldn't have made that comment about the Seventh Fleet.*

"Say hello to Louise, Tom. I want to talk to you later," the General said and turned to greet the other arriving guests.

"Have you seen Kim Ellis, Mother?" Ann asked.

"Yes, darling, she came in about five minutes ago with a handsome Navy Commander. She thought you'd be here."

"Tom and I stopped at the beach to watch the sunset," Ann said. "Kim and I found Tom and Joe at the main club and invited them over to say farewell to Father."

"Hello, Mrs. Curtis," Tom said and reached for her hand. "You get more beautiful everyday."

Louise Curtis hugged Tom. She kissed his cheek and said, "You're so handsome in your uniform, Tom. Please save a dance for me."

"Yes, ma'am," Tom said and followed Ann down the receiving line and to the bar. "What'd you like to drink, beautiful lady?"

"A Mai Tai," she smiled.

"Two Mai Tai's," Tom said to the bartender. A Mai Tai tasted like fruit juice but was a very potent drink. After this one he would switch to beer. He handed Ann a Mai Tai loaded with chunks of fruit, and they walked out to the lanai where Kim and Joe were talking in whispers.

"Did you two get lost?" Kim asked.

"No, we stopped at the beach to watch the sunset. Tom finally saw the green flash," Ann laughed.

125

"Yes, I saw it," Tom agreed. "It was a beautiful green flash that was gone in less than a second, but the memory will last a lifetime." Dinner was served at seven. Louise Curtis had the General's aide rearrange the seat assignments placing Ann, Kim, Tom and Joe at the head table. The waiter served from a platter of sizzling Kona steaks. They were very rare and very delicious. Dessert was a large wedge of chocolate cake topped with macadamia nut ice cream.

After dinner the girls headed for the powder room, led by Louise. "Would you gentlemen please join me outside for a cigar?" General Curtis said to Tom and Joe, as he walked toward the lanai.

"Thanks, General," Joe said as he accepted the cigar.

"No, thank you, General," Tom said refusing the offered cigar. "I stopped smoking two years ago."

"Well, good for you, son," Curtis praised. "Will this smoke bother you?"

"No, sir," Tom answered. "Please enjoy your cigar."

"When will your carrier sail for Vietnam?" Curtis asked and puffed on the cigar.

"Tomorrow, General," Tom said, "but she's going to the Sea of Japan instead of the South China Sea. Skipper Blackwell will take our squadron out there to track some Soviet submarines."

"Yes, I heard about the increased submarine activity in last Friday's brief to CINCPACAF," General Curtis said.

"That creates a major logistics problem for us," Tom continued. "We'll unload the SAR detachment tomorrow morning. I'll be taking them to Cubi Point Air Station on a C-130 out of Barbers Point. Then we'll shuttle the crew out to the *USS Concord* on the carrier's COD."

"Seems like I heard the briefing officer say that the *Concord* was about seventy-five miles off the coast of Da Nang. Is that about right?" Curtis asked.

Yes, General," Tom answered. "The carrier usually cruises around Yankee Station in a large circle, about seventy-five to two hundred miles from Da Nang."

"How many men in your detachment?"

"We have six aviators and sixteen enlisted, for a total of twenty-two, sir," Tom answered.

"Son, this is your lucky day," Curtis beamed. "I'm flying to Da Nang tomorrow afternoon in my KC-135, and we just happen to have twenty-five empty seats."

Turning to Joe, Curtis said, "Would it be okay if I gave your detachment a ride to Da Nang? Then we can get the Air Force helicopter detachment at Da Nang to fly them out to the carrier."

"Yes, thank you, General," Joe answered. "That would sure help us out of a tight bind. Are you going out for a duty assignment, sir?"

"Yes, Joe," Curtis said. "I finally wrangled a Deputy slot in the Wing at Da Nang."

"What time would you like us to report, General?" Tom asked.

"Let's see, take-off is fourteen-hundred," Curtis said. "You should have your detachment over at base operations by thirteen-hundred."

"We'll be there, sir," Tom assured him.

General Curtis looked up and saw the ladies returning from the powder room. He stubbed his cigar in the ashtray and said, "Enough shop talk, gentlemen. Here come the ladies." Turning to Tom, he said, "You'd better dance with Louise or she'll never forgive you."

SEVENTEEN

Waikiki Beach

Nimitz Highway
Honolulu, Hawaii

Tom leaned back in the soft seat and drove the Thunderbird down Nimitz Highway toward Waikiki. After dinner, he had danced with both Louise Curtis and Kim Ellis. As he danced with Ann, she complained of a migraine headache and asked him to drive her to the hotel. When they said good night to General Curtis, Louise was dancing with Joe Blackwell.

"Sorry about the headache, Ann. Do you get them often?"

"No, I haven't had a headache in a long time," she answered. "It feels better now. Too much damn cigar smoke in that place. Smoking should not be allowed in restaurants. Right, Tom?"

"You're so right, sweetheart," he agreed and turned right onto Kalakaua Avenue. "Which hotel?"

"The Moana. Remember the big banyan tree on the beach?"

"Sure do. God, I'm glad that you decided to play tennis today."

"Kim and I play tennis everyday. She's had a very rough time since Fred was shot down in Vietnam. Poor Fred's probably a POW in the Hanoi Hilton. She loves him very much."

"Well, she seemed to enjoy dancing with the Skipper. Maybe Joe will get lucky tonight," Tom laughed.

"If he doesn't get lucky, Kim will rape him! I know she hasn't had a man for almost eight months now."

"Oh, my God!" Tom exclaimed. "She's very close to going blind."

"Tom Colby, I know there's a little boy inside you saying all those things," she laughed. "Do you have a son or daughter?"

"One son, Thomas Edward Colby, the second. He's seventeen years old, quarterback and captain of his high school football team."

"Oh, God, don't tell me there's another Tom Colby," she groaned.

"Tommy's really a great football player. He loves to fly, but he doesn't want to go to the Naval Academy or any part of the Navy. He plans to be a doctor," Tom sighed.

"Well, good for Tommy," she said. "Quick, turn right."

Tom eased the Thunderbird into the circular driveway in front of the Moana Hotel and stopped behind the hotel shuttle bus. "Leave the keys in the car, and the valet will park it," Ann said and got out of the car. They rode the elevator up to the tenth floor of the Moana Towers. The Towers had been added between the Moana and the Outrigger hotels without distracting from the beauty and elegance of the 100-year old hotel. Ann's suite on the tenth floor overlooked the beach.

"God, what a snake ranch!" Tom exclaimed as Ann opened the drapes. He looked down at the famous Waikiki Beach that was crowded with tourists clad in tiny bikini's and multi-colored aloha shirts. "This would be the ultimate dream of any Naval aviator."

"Well, I'm glad that you approve of my little grass shack, sailor boy," Ann smiled and kissed him. "Come, I'll show you my snake ranch." She led him into the bedroom that contained a large king-size bed, vanity dresser and a chest of drawers. The bedroom had sliding glass doors that overlooked the ocean and opened onto the balcony. Between the bedroom and bathroom was a large walk-in closet. Ann walked into the closet and removed her silk skirt and blouse and draped them on a hanger.

"You can hang your clothes here next to mine. I'll check the champagne and meet you in the shower." She walked toward the small refrigerator clad in a black lace bra and matching garter belt.

Tom removed his white uniform shirt and trousers and hung them beside Ann's clothes and walked into the bathroom clad only in jockey shorts. Ann came in carrying two glasses and a bottle of champagne. "Would you pour, please?"

"Yes, my lady," Tom said and poured two glasses of champagne.

"Tom, please spend the night with me," she begged.

"Ann, I must go back to the ship. Skipper's in unofficial hack for missing ship movement in San Diego. He'll probably spend the night with Kim, and I should be there if some crisis develops."

"Don't you have a duty officer who can take care of any crisis?"

"Yes, we have a squadron duty officer, who's on watch twenty-four hours a day. I could call and let him know where to locate me in case of emergency. May I give him your telephone number?"

"Oh, yes, please do," she smiled. "Let's do it right now."

The duty officer answered, "Ready room, Lieutenant J.G. Jackson speaking, sir."

"Good evening, Rick, this is Commander Colby. I have some great news. Please get in touch with Chief Roberts and the other SAR pilots and tell them that we're flying to Da Nang tomorrow on an Air Force KC-135 out of Hickam Air Force Base."

"That'll be a lot faster than the C-130," Jackson agreed.

"Rick, I'm at General Curtis' suite at the Moana Hotel in Waikiki. Has the Skipper returned to the ship?"

"No, sir, he called in and left a number where he could be reached if we had an alert or emergency."

"Thanks, Rick. If you need me I'll be at this number." Tom read the telephone number to Jackson and asked him to repeat it to make sure he had copied it correctly. While he was talking to the duty officer, Ann walked into the room wearing a white silk kimono. She turned down the cover on the bed and propped on a pillow against the headboard sipping champagne.

"That was very discreet of you not to compromise a lady," she smiled when Tom hung up the telephone. "Joe's not back at the ship yet?"

"No, he called in and probably left Kim's telephone number."

Ann unfolded a grey silk kimono and held it while Tom slipped his arms through the large sleeves. "Compliments of the Moana. You may take this one to sea with you to help you through all those long, lonely nights. I hope you dream about me," she laughed.

Tom enjoyed the sensuous feel of the silk on his skin. "Damn, this feels good." He reached for the glass of champagne.

"Please make love to me, Tom. I need you now!"

He kissed her and said, "I love you, Ann."

"Don't get love confused with lust," she cautioned.

"Darling, I've had lust, and I've known love. I can assure you that the emotion I'm feeling is love. Is it possible to be in love with two women at the same time?"

"Yes, I suppose it's possible," she answered. They kissed gently at first, then their kisses became harder and longer. He listen to the surf hiss at Waikiki Beach as Ann pulled him down to the large bed. He thought about his dead brother's ghost as he made love to the beautiful blonde. *Yes, I will definitely tell Ann about Michael's visit, later.*

USS Shiloh
Pearl Harbor, Hawaii

Kim Ellis drove Joe Blackwell to the *Shiloh* at eleven o'clock. He directed her to the pier, and she parked by the officer's gangplank. Joe kissed her good night. She sat in the car and watched him walk up the gangplank, salute the duty officer and disappear inside the ship. Then she started the car and drove slowly back to her quarters at Hickam Air Force Base. Her sexual desires were completely satisfied, and she felt great.

Joe walked down to the wardroom for a cup of coffee. Two hours of marathon sex with Kim Ellis was exciting but not as satisfying as the one time he had made love to Sarah Wiseman at the beach cottage. *Jesus, the last thing I want to do is fall in love with Sarah,* he thought as he filled the cup with steaming coffee. CAG Boyd walked in as Joe was spooning sugar in his coffee. "Evening, CAG," Joe said. "Join me in a cup of coffee?"

"Sure thing, Joe," CAG answered and poured a cup of coffee from the steaming pot. "Have any luck finding a flight over at the MAC terminal?"

"CAG, I'm firmly convinced that young Colby's going to be an Admiral someday."

"I agree with you," CAG said. "Tom will probably be the first helicopter pilot to make Admiral. What did he do tonight that impressed you so much?"

"It was the way that he handled Major General Curtis. Tom and I went to the Hickam club for a beer before checking at the terminal. While I was on the phone calling the terminal, Tom's high school girlfriend walked in and invited us to a farewell dinner party for her father, Major General Curtis. He's flying to Da Nang tomorrow afternoon in his seven-oh-seven jet and taking our whole damn SAR detachment with him. Then he told Tom that he would have the Air Force SAR helicopters fly the detachment from Da Nang out to the *Concord*."

"That's great news, Joe," CAG said. "Is Tom still on the beach?"

"Yes, sir."

"Tell him to come by my office tomorrow morning after muster. I want to talk to him before the detachment leaves the ship."

"Yes, sir, do you know what time we're sailing tomorrow?"

"We'll know for sure by morning muster. We'll probably get underway at fourteen-hundred-hours. Good night, Joe, I'm going to try to get some sleep."

"Good night, CAG." Joe glanced at his watch as his thoughts returned to Sarah Wiseman. It was 11:40 p.m. *Damn, too late to call Sarah tonight,* he thought. *Well, by God, I'll call her first thing in the morning.*

EIGHTEEN

War Is Hell

Moana Hotel
Waikiki Beach

Tom lay on his stomach with his face buried in the pillow. The sheets were cool against his skin. The cool ocean breeze floated through the open sliding glass door. He heard the rumble as the ocean waves kissed the famous Waikiki Beach. He turned his head until he could see Ann's reflection in the closet door mirror. She was standing in the living room talking on the telephone. Tom smiled to himself, *God, it was a beautiful day to be flying to the war zone, but I would gladly postpone the trip a few days to enjoy the comforts of this beautiful lady.*

He heard the light tread of her feet as Ann entered the bedroom and crossed near where his head lay. He cracked his right eye and saw her reflection in the mirror. As she extended her hand to shake him awake, he grabbed her right hand with his left and rolled over. She landed on top of him. He smiled at the startled expression on her face and kissed her tenderly. Ann was breathless when he released her mouth.

"You bastard, you scared the hell out of me!" She scolded.

"Darling, never sneak up on a combat pilot," he said as his hand caressed her waist. "Why are you waking me at five?"

"We have to get you back to the big ship, sailor boy."

"I'm too pooped to move a muscle," he said.

"Well, you have to start moving and move fast," Ann tugged him out of the bed. "Grab a quick shower and shave. Room service is delivering breakfast in exactly twenty-two minutes."

Tom had showered, shaved and was dressed in his white uniform when the waiter wheeled the cart into the room and placed the steaming

133

breakfast on the lanai table. Ann had ordered a breakfast steak, scrambled eggs, hashbrown potatoes and wheat toast for Tom. On her plate was a poached egg and a crepe suzette.

"Thank you for the fantastic reunion, Ann," Tom said as he wolfed down the breakfast. "Were you really serious about trying to get the *Washington Post* to send you to Vietnam as a war correspondent?"

"Yes, most serious," she assured him.

"Well, I want you to reconsider. South Vietnam is a dangerous place to live and work. I understand that it's impossible to tell the good guys from the bad ones. Just last week a claymore mine blew up in a Saigon Catholic church killing and wounding scores of the worshipers."

"I do think you're concerned about my safety," she smiled.

"I am, Ann. I'm not sure what liberty ports the *Concord* has on her schedule. How about flying out to meet me in Manila or Hong Kong?"

"I'd love to, Tom. Just give me a call when you know which port your carrier is going to for rest and recuperation. Now, finish your breakfast, and we'll drive out to Pearl Harbor."

USS Shiloh, CVS-22
Naval Station, Pearl Harbor

The *Shiloh* was a beehive of activity as working parties made preparations for the carrier's departure. Ann parked near the forward gangplank and turned to face Tom. The ten-mile trip from Waikiki to Pearl Harbor Naval Station had been quiet and subdued as driver and passenger were remembering the past evening together. "Tom, promise me that you won't try to be a hero," Ann begged as she reached for his hand and brought it to her mouth. She kissed his hand.

"Okay, my lady, I promise not to take any unnecessary chances and try to be a hero," he answered. "If you'll seriously reconsider your plans to be a war correspondent."

"We have a deal," she lied. "Now get on your ship before you're late. I'll try to see you at noon before Daddy's jet leaves for Vietnam."

Tom got out and closed the car door. He gave Ann a smart salute then turned and walked up the gangplank. Ann sat and watched as he saluted the Officer of the Deck and disappeared inside the ship. Then she started the Thunderbird and drove back to Waikiki. She would call the *Post* today and start the ball rolling on her assignment as a war correspondent. The sun was rising over Diamond Head as she drove down Nimitz Highway. It was a beautiful Hawaiian day.

Tom's stateroom was on the main deck forward of the number one elevator. The forward hangar bay was packed with fourteen helicopters. Two helicopters sat on the flight deck where they could be quickly launched for search and rescue or a quick reaction ASW mission. Tom carefully walked around the parked helicopters, stepping high over the tiedown chains, and up the narrow passageway to his room. He picked up the telephone and dialed the squadron duty office. The phone was answered on the first ring, "HS-twenty-four duty office, Petty Officer Jackman speaking, sir."

"Good morning, Jackman. This is Commander Colby. May I please speak with the duty officer?"

"Yes, sir, Commander," Jackman answered. "Wait one, sir."

The duty officer came on the line, "Good morning, XO. This is Lieutenant J.G. Jackson, sir."

"Morning, Rick," Tom said. "Reporting myself back aboard. Have you heard from the Skipper?"

"Yes, sir. He got back to the ship about eleven last night. We had a quiet evening, all the squadron personnel are accounted for, and there are no messages for you, sir."

A damn efficient duty officer, Tom thought, "Thanks, Rick, I'll be in the wardroom having breakfast." He changed into the working, short sleeve khaki uniform and retraced his steps to the hangar deck, then down a ladder to the wardroom. CAG Boyd and Joe sat at the Commander's table. He walked forward and sat in an empty chair next to Joe.

"Good morning, gentlemen," he said.

"Morning, Tom," CAG replied. "Joe told me how you talked the Air Force into airlifting your detachment to Vietnam. Good job."

"Thanks, CAG. I've know General Curtis since he was a light Colonel. I dated his daughter, Ann, during our senior year in high school. The General's going to be Deputy at the Wing in Da Nang," Tom said as the steward placed a steaming cup of coffee on the table in front of him and took his order. He ordered one egg scrambled, bacon and wheat toast.

"Did you have dinner with Ann?" CAG asked.

"Yes, sir," Tom answered. "She was my dinner companion while the Skipper escorted her friend, Kim."

CAG Boyd looked across the table at Joe and said, "You forgot to brief me about your female dinner companion, Joe. Was she so ugly that you are trying to forget her?"

135

"God no, CAG," Joe answered. "Kim's a beautiful brunette with a very pleasant personality, but, she's a grieving widow," he lied. "Her husband was shot down about two months ago over North Vietnam. His wingman saw a chute, so there's a possibility that he's a POW."

"Ann's husband was killed in action, CAG," Tom said. "So you can see that the Skipper and I spent the evening consoling the Air Force widows."

"Bullshit!" CAG growled and sipped his coffee. "What time is your flight leaving Hickam?"

"Fourteen-hundred-hours, sir," Tom said and ate his second breakfast of the morning. "I told the General we'd be waiting at Base Operations at thirteen-hundred."

"That works out great," CAG said. "*Shiloh* will get underway at fourteen-hundred-hours, also. Enjoy your breakfast, gentlemen. I have a few things to check on before morning muster."

As CAG walked away from the table, Tom asked, "Did you get lucky, Skipper?"

"Hell, yes, Tom," Joe groaned. "Kim took me to her apartment and made love to me for two hours. Did you make out with Ann?"

"Three or four times, she has a suite at the Moana Hotel over-looking the ocean. What a place for a honeymoon."

"Damn, it's just not fair," Joe complained. "You and I have two of the most beautiful women in the Islands, and we're limited to a one-night stand. War is hell, my friend!"

Anderson Realty
Chula Vista, California

Linda Colby sat in her new office at Anderson Realty reading the *San Diego Union* newspaper. The headline screamed, *CONVAIR LOSES MISSILE CONTRACT, SEVEN THOUSAND TO BE LAID OFF.* Jackie Anderson walked into Linda's office and asked, "How do you like your new office?"

"It's very nice, Jackie," Linda answered. "But I think I picked a bad time to enter the real estate business." She held up the newspaper for Jackie to read.

"Linda, there's no good or bad time to get into real estate. That'll be seven thousand houses that we'll have a chance to sell if they decide to leave San Diego. Actually, you and I should buy all of those houses that we can afford and rent them. Those little twenty thousand dollar houses will be selling for forty to fifty thousand within ten years. We can double our investment."

Linda's telephone buzzed. She picked up the phone and heard the receptionist say, "Linda, you have a call on line one."

"Thanks, Lois," she said as she pushed button one and said, "Good morning, Linda Colby speaking."

"Good morning, Mrs. Colby, this is Glenn Carson. You were referred to our company by Commander Bob Wilson. We have an employee moving to the area who needs a house. Does your company sell houses in La Costa?"

"Please hold for a minute," Linda said and pushed the red hold button on the telephone. She turned to Jackie Anderson and said, "Mr. Carson wants to buy a house in La Costa. Can we sell a house in that area?"

"Linda, we'll sell him a house anywhere in the state of California," Jackie answered.

Linda pushed the button on line one and said, "Thank you for holding, Mr. Carson. Yes, we can sell you a house in La Costa. Would you like directions to our office?"

"No, thank you, Mrs. Colby," Carson answered. "I'd like to discuss the details with you during lunch. Will you meet me at twelve in the Sky Room of the El Cortez Hotel?"

"Yes I will," she said. "Thanks for calling Anderson Realty." Linda hung up the phone and jumped from her desk. "Jackie, my first customer wants to buy one of those expensive homes in La Costa."

"Don't count your chickens before they hatch," Jackie cautioned.

"Oh, I know," she smiled. "He wants to take me to lunch at the Sky Room. Since this is a business lunch, should I pay the bill?"

"Linda, a lady never pays the check. Let the gentleman buy you lunch, then take him to La Costa and sell him a very expensive house."

"Okay, boss," she laughed, "I want so much to sell a house to my very first customer. It would really be the icing on the cake to sell one of those mansions in La Costa."

NINETEEN

The Lady Is A Spy

Sky Room Restaurant
El Cortez Hotel
San Diego, California

Linda Colby entered the Sky Room of the El Cortez Hotel at exactly twelve noon. The maitre d' bowed and said, "Good afternoon, Mrs. Colby. Please follow me to your table." Linda was surprised that Andre had remembered her name. She followed him to a table near the piano.

Glenn Carson stood as Linda approached his table. "Good afternoon, Dr. Colby, my name's Glenn Carson. Thank you for meeting me on such short notice," he said and shook her hand. Linda noticed that his hand was soft and warm. His touch sent tingles up her arm. She estimated his age in the early forties. He was about the same as Tom's five feet-eight inch height, black hair speckled with grey, and dark brown eyes.

"Andre, bring Dr. Colby a glass of Chardonnay," Carson said.

"Right away, sir," Andre said and rushed off to the bar.

As Andre left the table, Carson said, "Please call me Glenn."

"All right, Glenn, if you will call me Linda," she smiled.

"We have a deal," he said as Andre placed the glass of wine in front of Linda and a tall glass filled with brown liquid in front of Glenn.

"What's that delicious looking drink?" She asked as Andre walked back to the maitre d' station.

"Cuban rum and Coke, I got hooked on it in Miami."

"You were with Bob Wilson when Sergeant Baker punched him in the eye last week, right?" Linda asked.

138

"Yes," he laughed. "Bob took me on a whale-watching tour in his airplane. When we landed at Brown Field, the Border Patrol arrested and cuffed us. The fat sergeant got mad and slapped Bob's face. Then a Border Patrol Commissioner came by and arrested Sergeant Baker and apologized to us."

"Sorry Glenn, I didn't mean to make such a big issue about it. Bob's a very special friend, and I don't want to see anyone hurt him."

"Linda, Bob recommends you most highly," he said and handed her his business card. The card read, AMERICAN FINANCIAL SERVICES, Glenn Carson, General Manager, and listed his telephone number. "One of our senior corporate officers wants to purchase this house." He handed her a piece of paper with the address.

Linda opened the paper and read the address, 55 La Costa Heights Road. "Glenn, I must confess that I'm not familiar with the La Costa area. Maybe you should select a Realtor in that area."

"No, we want you. The house is secluded on five acres over-looking the ocean. The market price is probably around a million and a half, but we're prepared to go as high as two. Will you please contact the owners and persuade them to sell?"

"Sure, I'll do my best."

"Well, that's all we can ask," he smiled. "You'll be amply rewarded for your labors. Your commission will be ten percent of the purchase price. If you can get the owner to sell within the next thirty days, you'll receive a ten thousand dollar bonus. Do we have a deal?"

Linda was stunned with the ten percent commission offer and bonus. The average real estate commission fee in San Diego was six percent. She reached for the wine glass. The glass was about one-third full. She drank the wine and sat the glass on the table. "We have a deal," she said and reached to shake his hand, "and I promise you that I'll give your project my full-time."

"I was hoping you'd say that," he smiled. The waiter suddenly appeared beside the table. "Now, let's order. Andre said the lobster tail was the chef's special for the day. Do you like lobster?"

"Oh yes, I love lobster."

Carson order lunch for them, and said, "Peter, bring a bottle of your best Chardonnay. We're celebrating a very important business trans-action."

"Yes, sir," the waiter said and hurried away to place the order and get the bottle of wine.

Da Nang Air Base
Republic of Vietnam

After refueling stops at Andersen Air Base in Guam and Clark Air Base in the Philippines, General Curtis' jet landed at Da Nang Air Base at 1720 local. Vietnam was ten hours ahead of Hawaii. The KC-135 was a Boeing 707 that was modified to carry both passengers and cargo. Prior to the landing, Tom had left the curtained VIP section and walked aft to the coach section where the SAR detachment was seated. The passengers were rumpled and stiff from the long flight. He told the men to remain in their seats until the VIP's had departed the aircraft.

General Curtis did not go out the exit door of the jetliner. Instead he walked back to the coach section of the aircraft and addressed the Navy group. "Commander Colby and men of the Navy SAR detachment, it has been my pleasure to have the Sea Devil crewmen on this flight. You men have a fine leader in Commander Colby. The only payment that I'm asking is for you gentlemen to rescue every Air Force pilot that bails out over the Tonkin Gulf. Take a few hours this evening and get to know your counterparts, the Jolly Green Giant helicopter rescue team of the Air Force, stationed here at Da Nang. Good luck and good hunting." He saluted the group.

As Tom stood and returned the General's salute, the twenty-one Navy men started applauding. Raising his hand to quiet the group, Tom said, "Thanks for the lift, General. This was a first class ride to the war zone. Good luck in your new job, sir." He shook hands with General Curtis and followed him toward the exit door.

After the Air Force VIP's were clear of the aircraft, Tom motioned for the detachment personnel to come forward. They filed off the aircraft and carried their bags to the waiting, blue Air Force bus. Tom asked the Vietnamese driver to take them to the 366th Helicopter Rescue Squadron. The bus was not air-conditioned, and the heat and humidity hit Tom like a fist as his lungs breathed in the steamy air. He felt sweat start to roll down the sides of his body. Before they reached the squadron area, his khaki shirt was soaked down the front and back, with circular dark patches under each arm. *Damn, it's going to be hot flying in those long sleeve, nomex flight suits*, he thought.

It was a three-mile bus ride to the 366th Helicopter Rescue Squadron. Major Greg King, USAF, met the detachment when the bus arrived. He saluted Tom and said, "Welcome to the home of the Jolly Green Giants. Please have your officers gather their bags and follow me to the BOQ. First Sergeant Walls will show the troops to their tent."

The BOQ was across the street from the squadron operations building. The building consisted of wood walls covered with a large tent. Inside the building was 10 rows of double-deck bunks, draped with mosquito netting. The temperature inside the room was 97 degrees. Major King yelled, "Throw your gear on an empty bunk and follow me across the street to the Officer's Club. It's air-conditioned."

Tom introduced the five officers in his detachment to Major King as Anah Thong, the Vietnamese bar girl, opened seven bottles of cold beer. The small club was air-conditioned as Major King had promised. The cool air was a welcome relief from the sweltering heat and humidity.

Anah smiled at the Navy pilots as she served the beer. She was five-feet-eight in height, tall for a Vietnamese. She wore a white silk shift with a slit up the left side almost to the waist. Her dark black hair hung in a smooth cascade down her back. She was Major King's girlfriend and slept in his hootch in the big double bed. Anah was eighteen but looked fourteen. She was a Vietnamese Nationalist who believed that liberation of her country was from Ho Chi Minh, not the Republic of Vietnam puppet army and the American President Lyndon Johnson.

Anah Thong was an active Viet Cong spy. When she returned to the bar, she carefully wrote the name of each of the six Navy pilots in the small ledger. After Tom's name, she wrote, *Commanding Officer of helicopter rescue on Concord ship.* She would add information later after she flirted with the handsome American pilots.

"Gentlemen, we have a compulsory brief for all visiting flight crews," King said. "The VC continually harasses us with mortar and sapper attacks. They try to get the mortars close enough to take out a fighter or a helicopter. The sappers sometimes get inside the base and throw satchel charges in buildings where troops are sleeping. Our alert system is very similar to your General Quarters alarm on the ship. Three blasts on the siren indicates that an attack is in progress, and all personnel are required to get in the bunkers as quickly as possible. Our bunker is out back between the club and the BOQ. Any questions?"

"Have you made contact with the *USS Concord*?" Tom asked.

"Roger that, Commander," King answered. "Ops got a message from the *Concord* this afternoon with an overhead time of ten-twenty hours tomorrow morning. We'll ferry your detachment out in two of our HH-3 helicopters."

"Have your pilots ever landed on an aircraft carrier?" Tom asked.

"No, sir," King answered. "I'd be happy to have two of your pilots as part of the flight crew."

141

"I'll fly with you, Greg," Tom said, "and Bull can ride shotgun on the second helicopter."

"Thanks Commander," King said. "After you gentlemen finish your beer, I'll drive you to the main club for dinner. Tonight is steak night, so we should get there early."

Major Greg King's Hootch
Da Nang Air Base
Republic of Vietnam

Major Greg King lay face down on the double bed in a drunken fog as Anah Thong struggled to undress him. She had been alarmed when Tom brought King to the door and helped her get him across the room to the bed. "Sorry Anah, we let Major King drink too much gin at the club."

"Not your fault, Commander," she said. "Major King should drink beer and not gin. Thank you for bringing him back to the hootch."

"Well, good night Anah, I'm exhausted. I'm going over to the BOQ and go to bed," Tom said as he walked toward the door.

"Wait Commander Tom," Anah called to him. "Captain Joe Smith has gone TDY to Bien Hoa. You can sleep in his room at the other end of the hootch." She took Tom's hand and led him through the bathroom to Captain Smith's room and turned up the air-conditioner. The room contained a double bed almost identical to the one that Major King was sprawled on in the other room.

"Are you sure this will be okay with Major King?" Tom asked.

"He's drunk, and I'm in charge, Commander Tom," she said and walked over and turned down the sheets. "Take a shower and sleep well."

"Thank you, Anah," he said as she walked back to King's room.

Anah sat on the bed and watched King. When she was satisfied that he was sleeping, she pulled the sheet up over him and walked back to Tom's room. He had showered and was laying on top the cool sheets when he heard Anah's bare feet padding across the floor. She sat on the side of the bed and rubbed his chest with her hand. She felt his nipples get hard. "He's drunk off his ass again, Commander Tom," Anah whispered. "Turn over and I will give you a very special massage."

Tom rolled over on his stomach and felt Anah straddle his legs. She pressed her nude body close to him, then began to massage his neck and shoulders. "Oh God, that feels great, Anah," Tom whispered. "Is there any chance that Major King will wake up and come looking for you?"

"No way, Commander Tom, he'll sleep for hours," she purred as she rubbed her breasts into his back. "Turn over," she ordered. Tom rolled over slowly. Anah mounted him and rocked back and forth.

Damn, she was so beautiful and sexy. He raised his head and kissed her small breast. Her nipples became erect, and she started moaning like Ann Curtis. Sex with those ladies was so similar, and yet so vastly different. Tom matched her rhythm. He felt her orgasm peak as he reached his climax. Anah rolled off him and collapsed on the bed. "Thank you, Anah, you're the best I've had since I got to Vietnam."

Anah was touch by his remark. This was the first American that had thanked her for loving him, and he said she was the best. She liked this Commander Tom. She went into the bathroom. Returning with a cool bath cloth she washed his manhood. Tom groaned and looked at the clock on the dresser, it read 11:45. "God, it's almost midnight, Anah. Will you please wake me at seven? I have to fly out to the carrier."

"Commander Tom, please hurry and put on your pants and shirt," she said, remembering that the sapper raid was scheduled to start at midnight. "There is rumor of a possible VC attack on the air base tonight. Sleep in your clothes and be ready to run for the bunker if you hear the siren." She walked to Captain Smith's closet and returned with a flak vest and lay it on the foot of the bed. "Remember to wear this flak vest," she said and leaned over to kiss his lips.

"Yes, dear," Tom laughed. "You're so beautiful, Anah," he said and got up and put on his shirt and trousers. He lay down and patted the bed, "Hold me until I go to sleep, please."

"Okay, Commander Tom," she said and snuggled up to him. Tom was asleep within five minutes. When he was snoring, Anah crept back to Major King's room and put on her clothes. She lay beside King and waited for the wail of the sirens to start.

143

TWENTY

Taste Of Combat

Da Nang Air Base
Republic of Vietnam

Tom lay in a deep sleep and dreamed about the Imperial Beach policeman. He was driving the Jaguar one hundred miles an hour down Palm Avenue and the policeman was closing on him with the siren going full blast. A loud explosion outside the hootch shattered him from the dream. He jammed his feet into his shoes and grabbed the flak vest. The clock on the dresser read fifteen minutes after midnight. He put on the flak vest and ran into Major King's room yelling for Anah. King lay on the bed snoring, while Anah tried to shake him awake. He jerked King into a sitting position. Kneeling on the floor beside the bed, he draped King over his shoulder in a fireman's carry and followed Anah to the bunker. Another explosion on his left shattered some windows in the Operations building. He felt debris strike his left arm as he ducked into the bunker and let King slide to the dirt floor. The bunker was bathed in dim light. Anah looked frightened, and he saw blood on her arm.

"Commander, you're bleeding," Ensign Tim Arnold yelled at him. "Is Major King dead?"

Tom looked at his arm and saw blood streaming down his elbow. "Ah crap, it must've been the window glass from the ops building that got me. Help me get the Major on the cot, Tim. He may have a few wounds,

144

but he's stinking drunk." As he and Arnold lifted King to the cot, he saw the blood. *Damn, I forgot to wear the magic white scarf,* he remembered the promise to his brother's ghost. *From this day forward brother Michael, I promise to wear your white scarf everyday.*

Anah ran over to Tom's side with some bandages. "Oh damn, you're wounded, Commander Tom," she said and pressed the bandage to his arm. "Come lay down. I'm sorry my people do this to you."

Tom felt dizzy and faint. He walked over and lay on the cot and let Anah nurse him. "It wasn't your people's fault, Anah," he said and caressed her back. "It was the damn Viet Cong."

"Tim, are all of our troops accounted for?" He asked Arnold.

"Yes sir, Commander," Arnold said. "Bull and Chief Roberts have a few wounds similar to yours. Everyone else is okay, sir."

The Air Force medic finished bandaging Ensign Walker's arm. He walked over to the cot where Tom lay and gently pushed Anah aside. "You did a fine job stopping the bleeding, young lady," he said to Anah. "Let me look at the Commander." The medic picked several pieces of shrapnel and glass from the wounds on Tom's left arm, and applied a tight bandage. "I'd better take a look at the Major. He took more of the blast than you did," the medic said to Tom.

The VC sapper raid was over in twenty minutes. The all-clear was announced by one long blast on the siren. The group walked from the bunker and looked at the shattered buildings. Major King's hootch was demolished. *It's a good thing I had time to carry out the drunk son-of-a-bitch,* Tom thought. *There's no way he could have lived through that.*

The ambulance arrived and took Tom, King, Bull, Chief Roberts and Anah to the base hospital. The Air Force doctor examined the medic's work and gave Tom a shot. "Get a good nights sleep, and you'll be okay in a few days if it doesn't get infected. You saved Major King's life carrying him out of that building. The Air Force thanks you, sir."

"I just want to get some sleep, doc. Will they attack again, tonight?"

"You're safe here, Commander," the doctor assured him. "The sappers have never been able to penetrate the security of our hospital. Sleep tight." He turned out the lights and walked out of the room. Tom thought about Anah's delicious small breasts and went to sleep.

Vice Admiral Colby's Stateroom
USS Providence, CLG-6
Sea of Japan

Admiral Thomas Colby sat at his large desk in the Flag Office. He breathed a sigh as his thoughts drifted back to his busy day, *I enjoyed the change of command on the fantail. The Providence is a Light Cruiser with guided missiles. She has a five inch gun mounted forward of the bridge. A helicopter flight deck is on the fantail where the H-2B Sea Sprite helicopter is tied down. It will be great having my own helicopter.*

Vice Admiral Robert Hollingsworth, my predecessor, offered his hand and said, "Thomas, she's all yours." Hollingsworth turned to Captain Lester and said, "John send a message to CINCPACFLT that Vice Admiral Thomas Colby has command of the Seventh Fleet."

"Yes, Admiral," Lester said and walked out of the Cabin.

"When are you flying back to CONUS?" I asked.

"I'm on the SAM Flight out of Tachikawa Air Base tomorrow afternoon at fourteen-hundred."

"Would you like a ride up in the helicopter?"

"Yes, thanks Thomas."

"Anything I should know about my Chief of Staff?"

"I guess you noticed that John's a black-shoe. I inherited him when I came aboard. He's a damn fine administrator, but feel free to replace him if you like."

The telephone rang, interrupting Colby's thoughts. He reached for the receiver and said, "Admiral Colby."

"Good evening, Admiral. This is Chief Hill down in comm. You have a secret personal message from Major General Curtis in Da Nang. I'll have the messenger bring it up to the Flag Cabin, sir."

"Thanks, Chief," Colby said and hung up the phone. *Damn, I hope something hasn't happened to Tom.*

Anderson Realty
Chula Vista, California

Linda drove into the lot and parked the Jaguar beside Jackie's Oldsmobile. She grabbed her briefcase and rushed into the building. "How was lunch?" Jackie Anderson asked.

"It was fabulous," Linda answered. "I love the Sky Room. The lobster was delicious, and I even splurged and had several glasses of wine." She removed a business card from her brief case and handed it to Jackie. "Mr. Carson wants us to buy this house in La Costa for one of the corporate officers at American Financial. He said to go as high as two million, and insists that we take a ten percent commission."

"Oh, I love these kind of clients," Jackie licked her lips.

"Glenn also promised me a ten thousand dollar bonus, if I can close the deal within thirty days."

"It gets better and better," Jackie said. "Tell me more."

"That's all, Jackie. How do we go about getting the listing from the current owners? Maybe they don't want to sell."

"It's called salesmanship," Jackie said reaching for the reference book that cross indexed addresses and telephone numbers. She turned to the La Costa section and found the address. "Fifty-five La Costa Heights Road is owned by James and Martha England. The first thing you do is call Mrs. England and compliment her on their beautiful home. All women like to be told that their homes are beautiful. Casually mention that you have a client who's interested in a home in that area. Then ask if you can come by and visit her and make a market analysis for her estate records."

"You make it sound so easy," Linda groaned.

"It is, Linda," Jackie said. "Go earn that commission."

"Okay, boss," Linda said as walked to her office and picked up the telephone. The maid answered on the first ring. Linda said, "Good afternoon, this is Linda Colby calling for Martha England."

"Just a moment, Miss Colby," she said. "I'll get Mrs. England."

Linda heard the British accent as Mrs. England said, "Hello, this is Martha England."

"Good afternoon, Mrs. England. My name's Linda Colby. I love your accent. My mother-in-law is also from England."

"Oh, is she now, do you know the town in which she lived?"

"Yes, the town of Eton."

"Eton is my hometown also," Martha said excitedly. "Linda, we must get together for tea and a chat."

"I'd love to meet you and see your beautiful home, Mrs. England. When would be a good time for you?"

147

"Please call me Martha. Can you make it for tea at four o'clock?"

Linda glanced at her watch, it was two forty-five. The drive to La Costa would take about forty minutes. "Yes Martha, I'd love to have tea with you at four. Good-bye." Linda hung up the telephone and walked into Jackie's office. "I'm having tea with Martha England at four o' clock."

"Way to go, Linda, want to celebrate with a diet Coke?"

"Certainly nothing stronger than a Coke," Linda agreed as she popped the top of the can. "How high should we go on the list price if I can convince Martha to sell?"

Jackie said, "The buyer has already established the market price. Now it's your job to convince Martha England that her beautiful home is worth two million dollars."

2000 feet above Julian Airport

Judy Anderson flew the Cessna 310 while Commander Bob Wilson sat beside her in the copilots seat. *Damn, she's a good pilot,* Bob thought and pulled the oil pressure circuit breaker.

Judy immediately noticed the oil pressure gauge for the number two engine dropping toward zero. "We're losing oil pressure on number two," she said. "Check the circuit breaker."

"Circuit breaker recycled," Bob lied. He looked at the number two engine out the right window. "Damn, we have oil all over the engine cowling."

"Securing number two," Judy said as she brought the throttle to number two engine toward idle cut-off.

Bob stopped her hand as she retarded the throttle to idle. "We have a simulated engine failure. I pulled the circuit breaker. Now, what's your plan of action?"

"We can maintain altitude on one engine, so we could fly back to Brown Field Airport, but we're right over Julian Airport. So I think we should make a single-engine approach to Julian."

"That's the correct answer," Bob agreed and watched as Judy trimmed the rudder to compensate for the yaw from the number one engine. Then she began the high altitude, single-engine approach. Her approach and landing was textbook perfect. On roll out Bob applied power to the number two engine. He took control of the airplane and

148

climbed out toward the mountains. "Well, you've learned all that I can teach you, Judy. You're dual-engine qualified in the Cessna three-ten."

"Thank you! Thank you, Commander Bob!" She yelled as she hugged him and kissed his lips. "You're a great instructor, and I just love flying your airplane."

"God, you taste good," he said licking his lips, "but you gotta remember never to kiss the pilot while he's trying to fly the airplane."

"Bullshit! You could fly this airplane with your eyes closed," she laughed. "Have you ever made love while you were flying?"

"No way, Judy," he lied. "That's against FAA regulations and has probably been the cause of several mid-air collisions."

"Well, did you think that the golden leg-spreaders would work on me when you gave them to Tommy?"

"Oh, yes, Judy, they always work," he boasted. "Didn't Tommy get lucky?"

"Only because I seduced him, but Tommy's a fast learner," she laughed. "Have you made love to Linda, yet?"

"No way! What makes you ask such a damn fool question," he snorted. "Anyway, if I had, I wouldn't tell. Gentlemen don't boast about their conquests."

"Do you think that Commander Colby's made love to my mother?"

Bob looked into her eyes and smiled, "No, I really don't think so. I'd say that the next door neighbor is too close to be messing around with."

Judy reached for her purse and handed him a package of photographs. "Look at these, Commander Bob."

"Jesus Christ!" He exclaimed as he looked at the photographs of Tom Colby and Jackie Anderson. "I would never have thought it." Cautiously he looked outside the airplane, the sky was clear, no other airplanes in sight. "Judy, I was going to tell you when we got back to Brown Field that I'm leaving for Vietnam this Friday. But I wanted to complete your dual-engine instructions before I left. So, today you graduated."

"Thanks, Commander Bob, can I make the landing at Brown Field?"

"I knew you were gonna ask that," he groaned. "Okay, pretty lady, you have the airplane," he said and raised his hands from the yoke. "May all your landings be smooth ones."

La Costa, California

Linda drove the Jaguar up Interstate 5 toward La Costa. She had planned to arrive at Martha England's promptly at four o'clock. Turning into the driveway at 55 La Costa Heights Road, she parked beside a black Rolls-Royce. She got out of the Jaguar and looked toward the ocean. *God, what a view! I'd love to have this house*, she thought. As she turned and walked toward the house, she saw an elderly lady sitting on the front porch. "Hello," she said. "I'm Linda Colby. Are you Martha?"

"Yes, darling," Martha answered as she stood and took Linda's hand. "You're so pretty. I love your red hair, and I love your motorcar. Come inside and we will have a spot of tea." Justine, the young black maid, served tea and cookies in the library. Linda enjoyed the tea and munched cookies as Martha told her about the house. "James and I planned to sell this house and move back to England. Then our doctor discovered that James had leukemia. He was gone within six months, and I do miss him so terribly much." The four bedroom house contained five thousand square feet of living space, a four car garage and maids quarters. The master bedroom had a balcony that overlooked the Pacific Ocean.

"How much do you want for your home?" Linda asked.

"Linda, I don't have the foggiest. The house down the street is on a two acre lot, and it sold for a million dollars. This lot has five acres. Do you think I can get a million?"

"Martha, if I were you, I wouldn't sell this house for one penny less than two million dollars," Linda said, "but please don't quote me on that. Real estate agents are not allowed to suggest listing prices for homes."

"Okay, darling, I've decided to sell for two million dollars," she smiled. "Can we get everything cleared up within a month? I want to get to Eton before the weather gets cold."

"Yes, we can close escrow in three weeks, if I push them. Please sign this listing agreement with my company, and I'll get started on it tomorrow." Martha signed the exclusive listing agreement with Anderson Realty, and Linda gave her a copy. "I really hate to run, but my son will be home from school and starved. Next time I promise to visit with you longer, Martha."

"I understand, dear," Martha answered and walked Linda out to the Jaguar. "Please drive carefully, and come back soon. Good-bye."

Linda drove slowly down the driveway thinking about her commission. Ten percent of two million was two hundred thousand dollars. She had a 60-40 commission split agreement with Jackie Anderson; $120,000 for her and $80,000 for Jackie. This was the most money that she had earned in her life. *I will have to think of some special way to thank Bob for recommending me to Glenn Carson.*

TWENTY-ONE

The Purple Heart

Seventh Air Force Headquarters
Da Nang Air Base
Republic of Vietnam

Major General Steve Curtis was in his office at Seventh Air Force Headquarters when the Viet Cong attacked the air base. He ran downstairs to the Crisis Action Center (CAC) and was briefed by the Command Duty Officer, Colonel Sam Jones, USAF. Curtis sat in the center and observed Colonel Jones as the action reports were received. Forty Viet Cong had penetrated the perimeter of the base. The thrust of the attack had been on the flight line. The Wing Commander, Lieutenant General Robert Blevins, USAF, was at Tan Son Nhut Air Base on an inspection tour. "Has the Wing Commander been notified of the attack?" Curtis asked.

"Yes, General, I was talking to him on the phone when you came in the center. He was pleased that you are here to assist me."

"Thanks, Sam," Curtis said. "This is all kinda new to me. So just carry on with your standard operating procedures."

"Thanks, General. We just got a report that six F-106D's were hit and one SAR helicopter. They blew up Major King's quarters and injured Major King, a Navy Commander Colby, two of his helicopter pilots and Anah Thong, a Vietnamese National."

"Son-of-a-bitch," Curtis swore. "That's Admiral Thomas Colby's son. He flew in on my VC-135 this afternoon. Keep me posted, Sam."

"Wilco, General," Jones said surprised at the show of compassion from General Curtis. "We have the quick reaction force in the area now, so it should all be over soon."

The VC attack was over in thirty minutes and the all clear was sounded. Colonel Jones made his report, "We have twenty-seven enemy KIA and two prisoners. A lot of the VC took off their black pajamas and faded back into the civilian force of the base."

"Wait one," Curtis interrupted. "Explain that last remark."

"General, we have over three-thousand gooks working and living here on the base," Jones explained. "Sir, I bet you that at least twenty percent of them are Viet Cong."

"What's security doing about this?"

"All they can, General," Jones said patiently. "The whole God damn Vietnamese military is so corrupt that it's impossible to do a proper security investigation."

"I appreciate your comments, Sam. Carry on with your report."

"Three troopers were killed in action and twenty-one wounded. All of the wounded are at the base hospital. That completes my report, sir."

"Thanks, Sam, I'll be upstairs if you need me. You did a good job."

"Thanks, General."

Curtis walked up the stairs. When he reached his office he dialed the base hospital. He told the duty corpsman to have Commander Colby's doctor call him after he had finished with the wounded. It was one o'clock in the morning when there was a knock on his door. "Come in," he called.

Major Ted Parsons, USAF, Medical Corps, walked into the room and stood in front of the General's desk. He saluted and said, "I'm Dr. Parsons, General. The corpsman said you wanted to talk to me."

"Please have a seat, doctor. You could've called. I didn't mean for you to make the trip up here at this time of the morning."

Dr. Parsons collapsed in the stuffed chair beside General Curtis desk. "I have the duty tonight General and have to stay awake all night anyway. So I thought I'd give you a first hand report." He produced two small bottles of whiskey from his pocket and sat one on the General's desk. "Compliments of your flight surgeon, sir."

"Thanks, doctor," Curtis said as he twisted off the cap and took a sip. "How serious are Major King and Commander Colby's wounds?"

"They were hit with some shrapnel and glass, nothing serious," Parsons answered. "But we have the makings of a bonafide hero in Commander Colby. You should recommend him for the Air Force Cross."

"What the hell are you talking about, doctor?" Curtis growled.

"General, we have a three star admiral's son who was personally promoted to Commander by the President of the United States. He hitchhikes a ride to Vietnam on a Major General's jetliner. In the middle of a sapper attack, all he has to do is run to the bunker. What does our Commander Colby do? He single-handedly saves the lives of Major King and a Vietnamese National."

"Did Commander Colby really save their lives?"

"Yes sir, he did," Parsons said and handed a Polaroid photograph to General Curtis. "Do you think Major King could've lived through that?"

Curtis looked at the twisted pile of lumber that was once Major King's quarters. "No, I agree with you, doctor. He would not have survived that explosion."

Parsons handed him another photograph. "This is the Vietnamese National that Commander Colby saved. Her name is Anah Thong."

Curtis looked at the photograph of Anah Thong and felt a stirring in his groin. She was beautiful. "What was she doing in Major King's quarters?"

"She's the bar maid for the Jolly Green Giant Officer's Club. She's probably Major King's mistress," Parsons answered.

"Jesus Christ, does every Air Force pilot out here have a mistress?"

"No, sir," Parsons laughed. "Just Field Grade Officers and above."

Curtis knew when his leg was being pulled and laughed along with the doctor. "You may have an angle on this hero thing, doc. Let me sleep on it and I'll get back to you in the morning. The least we can do is pin the Purple Heart Medal on them in the morning, right?"

"Yes, General," Parsons answered. "I've made the proper entries in their medical records. Will the General be available for an eight o'clock award presentation in the hospital ward?"

"Yes, I'll be there, doc," Curtis said and sipped the bourbon. "This is the best Jim Beam I've tasted."

"That's not Jim Beam, General," Parsons said. "I keep the empty Air Force bottles and refill them with Jack Daniels whiskey. It's only two dollars a fifth at the package store."

"Why did Major King need to be rescued, doc?"

"Because he was drunk. He's an alcoholic, sir."

"Well, I'll have to something about him and Miss Thong. I wonder if she can type. Maybe we can find a job for her here at Headquarters."

Parsons sat another small bottle of whiskey on the desk and stood. "I must get back to the hospital, General. See you in the morning, sir." He saluted and walked out of the office.

General Curtis stared at the photograph of Anah Thong. He would talk to her tomorrow about a job at Headquarters. He began to draft a personal message to Vice Admiral Colby and thought about the Air Force Cross recommendation for Tom Colby. It would be a fitting tribute for a brave heroic act under enemy attack, he decided.

Flag Mess
USS Providence, CLG-6
Sea of Japan

Vice Admiral Thomas Colby and Captain John Roy Lester finished eating breakfast in the flag mess and lingered over a second cup of coffee. Colby unbuttoned his shirt pocket and removed a folded piece of paper. He handed the paper to Lester and said, "John, I'd like for you to read this message from the Deputy Commander at Seventh Air Force." Lester unfolded the sheet of paper and read:

SECRET
OPERATIONAL IMMEDIATE, 180128Z OCT 65

FM: DEPUTY COMMANDER, SEVENTH AIR FORCE
TO: COMMANDER, SEVENTH FLEET

PERSONAL FOR VICE ADMIRAL THOMAS COLBY, USN

COMMANDER TOM COLBY RECEIVED SEVERAL MINOR
WOUNDS DURING A VIET CONG ATTACK ON DA NANG AIR BASE
TONIGHT. IGNORING HIS WOUNDS, TOM SAVED THE LIVES OF
MAJOR GREG KING AND A VIETNAMESE NATIONAL, MISS ANAH

THONG. THE BASE FLIGHT SURGEON ASSURED ME THAT TOM
WILL BE ABLE TO FLY OUT TO THE CONCORD THIS MORNING. I
HAVE ARRANGED FOR TWO HH-3 SAR HELICOPTERS TO FLY THE
NAVY SAR DETACHMENT TO THE CONCORD ON AT 0900 LOCAL.
AT 0800 LOCAL, I WILL AWARD THE PURPLE HEART MEDAL TO
COMMANDER TOM COLBY, ENSIGN WILLIAM WALKER AND CHIEF
PETTY OFFICER ROY ROBERTS.

UNDER SEPARATE CORRESPONDENCE, I AM RECOMMENDING
THAT COMMANDER TOM COLBY BE AWARDED THE AIR FORCE
CROSS FOR HEROISM PERFORMED DURING HEAVY ENEMY
ATTACK. DISREGARDING HIS PERSONAL SAFETY HE SAVED THE
LIVES OF MAJOR KING AND MISS THONG AND CARRIED THEM TO
SAFETY.

CONGRATULATIONS ON YOUR THIRD STAR AND COMMAND AT
SEVENTH FLEET. (ARMY BEAT NAVY).

SMOOTH SEAS AND FOLLOWING WINDS
MAJOR GENERAL STEVE CURTIS, USAF
DEPUTY, SEVENTH AIR FORCE
SECRET

Lester was visibly shaken after reading the message. Admiral
Hollingsworth had never shared the personal messages that he often
received. "I'm sorry that your son was wounded, Admiral. Would you like
for me to send a message of inquiry to the base hospital at Da Nang?"

"No, John," Colby answered. "This was Steve's way of letting me
know that Tom had received some minor wounds during an attack on the
base. Steve was at West Point while I was at the Academy. They beat us
three straight years in the Army-Navy game, and he'll never let me forget it.
General Curtis is Tom's godfather. He only has one child, a daughter, and
he thinks of Tom as his son. When will we be back on station in the Gulf
of Tonkin?"

"About noon tomorrow, Admiral."

"Excellent, after you read the morning messages, please give me a
brief on my schedule for the remainder of the month."

"Aye, aye, sir," Lester answered as they rose from the table and
went to their offices to start the work day.

The Colby Residence
Bonita, California

At 9 o'clock Linda Colby dialed the number on Glenn Carson's business card. She heard the receptionist say, "American Financial Service, how may I help you?"

"Good morning, my name is Linda Colby. May I speak to Mr. Carson?"

"Yes, Miss Colby. Hold the line, please," the receptionist said.

Then she heard the baritone voice of Glenn Carson saying, "Good morning, Linda. This is Glenn."

"Hi, Glenn. I have great news about the La Costa house," she beamed.

"Will the owners sell?"

"Yes, Mrs. England has agreed to list her home with my company for two million dollars. The house will be available to close escrow within the next thirty days."

"Excellent work, Linda, the boss and Mrs. Salvatorie will be very pleased with your work."

"When would the Salvatorie's like to see the house?"

"Maybe this afternoon," he answered. "Let me check their schedule and get back to you, okay?"

"That'll be fine, Glenn. Mrs. England will probably insist that they come for tea like she did me."

"Georgia would love the tea bit, but I'm not too sure about the boss," he laughed. "I will get back to you as soon as I can Linda."

"I'm not going to the office before eleven," she said. So if you need me before then, call my home number on my business card."

"Please hold the line, Linda," Carson said. "Boss just walked in, and I'll check his schedule." Within minutes Carson was back on the phone, "Boss wants you to set up the tea bit with Mrs. England for four o'clock this afternoon. Can you pick up Boss and Georgia at the El Cortez Hotel at three-thirty?"

"Yes Glenn, I'll see you at three-thirty. Good-bye."

Base Hospital
Da Nang Air Base
Republic of Vietnam

Captain John Jasper, USAF, the aide-de-camp to General Curtis, briefed Commander Tom Colby, Ensign Bull Walker and Chief Roy Roberts about the awards ceremony. "Gentlemen, when I call your name, you'll come forward and stop in front of the General and salute. I'll read the citation. General Curtis will pin the medal on you and shake your hand. You'll salute again, do an about-face and march back to your chair."

Tom said, "Captain Jasper, the Navy does not salute indoors."

Jasper looked bewildered and said, "You're right, Commander. I forgot all about that since we haven't pinned a lot of medals on Navy personnel. Ah, man, this is gonna screw up everything. Couldn't you guys just fake it and do it the Air Force way this time. It sure would make everything flow much easier, sir."

"Yes, Captain," Tom said. "We're very capable of doing it the Air Force way, if it'll get this facade over with so we can get out to the *Concord*." Turning to Walker and Roberts he asked, "Bull and Chief Roberts, do you need to practice on the saluting bit?"

"No, sir," Bull answered for the two of them. "We'll follow Captain Jasper's directions."

Major Ted Parsons walked into the room and said, "John, can I see you a minute before General Curtis gets here?"

"Yes sir," Jasper said. They walked to the other end of the room.

"John, I was talking to General Curtis last night about Miss Thong. He wants to find a clerical job for her at Wing Headquarters. You know that would be a fiasco. So I suggest that you talk Miss Thong into becoming a member of the General's personal staff at his quarters."

"Is she the pretty lady sitting beside Commander Colby?"

"Yes," Parsons said. "Don't you think Anah would brighten up the General's quarters?"

"Yes sir, she would," Jasper answered. "Thank you, doctor. I'll go over an talk to her before the General gets here."

Captain Jasper walked over to where Tom was sitting beside Anah. "Excuse me, Commander," he said. "May I talk to Miss Thong?"

"Why certainly, Captain," Tom answered as he introduced them. "Anah, this is Captain John Jasper, the aide to General Curtis. Captain, this is Anah Thong."

Anah reached for his hand and said, "So pleased to meet you, Captain John."

"Thank you, Miss Thong, General Curtis needs a maid in his quarters, and I was hoping you would consider taking the job. There would be a room for you."

Anah glanced at Tom who nodded his head. "Yes, Captain John, I will take the job. Can I start today?"

"Yes, Miss Thong. Please see me after the ceremony," he answered as General Curtis walked into the room. **"Attention in the room**!" he yelled and everyone stood.

General Curtis was very surprised to see the beautiful Vietnamese lady talking to his aide. "Please be seated," Curtis said as he walked over and shook hands with Tom. "How's the arm?"

"Just a few scratches. Nothing to make a fuss about, sir," he answered. "General, I'd like you to meet Miss Anah Thong. Anah, this is my godfather, General Steve Curtis."

General Curtis took Anah's hand and said, "I'm so very pleased to meet you Miss Thong. I'm sorry that you were injured in the last attack."

"Good morning, General Steve," Anah smiled. "I'm so honored to meet Commander Tom's father."

"The godfather bit was probably too much for her to comprehend, General," Tom said. "Sorry that I brought it up."

"It's like being an honorary father, Miss Thong," Curtis smiled at her.

"Thank you, General Steve, for explaining it so eloquently," Anah said and released his hand.

"Please be seated, Miss Thong," Curtis said. "I know Commander Colby is anxious to get this awards ceremony over so he can fly out to his ship." He walked to the podium as Captain Jester said, "Commander Colby, please come front and center." Tom stood, walked to the podium and saluted the General.

Curtis was surprised to see Tom salute. "When did the Navy start saluting indoors?" He asked Tom and returned the salute.

"Just following the orders of your aide-de-camp, sir," Tom said.

"Well, we don't have to make this thing so formal," Curtis said as he motioned for Ensign Walker and Chief Roberts to come forward. Bull and Chief Roberts walked to the podium, stood on Tom's left side and saluted the General. Curtis returned their salute and said, "Please stand at ease, gentlemen." He turned to face Anah, "Miss Thong, would you join us, please?"

Anah rose from her chair and walked to the front of the room and stood on Tom's right side. Captain John Jasper was sweating. This was the most screwed up awards ceremony that he had ever seen. He started to read the citation for Commander Colby's Purple Heart.

"Captain, we're not going to read all of the citations. Instead I would like to say a few words about this medal that we all admire, but no military man wants to earn," Curtis laughed and the group in the room joined him. He talked for about five minutes on the origin of the medal then turned to Jasper and said, "Please bring the medals."

Jasper walked to the podium holding a tray on which the three medals lay. Curtis pinned the medals on Tom, Ensign Walker and Chief Roberts. He turned to Captain Jasper and said, "Do you have an extra Purple Heart, John?"

"Yes, sir," Jasper said as he did an about-face and walked to the table to get another medal. *God damn, the General is really screwing up if he awards a Purple Heart to this Vietnamese woman*, he thought. He returned to the podium and handed the medal to General Curtis.

"Miss Thong, the United States Air Force cannot award a medal to a foreign national, but I would like you to have this medal in remembrance of your part in the attack last night. I was informed that you led Commander Colby through the dark to the bunker while he was carrying the wounded Major King on his back. The Air Force is proud of you," he said and pinned the medal on her blouse.

"Thank you General Steve," Anah squealed and kissed his cheek.

"You are quite welcome, Miss Thong," he smiled. Turning to the officers in front of him, he said, "That concludes the award ceremony. You gentlemen are excused."

Tom whispered in a low voice, "Sea Devils, attent-hut, hand salute." After General Curtis returned their salute, Tom said, "Ready-two, about-face, follow me." He led them single file to the back of the room where the remainder of the SAR detachment was seated. "Okay troops, it's time to go to war and earn some medals," he said as he led them out of the hospital.

TWENTY-TWO

The USS Concord

The Gulf of Tonkin
Yankee Station

Commander Tom Colby flew the lead helicopter. Captain Steve Smith, USAF, from the Jolly Green rescue squadron, sat in the copilot seat. Ensign Bull Walker was flying the second helicopter in a loose formation on Tom's wing. At five-thousand-feet above the Gulf the temperature was a comfortable 74 degrees. Tom tuned in the frequency for the *USS Concord's* TACAN. The bearing needle spun slowly around the dial of the instrument and locked on to a bearing of 87 degrees. The mileage indicator continued to spin and finally stopped on 48 miles. "That's the carrier," Tom said to Steve. Glancing at the air speed indicator, he read 120 knots. "We should be there in about twenty minutes."

Tom saw the trail of smoke on the horizon. "That's the *Concord*, at twelve o'clock." He pressed the radio switch and said, "Jolly Green flight, switch to homeplate frequency, over."

In the second helicopter, Bull said, "Green-Two switching, out." Steve switched the UHF radio to the carrier's frequency. In his ear phones, Tom heard Bull say, "Green-Two, in."

Tom keyed the mike and said, "War Chief tower, Air Force helo Seven-Seven-Five, over."

The Air Boss in Pri-Fly reached for the mike hanging from the ceiling over his chair and said, "Air Force Seven-Seven-Five go ahead."

"Roger, tower, Seven-Seven-Five is flight of two HH-3 helo's on your 267 at thirty-eight miles. Request low pass and passenger stop."

Commander Red Barber, USN, was Air Boss of the *USS Concord*. "Negative low pass, Seven-Five," he growled into the mike. "Respot of flight deck in progress. Your signal on arrival is starboard delta, and we'll try to fit you in as we respot."

"Roger, starboard delta, Boss," Tom said.

"Seven-Five, are you carrier qualified?" Barber asked.

"Roger, Boss, both helo's have Navy flight crew aboard."

"Seven-Five, say pilots name," Barber ordered.

"Commander Colby in lead. Ensign Walker on my wing."

Jesus Christ that has to be Admiral Thomas Colby's son, Barber thought. He had read in the *Stars and Stripes* where Vice Admiral Thomas Colby had taken command of the Seventh Fleet. Keying the mike, he said, "Seven-Five, you and your wingman are cleared for low pass and Charlie on arrival. Say how long passenger stop, over."

"Thanks for the low pass, Boss. Estimate passenger stop five minutes. Please notify the First Lieutenant that we have the replacement SAR detachment of twenty-two crewmen and baggage to unload, over."

"He's going to love that, Tom," Barber said. "Call two miles, out."

"The Air Boss knows me, but I don't recognize his voice," Tom said to Steve over the intercom. Then pressing the mike, he said, "Green-Two, Green lead, you copy War Chief, over."

"Roger, lead," Bull replied.

"Hang tight, Bull," Tom said. "Climbing left break after we pass the island." Bull clicked the mike to acknowledge that he had received the message.

Damn, those guys have good radio discipline, Barber thought and dialed the bridge to speak to the Commanding Officer of the *Concord*, Captain Samuel Streeper. He heard the Captain say, "What do you need, Red?"

"Captain, we have two Air Force choppers about fifteen miles out with the Navy SAR detachment aboard. Admiral Colby's son is leading the

163

flight of two. I just cleared him for a low pass and thought you might like to watch it."

"Thanks, Red," Streeper said and hung up the phone. He and Red Barber had flown with Admiral Colby when he was CAG on the *USS Essex* during the Korean War.

Tom started descending from 5,000 feet when they were 10 miles from the carrier. He leveled the helicopter at 200 feet and kept the air speed at 140 knots. Bull tucked in close on his right wing. When they reached the two mile marker on the TACAN, he pressed the mike and said, "War Chief tower, Seven-Five at two miles."

"Roger, Seven-Five, cleared low pass, call with gear after break."

Tom passed over the fantail of the *Concord* at 145 knots. His altitude was level with Pri-Fly. After passing the island of the carrier, he rolled the helicopter into a 45 degree climbing, left break and did a wingover to 300 feet, then pressed the mike and said, "Seven-Five with gear."

"Roger, Seven-Five, you have Charlie near the number two elevator."

"Roger, Charlie," Tom said as he lowered the collective and pulled back on the cyclic to reduce air speed.

Bull executed his break approximately three seconds after Tom. He called the tower, "Seven-Nine with gear."

"Roger, Seven-Nine, you have Charlie behind Seven-Five."

"Seven-Nine, roger Charlie," Bull said.

Tom spotted the Landing Signal Officer and followed his directions as he slid across the deck of the carrier at 10 feet of altitude. When the LSO crossed the wands over his head, Tom gently landed the big helicopter. He keyed the radio transmit button and said, "Boss, we would like to keep turning while we unload. These HH-3's rotor blades do not fold like the Navy H-3."

"Jesus Christ, those are big motherfucker's," Barber exclaimed. "Okay, keep them turning, but expedite the unloading."

Tom pressed the intercom mike and said to Captain Smith, "Thanks for the air-lift, Steve. Call the tower for takeoff and watch the LSO. Don't takeoff until he gives you the wind-up and launch signal." He unplugged his helmet, released the shoulder straps and seat belt and walked to the passenger door of the helicopter. The crewman handed him a bag as he walked down the steps. Bull stepped out of the helicopter behind him. Together they ran toward the island of the carrier. The SAR crew also grabbed bags and ran across the flight deck.

Tom heard the flight deck speaker boom, **"STANDBY TO LAUNCH HELO'S."** They had been on deck less than four minutes when the LSO raise the wand in his right hand over his head and give the wind-up signal to launch. The LSO dropped to his knees and pointed the wand toward the bow of the carrier. Steve lifted the big HH-3 into a 10 foot hover and checked the gauges. He then dove the helicopter over the left side of the carrier as Tom had briefed. Seven-Nine was close behind him. They joined on climb out and flew toward Da Nang Air Base.

Interstate 5 Freeway
San Diego, California

Linda drove the Jaguar north on Interstate 5 Freeway. She took the Sixth Avenue exit and drove toward the El Cortez Hotel for the three-thirty appointment with the Salvatories. When she pulled into the circular drive at the entrance of the hotel, she saw Glenn Carson. He was dressed in a dark blue suit and a red tie. She rolled the window down as Carson walked to the car. "Good afternoon, Glenn," Linda said as he leaned down and looked in the car. She was wearing a green silk suit, white blouse and five strands of gold chains around her neck.

"God, you're beautiful, Linda," he gasped.

"Well, thank you, kind sir," she said. "You're also very handsome in that nice suit. I really like your beautiful tie."

"Ah, hell, that was so unprofessional!" He said. "Please forgive me, Linda."

"Glenn, you never have to apologize for telling a lady that she's beautiful," Linda laughed. She breathed deeply as she smelled his cologne and said, "You smell so good, now that makes us even. Are the Salvatorie's ready to go look at their new home?"

"Here they come," Glenn said as a couple approached the Jaguar. Linda was shocked at the age difference in the couple. Samuel Savatorie was in his mid-sixties while Georgia appeared to be thirty. He was 6-feet-2 and weighed 180 pounds. His long white hair waved in the wind. Georgia appeared to match Linda's 5-foot-4 height and had long black hair that hung down her back. She wore a blue linen suit and a white silk blouse that was stretched very tightly over her large breasts. Glenn made the introductions, "Linda, this is Georgia and Mr. Salvatorie. Boss, this is Linda Colby."

"I'm pleased to meet you both," Linda said and shook hands with Georgia and then Salvatorie.

"You may call me, Boss, Miss Colby," Salvatorie said.

"Alright, I'll call you Boss, if you'll call me Linda," she smiled.

"We have a deal, Linda," Salvatorie said and opened the back door for Georgia. Glenn hurried around the Jaguar and held the driver's door for Linda. Then got in the passenger seat and buckled the seat belt.

Linda started the Jaguar and drove toward the freeway. She noticed a black limousine pull away from the hotel and follow her down the freeway. "Are we being followed, Glenn?"

"No, Linda," he laughed. "Boss and Georgia are going to Los Angeles after the tea with Mrs. England. The limo will trail us to La Costa then take them up to L.A."

Linda looked in the rear view mirror and said, "Georgia, Mr. England had the house built for Martha, and she's very proud of it. If you see anything you don't like, please make a mental note to tell me later."

"That's excellent advice, Linda," Salvatorie said from the back seat. "In other words, Georgia, keep your trap shut."

"Okay, Boss," Georgia said, "but I just know I'm just gonna love the house. I promise that I won't sour the deal, Linda."

Gosh, I sure hope not. Everything is going perfect in my first real estate transaction, Linda thought. Traffic was light on the freeway. She reached the La Costa exit at three forty-five. Turning to Carson she said, "Glenn, would you and Boss prefer a beer instead of tea?"

"Oh, yes," Glenn said, "if Mrs. England wouldn't be offended."

Linda pulled into the parking lot of a 7-Eleven store and said, "Run in and get the brand of beer that you like."

Glenn jumped from the car and ran into the store. He was back within minutes with a paper bag. "Boss likes Coors light. So I bought two six-packs."

166

"Let's go have some tea and beer," Linda said as she backed out of the parking lot and drove down La Costa Avenue toward La Costa Heights Road.

Pacific Air Force Headquarters
Hickam Air Force Base
Honolulu, Hawaii

General Scott, Commander of Pacific Air Force, sat at his desk on the second floor of the Headquarters Building reading a personal message from Major General Curtis. The Deputy of Operations had briefed him that Major General Curtis had given Commander Colby and the Navy SAR detachment a ride to Da Nang on the KC-135. He read the message a second time.

SECRET
OPERATIONAL IMMEDIATE, 180624Z OCT 65

FM: DEPUTY COMMANDER, SEVENTH AIR FORCE
TO: COMMANDER, PACIFIC AIR FORCE

PERSONAL FOR GENERAL R. L. SCOTT, USAF
SUBJECT: REPORT OF VC ATTACK ON DA NANG AIR BASE, 18 OCT 65.
DAMAGE TO USAF: SIX (6) F-100-D STRIKE DAMAGE, ONE (1) HH-3 HELICOPTER STRIKE DAMAGE, THREE (3) PERSONNEL KIA, AND THIRTY-SEVEN (37) WOUNDED. VC LOSS: TWENTY-SEVEN (27) KIA, AND TWO (2) POW.
COMMANDER TOM COLBY, USN, THE SON OF VICE ADMIRAL THOMAS COLBY, USN, COMMANDER SEVENTH FLEET, WAS WOUNDED DURING A VIET CONG ATTACK ON DA NANG AIR BASE. COMMANDER COLBY SAVED THE LIVES OF MAJOR GREG KING AND A FOREIGN NATIONAL, MISS ANAH THONG. THIS IS POLITICALLY SENSITIVE, SINCE COMMANDER COLBY WAS PERSONALLY PROMOTED BY LBJ TWO WEEKS AGO.
THE PURPLE HEART MEDAL WAS PRESENTED TO COMMANDER COLBY AND TWO OF HIS CREW MEMBERS THIS MORNING AT THE BASE HOSPITAL. IT IS RECOMMENDED THAT COMMANDER COLBY BE AWARDED THE AIR FORCE CROSS FOR HIS HEROIC DEEDS ABOARD THIS AIR BASE WHILE IN A TRANSIT PASSENGER STATUS.
COMMANDER COLBY IS THE OFFICER-IN-CHARGE OF THE NAVY COMBAT SEARCH AND RESCUE HELICOPTER UNIT ABOARD USS

CONCORD, CVA-51. CITATION WILL BE FORWARDED UNDER
SEPARATE CORRESPONDENCE.

MY BEST TO SUSAN. THANKS FOR THE ASSIGNMENT.

MAJOR GENERAL STEVE CURTIS, USAF
DEPUTY, SEVENTH AIR FORCE
SECRET

General Scott pushed a button on his desk to summon his flag secretary, Lieutenant Colonel Charles Johnson. "Yes, General," Johnson said as he walked into the office.

He handed the message to Johnson and said, "Sit down, Charlie, and read that message from General Curtis."

Johnson sat in the chair next to General Scott's desk and read the personal message from Major General Steve Curtis. "Miss Thong must've been Major King's hootch girl, sir, " he said.

"Dammit to hell, Charlie, I don't need you to analyze that," Scott exploded. "Do we recommend the Navy fly boy for our big medal? Seems like to me that the Distinguished Flying Cross would be more appropriate."

"The Air Force Chief of Staff is a personal friend of LBJ's," Johnson said. "We could possibly put another feather in the Boss's hat by routing this to the Commander-in-Chief through the Chief of Staff." He sat and thought for a minute, then said, "Sir, I think we should recommend the squid for the Congressional Medal of Honor. LBJ won't care a tinkers damn for the Air Force Cross."

"Well, I don't agree," Scott said. "Draft a personal from me to the Chief of Staff recommending the Air Force Cross for Commander Colby. Also recommend that General Curtis be promoted to Lieutenant General and assigned as Commander of the Seventh Air Force. He has earned his third star."

"I agree, General," Johnson said, "but what're we going to do with General Blevins?"

"We can always hope that he'll retire, Charlie," Scott said. "For some God damn reason the Chief of Staff likes him. They'll find him a nice, soft job in the Pentagon."

168

Interstate 5 Freeway
San Diego, California

Linda Colby drove the Jaguar south on Interstate 5 Freeway. The traffic was heavy in the evening rush hour commute. Martha England's tea party had been a success. She was delighted that Glenn had brought beer, and she ordered Justine to bring James' beer mugs. Martha, Boss and Glenn drank beer while Linda and Georgia drank tea. She glanced at Glenn and said, "What do you think of Martha England?"

"She's a very charming English lady. I think she's real pleased that Boss and Georgia are buying the house."

"Yes, I guess so. I'd love to have that house, wouldn't you?"

"No, Linda," he answered. "I'd much rather live at the El Cortez. Please come by for a glass of wine and an early dinner in the Sky Room."

"I'd love that," she said, "but I need to call my son, and let him know that I'm going to be late."

"You can call from the Sky Room," Glenn said as Linda turned into the hotel driveway. "Leave the keys in the ignition and valet will park it." Glenn got out of the Jaguar and walked around to open Linda's door. A valet dressed in a red uniform rushed up to the car. "Bobby, park the car for Dr. Colby," he said and handed the valet a tip. *Glad, I remembered to use Linda's professional title,* he thought.

"Thanks, Mr. Carson," the valet said.

Linda and Glenn were alone in the glass elevator as they rode up to the Sky Room. "Glenn, you don't have to call me, doctor."

"Well, I like the sound of it, and it impresses the hired help. Boss was very pleased with the job you did, Linda. He wants you to work for our company. We'll offer you fifty thousand a year retainer to handle the company real estate. Of course, you'll also get a ten percent commission on all transactions," he said as the elevator reached the top floor. Before Linda could answer, the maitre d' appeared and ushered them to Glenn's table by the piano. "Andre, bring Dr. Colby a glass of Chardonnay and a beer for me. Oh yes, please bring a telephone."

"Right away, sir," Andre said and brought the telephone from the piano and sat it on the table by Linda. Then he hurried away to get the drinks.

169

Linda dialed the telephone. Tommy answered on the first ring. "Hi, Tommy," she said. "I'm having a business dinner at the Sky Room of the El Cortez Hotel and may be late getting home."

"That's okay, Mother," he said. "I've finished my homework and was going to call Judy and take her out for hamburgers."

"That'll be fine, dear," she said, "don't stay out too late."

"We won't, Mother. Good-bye."

Linda replaced the receiver on the phone and looked up at Glenn. "That was my son, Tommy. He said he was in the house alone, but he was breathing hard just like he and Judy were making love."

"How old is Tommy?"

"Seventeen."

"Hold old were you the first time you made love, Linda?

She saw the twinkle in his eyes, and said, "Seventeen. How old were you?"

"I was fourteen, with a perpetual erection. Susie was sixteen and she taught me all about sex. What a teacher!" The waiter arrived with their drinks and carried the telephone back to the piano. Glenn lifted the glass of beer and touched the rim of Linda's glass. He said, "Here's to the start of a beautiful friendship, Linda."

Linda raised the glass to her lips and took a sip. "Thank you, Glenn. I know we can be good friends."

"Will you take the job, please?"

"How could I possibly refuse a generous offer like that," she answered, "but I should have my broker's license to be your agent."

"Thanks, Linda. Let's order dinner, then I want to show you some of the fringe benefits that come with the job," he smiled and waved at the waiter. Linda ordered the lobster tail while Glenn ordered a rare Porterhouse steak. After dinner, Glenn and Linda rode the elevator down to the tenth floor. They walked along the hallway until he located Suite 1016. He unlocked the door and motioned Linda inside. "Your suite, my lady," he said as he handed her the key.

"**You have to be kidding**!" She yelled and looked at the suite of rooms. She threw her arms around his neck and kissed him hard on the lips. "Oh, Glenn," she moaned. "It's like a dream come true." She opened the drapes on the sliding glass door that led to the small balcony. She opened the door and Glenn followed her out to the balcony. "Look at that beautiful sunset."

Glenn took her hand and led her back inside the suite and sat beside her on the couch. He removed a thick envelope from his suit pocket and handed it to Linda. "This is your bonus. You earned it."

Linda opened the envelope and stared at the thick stack of one-hundred-dollar bills. "I can't take many more surprises like this, Glenn," she laughed.

"I have just one more," Glenn said and got up and walked to the small refrigerator in the kitchenette. He opened the door and brought out a bottle of cold champagne. He popped the cork and poured two glasses. Returning to the couch, he sat beside Linda and gave her one of the glasses and asked, "Would you like to make a toast?"

"Yes, Glenn," she said as she raised her glass of champagne and looked into his eyes. "Here's to our friendship, may it last forever." She raised the glass of champagne to her lips, took a sip and kissed him softly on the lips. As she broke the kiss, she said, "You make me feel like a seventeen year-old again."

Glenn got up and lifted her into his arms. He walked into the bedroom, placed her on the big bed and lay beside her. "I love you, Linda," he said as he took her in his arms and kissed her. He felt her tongue probe his mouth. *This is indeed my fantasy come true*, he thought as they rolled on the soft bed.

TWENTY-THREE

The Seduction of General Curtis

USS Concord
Yankee Station

After unloading from the Air Force helicopters, the Sea Devil SAR detachment assembled on the hangar deck, outside the HS-26 workshop. Lieutenant Commander Arthur Goldberg, officer-in-charge of HS-26 detachment, shook hands with Commander Colby and welcomed the group to the *Concord*. He asked Chief Madison to escort the enlisted crew members to their berthing space on the third deck, and show Chief Roberts to the Chief Petty Officer quarters.

Tom waited until his detachment personnel had carried their bags down the ladder to the second deck, then turned to Goldberg and said, "Sorry to hear about all your bad luck, Art. What's the condition of your last two helicopters?"

"They're in bad shape and should be grounded," Art answered. "The carrier will not give us enough fresh water to wash off the salt spray, and we have severe corrosion. I grounded all three helicopters the week before Admiral Perkins and Captain Stoddard were killed. The Air Boss put them back in a ready status."

"What did CAG have to say about it?"

"CAG Dick Brown doesn't want to get involved with helicopter operations. We work for the Air Boss."

"Well, I can see why things are screwed up, Art. Please show us to our quarters so we can stow this gear, then we'd like to look over the helicopters."

Art looked at the deck and said, "Commander, there aren't any staterooms left for your officers. The civilian tech reps from Grumman and Chance Vought took the last staterooms. The First Lieutenant assigned your officer's bunks in the hospital ward. There's an empty bunk in my stateroom, and you're welcome to that, sir."

"I appreciate the offer, Art, but I'd like to stay with my officers until I get this mess straightened out. Lead us to the dispensary," he said as he lifted his bag and flight gear. He followed Goldberg down the steep ladder to the second deck. His left arm was beginning to hurt. He looked at the bandage. *Well, at least we can get our bandages changed while we are sleeping in sick bay*, he thought.

Art escorted Tom and the five pilots down to the third deck, and aft to the hospital ward. The room contained ten double-deck hospital beds. The pilots were stowing their clothes in the wall lockers between the bunk beds when the ship's loud speaker announced, "**NOW HEAR THIS! SET SPECIAL FLIGHT OPERATIONS TO LAUNCH THE SAR HELO. PILOT'S MAN THE HELO.**"

The flight deck of the *Concord* became organized bedlam. The Flight Deck Officer halted the arming and refueling activities, and plane handlers began to clear the flight deck in front of the island. The helicopter was towed from its parking space behind the island to the center of the flight deck as the ship turned into the wind. The crew chief started the number one jet engine and began the rotor blade spreading process. The duty SAR pilots raced to the big helicopter, climbed into the cockpit, started the number two engine and called Pri-Fly for permission to engage rotors. Nine minutes after the order was given, the helicopter lifted into a hover and flew over the left side of the ship.

"Damn," Art groaned. "We must've lost a jet on that last strike. Come on, guys, we'll go up to CIC, and get briefed." He led the way up seven ladders to the O-3 level, one deck below the flight deck, to a door marked Combat Information Center. The helicopter pilots stood in the back of the room until their eyes adjusted to the dim light. CIC was lit entirely by dim red lights. A large plexiglas status board listed every sortie

173

that the carrier had airborne and all of the aircraft on the flight deck, waiting to be launched on the next strike. The board operator wearing sound-powered telephone headset stood behind the board and circled the aircraft side number, BF-202, with a red grease pencil.

*   *   *

In the cockpit of BF-202, Lieutenant Tony Parker felt the Phantom shudder as he climbed through the flak. He rolled the wings level and looked at the brilliant red glow of an engine fire-warning light. A quick glance in the rear-view mirror showed no visible fire. He glanced at the exhaust gas temperature gauge and saw it rise to 750 degrees. He shut off the flow of fuel to the right engine. The F-4 Phantom flew south toward the Gulf of Tonkin. "Blue Flight, this is Blue Leader," Tony began calmly as he flew toward the beach. "I'm hit. I'm hit!"

His wingman, Lieutenant Joe Brady, flew through the flak unscratched and followed Parker toward the beach. "Blue Leader, this is Two-Zero-Four," Joe said. "I'm coming up behind you. Stay level and I'll look you over."

"Roger, Four," Tony said. "Right engine's gone, but we still have a fire warning light."

Joe flew underneath the crippled Phantom and saw the gaping holes in the fuselage near the right engine. "Negative fire, Blue Leader," Joe said. "You're losing hydraulic fluid and fuel, Tony. Do you want to try to ride her to the water?"

"Affirmative Four," Tony answered. "Joe, don't get too close in case we blow up, but please let me know if you see fire."

"Wilco," Joe said then continued, "Tony, you have three bombs on the racks. Recommend you jettison."

"Thanks, Joe," Parker said and pushed the salvo switch. The three, 500-pound, bombs dropped from the Phantom and exploded in the dense forest four miles below the jet.

*   *   *

"Give me the status of his battle damage," the Air Operations Officer said to the air strike controller over his hot-telephone line.

174

In the next compartment the air strike controller stepped on his mike switch and said, "Blue Fin Two-Zero-Two, War Chief Strike. State extent of battle damage, over."

Lieutenant Parker's voice came over the public address speaker in CIC, "Two-Zero-Two sustained heavy damage from anti-aircraft over the target. Right engine's gone, possible fire in right engine compartment."

"Roger, damage. We have you radar contact. Your steer to War Chief is One-Seven-Two. Squawk One-Seven-Zero-Zero."

"Wilco," Tony answered as he switched the IFF numbers to 1700. He glanced at the tail-pipe temperature of the right engine. It steadily rose to 900 degrees centigrade. He looked below and saw the white sand of the beach flash beneath the Phantom. He pressed the mike and said, "Two-Zero-Two, feet wet."

"Roger, feet wet," the controller said. "Be advise SAR helo closing your position, over."

"TONY, YOU'RE ON FIRE!" Joe screamed into the mike, **"EJECT! EJECT!"**

Tony looked in the rear-view mirror and saw fire shooting out of the exhaust of the right engine. "**MAYDAY! MAYDAY! MAYDAY**!" He yelled into the mike. "War Chief, we have a fire and are ejecting, out." He keyed the intercom switch to talk to Lieutenant Gary Russell in the back seat. "Gary, we have a fire in number two. Prepare for ejection. Good luck, buddy." He reached up with both hands and grasp the primary ejection handle and pulled it down over his face. Instantly they were shot out of the cockpit in a thunderclap of noise, plexiglas and hurricane-force wind.

After the deafening thunderclap of the rocket seat and rush of wind on ejection, there was complete silence. Tony felt the straps rising from his shoulders as he swung beneath the parachute. He looked up and saw the Phantom explode into a brilliant fireball. Then he glanced over his left shoulder and saw Gary's white parachute. He reached for his emergency radio and turned on the beacon. This would allow the SAR helicopter to home-in on him. He looked to the east and saw the helicopter flying toward them. He silenced the beacon and put the radio on transmit/receive. "SAR helo, this is Blue Fin Two-Zero-Two," he said into the radio.

"Blue Fin Two-Zero-Two, helo Seven-Eight, have two parachutes in sight, over," Lieutenant Larry Wallace said from the command seat of the H-3 helicopter.

"Roger, Seven-Eight," Tony said as he looked below and saw the junks. "Looks like we're landing right in the middle of a dozen junks. Stand clear and give my wingman a chance to scare them off."

"Roger that," Larry said and banked the helicopter into a steep right turn. He saw Tony hit the water in his parachute. Two of the junks turned and headed for Tony. The other parachute was almost a mile away, closer to the junks. Larry turned to his copilot, Lieutenant Bob Welch, and said, "We can't wait for the Spads to get here. We've gotta get the pilot before the junks get there."

Bob gripped his M-16 rifle and nodded agreement.

Lieutenant Joe Brady had continued to circle as the parachutes descended toward the water. War Chief strike advised that a flight of four Spads would be on scene within ten minutes. "That's too late," Joe said. "There's a junk going toward the pilot. I'm gonna to take him out."

Joe reefed the Phantom around, and got the junk in his sights. The junk turned as he fired. The 20 mm bullets tore up the sides of the wooden boat and cut-off one of the three masts. The boat was low in the water, as Joe pulled a hard four-G turn and flew toward the second parachute.

Lieutenant Gary Russell, the back seat radar operator, hit the water near three of the large fishing junks. He removed his .38 caliber pistol from his shoulder hostler and dropped it in the water. Then he pressed the mike of his radio and said, "Tony, the gomers will capture me in about ten seconds. Keep your powder dry, my man, and send my Christmas card to the Hanoi Hilton. Destroying my radio, good luck, shipmate."

A man on the front of the junk fired an AK-47 into the water near Gary and yelled something in Vietnamese. Gary released the survival radio and let it sink as he raised his hands above his head. Three men jumped into the water and quickly pulled him aboard the junk. Joe flew over the junks at 420 knots. He saw Russell's parachute in the water, but he could not tell which junk had captured him. In frustration, he turned and flew back toward the pilot, as the helicopter slowed to a 30 foot hover over Parker.

The second junk raced by the boat that Joe had shot. Three men were standing on the bow firing AK-47 rifles at the helicopter. The copilot fired his M-16 at the junk. He saw one of the men clutch his chest and fall. He continued to spray the junk with bullets until one of the bullets from the AK-47's sliced into his neck. The M-16 slipped from his lifeless hands, and he slumped forwarded in his shoulder harness.

Joe saw the second junk firing at the helicopter. He dove at the boat and pressed the trigger. The twenty-millimeter bullets chewed up the front of the junk. He pulled a three-G turn to the right and saw Tony being hoisted aboard the helicopter.

When Tony was in the helicopter, Larry dropped the nose and quickly accelerated away from the junks at 120 knots. He glanced at Bob and saw the blood running down his neck. He yelled into the intercom, **"Stu, get up here! Mr. Welch's been hit!"**

Petty Officer Stewart ran forward and checked Lieutenant Welch's pulse. He shook his head at Wallace and saw the blood on the pilot's left arm. He pressed his mike and said, "Mr. Wallace you've been hit, too." He grabbed his survival knife from its scabbard and slit the left arm of Wallace's flight suit. One of the AK-47 bullets had sliced a hole in his left shoulder and buried itself in the padding of the pilots seat.

"How bad is it, Stu?" Larry asked.

"Doesn't look like the bone was hit, but you have a nasty wound, sir," Stewart answered. He grabbed the first aid packet and selected a thick bandage. He pulled the strings to the bandage tight, and the flow of blood stopped. "I put that on pretty tight to stop the flow of blood. Let me know if it gets too uncomfortable. How does the arm feel, sir?"

"I don't feel a damn thing, Stu," Larry said, "but I know it'll be hurting like hell by the time we get back to the carrier."

"Sorry, sir," Stewart said as the turned and walked back to the cabin and sat on the bench seat beside Lieutenant Parker. The jet pilot was still wearing his helmet. He plugged Parker's helmet cord into the second crewman station. Now Parker could listen in on the intercom and radio.

Lieutenant Joe Brady climbed his F-4 back to twenty-thousand feet. He pressed the mike switch and said, "War Chief Strike, this is Two-Zero-Four with sitrep, over."

"Go ahead, Two-Zero-Four," the strike controller said.

"SAR helo enroute with pilot of Two-Zero-Two. The navigator was captured by the junks. You can recall the Spads, over."

"Roger, Two-Zero-Four," the controller said and then continued, "Break-break, SAR Seven-Eight, do you read? Over."

"Roger, Strike," Larry said. "See you at twenty-two. Lieutenant Parker's not injured. Advise that SAR pilot is wounded in left arm. My copilot was killed in action. Request Charlie on arrival, over."

"**Son-of-a-bitch**!" the controller yelled before he caught himself. "Sorry, sir. Call War Chief tower for landing clearance. Winds are twenty-five degrees port at sixteen knots, over."

"Roger, winds," Larry said and flew toward the carrier. *Our last flight on the Concord, and Bob had to buy the farm*, he thought. God, he hated the thoughts of inventorying Bob's personal effects. He placed the landing gear handle in the down position as he passed over the plane guard destroyer one mile behind the *Concord*. "War Chief Tower, Seven-Eight, one mile with gear, over," he said as he held the altitude at 200 feet and airspeed of 120 knots.

"Roger, Seven-Eight, your signal Charlie abeam the island," the Air Boss said.

"Roger, Charlie," Larry said. "Have unsafe indication on left gear. Request fly-by for visual inspection, over."

"Roger, fly-by," Commander Barber said and reached for his field glasses. He focused on the helicopter and saw that both main gear were extended. *God damn helo pilot wanted to sneak in a fly-by on the ole Air Boss*, he thought and smiled. *Well, this helo pilot had earned his fly-by*. Barber pressed the mike and said, "Seven-Eight, gear looks good to me. You're cleared for fighter-pilot break after you pass the island."

"Roger break, Boss," Larry said and rolled the H-3 into a 45 degree bank to the left. The five rotor blades of the big H-3 began a loud popping series as the rotor tips bit into the humid gulf air. Larry held the helicopter in a tight 360 degree turn and landed in the middle of the flight deck near the island. He could see people running toward the helicopter from the island. He secured the number two engine and disengaged the rotor system. He applied the rotor brake, and the rotors were stopped before the corpsman could reach the aircraft. He pushed the blade fold button. The number one blade positioned itself over the tail of the helicopter. The other four blades began to fold back along the fuselage. The flight surgeon ran up and jumped into the cabin door. A yellow tow tractor hooked onto the tail wheel and pulled the H-3 clear of the flight deck to its parking space behind the island.

A corpsman in a white shirt with a red cross on his chest walked to the cockpit area. He raised the copilot's head and looked at his neck. More men climbed up the side of the H-3 and released the fastenings that held the copilot to the seat. They lifted his body out of the cockpit and passed him to the people waiting below. His body was placed on a yellow tractor that raced for the number two elevator. The flight surgeon unwrapped the tight bandage and looked at the wound in Larry's left arm. He jabbed a needle into the fleshy part of Larry's shoulder in injected a shot of morphine. Then he replaced the bandage. "Come on, men. We're all going down to sickbay for a check-up. I might be able to find some bottles of bourbon," he said and led the group toward the island.

Major General Curtis' Quarters
Da Nang Air Base
Republic of Vietnam

Captain John Jasper, USAF, drove Anah Thong from the Base Hospital to the General's quarters. He told her to get some rest and he would assign her duties later. After Jasper drove away in the jeep, Anah walked through the spacious, six-room house. She met the two other members of the staff. Tuie Ky, the cook, and Dan Tran, butler and chauffeur. She informed the two that she was the General's mistress and they would take orders from her.

When General Steve Curtis walked into his quarters, he was pleasantly surprised to find Anah waiting for him in the living room. She wore a white silk shift with a slit up the left side. She stood as Steve entered the room and said, "Good evening, General Steve. It is so good to see you again. Please sit by me on the couch." Anah picked up a small silver bell and rang it. Tuie Ky entered the room with two glasses of French wine. She placed the glasses on the coffee table in front of the General and Anah. "Thank you, Tuie," Anah said as she picked up one of the glasses and held it to General Curtis' lips.

Curtis sipped the wine and said, "That's so delicious, Anah. Much better than my usual martini."

Anah smiled at him, "That's French Chardonnay. I bought it today in the marketplace." Anah's trip to the market had been a cover for her to report to her superior, Huey Ky, that she was now in a responsible position in General Curtis' quarters. Ky was pleased with the news. Tuie Ky, his niece, was also an agent for the Viet Cong. Now he would have to think about moving Tuie. He heard that a general at MACV was looking for a French cook. MACV was an acronym for Military Assistance Command, Vietnam, the 3,500-man unified command at Tan Son Nhut Air Base, under control of the Commander-in-Chief of the Pacific Command (CINCPAC), based in Hawaii. *Yes, Tuie will be perfect for the job at MACV*, he thought.

"You didn't have to go to the market," Curtis protested. "You should've been resting after your terrible experience in the raid last night."

"I feel fine," she laughed. "Captain John brought me to your house this morning, and I decided you needed a mistress to manage your servants. So I am your new mistress."

"I'll drink to that," Curtis said as he reached for his glass and took a drink. He felt a stirring in his groin. *God, she's so beautiful and so young.* "You're tall for a Vietnamese girl, Anah. Does your family live in Da Nang?"

"No, my mother was Vietnamese. My father was a Colonel in the French Foreign Legion. He was killed in the Viet Minh war when I was young. Mother said I get my height and blue eyes from him."

"You've suffered so much for such a young lady," Curtis said and took her hand in his. Her skin was so soft and her touch sent tingles up his arm. "Come on, let's have dinner."

"Okay," she said as she jumped up from the couch and led him to the dining room. Tuie served their dinner and was always ready to refill General Curtis' wine glass as Anah signaled to her. When Curtis finished his dessert, Anah stood and tugged at his arm, "Come, I have a very nice surprise for you." She led him to the bedroom and unbuttoned his shirt. He sat on the bed as she took off his shoes and socks.

"Take off your trousers and shorts," she said as she walked to his closet and returned with a silk robe. "You are so handsome," she said as she draped the robe around his shoulders and kissed his cheek. Then she quickly removed the white silk shift. Curtis was surprised to find that she was nude underneath. He decided that she was intoxicatingly seductive. She put on a silk robe, and said, "Come with me."

She led him out of the quarters toward the bath house. Inside was a large California style hot tub. "A warm bath will relax you after a hard day at the office," she laughed and removed his robe. Curtis climbed into the tub and sat on the bench. The water came up to his neck. Anah removed her robe and climbed in beside him.

"Is the water too hot?"

"No, it's perfect, Anah. Just like you." He reached for her and brought her into his arms.

Anah's hands caressed his body.

Curtis moaned as he felt her massage his manhood. He kissed her and felt her tongue quickly probe his mouth. *Damn, this is going to be one tour of hazardous duty that I will never forget,* he thought and kissed her again.

TWENTY-FOUR

Collision At Sea

USS Concord
Yankee Station

Lieutenant Bob Welch's body would be flown to NAS Cubi Point in the Philippines on the afternoon COD flight. COD was an acronym for Carrier Onboard Delivery. The COD was the C-IA Grumman twin-engine, propeller-driven aircraft that flew personnel, mail and air freight from Cubi Point to the carrier in the Tonkin Gulf. Lieutenant Larry Wallace's wound was superficial enough to allow him to accompany Welch's body to San Diego. Then Wallace could recuperate at the Balboa Naval Hospital. The COD would launch after the last air strike of the day.

Tom had inspected the two H-3 SAR helicopters with LCDR Art Goldberg and agreed that both helo's should be grounded for extensive corrosion. Tom asked Chief Roberts, to conduct an inspection of the tail rotor drive shaft and tail rotor gear boxes. "The Air Boss will be busy with the launches and recoveries until fourteen-hundred," Tom said to Art. "Want to go up to Pri-Fly and have a change of command with him after the last launch?"

"Good idea," Goldberg said. "Do you know Commander Barber?"

"Oh yes, he's an old friend of the family. He flew with my father during the Korean War. Dad was CAG on the *Essex*. I know that Barber will be upset, but the first thing I must do is ground the helicopters."

"I agree with you, sir, but I bet you a case of beer that CAG Brown just puts them in an up status again."

"You're probably right, Art. He has that option, but he must also assume the responsibility that goes along with the decision. Someone is gonna get killed unless those helo's are grounded and repaired. I gotta try to try to convince him that those helicopters are unsafe to fly, especially in a combat situation like this morning."

The ship's public address system announced, "**NOW HEAR THIS. SET FLIGHT QUARTERS**." Several junior officers got up from the tables and hurried to their duty station. *God, I hope we don't lose a jet on this launch*, Tom thought as he sipped the black coffee.

Officer's Club
NAS, Ream Field

Lieutenant Commander Bob Wilson and Tommy Colby ate lunch at the Ream Field Officer's Club. "Tommy, I won't be able to make it to the game tomorrow night," Wilson said. "I sure hope you win and keep your undefeated season intact."

"We're playing the Imperial Beach Mariners," Tommy said. "I'm confident that we can beat them, Commander Bob. You have a hot date, Friday night?"

"No," Wilson laughed. "I'm shipping out tomorrow for Vietnam on the *USS Belknap*. Lieutenant Terry Fox and I are taking a H-2 helicopter aboard the *Belknap* to fly combat search and rescue mission in the northern part of the Gulf of Tonkin."

"I'm not familiar with the *Belknap*. Is that a small aircraft carrier for helicopters?"

"No," Wilson said. "The *Belknap's* a Navy destroyer armed with missiles. She has a landing area on the fantail large enough for H-2 operations. The only thing that worries me is she doesn't have a hangar. We may have some problems with corrosion from the salt spray."

"You may also have some problems with the North Vietnamese gunners. Dad told me that HS-twenty-six lost thirteen helicopters in combat search and rescue operations. That's some pretty bad odds, Commander Bob."

"Yeah, I agree. First of all, I want to say that I have complete faith in the H-2 Sea Sprite and my aviator skills to survive the missions in the

Tonkin Gulf. Did Judy tell you that I checked her out in my Cessna three-ten?"

"She hasn't talked about anything else," Tommy laughed.

"I want you and Judy to fly my three-ten occasionally to keep her in good shape. Also, I'd appreciate it if you'd take care of my beach cottage."

"I'll fly the three-ten as often as you think I should, and I would be most happy to check on the beach cottage."

Wilson handed Tommy a key and said, "Now, just in case that I don't come back, I want you to have the three-ten and the cottage. I gave your mother power of attorney to make it happen."

"Jesus, Commander Bob. I wish you wouldn't get so morbid and let negative thoughts creep into your mind. I really believe in the power of positive thinking. Don't you?"

"Yes, I do, Tommy. I know I'll survive this little cruise to Vietnam, but I wanted you to know how I feel. You've been like a son to me."

"Thanks, Commander Bob," Tommy said. *It will be great flying Commander Bob's Cessna 310*, he thought as he chewed the steak. "What time is your ship leaving tomorrow?"

"At zero-nine-hundred Navy time. Terry and I will fly the H-2 aboard as the ship cruises out the harbor."

"I sure hope this war is over soon," Tommy said as finished his steak and drank the Coke. "Thanks for lunch. I gotta run back to school before I get marked tardy." He stood and shook hands with Wilson then put his arms around him and embraced him and said, "Take care, and fly safely."

"Thanks, Tommy, win the game for me tomorrow night."

"Sure will, Commander Bob," Tommy said as he turned and rushed out of the room to the Mustang. *Damn, I'm going to miss Commander Bob*, he thought as he started the car and drove back to Otay High School.

USS Concord
Yankee Station

Tom Colby and Art Goldberg walked into Pri-Fly as the last two jets were being launched from the bow catapults. Commander Red Barber jumped out of his chair and rushed over to shake hands with Tom. "God, it's good to see you," Barber said and pumped Tom's hand. "Welcome to

Yankee Station. Take a seat and watch the recovery of the last strike." The Pri-Fly room was almost twice the size of the one on *Shiloh* and contained two large barber-type chairs, placed side-by-side, for the Air Boss and Assistant Air Boss. Tom climbed into the seat stenciled ASST. AIR BOSS.

The COD, spotted on the fantail of the carrier, was completing the engine warm-up and checkout. Today, the COD was not heavily loaded and had elected to make a deck-run takeoff. When the last two strike aircraft were launched, the COD called ready for takeoff. Barber reached for his mike and cleared the COD. Then he called the strike aircraft circling overhead the carrier, "Blue Flight, War Chief tower, your signal Charlie."

The F-4 Blue Flight leader answered, "Roger Charlie, leaving Delta this time."

Tom watched as the COD released its brakes and started the take-off roll. The *Concord* was cruising at 31 knots. The South China Sea wind was from 120 degrees at 18 knots. The wind added to the carrier's speed equaled 49 knots of wind across the deck, the secret of carrier aviation. The COD only had to accelerate to 31 knots, and she would be flying. The COD continued to accelerate rapidly and was airborne near the number two elevator. The COD turned left and headed east toward NAS Cubi Point.

The flight of F-4 jets flew over the carrier at 400 feet. When the leader passed the bow of the ship, he broke to the left in a 90 degree bank. The rest of the flight followed at four second intervals. The result was a racetrack-type pattern that allowed the trapped aircraft to clear the landing area before the next aircraft rolled onto final and called the meat-ball in the landing signal mirror. The F-4's were first to land, followed by the F-8 Crusader's. Next came the A-1 Spad's, and finally the Grumman twin-engine, jet turbo-propeller E-2 with the large radar dish on top of the wings. The recovery was completed without incident. *Concord* reduced speed to 18 knots and turned west toward the coast of Vietnam.

Red Barber reached for the mike and said, "**SECURE FROM FLIGHT QUARTERS**." He replace the microphone on the rack above his chair and turned to face Tom. "We heard that you were wounded in the raid last night at Da Nang. How did the Air Force treat you?"

"Just great, Boss," Tom answered. "We flew from Hawaii to Da Nang on General Curtis' jet liner and had a delicious steak at the club last night. Then the Jolly Green Skipper got drunk and passed out, so I got to sample his hootch girl. Sure was some great R and R."

"Hell, it was worth getting shot, if you got laid," Barber laughed. "Gee, I still can't believe you're a full Commander."

"Did you hear that Dad got three stars and has command of the Seventh Fleet?"

"Yeah, I read about it in *Stars & Stripes*," Barber said. "Damn, that's great. Now maybe we'll get to hit some good targets."

"I wouldn't count on it," Tom cautioned. "The targets are still selected by Mr. McNamara and his Pentagon whiz team."

"You wouldn't believe some of the shit that he has selected as targets for us," Barber said.

"Boss, about the SAR helicopters. They're in bad shape, and I had to ground them."

"Yeah, I know," Barber answered. "Flight Deck Control called up awhile ago and told me that you had grounded the helos."

"We have three SAR helicopters on the *Shiloh* that are in mint condition," Tom said. "They have the new gold strip engine and armor plating around the pilot and copilot's seats."

"Where's the *Shiloh*?" Barber asked.

"In the Sea of Japan, playing hide and seek with five Russian nuke submarines."

"Damn, I wish there was some way we could get those birds out here to Yankee Station," Barber said. "Did the First Lieutenant find some staterooms for your pilots?"

"No, sir, we're sleeping in a wing of sick-bay."

"Damn, that's totally unsat," Barber said and reached for the telephone. He dialed the office of the First Lieutenant. "Mr. Smith, this is the Air Boss," he said. "What's this crap about assigning my SAR pilots to sleep in sickbay?" Barber listened to Lieutenant Smith's reply and said, "Yes, that'll be satisfactory. Thank you, Mr. Smith." He hung up the phone and said, "The First Lieutenant found your pilots an eight-man J. O. bunk room on the o-three-level, just aft of the aviator wardroom. Would you like to bunk with your crew?"

"Yes, sir," Tom answered.

A messenger walked into Pri-Fly. "Commander, I have a flash message for you, sir," he said and handed Barber a folder.

Barber read the the message and swore, "Those God damn black-shoes should not be allowed to drive ships." He passed the folder to Tom and said, "Read this." Tom read the message.

TOP SECRET
FLASH 191432Z OCT 65

FM: USS WADDELL
TO: USS CONCORD
INFO: CINCPACFLT
    COMMANDER, SEVENTH FLEET
    COMMANDER, TASK FORCE, SEVEN SEVEN POINT SEVEN
BT
SUBJ: COLLISION AT SEA.
1. COLLISION OCCURRED BETWEEN WADDELL AND BRINKLEY BASS DURING REFUELING OPERATIONS. BRINKLEY BASS LOST TWENTY-TWO FEET OF HER BOW.
2. BRINKLEY BASS IN DANGER OF SINKING. REQUEST CONCORD TRANSFER SHIP REPAIR PARTY VIA HELO ASAP. CASUALTY REPORT TO FOLLOW.
ET
TOP SECRET

"Do we send our SAR helo to save the black-shoes' ass, Tom?" Barber asked as Tom finished reading the message.

"How far away are those ships?"

"Oh, about a hundred and fifty miles up the Gulf at PIRAZ station," Barber answered. PIRAZ was an acronym for Positive Identification Radar for Aircraft Zone."

"It would be great to have a Spad escort the chopper," Tom said.

"Let me check on it," Barber said and reached for the red telephone that would connect him with the bridge. "Good afternoon, Captain. Commander Colby and I were discussing the message from the *Waddell*. Tom wants a Spad to escort the chopper." He listened for a few minutes, and said, "Aye, aye, sir."

He replaced the telephone and turned to Tom. "The Captain wants your helo to take a repair party of fifteen to the *Brinkley Bass*. Negative escort."

"Boss, the H-3 only has twelve passenger seats," Tom complained. "Three of those guys won't even have seats much less seat belts."

"Welcome to the *Concord*," Barber said. "Can your pilots be ready for launch in fifteen minutes?"

"Yes, sir," he said as he walked out of Pri-Fly and rushed down the ladders to brief Chief Roberts and the flight crew, Ensign Bull Walker and Lieutenant (j.g.) Rick Jackson.

TWENTY-FIVE

Death of Sea Devil 78 and 72

USS Brinkley Bass (DE-671)
Tonkin Gulf

Ensign Bull Walker hovered Sea Devil 78 thirty-feet above the fantail of the *USS Brinkley Bass*. The repair party had welded steel plates over the gaping hole in the bow of the ship. With the new stubby nose, the *Brinkley Bass* looked more like a landing ship tank than a destroyer escort. The copilot, Lieutenant (j.g.) Rick Jackson stared at the twenty foot waves. The H-3 was an amphibian helicopter with a seaplane hull, but it would be difficult to stay afloat in those waves.

As the crewman hoisted the last person of the repair party aboard the helicopter, the tail-rotor gear box began to fail. Bull lowered the nose of the helicopter to gain forward speed. When the helicopter was 200 feet from the *Brinkley Bass*, the tail-rotor flew off the helicopter and whirled away like a giant frisbee. The helicopter began a rapid, uncontrolled spin to the right. The helicopter struck the ocean in a level attitude and flipped over on her back. She floated upside down for five minutes and slowly began to sink.

While the helicopter floated upside down, Bull took charge of the rescue operations. He yelled at the passengers to hold onto each other and wait for the *Waddell's* lifeboat to pick them up. He counted heads. Three of the men were missing.

USS Concord
Yankee Station

Tom Colby was sitting in Pri-Fly beside Red Barber when the messenger delivered the flash message from the *USS Waddell*. Barber quickly read the message and handed it to Tom. He said, "We lost another helicopter." Tom read the message with a heavy heart.

FLASH SECRET 191623Z OCT 65

FR: USS WADDELL
TO: USS CONCORD
INFO: CINCPACFLT
    COMMANDER, SEVENTH FLEET
    COMMANDER, TASK FORCE SEVENTY-SEVEN POINT SEVEN

SUBJ: CRASH OF NAVY HELO NUMBER 78 AT SEA.
1. NAVY HELO, SIDE NUMBER 78, LOST AT SEA WHILE HOISTING REPAIR PARTY FROM BRINKLEY BASS.
2. OBSERVER SAW TAIL ROTOR LEAVE HELO PRIOR TO CRASH. HELO CREW AND TWELVE (12) REPAIRMEN ABOARD WADDELL. THREE (3) REPAIRMEN MISSING AT SEA.
3. BRINKLEY BASS IS SEAWORTHY WITH TEMPORARY BOW AND CONDUCTING SEARCH FOR SURVIVORS AT CRASH SITE.
ET
FLASH SECRET

"Son-of-a-bitch," Tom swore. "I was afraid we'd kill somebody in this operation."

"Easy, Tom," Barber said. "The *Waddell* and *Brinkley Bass* may find them."

"They may find their bodies, Boss. If they didn't get out of the helicopter within five minutes, they're dead. They're probably still in the cabin of the helicopter."

"What do we do now, Tom? Launch your last helicopter?"

"I don't see any other choice, Boss. I'll go brief the flight crew while you set fight quarters."

As Tom walked out of Pri-Fly and down the ladders he heard the ship's public address system announce: **"NOW HEAR THIS. SET FLIGHT QUARTERS TO LAUNCH THE SAR HELO."** He wanted to fly this mission, but Lieutenant's Paul Webb and Tony Olson were next on the flight schedule rotation. Tom and Ensign Tim Arnold would fly the next mission. *If there are any helicopters left to fly*, Tom thought.

USS Waddell
PIRAZ Station
Tonkin Gulf

Lieutenant Paul Webb made the 116 mile trip from the *USS Concord* to the *Waddell* in one hour and five minutes. One of the five rotor blades was out of track, producing a vertical bounce to the airframe on every revolution of the rotor. The number three rotor blade would not track to match the other blades. Paul looked down at the *Waddell* and *Brinkley Bass* rolling and pitching in the rough sea. "God, it's going to be tough sitting this big mother down on the small, rolling flight deck," he said to his copilot, Tony Olson.

"Maybe she'll stabilize when she turns into the wind," Tony said.

"Sure hope so, switch to *Waddell* frequency and look up her call sign. I think it's Sentry." Olson switch the UHF radio to *Waddell* frequency. He looked at his knee note pad for the ship's call sign and gave a thumbs-up sign. Pressing the mike switch, Paul said, "Sentry, this is Sea Devil Seven-Two, five miles south for landing, over."

"Roger, Sea Devil Seven-Two. Your signal Charlie on arrival, out," the *Waddell* flight tower acknowledged. Paul saw the destroyer turn to the right to place the relative wind 30 degrees off the port bow. He started his landing approach as the ship's radio announced, "Sea Devil Seven-Two, your winds 30 degrees port at 42 knots. Advise deck is pitching fifteen to twenty feet, over."

"Roger winds," Paul acknowledged as he saw the fantail rise and fall in the large waves. The secret of landing in rough waves was not to dive for the deck. He hovered ten feet in the air over the circle on the flight deck and slowly lowered the helicopter. When he felt the left main gear and tail wheel touch the deck, he bottomed the collective and planted the helicopter to the deck. The helicopter began to slide toward the right side of the flight deck. The deck crew swarmed around the helicopter. Tiedown chains were snapped to mounting points on the fuselage of the helicopter, and the slide stopped. The helicopter was locked to the rolling flight deck.

The Executive Officer of the *Waddell*, Lieutenant Commander James Jones, was in the flight deck control station. He pressed the mike and said, "Nice landing, Seven-Two. Would you like to shut down and have a cup of coffee in the wardroom before the flight back?"

"Negative, Sentry," Paul replied. "I don't want to take a chance of shutting down the rotors in this high wind. Are my passengers ready?"

"Roger that," Jones replied. "They're on their way to the flight deck."

Paul saw the four flight crew members and twelve passengers of Sea Devil 78 come around the left side of the ship and head for the helicopter. Bull was in the lead. They quickly filled the twelve seats. Four of the passengers sat on the deck of the helicopter. The hoist operator reported to Lieutenant Webb that they were ready for takeoff. "Jackman, I want the passengers who don't have a seat to wear the gunner's belt," he said over the intercom.

"Roger, Mr. Webb, they have on gunner's belts."

"Thanks," Paul said and called the tower for takeoff, "Sentry, Sea Devil Seven-Two is ready for takeoff."

"Roger, Seven-Two. You have a green deck. Your winds are thirty degrees port at 45 knots. Have a nice flight," Jones said.

"Thanks, Sentry," Paul said and gave the pull chocks and tiedown sign. Tony pushed the throttles to 104 percent, glanced at the gauges and gave a thumbs-up signal. Paul eased up on the collective lever, and the helicopter became airborne. He lowered the nose and quickly accelerated away from the ship. They were two miles south of the *Waddell* when Paul noticed the trouble. He pushed the left rudder pedal and got no response. He pushed the right rudder pedal and the helicopter turned slowly to the right. It took full left rudder to stop the turn and maintain straight flight. **"Jackman, let me talk to Bull!"** he yelled over the intercom.

"Yes, sir," Petty Officer Jackman said and handed his mike to Ensign Bull Walker.

"What's up, Paul?" Bull asked.

"Bull, I have very little rudder control on this bird. Did it happen like this on Seven-Eight before the tail rotor broke off?"

"No, we had no warning at all. She just started spinning to the right, so I had to enter autorotation and try to land in the ocean. Can you land back aboard the ship?"

"No way," Paul answered. "I have full left rudder in now just to maintain straight flight. I recommend that we ditch beside the *Waddell*. What do you think?"

"That's the only thing that you can do, Paul. God, I hate to go into those big waves again," Bull moaned.

Paul turned the helicopter toward the *Waddell*. He pressed the mike and yelled, "**MAYDAY**! **MAYDAY**! **MAYDAY**! Sentry, this is Sea Devil Seven-Two declaring an emergency, over."

Lieutenant Commander Jones grabbed the microphone and said, "Seven-Two, this is Sentry. Are you requesting a Green-deck?"

"Negative, Sentry," Paul answered. "We're losing tail rotor control and will not be able to land on the ship. Plan to ditch along side *Waddell*, over."

"Roger, Seven-Two. We will make a left turn and block the wind as much as possible for you," he said as he pushed the crash alarm button. The Captain on the bridge saw the red crash alarm light and ordered the ship to General Quarters.

"Thanks, Sentry," Paul said as he saw the ship begin a left turn. The waves on the leeward side of the ship were only ten feet high. *Damn, we might just be able to make it,* he thought and remembered the one emergency water landing that he had practiced at Otay Lake in San Diego. He didn't like to land on the water. "Bull, I might not have enough left rudder to stop the right rotation of the nose on landing," he said into the intercom. "What do you recommend?"

"Paul, I think you should plan a low, slow approach," Bull said. "If she starts turning then you bring in the collective, just ease it off and let the tail wheel drag in the water. Once you get the tail wheel in the water, that will act like a sea anchor and stop any turning."

"Thanks, Bull," Paul said. "After we get on the water, I want you to get those passengers out as quickly as possible. She's gonna be hard to keep upright in those big waves."

"I read you," Bull said. "I'll get these sand-crabs out, don't worry about that."

193

Webb was 10 feet above the waves flying at 40 knots when the nose began to yaw to the right. He lowered the collective and the yaw stopped. He felt the tail wheel strike a wave and cushioned the landing by raising the collective.

When the helicopter touched the water, the crew of Sea Devil 78 jumped out the cabin door. Bull unlocked his seat belt and yelled for the passengers to unstrap and get out. He threw three of them out the door. He reached for the microphone and said, "Nice landing, Mr. Webb. All of the passengers are out of the helo, and I'm next. See you on the *Waddell*." Bull jumped into the water and inflated his Mae West.

The helicopter was riding the large waves like a roller coaster. Paul pressed the intercom mike and said, "Tony, let's try to shut her down." He was afraid of the whirling rotor blades. He had seen photographs where rotor blades had sliced through a foot-thick pine tree. Tony secured the number two jet engine and disengaged the rotor system. Paul gently applied the rotor brake and the helicopter began a slow turn to the right. The helicopter made five circles before the rotor blades stopped and began to slap against the waves. Paul quickly shut off the number one engine and secured all the switches.

"Let's get out of this bird," Paul yelled as he unsnapped his helmet cords and stepped out the pilot's window. They inflated their Mae West life jackets and floated away from the helicopter. The lifeboat from the *Waddell* had collected the passengers and was headed toward the two pilots. "I guess we'll get to have coffee in the wardroom with the ship's officers after all, Tony," Paul said as they were pulled aboard the lifeboat.

TWENTY-SIX

The Borrowed Angel

USS Concord
Yankee Station

Red Barber sat at his desk in Air Operations trying to get caught up on the volume of paperwork that was piled in the IN basket. Tom Colby sat at a desk nearby reading the latest issue of *Navy Times*. The messenger walked in with the message file under his arm. "Is that from the *Waddell*, Williams?" Barber asked.

"Yes sir, Commander," Petty Officer Williams said. "Flash, top secret."

"Williams, I just can't take anymore bad news. If we've lost another helicopter, I'm going to be mad as hell," Barber snorted.

"Please don't shoot the messenger, sir," Williams begged. "We don't make the news. We just deliver it."

"Give it to Commander Colby. The helicopters belong to him." Petty Officer Williams smiled and handed Tom the manila folder. Tom opened the folder and read:

TOP SECRET
FLASH 191754Z OCT 65

FM: USS WADDELL
TO: USS CONCORD

INFO: CINCPACFLT
    COMMANDER, SEVENTH FLEET
    COMMANDER, TASK FORCE SEVENTY-SEVEN POINT SEVEN

BT
SUBJ: CRASH OF NAVY HELO NUMBER 72 AT SEA.
1. NAVY HELO, SIDE NUMBER 72, CRASHED AT SEA. HELO LOADED
PASSENGERS AND DEPARTED WADDELL FOR CONCORD. RUDDER
CONTROL WAS LOST AND PILOT ELECTED TO DITCH ALONG SIDE
WADDELL. ALL PASSENGERS AND FLIGHT CREW RESCUED BY
LIFEBOAT. HELO SANK IN HEAVY SEAS.
2. FLIGHT CREWS OF HELO 72 AND 78 ARE COMMENDED FOR THEIR
SUPERB SKILL AND TIMELY ACTION TO EMERGENCY SITUATIONS.
FLIGHT CREWS OF BOTH HELO'S ARE RECOMMENDED FOR THE AIR
MEDAL. CITATIONS WILL BE FORWARDED.
3. SEARCH FOR THREE MISSING PASSENGERS OF HELO 78 CRASH IS
SUSPENDED. WADDELL AND BRINKLEY BASS ENROUTE TO
YANKEE STATION AT TEN KNOTS. TRANSFER OF HELO FLIGHT
CREWS AND PASSENGERS VIA YOUR PLANE GUARD HELO AFTER
FIRST LIGHT.
ET
TOP SECRET

Tom closed the folder, passed it to Barber, and said, "Well, Boss, we're out of the combat SAR business."

"Son-of-a-bitch," Barber swore and read the message. "I should've listened to you Tom. Those helicopters were in horrible condition. We've killed five people including Admiral Jim Perkins and his Chief of Staff by continuing to fly them."

"Boss, it was a command decision in a combat situation," Tom tried to console him. "Anyway, what we need are my three combat SAR helo's that're sitting on the *Shiloh*."

"You're right, Tom," Barber said, "but they have a mission with the Soviet submarines. Maybe we can borrow a helo from the Air Force rescue squadron in Da Nang until the *Shiloh* gets to Yankee Station."

"**Boss, you hit the nail on the head**!" Tom yelled. "I know General Curtis will loan me one of the Jolly Green helo's until the *Shiloh* finally gets on station. I'd like to send him a message."

"Go ahead and draft one, and I'll clear it through the Captain."

Tom grabbed a pad and started drafting a message to the Seventh Air Force.

Seventh Air Force Headquarters
Da Nang Air Base
Republic of Vietnam

Major General Steve Curtis sat at his desk in the Seventh Air Force Headquarters thinking about Anah Thong. Maybe it wasn't such a bad idea to have a hootch girl, he smiled as he read the message from the *USS Concord*:

SECRET
OPERATION IMMEDIATE 191822Z OCT 65

FM: USS CONCORD
TO: COMMANDER, SEVENTH AIR FORCE
INFO: CINCPACFLT
        COMMANDER, SEVENTH FLEET
        COMMANDER, TASK FORCE SEVENTY-SEVEN POINT SEVEN
        USS SHILOH (CVS-22)
BT
SUBJ: LOAN OF ONE USAF HH-3 HELO TO USS CONCORD SAR UNIT.
1. CONCORD HAS URGENT NEED TO BORROW ONE HH-3 HELO
FROM 366TH USAF HELICOPTER RESCUE SQUADRON AT DA NANG
TO CONTINUE SAR COVERAGE IN THE TONKIN GULF FOR NAVY
AND AIR FORCE PILOTS. CONCORD'S TWO H-3 SAR HELOS LOST AT
SEA DURING RESCUE OPERATIONS IN THE NORTHERN GULF.
2. CONCORD'S REPLACEMENT H-3 HELICOPTERS ONBOARD USS
SHILOH ON CLASSIFIED MISSION. ETA YANKEE STATION IN NEXT
TWO MONTHS.
3. COMMANDER TOM COLBY, USN, ENROUTE TO DA NANG ON
CONCORD C-1A COD TO DISCUSS TRANSFER WITH SEVENTH AIR
FORCE. ESTIMATED TIME OF ARRIVAL AT DA NANG IS 1845 LOCAL.
ET
SECRET

Curtis smiled as he finished reading the message. He pressed a button on his desk that would summon his aide. Then he dialed the number of the 366th Helicopter Rescue Squadron. The duty officer answered.

"This is General Curtis at Seventh Air Force Headquarters. Let me speak to your commanding officer."

"Sorry, General," the duty officer said. "Major King's in the hospital."

"**I know that, Lieutenant!**" Curtis roared. "Do you have an acting commanding officer?"

"Yes, General," the duty officer said. "Captain Steve Smith will be with you in a minute, sir. Please hold."

Curtis sat and held the telephone while Captain Jasper walked into the room. Smith came on the line, "Good evening, General Curtis. This is Captain Smith. How can we be of service, sir?"

"Steve, did you meet Commander Tom Colby from the Navy SAR detachment on the *USS Concord?*"

"Yes, sir, General. Commander Colby and I flew the detachment out to the *Concord* yesterday morning."

"Well, Steve, the *Concord* just lost their last two helicopters and wants to borrow a Jolly Green HH-3. I sure would like to accommodate the Navy if it doesn't place you in a bind. Do you have one that we could loan them?"

"Yes, General, we have eight birds left in the detachment. We could loan them one for a month or two, sir."

"Thanks, Steve. I appreciate your help and understanding. Oh, by the way, I want you to pick out the best HH-3 on the line and have it ready to go within the hour. Commander Colby's flying in on the *Concord* C-1A in forty-five minutes. He might want to fly back out to the *Concord* tonight."

"I understand, General. The bird will be ready, sir."

Curtis turned to Captain Jasper and said, "I guess you heard that Commander Colby will be landing here in forty-five minutes. Pick him up at the terminal and bring him out to my quarters for dinner. Oh yes, go by the 366th helo squadron and pick up Captain Smith. Tell Smith that he's having dinner with me and Colby."

"Yes, General," Jasper said as he turned and walked out of the office to carry out the orders. He couldn't understand why his general was treating Commander Colby like a Navy Admiral.

Seventh Fleet Flag Office
USS Providence
Tonkin Gulf

Vice Admiral Thomas Colby finished reading the messages from the *USS Waddell* and the *USS Concord*. He turned to his Chief of Staff, and said, "John, we need to appoint a board of inquiry to look into those helicopter accidents. Do we have someone on the staff who can do it?"

"Admiral, I recommend that we ask CINCPACFLT to appoint an officer to investigate it," Lester replied. "That way, it doesn't look like we're trying to hide our dirty laundry."

"Good idea, John," Colby replied. "Draft the message."

"Aye, aye, sir," Lester said and left the office.

USS Shiloh (CVS-22)
Sea of Japan

Commander Joe Blackwell was summoned to the Bridge by Captain Red Roberts. He stood beside the Captain's chair and read the message from the *Concord*. "What the hell is going on, Joe?" Roberts asked.

"Captain, we were briefed by Lieutenant Don Becker that HS-26 helo's had severe corrosion. When Admiral Perkins was killed in the crash, personnel on the *Turner Joy* saw the tail rotor break off. It must be poor maintenance, sir," Joe answered.

"Would your SAR pilots fly an unsafe helicopter?"

"No, sir," Joe answered. "Not unless they were ordered to, or if it was a life or death situation. I wish we could end this fiasco with the Russian submarines and get to Yankee Station." The *Shiloh* had been conducting around-the-clock flight operations for the past 72 hours tracking the five Russian submarines. Joe had met the flight schedule and kept three H-3 helicopters airborne in four hours shifts.

"Thanks for coming up to the bridge, Joe," Roberts said.

"Yes sir, Captain," Joe said and left the bridge. He thought about the two missing SAR helicopters and wondered if the flight crews were okay as he walked down the ladders to the wardroom.

MAC Terminal
Da Nang Air Base
Republic of Vietnam

Captain Jasper parked the sedan in front of the MAC terminal. On the license plates were the two chrome stars of a Major General in the Air Force. Jasper liked being an aide-de-camp. He watch as the Navy C-1A taxied to the parking ramp. He read the letters stamped on the fuselage, USS CONCORD. He started the sedan, drove out on the ramp and parked behind the C-1A. The sun was setting behind Monkey Mountain as Jasper walked toward the parked aircraft. He saluted as he recognized Commander Colby, and said, "Good evening, Commander. General Curtis would like you to join him at his quarters for dinner."

Tom Colby and Ensign Tim Arnold were dressed in the Navy short sleeve tropical khaki uniform. He returned Captain Jasper's salute, and said, "That's very kind of General Curtis. If we have time, I'd like to take our two crewmen by the 366th Helo Squadron."

"We'll be going right by there, Commander," he answered. "Captain Smith is also invited to dinner with General Curtis."

The pilots and crewmen grabbed their flight bags and walked toward the sedan. Tom rode in front beside Jasper. Ensign Arnold and the two crewmen got in the back seat. The air-conditioned car was a welcome relief from the hot, humid air on the parking ramp. Jasper drove across the ramp and turned right on the street leading to the 366th Helicopter Rescue Squadron.

Captain Smith saluted as Tom got out of the sedan, and said, "Welcome back to Da Nang, Commander."

"Steve, I'd like you to meet the best copilot in the United States Navy, Tim Arnold."

"Happy to meet you, Tim," Smith said and shook Tim's hand.

"Did General Curtis decide to loan us a helicopter, Steve?" Tom asked.

"Yes sir. You're getting the best bird on the line," Smith said, "number Seven-Seven-Five."

"That was the bird we flew out to the *Concord* the other day," Tom remembered. Turning to his crew, Tom said, "You troopers take the gear out to Seven-Seven-Five and start the preflight. Mr. Arnold and I'll be back just as soon as we finish with General Curtis."

"Yes, sir, Commander," the crewmen said and lugged the bags toward the big, green helicopter.

"We're ready to go, Captain Jasper," Tom said and got in the car.

"Okay, Commander," Jasper said as he got behind the wheel and started the car. General Curtis certainly did not invite this black Navy officer to dinner. He would leave that problem for the General to handle. He backed out of the space and drove toward General Curtis' quarters.

Yankee Station
The Gulf of Tonkin

Ensign Tim Arnold flew the Air Force HH-3 helicopter at three-thousand-feet above the Gulf. For the past four hours, the *Concord* had been cruising toward Da Nang Air Base at 20 knots. Commander Red Barber had visited the bridge and suggested that Captain Streeper steam toward Da Nang to reduce the long over-water night flight from Da Nang to the carrier.

Tom switched the TACAN to *Concord's* frequency. The bearing needle pointed straight ahead on a bearing of 91 degrees. The mileage indicator stopped at 62 miles. Tom pressed the intercom mike and said, "Captain Streeper's been driving the carrier straight toward the beach. What's your ETA, Tim?"

Arnold glanced at the doppler ground speed indicator that showed 122 knots, and said, "Twenty-nine minutes, Commander."

"Sounds about right," Tom said. He pressed the radio mike and said, "Da Nang departure control, this is Air Force Helo Seven-Seven-Five leaving your frequency for War Chief, over."

"Seven-Seven-Five, frequency change approved," departure control answered. "Have a nice flight."

Tom switched the radio frequency and said, "War Chief tower, Air Force helo Seven-Seven-Five, over."

Red Barber was waiting in Pri-Fly for the radio call. He pressed the mike and said, "Go ahead, Seven-Five."

"Roger, Boss, on your two-seven-one radial at fifty-eight. ETA is two-seven minutes."

"Seven-Five, expect Charlie on arrival. Call at five miles with gear," Barber said. He reached for the public address microphone and said, **"NOW HEAR THIS. SET FLIGHT QUARTERS FOR HELO RECOVERY."**

Tom pressed the intercom mike and said, "Sounds like the Air Boss was sitting in Pri-Fly waiting for our call, doesn't it?"

"Sure does," Tim agreed. "Commander Barber was pretty shook up after Seven-Two lost tail rotor control and had to ditch."

"Yeah, he's blaming himself for the loss of all three helicopters," Tom agreed. "Tim, we gotta take care of this bird. I don't want to see one spot of corrosion on her."

"Make me the Maintenance Officer, and I promise you that she'll get a fresh water bath every day," Tim boasted.

"You got the job," Tom said and slapped him on the shoulder. "What do you think of Miss Anah Thong?"

"God, she's one beautiful woman," Arnold groaned. "I got a hard-on just gazing into her sexy blue eyes."

"Those are French eyes," Tom said. "Her father was a Colonel in the French Foreign Legion."

"Do you think that General Curtis is sleeping with her, sir?"

"If he isn't then he's impotent," Tom laughed. "She seduced me about thirty minutes before the sapper raid the other night."

"Do you think she's ever made love to a black man?"

Tom thought for a minute and then said, "No, Tim, Anah's probably never had that pleasure. Tell you what I'm gonna do. If you keep the corrosion off this bird, I'll fix you up with Miss Thong when we return this Jolly Green helo to the Air Force."

"We got a deal, Commander," Tim said as he switched hands on the cyclic stick and reached over to shake Tom's hand. *This was one sweet deal that he want to make sure was sealed with a hand shake.*

TWENTY-SEVEN

Commander Bob Goes To War

The Crown Room
Hotel Del Coronado
San Diego, California

Linda Colby had asked Bob Wilson to join her for breakfast at the Crown Room. She ordered the champagne breakfast for two. Linda raised her glass and said, "I have a toast for you, Commander Bob."

Bob put down his fork and reached for the glass of champagne. "Okay, pretty lady, proceed with your toast."

"To a safe and successful voyage on the *Belknap*. May you have many rescues and come home safely," she said and gazed into his brown eyes. They touched the rims of their glasses and drank champagne. As soon as the glasses touched the table, they were refilled by the waiter.

"My turn," Bob said. "To my very special redhead. I'll always love you, pretty lady," he said as he touched her glass and drank champagne.

"Did you make love to Jackie Anderson last night?" She asked and saw him flinch.

"My God, you must have spies everywhere," he laughed.

"No, I just know that Jackie usually gets what she goes after."

"Well, she sure shocked the hell out of me last night. Sure you want to hear all the gory details?"

"Yes," Linda said and reached for a piece of toast.

"We had dinner at the Sky Room," Bob began. "I coaxed Linda down to my room and was really shocked when, Valerie, the young redhead from room service crawled in bed with us."

"Bullcrap, Bob!" Linda exclaimed. "You don't have to make up sea stories to impress me."

Bob raised his hand in a mock salute and said, "Scouts honor, Linda. This is the honest truth. I made love to two women last night. God, I've had that fantasy for years. I just wish the redhead had been you."

"Thanks," she said as and took his hand. "When you get back from playing war games, Jackie and I will arrange a very special treat for you in Suite 916."

"God, I can hardly wait," he groaned and squeezed her hand. "That's a promise that I intend to hold you to, Linda Colby."

"I've never broken my word, Commander Bob," she said as she released his hand and started eating her breakfast. "What time are you leaving this morning?"

"Lieutenant Terry Fox and I will fly aboard this morning at ten o'clock as the *Belknap* cruises out the channel."

"Are there any last minute things I can do for you?"

"No, thanks, Tommy and Judy will fly my three-ten occasionally and check on my beach cottage."

"You gave Tommy a key to your beach cottage?" She asked. "He and Judy will be making love over there every night."

"Oh, I doubt that, but they would be safer there than going to a motel or the back seat of a car."

"I'm sorry Bob," she said and reached for his hand again. "You're so thoughtful, sweet and kind."

"Okay, you're forgiven," he said and squeezed her hand. He looked into her gray-green eyes and said, "Please take care of my money."

"I promised that I would. If you're so worried about the state of California getting your money, we should have put it in my safe deposit box the other day."

"I wish we had done that," he said. "Promise me that you'll make the transfer as soon as the bank opens today."

"Okay, I promise," she folded her napkin and stood. "Now, walk me out to the Jaguar so I can kiss you good-bye." Bob threw some money on the table to cover the check and followed Linda to the parking lot. He opened the door of the Jaguar for her and stood waiting for his kiss.

"Get in the car, Bob. I don't kiss in public."

Bob ran around the Jaguar and got in the passenger side. Linda started the car and drove to the deserted end of the lot. The sun was just beginning to rise when she kissed him. "Think about me when you're on your ship fantasizing about making love," she said and kissed him again.

Jesus Christ, what a way to go to war, he thought and caressed her soft red hair.

USS Concord
Yankee Station

Tom Colby and Tim Arnold were on the flight deck of the *Concord* conducting a preflight inspection of the HH-3 helicopter as the sun rose above the Tonkin Gulf. The helicopter had become known to the *Concord* as side number Seven-Five and was assigned a parking space behind the island super-structure. Tom pointed to the horizon where the *Waddell* and the blunt nose *Brinkley Bass* were coming into view. "There's our SAR crew, Tim. Let's get this bird in the air and go get them." He climbed in the cockpit and sat in the pilot's seat. A yellow tractor towed the helicopter to the center of the flight deck. The plane captain plugged the auxiliary power into the nose of the helicopter. Tom held up one finger in a winding motion above his head. This signal told the flight deck operator that the crew was ready to start the jet engines.

The flight deck director wore a portable radio. He called Pri-Fly for permission to start engines. The director moved a lighted wand above his head in a waving motion. Tom pressed the starter of the number one engine, and the turbine started to whine. He quickly brought the number one engine to 104 percent and turned on the generators. "Pull the power," Tom ordered.

Ensign Arnold held up both hands and gave the unplug sign to the plane captain. He pulled the power cable from the nose socket and ran across the flight deck.

Tom started the number two engine and brought the turbine up to 56 percent power. He called the tower and requested permission to engage the rotors. After the Air Boss gave permission, Tom engaged the rotor system with the number two engine. In less than three minutes the helicopter was ready to launch. Tom pressed the mike switch and said, "Tower, Seven-Five, ready for takeoff."

"Seven-Five, you have a green-deck. Your wind is down the deck at thirty-two."

"Roger, tower. Seven-Five lifting," he said as Ensign Arnold gave the "pull chocks" sign. Tom lifted the helicopter into a 10 foot hover, lowered the nose and quickly accelerated toward the *Waddell*. He pressed the mike switch and said, "Seven-Five switching to Sentry, over."

"Roger, Seven-Five," Barber answered. Arnold switched the UHF radio to the *Waddell* frequency.

Tom pressed the mike and said, "Sentry, this is Helo Seven-Five for passenger pickup, over."

"Helo Seven-Five, your signal Charlie. Call at two miles with gear," *Waddell* tower answered. "Can you carry all passengers in one load?"

"That's affirmative, Seven-Five, gear down and locked."

"Roger, Seven-Five, you have a green deck. Wind is thirty degrees port at twenty-eight knots, over."

"Roger," Tom said as he lowered the collective and started the approach to the small helicopter deck on the fantail. "Looks small compared to the *Concord*, right Tim?"

"Sure does," Arnold agreed. "Are you sure we'll fit on that small flight deck?"

"Yes, she'll fit," Tom assured him. "This bird is not that much larger that the SH-3." Tom brought the helicopter to a stable 10 foot hover and followed the directions of the LSO. He felt the wheels touch the deck and bottomed the collective. The flight deck crew attached the tiedown chains. The passengers followed Bull Walker single file to the big helicopter. Some were very apprehensive about another helicopter flight after surviving two crashes in the large waves.

After the passengers were locked in their seats, Tom called for takeoff and was back aboard the *Concord* within ten minutes. He quickly secured the engines. The yellow tractor towed the helicopter to the parking spot behind the island. Tom informed the two flight crews and passengers to meet in the wardroom. Commander George Parker, the

Operations Officer, was conducting an investigation of the two accidents, and needed statements from the crew and passengers. "Come on, Tim," Tom said. "We might as well get a cup of coffee and listen to the debriefing about the accidents."

"Yes, sir," Tim said. He yelled over his shoulder to the plane captain, "Be sure to wash off all the salt spray. I'll be back up to inspect this bird within the hour."

Tom knew he had made a wise decision appointing Ensign Arnold as maintenance officer of the HH-3. There wasn't going to be any corrosion on this helicopter. He intended to keep his part of the bargain with Arnold. Anah Thong would seduce Arnold if Tom asked her, nicely.

California First Bank
San Diego, California

Linda Colby drove into the parking lot of the bank and parked the Jaguar. She walked to the safe deposit box section and unlocked her box. Then she unlocked Lieutenant Commander Wilson's box, and transferred the one hundred packages of cash. Each package contained ten thousand dollars. Quickly, she made a decision and stuffed four packages in her purse. *It is just plain stupid to keep this money locked away when it could be earning six to eight percent interest,* she thought. She would deposit the money in savings accounts in several banks and savings and loan companies around the area. She walked from the bank thinking about Commander Bob. She hoped that he and Tom would make it home safely from the War.

TWENTY-EIGHT

Beeper Mayday

USS Concord
Yankee Station

Tom Colby and Tim Arnold ate Sunday dinner in the dirty-shirt aviation wardroom on the O-3 level. They were dressed in green nomex flight suits and high-top leather flight boots. They had just finished dinner when the ship's public address system announced, "**PILOTS, MAN THE SAR HELO**." Tom and Tim ran up one ladder and out onto the flight deck as the HH-3 was towed to the launch area near the island. Tom started the jet engines while Arnold followed the checklist. After takeoff, Commander Barber ordered them to switch to strike control channel. Tom pressed the mike and said, "War Chief strike, Sea Devil Seven-Five, over."

"Seven-Five, come right to one-two-six. We have several beepers on a bearing of one-two-six degrees. Unknown mileage."

"Roger, strike," Tom said." He pressed the intercom mike and said, "Tim, it'll be too dark soon to see anything. Keep a look-out at our twelve o'clock position for strobe lights."

"Yes, sir," Arnold said and switched off the guard channel to silence the high pitch squeal of the beepers. "Damn, those beepers have a nauseating pitch."

"Tim, you may have heard your last mayday the old-fashioned way," Tom said. "Now, the emergency rescue alert is an electronic beeper signal. Man, they sure do clobber guard channel."

In the cabin behind the cockpit, Petty Officer Steve Jackman and Airman Roy Lewis checked the rescue hoist. Jackman removed his flight suit and dressed in a two-piece divers wet suit. He slipped on the swim fins and checked his face plate. He would jump into the water and check the downed pilot prior to rescue. He would check for injuries, but most importantly, he would ensure that the pilot was clear of his parachute.

"I have two strobe lights at one o'clock," Tim said.

Tom pressed the mike and said, "Looks like two or possibly three strobe lights. Are you all set for a pick up, Jackman?"

"Yes, sir," Jackman said. "I'm the swimmer and Lewis is hoist operator."

"Okay, Jackman," Tom said. "Keep a look out for junks. This could be a trap. Don't jump into the water until I give the word."

"Yes, sir," Jackman said and smiled at Roy Lewis. He felt the helicopter start its descent toward the first man in the water.

Tom turned the UHF radio to guard and tried to call the pilots in the water. If they would turn the radios from beeper to voice they could talk with the helicopter. All he heard was the high pitch wail of the beeper. He turned-off guard channel as a pilot in the water ignited a smoke flare. Tom was descending to fifty feet over the pilot and counted four more strobe lights on the water. He lowered the helicopter to a 10 foot hover over the pilot and said, "Lewis, tell Jackman to jump."

"Yes, sir," Lewis said.

Jackman sat in the cabin doorway. When Lewis tapped his shoulder, he jumped. He splashed in the water near the pilot and swam under water. The pilot was clear of his parachute. He surfaced near the pilot and said, "Are you injured, sir?" He gave Lewis the thumbs-up signal.

"No," the pilot answered. "What are you guys, some kind of new Air Force seal team?"

"No sir, just your standard Navy combat rescue team," Jackman said. "Put down your helmet visor. The salt spray will hurt your eyes during pickup." Lewis lowered the hoist. Jackman let the hoist enter the water before he reached for it. A hovering helicopter builds up a large

209

charge of static electricity. Jackman grabbed the hoist cable and hooked the snap to the pilots torso harness. He gave Lewis the pick-up signal and swam toward the next strobe light. After the first pilot entered the cabin, Tom air-taxied to the next light. Within ten minutes, five Air Force officers were in the cabin of the helicopter.

Tom departed the hover and flew toward the *Concord*. He pressed the mike and said, "War Chief strike, helo Seven-Five."

"Go ahead, Seven-Five," the air controller said.

"Roger strike, Seven-Five inbound at twenty-five. Have five Air Force pilots aboard. Negative injuries, over."

"Thank you, Seven-Five. Charlie on arrival near the island." As Tom approached the *Concord*, he was surprised to see the flight deck bathed in white light. The red floodlights mounted above Pri-Fly were usually on during night operations. Then he saw the large welcome committee huddled behind the island led by Captain Samuel Streeper, to personally welcome the Air Force pilots aboard the *Concord*.

Tom stopped the rotors and shut off the jet engines. This was his first rescue in the combat area, and he felt great. After Captain Streeper shook hands with the five pilots, the carrier's doctor insisted they go down to the hospital for a check-up. The check-up consisted of five small bottles of whiskey and a cool shower. The pilots were dressed in the Navy international orange flight suits and escorted to the dirty-shirt wardroom to meet the Air Group. The stewards were busy serving ice cream and coffee.

Captain Streeper tapped on his coffee cup with a spoon and stood. The noise in the room stopped and he said, "Gentlemen, it's a pleasure to have these brother fliers aboard the *Concord*. First, I'd like for us to give Commander Colby and the SAR crew a hand for a job well done."

The wardroom erupted into applause as several of the junior officers stood and yelled, "**WAY TO GO, ROTORHEADS**."

Streeper raised his hands to quiet the room, and said, "This is the story of a rescue that almost didn't happen. I'd like to introduce Lieutenant Colonel Will Boyd, who will fill you in on the details." He turned to the group of Air Force pilots and said, "Colonel Boyd, please introduce your flight crew and tell us how you guys were shot down."

Boyd stood and said, "I want to personally thank Commander Colby and his helo crew for our rescue. I was completely unprepared when the Navy seal crewman jumped into the water beside me and checked me over. He had me hooked-up to the rescue hoist, and I was inside the helo before I knew what was happening. I'm gonna recommend that the Air Force helicopter crewmen adopt these tactics."

Boyd continued with his briefing, "We were flying a B-66 on a wild weasel mission when a SAM almost knocked us out of the sky. My copilot, Major Bill Lassen, figures that a SAM exploded when it locked onto the chaff that had just been ejected. The explosion jammed the elevator in the full nose-up position. We were headed out to sea and ejected as the B-66 was climbing through thirty-thousand feet. That sure was one hell of a long six mile parachute ride."

Boyd turned to face his flight crew, and said, "Gentlemen, Major Bill Lassen, my copilot. Captains Jack Preston, Phil Weston and Cowboy Jackson are the electronic warfare operators. The sixth member of our crew, Captain Marion Molino, didn't get out of the bird. We were hit at fifteen-hundred hours and floated in the water for almost two hours when Captain Streeper drove this big aircraft carrier near enough to pick up our beepers." Boyd finished and sat in his chair.

Captain Streeper stood and said, "Gentlemen, that concludes the briefing. The COD will launch at nineteen-thirty to take these officers to Da Nang." The buzz of conversation returned to the wardroom as the Air Group aviators talked about the rescue. *Those Air Force pilots were in for one hell of a surprise when they experienced their first carrier CAT shot, sitting in the rear-facing seats*, Tom thought and sipped the hot coffee.

Seventh Air Force Headquarters
Da Nang Air Base
Republic of Vietnam

Major General Steve Curtis sat at his desk and read the message from the *USS Concord*.

SECRET
OPERATION IMMEDIATE 212255Z OCT 65

FR: USS CONCORD
TO: COMMANDER, SEVENTH AIR FORCE
INFO: CINCPACFLT

COMMANDER, SEVENTH FLEET
COMMANDER, TASK FORCE SEVENTY-SEVEN POINT SEVEN
USS SHILOH, CVS-22
BT
SUBJ: RESCUE OF AIR FORCE B-66 FLIGHT CREW
1. COMMANDER TOM COLBY, FLYING AIR FORCE HELO NO. 775
RESCUED FIVE AIR FORCE PILOTS, AS FOLLOWS:
    LTCOL WILL BOYD
    MAJ BILL LASSEN
    CAPT JACK PRESTON
    CAPT PHIL WESTON
    CAPT COWBOY JACKSON
    CAPT MARION MOLINO DID NOT EJECT FROM THE AIRCRAFT.
2. ABOVE FLIGHT CREW ON CONCORD COD. ETA DA NANG AT
TWENTY HUNDRED HOURS.
ET
SECRET

Curtis was pleased that the *Concord* had rescued the flight crew of the Air Force B-66. He reached for the telephone and dialed the squadron commander, Colonel John Philips. He said, "John, this is General Curtis. Have you seen the message from the *Concord*?"

"No, General," Philips answered.

"Well John, the *Concord's* helicopter just fished your B-66 wild weasel crew out of the Gulf. They are inbound on the *Concord's* COD. Can you meet me at the terminal at twenty-hundred hours?"

"Yes, sir, General. Damn, it's great that they got out."

"Sorry John, you have a letter to write. Captain Molino didn't get out of the aircraft."

"Son-of-a-bitch!" Philips swore then said, "Sorry General, Molino was a great guy."

"That's okay, John. See you at the terminal in thirty minutes," Curtis said and broke the connection.

USS Shiloh (CVS-22)
Sea of Japan

Commander Joe Blackwell sat beside CAG at the Commander's table in the wardroom. A Marine Corps sentry, wearing a .45 caliber pistol, entered the wardroom and walked to the table. "Excuse me, CAG," the sentry said to Commander Boyd. "We have an operational immediate from the *Concord*, sir."

"Jesus, I hope they haven't lost another helicopter," CAG said as he reached for the folder. He read the message and handed it to Blackwell. "I can't understand this, Joe. The other day, Commander Colby rescued an Air Force Major and was recommended for the Air Force Cross. Today, he rescued a light colonel, a major and three captains, and they didn't even recommend him for the Good Conduct Medal."

Joe read the message. "Thank you, sentry," he said to the Marine and returned the message folder. The sentry tucked the folder under his left arm, executed a smart about-face and marched from the wardroom. Joe turned to Boyd and said, "CAG, the Sea Devil's aren't virgins anymore. They've been wounded in combat and made their first five rescues. I have a feeling that Tom will wield them into a mean, fighting rescue detachment. I just wish I could be flying with them."

"Take it easy, Joe," CAG said. "After we get through playing games with the Russian subs, you can fly all of the combat search and rescue missions that you want too."

"I'm going to hold you to that promise, CAG. I have a midnight launch, so I'd better get some sleep," Joe said and walked from the wardroom.

Twenty-Nine

CIA Mission

USS Concord
Yankee Station

Commander Joe Blackwell's prediction about the Sea Devil's was correct. In the first eight weeks of operations, the detachment rescued 31 pilots with the borrowed Air Force helicopter. Ensign Arnold supervised the maintenance and upkeep of the helicopter. He was constantly looking for corrosion. Petty Officer Steve Jackman and Airman Roy Lewis were waxing a section of the fuselage when Tim made his inspection. This line period would be over in three more days. The ship would then leave Yankee Station and celebrate Christmas at the Naval Station, Subic Bay in the Philippines. The carrier would dock at the NAS Cubi Point carrier pier. Five days of rest and recuperation awaited most of the men.

After 90 days on the line, the sailors and airmen were looking forward to the sexual delights of Olongapo City. A small river separated Subic Bay Naval Station from Olongapo City. Sailors, on liberty, could walk across the bridge to the city of 156,000 people who catered to their every need. The city offered cheap booze and young, brown bar girls who would perform almost any sex act for a price. The ultimate prize the bar girls sought was marriage, their one-way ticket to the United States and citizenship. "Are you going to treat us to a drink in Po City, Mr. Arnold?" Jackman asked.

214

Tim looked at Jackman, and said, "You guys keep this bird free of corrosion, and the first round of San Miguel is on me."

"You have a deal, Mr. Arnold," Jackman said. "Sir, is it true that one can buy a piece of tail for five dollars in Po City?"

"I don't know. I've never been to Olongapo," Tim answered, "but a five dollar piece of sex will probably give you of a dose of clap. I heard that over half of the bar girls have VD."

"Oh, God, I didn't realize it was that high," Jackman groaned. "It's some consolation to know that one can't catch the clap from a blow job, right Mr. Arnold?"

"Yes, I guess you're right," Tim said as he resumed his inspection of the helicopter. What he needed was to get laid by one of the bar girls in Po City so he could forget about his fascination with Anah Thong. Tim smiled as he rubbed his hand along the metal of the fuselage. One day soon, Anah Thong would be his sex toy. "The bird looks good, troops," he said and walked toward the island. He descended the ladder to the O-3 level and walked forward to the bunk room. Tom lay on his bed reading two letters. "Get some mail on the afternoon COD, Skipper?"

"Yes, my former high school girlfriend is flying to Manila to celebrate Christmas with me."

"That's fantastic!" Tim exclaimed. "Is she the cute blonde that came by to see you just before the General's plane left Hawaii?"

"That's the one. Ann is General Curtis' daughter. Her husband was killed in action a few months ago."

"Oh, that's too bad, sir. Are you going down to see the movie? I think it's an Elizabeth Taylor flick."

"No, I don't think so. Think I'll stay here in the room and write some letters. Enjoy the movie."

"Thank you, sir," Tim said and walked out of the bunk room. Tom reached for Ann's letter and read it again. He had written her a month ago giving the dates that the *Concord* would be in the Philippines. Her letter stated that she had made reservations for them at the Army-Navy Club in Manila from December 22nd to the 26th. He relaxed as he thought about the beautiful blonde and drifted off to sleep.

It was 11:45 p.m. when the telephone rang. Lifting the receiver, Tom said, "SAR stateroom, Colby speaking."

215

"Tom, this is Red Barber. Please come down to the war room."

"I'll be right down, Boss," Tom said. He hung up the telephone and slipped on his shoes. The war room was located on the O-3 level, forward of strike operations. The Navy Captain in charge of the war room was in constant contact with the White House. He received a list of targets from the Secretary of Defense and passed these orders along to strike operations. An air plan covering the next twenty-four hours was published and distributed throughout the carrier. The door of the war room was guarded by a Marine Corps sentry. A top secret clearance was required for admittance. Tom handed his military identification card to the sentry and said, "Commander Barber asked me to meet him in the war room."

The sentry examined the identification card and checked the signature on the reverse side of the card. "Wait one, Commander," the sentry said as he lifted the receiver and dialed the telephone. "Commander Barber, please," the sentry said when the clerk answered the telephone. When Barber answered, the sentry said, "Commander Colby to see you, sir." The sentry replaced the receiver and unlocked the door. He said, "You may go in, Commander."

"Thank you," Tom said and walked by the armed sentry. He was surprised that the room was so small. Inside were four people. Barber introduced the people to Tom, Captain Mac Magarity, Jack Warner and Yeoman Chris Chalmers. Warner wore civilian clothes. He flashed a CIA badge to Tom and took charge of the meeting.

"What level of clearance do you have, Commander?"

"Top secret," Tom answered.

"Have you ever had a SCI or Q clearance?"

"No."

"Damn, this is gonna be difficult," Warner said turning to Captain Magarity. "Mac, this goes way above top secret. I'm not sure that we can disclose any of it to Commander Colby."

"Mr. Warner, I'm not so sure that I want to hear your classified brief unless it pertains to my detachment or my family," Tom said.

"Easy, Tom," Barber cautioned. "The spook boys need your help. Just be patient and listen to Jack."

"Commander Colby has the only helicopter on the *Concord* that can reach your people, Jack," Magarity said. "I suggest you give him a briefing of the details that he'll need for the rescue."

"Okay, Captain," Warner said. Turning to Tom, he asked, "Have you heard of an operation called Get Even?"

"No," Tom said.

Warner made a decision and started the briefing, "This evening some of our people made a strike on Haiphong Harbor. During the withdrawal, our boat was damaged by enemy fire and can only make twenty knots. They have five wounded aboard and are headed for the hospital at Da Nang. We'd like for you to rendezvous with the boat and pickup the wounded."

"What type boat?" Tom asked.

"Classified," Warner said.

"What nationality are the agents?" Tom asked.

"Classified," Warner said.

"Can anyone on the boat speak English?" Tom asked.

"I don't know, Commander," Warner said, "We don't think so."

"Jesus Christ, Warner!" Tom exploded. "You should listen to your briefing from my side of the table. You're asking me to make a night rendezvous with some kind of boat in the northern part of the Gulf. The people onboard may not be able to talk to me. It doesn't feel like a fifty-fifty chance of survival to me. For your information, the Commander-in-Chief personally ordered me not to fly a mission unless we had a fifty-fifty chance to make it."

"Okay, Commander, I apologize," Warner said. He didn't know that Colby had been personally briefed by the President of the United States. "The craft is a 54-foot PT boat. Twelve of our agents went north tonight to take out some people. We don't know how serious their wounds are, but we need to get them to the hospital as soon as possible."

"Okay," Tom said. "We'll launch the helo to be overhead the boat at first light. We'll fly the wounded to the hospital at Na Nang. I'll brief my flight crew."

"No way, Colby," Warner said. "You fly the mission, and none of your crew has the need to know any of this classified information."

"Now, wait just a damn minute," Tom said. "I don't work for CIA, and I don't particularly want to fly your mission. I work for Commander Red Barber."

"Tom, I want you to fly the mission and please cooperate with Jack," Barber said.

"Okay, Boss," Tom said. "What's their call sign?"

"General Lee," Warner answered. "They'll monitor UHF channel 255.5 and Navy guard channel."

Tom wrote the information on his note pad and said, "We'll do our best to find your agents." He stood and turned to Barber. "Boss, call me about thirty minutes before you want us to takeoff. I'm gonna try to get some rest."

Colby Residence
Bonita, California

Linda Colby served chocolate cake and vanilla ice cream to Tommy, Judy and Jackie Anderson. Tommy and Judy were looking at the sectional flight charts and notes that Tommy had made at Brown Field Flight Clearance. "It'll be approximately nine hours of flight time between here and the Flying C Ranch in Virginia," he said. "I recommend that we stop in St. Louis to refuel and have lunch. If we can get airborne by eight o'clock Saturday morning, we can make it to the Flying C before dark."

"Okay, with me," Linda said. "How does it sound to you, Jackie?"

"I don't know," Jackie said. "Do you think we can trust these two teenage pilots to fly us all way across the United States and find a ranch somewhere in Virginia?"

"Oh, Mother," Judy scolded. "Tommy and I are excellent pilots."

"I was just kidding, dear," Jackie said. "The plans sound okay to me Linda." Jackie was looking forward to celebrating Christmas at the Colby ranch. Maybe the President would come by for a drink, or invite her to Camp David.

"Okay, I'll call Grandma Colby and brief her on our plans," Tommy said and reached for the kitchen telephone.

"Colby residence," Samuel Watson answered on the first ring.

"Hey, Sam, this is Tommy. May I speak to Grandma?"

"Yes sir, Mr. Tommy," Watson said. "Your grandma's gonna to be tickled pink. Wait a minute, and I'll fetch her."

"Hello, Tommy," Margaret Colby said.

"Hey, Grandma, I wanted to call and let you know that we'll be flying out in Commander Bob's Cessna three-ten on Saturday. We'll leave San Diego about eight o'clock and refuel in St. Louis. Then we should make it to the Flying C by four, depending on the weather and winds."

"That's marvelous news, Tommy," Margaret said. "Have a safe flight. Please let me speak to Linda."

"Okay, Grandma, hold on a minute," he said and placed his hand over the mouthpiece. "Grandma wants to talk to you, Mother."

"I'll take in on the living room phone," Linda said and rose from the table. When Tommy heard his mother's voice, he hung up the receiver.

"Judy, will you please get me some more ice cream?" He asked.

"Yes, master, if you'll let me make the takeoff."

"Okay, you can make the takeoff, but I'll back you up on the controls just in case you get flustered or have tingling feelings," he said.

"Thanks," Judy said as rose from the table and kissed his cheek. She was blushing as she walked to the refrigerator to get the ice cream. Jackie felt that she had missed something that was very important to these kids. *It must be young love*, she thought. *It was indeed going to be a lovely Christmas in Virginia. Maybe even some snow.*

Sea Devil 775
Two thousand feet above the Tonkin Gulf

Tom flew the helicopter north, toward Haiphong. They had launched thirty minutes before sunrise. He briefed the crew that this was a top secret mission. They were looking for some wounded crewmen on a PT boat. Ensign Tim Arnold sat in the copilot's seat. Steve Jackman and Roy Lewis were hoist operators. Tom had suggested that the ship's flight surgeon, Commander Jim Davenport, be assigned to the mission. Davenport volunteered to be a member of the crew. He wore his old international orange flight suit and clutched his doctor's bag. The morning sun rose up out of the Gulf like a large orange ball of fire.

Tim scanned the horizon ahead of them with binoculars. "I see a small boat at eleven o'clock, Commander," Tim said over the intercom.

Tom altered course ten degrees to the left and started descending. He switched to channel 255.5 and called, "General Lee, this is Sea Devil Seven-Five. Do you read, over?" There was no answer. Tom continued descending and saw the boat ahead in their twelve o'clock position.

"That's our boat, Commander," Tim said and continued to look through the binoculars. "She's flying the flag upside-down. That's the international sign of distress."

Tom tried to reach the boat several more times on the radio, but there was no answer. He switched to the *Concord* frequency and said, "War Chief strike, Sea Devil Seven-Five, over."

"Go ahead, Seven-Five," strike operations said.

"Roger, we have the PT boat in sight. We may lose radio contact when we descend for the pickup."

"Roger, Seven-Five," strike operations said. "Good luck."

Tom circled the PT boat. It was painted camouflage green without any numbers or markings except for the flag, flying upside-down from the mast. Tom saw several members of the crew on the deck dressed in the camouflage clothes like the Marines wore. He estimated that the boat was cruising at 20 knots. If it just held that course, the pick-up would go great. When he brought the helicopter into a hover thirty feet above the craft, the boat suddenly stopped dead in the water.

"**Damn it to hell**!" Tom yelled into the intercom as he overshot the boat. He waved-off his approach and circled the boat. Looking over at Tim, he said, "Just as I came into a hover, the boat stopped."

"He has probably never been hovered over before by a helicopter this big, Commander," Tim said. "We're larger than the boat."

"We may capsize him if he doesn't keep up some speed," Tom said. He keyed the mike and said, "Jackman, put the doc on the intercom."

"Roger, wait one, sir," Jackman said.

"This is Davenport," the flight surgeon said over the intercom.

"Hey doc, I'm gonna have Jackman lower you down to the boat on the hoist so you can check on the wounded men. Tell the coxswain to keep the boat heading south at twenty to thirty knots, understand?"

"Roger," Davenport said, "switching you back to the crewman."

Tom approached the PT boat again. Just as he expected, the moment he hovered over the boat, it stopped. The eighty knot wind from the five large rotor blades blew the boat around like a beach ball. Tom raised the helicopter to a 60 foot hover and managed to stay over the deck long enough for Jackman to lower the doctor to the pitching deck. Then he backed off to one side and hovered as the doctor checked over the wounded crewmen.

Davenport talked to the coxswain and pointed south. Suddenly, the PT boat headed south at 20 knots. Tom smiled and moved in closer. Now, the rotor wash was not blowing the boat all over the gulf.

Davenport raised his right hand showing four fingers. He quickly dropped his hand and made a slashing movement across his neck. He raised his right hand again showing one finger, and gave a thumbs-up.

"Doc's telling us that four of the guys are dead, and he has one for pick-up," Tom said and moved the helicopter over the boat. Jackman lowered the hoist to the deck. Davenport grabbed the sling and put it around the injured man. As Jackman started hoisting the man aboard, Tom keyed the mike and said, "Jackman, watch that gook very closely. If he has any weapons or grenades, take them from him as soon as he's in the helicopter. If he makes any move to damage the helicopter, throw him out the door."

"Yes, sir," Jackman said. He and Airman Roy Lewis stared at the man as he approached the helicopter. Jackman stopped the hoist six feet below the bottom of the helicopter. He pressed the mike and said, "Commander, the guy has an automatic rifle, a .45 caliber pistol and three grenades that I can see. Oh, shit! Looks like his left arm's been shot off."

"Easy, Jackman," Tom said. "Bring him inside the helicopter and tie him to the stretcher. Make sure that he can't reach those weapons or grenades."

"Roger, sir," Jackman said as he continued to raise the hoist. Lewis pulled the man into the helicopter. Jackman and Lewis quickly lowered him to the stretcher and strapped his right arm and both legs to the stretcher. Jackman pushed the rifle and pistol away from the stretcher. He tossed the grenades out the cabin door. He searched the man's pockets and found two more grenades. Both pins had been pulled. He threw the grenades out the cabin door as he pressed the mike and said, "Commander, the bastard had two grenades in his pocket with the pins pulled. He was gonna blow us out of the sky."

The grenades exploded just before they hit the water near the PT boat and blew plumes of water from the Gulf. Tim prayed that none of the shrapnel struck the skin of his precious helicopter.

"Okay, Jackman," Tom said. "Search him again, if you find another grenade, you and Lewis toss him out the cabin door, understand?"

"Yes, sir," Jackman answered. He and Lewis searched every inch of the man's body. "No more weapons on him, Commander."

"Roger, Jackman, it's time to pick up doc and head for the bird farm," Tom said and slid the helicopter back over the boat. Jackman lowered the hoist for the doctor. As Davenport stepped into the cabin, Airman Lewis saw blood on the seat of his flight suit.

Lewis pressed his mike and said, "Commander, the doc's been wounded. There's blood all over his flight suit."

Jackman led Davenport to a stretcher and motioned for him to lay on his stomach. He pulled down the doctor's flight suit and saw several wounds where the shrapnel from the grenades had entered Davenport's buttock. He pressed a thick bandage to the wounds to stop the flow of blood.

"**Jesus Christ, Jackman**!" Tom yelled into the mike. "You almost killed the doctor with those damn grenades."

"Sorry Skipper," Jackman said. "When I saw that he had pulled the pins and intended to blow us all to hell, I just tossed them out the door without aiming at anything. Want us to throw him out the door?"

"No, you did the right thing," Tom assured him. "We're grateful that you saved our lives. Do you want Mr. Arnold to help you patch up the doc?"

"No, sir," Jackman said. "Doc Davenport has three lacerations on his left buttock. Lewis and I will patch him up with some of his tape."

Tom had slowed the helicopter to a hover as the PT boat sped away to the south. "I don't trust those guys anymore," Tom said into the intercom. Then he lowered the nose of the helicopter and headed toward the *Concord*. He was not flying this gomer to the hospital. Switching to Pri-Fly frequency, he said, "Seven-Five inbound at twenty-five."

Red Barber reached for the microphone and said, "Roger, Seven-Five. Your, signal Charlie on arrival. Do you have the wounded crewmen onboard?"

"Negative, Boss," he answered. "Dr. Davenport was wounded during the pickup. He lost a little blood, but he's okay. We also have a wounded prisoner of war onboard. Please have the Marines and Mr. Jack Warner meet us on the flight deck. This bastard tried to blow us out of the sky with two grenades."

"Roger, Seven-Five, call one mile with gear," Barber said and reached for the red telephone that would connect him with the bridge. He explained the situation to Captain Streeper. "Yes, Skipper, it looks like Commander Colby's bringing the *Concord* her first prisoner of war. The gook tried to grenade the chopper. I'd better go down to the flight deck and keep Tom from shooting the CIA agent after he lands." Barber reached for his blue baseball cap and raced down the twelve ladders to the flight deck.

THIRTY

Alpha Strike

Tom walked into the hospital and stopped at Chief Felter's desk. He grinned at the Senior Chief and said, "I'd like to pay my respects to Dr. Davenport. Is he well enough to receive visitors?"

"Yes, Commander," Felter said and led Tom to a small hospital room. Commander Jim Davenport wore green pajama pants and a bright orange University of Tennessee sweat shirt. He lay on his stomach reading the *Stars & Stripes* newspaper.

"I like your uniform, doc," Tom said and sat in a chair near the bed. "How're they treating you in this place?"

"The food is lousy, and I'm freezing my ass off," Davenport complained.

"Well, I have something that will cheer you up," Tom said and handed Davenport a small squadron patch. On the yellow patch was a green dog with three heads. "Dr. Jim, you're hereby an honorary member of the Sea Devils, and we'd like for you to fly SAR missions with us."

"God, that's a mean looking dog," Davenport said as he gazed at the squadron patch. "Does he have a name?"

"Yes, his name is Cerberus. He's the dog that guards the gates of Hades."

"Senior Chief, this is a very special occasion for me to be made a member of the world-famous Sea Devil combat rescue squadron," Daven-

224

port said. "Do we have something appropriate to celebrate this very special day?"

"Yes, doctor," Felter said as he unlocked a cabinet and produced three small bottles of medicinal bourbon. He handed a bottle to Tom and Dr. Davenport. He unscrewed the top to his bottle and said, "Gentlemen, a toast. To Dr. Jim and the Sea Devil rescue squadron. May you have many successes." He raised the bottle to his lips and emptied it in three swallows. "Now, if you'll excuse me, I have to get back on duty," he said. He walked out of the room and closed the door behind him.

"Chief Felter and I have been together a long time, Tom," Davenport said. "He was a farm boy in west Tennessee before he joined this man's Navy."

"Are you in much pain, Jim?"

"No, Felter put enough morphine in my butt to last a week. I just get mad as hell when I think about that gook. He was willing to commit suicide to blow us out of the sky. What was he, a Viet Cong?"

"I don't know. He was probably a North Vietnamese regular who infiltrated the South and became a trusted agent of the CIA. They just love to blow-up our helicopters. The Captain put Mr. Warner and the gook on the evening COD for Da Nang. I'm sure glad they're off the ship."

"Me, too," Davenport agreed and sipped the bourbon.

"Doc, I heard that the Air Group is planning a big alpha strike on the POL tanks near Haiphong tomorrow. There are a lot of SAM's in that area, so they'll probably be needing our services."

"Sure wish that I was able to fly crew with your team," Davenport said as he shook Tom's hand. "Thanks for the squadron patch, and good luck."

"So long, Jim," Tom said and closed the door. He walked back into Chief Felter's office and said, "I'm putting Dr. Davenport in for the Silver Star medal."

"Thanks, Commander, I really appreciate that. Dr. Jim deserves it. Come back and see us any time," Felter said as Tom walked out of the hospital and climbed the ladders to Pri-Fly.

Red Barber was sitting in his Pri-Fly chair reading *Stars & Strips.* "What brings you up to Pri-Fly?" he asked.

"Boss, I'd like some time off to visit with friends in Manila while we're in Cubi," Tom said and thought about Ann Curtis.

"You can have off all the time you need. Beth's flying to Manila on the 22nd. We have reservations at the Army-Navy Club Hotel."

"I also have reservations there," Tom said. "Would you like to fly across Manila Bay to the Army-Navy Club in the SAR helo? It'll save you a four-hour car ride around the bay and through the jungle."

"No thanks, the plane guard Officer-In-Charge (OIC), Jack Rand, is gonna fly me over in the two-charlie helo."

"Boss, I don't trust those two-charlie helicopters. I wish you'd ride over with me in the HH-3. I'll even let you ride shotgun."

"I'm gonna ride shotgun with Jack Rand. It's all settled, Tom."

"Roger, Boss, new subject. I'd like to pre-position Seven-Five up to the *Waddell* before the Alpha strike in the morning. That way we'd be within twenty to thirty miles if a jet gets hit."

"How'd you hear about the Alpha strike?

"On the mess deck," Tom grinned. "It just makes sense to be as close as possible to the action if a pilot needs to be picked up."

"It does sound like a good idea, Tom. I'll have to clear it through the Captain and CAG. For some reason, CAG Brown doesn't like helicopters."

"I'll tell you one thing, Boss. CAG's gonna fall in love with our angry flying-palm-trees if he ever needs to be rescued from those North Vietnamese junks. I heard that the North Vietnamese military are offering the junk's ten-thousand-dollars in gold for every pilot they capture."

"Good God, I didn't realize the reward was that high. No wonder they fight so hard to capture our pilots. After the COD gets back from Da Nang, I'll talk to the Captain and let you know about positioning Seven-Five up to the *Waddell*."

"Thanks, Boss, I'll be in the wardroom," Tom said as he walked out of Pri-Fly and started down the ladders. *It's a Commander's night to fly,* Tom thought as he gazed at the full moon.

Tennis Court
Hickam AFB
Honolulu, Hawaii

Ann Curtis and Kim Ellis played tennis on the number one court near the Hickam Officer's Club. "Forty serving thirty, set point," Ann called as she pitched the yellow tennis ball high above her head. She slammed her racket into the ball and sent a rocket serve toward Kim Ellis. Kim took one step to her right and returned the ball.

"Damn," Kim swore as the ball struck the top of the net and fell back on her side of the court. "Good game, Ann," she said as she walked to the side of the court and wiped her face with the towel.

"Let's go over to the Sea Breeze and have a cold Mai Tai," Ann said, "and I'll tell you about our trip to the Philippines."

"Okay," Kim said as she gathered her tennis rackets and followed Ann to the Thunderbird. Ann started the car and turned the air-conditioner to maximum cold. The blast of cold air was a welcome relief after two hours of tennis in the late afternoon Hawaiian sun.

"Have you heard from Joe Blackwell?" Ann asked as she parked the Thunderbird.

"Yes," Kim answered as they walked toward the club. "He wrote that the *Shiloh* probably won't get to the Philippines until after the first of the year."

"That's too bad, I know you would enjoy seeing Joe again."

"I don't think Joe was all that thrilled with me. It was probably a one-night stand for Joe."

"Well, that'll give us more time to double up on Tom," Ann said.

"Do you really think it's a good idea?"

"Hell, yes," Ann said. "Tom told me that his fantasy was to make love to two women. I told him that you and I would meet him in Hong Kong. So we'll surprise him and move up the date to the Philippines. You and I will be a nice Christmas present for Tom?"

"Were you able to get adjoining rooms?"

"Yes, darling," Ann cooed and waved to the waitress. "Please bring us two more Mai Tai's." She turned back to Kim. "Did you know that Tom was wounded?"

"Oh God, no!" Kim said. "What happened?"

"It wasn't serious. Tom saved some major's life, and was wounded in his left arm on the way to the bunker. Father nominated him for the Air Force Cross medal."

"Sounds like Tom is a hero," Kim agreed.

"Yes, darling, Tom is a hero. I can hardly wait to make love to our handsome hero," Ann licked her lips and sipped the second Mai Tai.

"Me, too," Kim said and sipped her Mai Tai. She looked across the table at her friend, "This will be a Christmas that Tom Colby will remember for the rest of his life."

USS Belknap
North SAR Station
Gulf of Tonkin

Lieutenant Commander Robert Wilson and Lieutenant Terry Fox sat in the combat information center on the *Belknap* and listened to the air briefing. *Belknap* was the flag ship of Commodore Fillmore. Her station was in the northern part of the Gulf between PIRAZ and Yankee Station. Her missiles protected the aircraft carrier and other ships in the area from MiG attacks. Her secondary mission was to rescue Navy and Air Force pilots who were shot down during attacks on North Vietnam.

Bob listened intently as the briefing officer explained the Alpha strike of 90 aircraft from the *Concord* and Air Force that would hit the POL tanks at Haiphong. The area around Haiphong was ringed with Surface to Air Missiles (SAM's) and anti-aircraft batteries. *Jesus, I would hate to be flying those A-1's and A-4's*, Bob thought.

The Kaman H-2B helicopter was in top shape and ready for action. Bob and Terry had practiced the tactics that he and Tom Colby had discussed in the gedunk at NAS Ream Field. Bob had qualified three of the combat air crewmen as rescue swimmers. He had a feeling that the Alpha strike would be their first taste of combat. He knew that his SAR crew was ready.

THIRTY-ONE

Rescue of CAG Brown

USS Waddell
PIRAZ Station
Gulf of Tonkin

Tom Colby held the map of the North Vietnam coastline while Tim flew the helicopter toward the PIRAZ Station. They had launched from the *Concord* at four-thirty that morning for the hour's flight to the *Waddell*. They would be on station when CAG Brown led the first flight of twenty A-4's against the oil storage depot in Haiphong at 5:30. "Tim, I hope we don't have to cross that beach today," Tom said as he studied the anti-aircraft and SAM sites the intelligence officer had marked on their map.

"We shouldn't have to, Commander, since Haiphong's so close to the Gulf. If anyone gets hit, they should make it to the water."

"Give the *Waddell* a call and let them know we're entering their radar control zone."

"Yes, sir," Tim said and switched the radio to the *USS Waddell* frequency. He pressed the mike and said, "Sentry, this is Sea Devil Seven-Five on your one-seven-eight radial at fifty-five, over."

"Roger position, Seven-Five," the air controller said. "Squawk zero-zero-seven-one, over."

Tom switched the IFF/SIF channel to 0071 and gave a thumb's-up. Tim pressed the mike switch and said, "Seven-Five squawking."

"Roger squawk, your steer to Sentry is zero-zero-five, over."

"Roger steer," Tim said and turned the helicopter three degrees to the right. "She must be steaming away from the beach," he said and stared through the windshield at the black night. Thousands of stars cluttered the early morning sky.

Tom saw the red running light of a ship at his two o'clock position. He looked at the brief sheet on his knee pad and switched the TACAN channel. The bearing needle made a complete sweep of the dial and steadied on a bearing of 025 degrees. The mileage indicator was showing 22 miles. Tom pressed the mike and said, "Sentry, this is helo Seven-Five. Request frequency shift to Red Baron, over."

"Roger, Seven-Five, frequency change approved, out."

"That's the *Belknap*," Tom said pointing toward the red light. "My buddy, Bob Wilson, has a Hukie-Two helicopter detachment aboard her." He switched the UHF channel and said, "Red Baron, this is Sea Devil Seven-Five, over."

"Aircraft calling Red Baron, say again side number," the *Belknap* air controller said.

"Roger, Red Baron, this is Navy helo, Seven-Five. How do you read me?" Tom asked.

"Loud and clear, Seven-Five, go ahead your message, over."

"Let me speak to the H-2 SAR helo pilot, please."

"Stand by, sir," the controller said. "I think he's in CIC."

"I have the aircraft," Tom said as he took the controls and turned right to circle the *Belknap*. "I have a feeling that we're going to need the H-2 to back us up today. Bob's one of the best rescue helo pilots in the business."

"Seven-Five, this is Red Baron," the *Belknap* controller said.

"Seven-Five, go ahead," Tom said.

"This is the H-2 pilot, BW," Bob Wilson said.

"Morning Commander Bob, this is TC," Tom said into the mike. "Suggest you get airborne ASAP and rendezvous with me over PRIAZ."

"Roger that," Bob said. "See you in fifteen minutes, out."

USS Concord
Yankee Station

CAG Dick Brown loved the A-4 Skyhawk. He had flown 105 combat missions in the attack jet, and she always brought him home safely. He sat in the cockpit and looked through the windshield past the bow of the flight deck into the blackness beyond. He hated night catapult shots. So many things could go wrong as the aircraft was hurled down the cat. He glanced at the standby gyro. He checked the engine gauges, they were all in the green areas marked on the instruments. He reached between his legs and felt the position of the alternate firing handle for the ejection seat.

The taxi director gave the signal to come forward. CAG released the brake and eased the throttle forward. He felt the jolt as the A-4 mated with the waiting shuttle. The jet was locked to the catapult. The carrier began to turn into the wind. The flight deck crew leaned into the 50 knot wind as the ship steadied on a launch course.

The launch director held his wand over his head and gave CAG the wind-up signal. CAG pushed the throttle to the forward stop with his left hand and curled his fingers around the catapult grip. He glanced quickly at the gauges, and saw that everything was go. He placed his head back in the headrest and flipped the exterior-light switch on the catapult grip.

The catapult officer saw the light on top of the tail come on. He swung his yellow wand in a long arc pointing down the flight deck. The catapult fired and CAG was flying. Five seconds later, the number two catapult fired CAG's wingman. The other strike aircraft taxied forward to the catapults as the number three and four catapults fired at five-second intervals. The Alpha strike had started.

PIRAZ Station
Gulf of Tonkin

Tom flew the HH-3 in a lazy race track pattern, three-hundred-feet above the *Waddell* as the H-2 Sea Sprite joined on his right wing. In the early morning light, Tom could read the numbers - **22**, painted on the tail. The sun would be rising in another 10 minutes. Tom pressed his mike and said, "Two-Two, switch to Ream frequency."

In the cockpit of the H-2, Lieutenant Commander Bob Wilson told his copilot, Lieutenant Terry Fox, to switch to 236.4. Fox set the numbers in the UHF radio and clicked his mike twice. Bob pressed the mike and said, "Two-Two in. Is that you in the Air Force Jolly Green Giant, Tom?"

"Roger that, Two-Two, stay on my wing. Our services may be needed soon. Switch back to Sentry." Bob clicked the mike twice and switched the UHF radio back to the *Waddell* channel. The two helicopters flew toward the beach as the Alpha attack roared toward Haiphong at twenty-two-thousand feet.

Alpha Strike
22,000 feet above Haiphong
Democratic Republic of Vietnam

CAG Dick Brown had inspected the aerial photographs of the four SAM sites that ringed the POL complex at Haiphong. Each site had six SA-2 surface-to-air missiles. The missiles sat on their trailer launchers. The trailers were arranged in circle around a control van with the radar antenna. The secret of defeating the SAM was to destroy or jam the radar. The F-4, nicknamed the Wild Weasel, could protect itself from SAM's by using the radar homing and warning instruments, called RHAW. The F-4 would provoke the SAM site to turn on their radar. Then the F-4 would launch their Shrike missile that flew down the beam of the enemy radar and destroyed the SAM site. Four of the Wild Weasels flew in the Alpha strike. They would attack first.

Haiphong Radar Defense Base
Democratic Republic of Vietnam

Captain Huey Toon sat behind the radar operator and stared at the large radar screen. He counted twenty green blips over the northern part of the Gulf of Tonkin. The operator alerted Hanoi Air Base to have the MiG's ready for intercept. Huey was the brother of North Vietnam's first air ace, Major Victor Toon. Yesterday, his brother had scored his sixth kill as the American jets circled around Haiphong and attacked the railroad yard in Hanoi. The Haiphong SAM site had fired two missiles and turned off the radar. The radar tacticians were afraid of the American missile that flew down the beam of the radar.

Toon sipped the strong green tea and finished his rice breakfast. He seriously doubted that the Yankee missiles had this capability. Today, the radar would not be turned off. The Haiphong defense team would fire their missiles and drive the Yankee pilots from the sky before they reached Hanoi. He watched as the fire-control radar operator pushed the red button below the radar screen. A siren wailed in the distance, warning personnel to stay clear of the blast area of the missiles. "Captain Toon, the missiles are ready," he reported as his hand hovered over the fire control button.

"Wait until the jets start turning in toward Hanoi," Toon ordered. "I want you to hit an American jet with each missile you fire, comrade."

Alpha Strike
22,000 feet above Haiphong
Democratic Republic of Vietnam

CAG Brown heard the steady RHAW warning in the earphones of his helmet. The Haiphong SAM radar was painting the flight. He glanced over at the F-4 Phantom that was flying on his wing. He tapped on his helmet with his right hand and saluted. This signal had been used for 75 years in Naval aviation to pass the lead from leader to wingman. Lieutenant Tony Parker was flying the Phantom. He returned CAG's salute and gently added throttle to move up and take lead of the flight. Naval Flight Officer, Lieutenant Jim Ryan, sat in the back seat of the F-4 operating the electronic warfare gear. Tony watched as CAG slowed the A-4 then slid under his aircraft to emerge on his right wing. This maneuver was performed in the other three sections of the flight. Now the Wild Weasel aircraft were leading the flight. Tony turned the flight toward the beach. He pressed the mike and said, "Strike ops, Alpha flight, feet dry."

"Roger, feet dry. Good hunting," the strike operations controller said.

Tony raised his left arm to signal CAG to move over to left echelon. CAG flew under Tony's aircraft again and assumed his position on the left wing of the F-4 between Tony and the number three aircraft. Tony clicked his mike switch twice. He rolled the Phantom into a 120 degree break and dived on the SAM target. The A-4's followed his attack at one-second intervals. Tony pressed the intercom switch and said, "You can fire at will, Jim. I'd like to take out that radar before they launch a missile."

Ryan pressed his head to the hood of the radar set. He pressed the fire button and said, "Shrike, away."

* * *

Captain Toon sat in the control van and watched the aircraft turn toward the beach. "Get ready to fire, comrade," he said to the radar controller. Then he saw another blip emerge from the lead aircraft and accelerate toward the van. "**FIRE! FIRE!**" Toon yelled as he raised the trap door beneath his chair and dropped into the bunker below. The radar tactician launched two missiles then turned and ran toward the bunker. The Shrike missile exploded when it hit the top of the radar antenna. The explosion vaporized the van before the controller could reach the bunker. The remaining four SAM's were useless without the guidance of the radar.

* * *

CAG was diving through 12,000 feet when Tony yelled over the radio, "**SAM LAUNCH! SAM IN THE AIR.**" CAG saw the POL tanks fill the bomb sight. He pushed the switch that released six, 500 pound bombs and turned toward the second SAM. He saw Lieutenant Parker dive toward the first SAM. The F-4 went into afterburner and accelerated to Mach-1. CAG wished this stubby little Skyhawk had the speed of the Phantom. Still, he had a chance of defeating the SAM. He dived and twisted the Skyhawk then pulled six G's as he tried to out-maneuver the missile.

"**I'm going to make it**!" CAG yelled into his oxygen mask. "**I'm going to beat that damn missile!**" The SAM exploded in blast of thunder that engulfed the little Skyhawk, blinding and deafening CAG. He was semi-conscious as he struggled to regain control of the aircraft. His vision returned and he saw the cockpit full of warning lights. He battled the controls and stopped the spin. He was falling toward the Gulf, but he knew from the feel of the controls that the A-4 was dying. He scanned the cockpit gauges and saw the hydraulic pressure falling. *This bird's not going to make it back to the ship*, CAG thought. He looked around for his wingman and saw the black smoke rising from the ruptured oil tanks.

Pretty good bombing for an old fart, he thought and switch the radio to guard channel. "**MAYDAY**! **MAYDAY**! **MAYDAY**!" He yelled, "Alpha One ejecting over Haiphong harbor."

Tom was 12 miles from Haiphong when he heard CAG broadcast the mayday. He pressed the mike and said, "Let's go get him, Bob." He heard the double click of Bob's radio as he lowered the nose of the big HH-3 and accelerated to 140 knots. At this speed they could reach the crash site within five to six minutes.

"It's time call in the Spads," Tom said to Tim as he thought about the junks in Haiphong Harbor. They would be fighting each other for the $10,000 reward for the capture of an American pilot. Tom keyed the mike and said, "Strike ops, Seven-Five and Red Baron helo enroute to pick up Alpha One. Request Spads buster to crash site for close-air support."

"Roger, Seven-Five, Spads will be on station in five minutes," the strike operations controller said. Four A-1 Skyraiders had launched after the Alpha strike. They were orbiting the Gulf, 20 miles south of Haiphong at 10,000 feet.

*   *   *

CAG Brown struggled to move the flight controls of the crippled A-4. Lieutenant Chris Sawyer, his wingman, joined on CAG's right wing. Chris keyed his mike and said, "Good bombing, Boss. You started a beautiful fire down there."

CAG looked out of the cockpit and saw Sawyer in a tight formation on his right wing. His left arm was hurting like hell. He saw blood dripping down his elbow. *Must be some shrapnel from the SAM*, CAG thought. He pressed the mike and said, "Chris, this bird is getting hard to fly, and my left arm is bleeding like a stuck pig. Look me over. Can you see any fire?"

"Roger, Boss," Sawyer said. "Fire's coming out the tailpipe. Recommend you eject before she blows. I'll follow you down and stay with you until the chopper arrives."

"Thanks Chris, I'm punching out now," CAG said as he felt the hydraulic pressure go. The A-4 started a slow roll to the right. He hunched down and pulled the hand grips to release the canopy. As the canopy blew away, a hurricane wind whipped through the cockpit and ripped the briefing charts from his knee pad. CAG reached up with both hands, grasped the face curtain and pulled it down over his head in a swift motion. Instantly he was shot out of the cockpit in the Martin-Baker seat. The seat harness automatically released, and a small explosive charge kicked CAG free of the chair. The parachute deployed and the bone-jarring jolt slowed his downward plunge. CAG swung like a pendulum beneath the billowing parachute. He looked down and saw his A-4 plunge into the harbor. He also saw two helicopters racing toward the spot where his Skyhawk splashed. He hoped that Commander Colby could get to him before the damn junks got there. He was startled as Lieutenant Chris Sawyer's A-4 zoomed by his parachute and did a victory roll.

Chris rolled the A-4 over and dived on the junks in the harbor. He had four bombs remaining on the pylon underneath his wings. He released his first bomb at 1500 feet. The bomb was a direct hit and blew the wood-hull junk into a thousand pieces. He pulled the Skyhawk up into a 5-G climb and locked on the second junk as he came over the top to the loop. His bomb was short by 10 feet, but the concussion overturned the junk.

The Vietnamese anti-aircraft batteries locked onto the A-4 as Chris climbed out of his second bombing run. Tracers rose ahead of him in a shimmering curtain of fire. He felt thumps hitting the tail section of his jet. The engine flamed out and he saw the fire-warning light glow red on the instrument panel. Chris swung the A-4 into a hard right turn and pointed the nose toward the Gulf. He was afraid to drop the remaining bombs. He might hit the rescue helicopters. Chris depressed the mike and yelled, "MAYDAY! MAYDAY! MAYDAY! Red Eagle 307 ejecting."

CAG was 500 feet above the water when Chris ejected from the burning Skyhawk. He concentrated on preparing himself for a parachute landing in the water. He reached up for the quick disconnect fittings that would release him from the parachute. The moment he felt his feet touch the water, he pushed the quick-release fittings with all his might. He screamed as pain shot through his elbow up to the shoulder. The plunge carried him 10 feet below the surface of the water. He pulled the toggles that inflated the Mae West life vest and shot to the surface.

The large green helicopter with the numbers 775 painted on the side hovered over CAG as he surfaced. Petty Officer Steve Jackman jumped from the helicopter and splashed into the water near him. CAG watched in shock as the helicopter lower its nose and flew away, just skimming the top of the water. Jackman surfaced beside CAG, raised his face mask and said, "Are you wounded, CAG?"

"Yeah, I took some shrapnel in my left arm. Where in the hell did the damn helicopter go?"

"Commander Colby's making a circular approach for a pickup in two minutes, sir," Jackman said as he snapped his torso harness to CAG's. "Lower the visor on your helmet because the wind from the rotor blades will blind you."

CAG lowered his visor as he saw Jackman replace his face mask. He looked up and saw Lieutenant Sawyer's parachute descending toward the harbor. The H-2 helicopter flew toward him.

The water around CAG became a hurricane as the big HH-3 dropped into a 10-foot hover. Airman Lewis pitched the cable to Jackman. He watched as Jackman snapped the cable to his torso harness, then yelled into his hot microphone, "**CLEAR TO LIFT, COMMANDER**." Tom yanked up on the collective and jerked the two men out of the water as the enemy shells exploded around them. CAG and Jackman dangled on the hoist cable, 30 feet behind the helicopter, as Tom accelerated through 100 knots. When they were 15 miles from the beach, Tom slowed to 40 knots, and Lewis reeled the two men inside. Jackman insisted that CAG lay on the stretcher as he examined his wounds.

Jackman put on his flight helmet and plugged in the cords. He pressed the intercom mike and said, "CAG's wounded in his left arm, and he may have a fracture. I'm putting on a temporary splint, Commander."

"Roger, Jackman," Tom said. He unstrapped the seat belt and walked back to the cabin. Kneeling beside the stretcher, he plugged CAG's helmet cord into the helicopter intercom. "Welcome aboard Sea Devil helo rescue service, CAG. We're about twenty minutes from the *Waddell*. She has a doctor onboard who can patch you up. The *Concord's* over an hour away. I'd like to stay on station in case someone else in your flight needs our services."

CAG Brown nodded in agreement. He pressed the mike and said, "I agree, take me to the *Waddell*." Then he reached over with his right hand and grasped Tom's hand. "You really scared the hell out of me, but thanks for saving my life, Tom. Did the other helicopter pick up my wingman?"

"Yes, sir. My buddy, LCDR Bob Wislon, is pilot of the H-2. He will pick up your wingman and land on *Waddell* after us," Tom said and hurried back to the cockpit. They landed on the fantail of the *Waddell* as Lieutenant Commander Bob Wilson hoisted Lieutenant Chris Sawyer out of Haiphong Harbor. The A-1 Skyraiders arrived on station. Their twenty-milimeter guns and 2.75-inch rockets scattered the junks. Alpha flight continued to dive bomb the oil storage tanks and black smoke billowed into the sky.

THIRTY-TWO

R & R In The Philippines

USS Concord
Yankee Station

CAG Dick Brown sat in Pri-Fly beside Commander Red Barber and watched the recovery of the strike aircraft. This was the last combat mission for the *Concord* on this line period. After the aircraft landed, the carrier would turn west for the thirty-eight hour trip across the South China Sea and six days of rest and recuperation at Subic Bay. CAG stared out the large glass window of Pri-Fly as the A-4 Skyhawk's tailhook caught the last arresting-cable called, the number four-wire. The Skyhawk was jerked to a stop on the wet flight deck.

"**DOUBLE-DAMN**!" CAG yelled as he picked up his binoculars and read the pilots name that was printed below the canopy, LTJG. TOM FORD. "Red, I'm gonna schedule Mr. Ford for several sessions of Pri-Fly duty," CAG said. "That's the third time he's caught the four-wire this week." Throughout the deployment, each of the junior aviators took his turn in Pri-Fly, standing four-hour watches and observing the landings of the Air Group.

"I'd be glad to have Mr. Ford up here, CAG," Barber said as he reached for the microphone and cleared the A-1 Spads to land. "Sure hope we can get the Spads and the helo aboard before Captain Streeper runs into that next rain squall."

239

"I just hope we have some nice weather in Cubi," CAG said as he adjusted the sling on his left arm. His arm was not broken, but he had received several deep lacerations when the SAM exploded near his aircraft. Dr. Davenport had applied a soft cast to immobilize CAG's arm. An itch near his elbow was begging to be scratched.

"Too bad you won't be able to fly to Cubi Point with the Air Group tomorrow."

"Like hell, I won't!" CAG exclaimed. "I'm riding shotgun on the COD. I'll have a cold beer waiting for you when the carrier docks at Cubi Point."

"Thanks, Dick," The last Spad was turning downwind, when Barber ordered the plane guard helicopter to land after the Spad trapped.

"Is the SAR helo still up at PIRAZ station?" CAG asked.

"Yes, CAG, Tom probably started heading south after the last aircraft left the target. Did you enjoy your first ride in the Sea Devil helo?"

"Red, those great guys saved my ass. The North Vietnamese artillery put five shells within one hundred feet of the chopper. If Tom had stayed in the hover another twenty seconds, they'd have blown us out of the sky. Petty Officer Jackman hooked me to his torso harness, then Tom literally jerked us out of the water. Jackman and I were dangling thirty feet behind the chopper while Tom evaded the artillery shells. I don't mind telling you that I was scared to death."

"The hell you say," Barber laughed.

"Red, those helo pilots are truly heroes. I've recommended the Navy Cross for Colby and Arnold, and the Silver Star for the crewmen. Was it your idea to position them on the *Waddell*?"

"No, I can't take credit for that. Tom came up with the idea of being as close to the action as possible and using the Spads for close air support."

"Those old Spads were truly a beautiful sight," CAG smiled. "Two big junks were headed toward my wingman when the Spads rolled into their attack. The flight leader took out the first junk, and his wingman blew up the second one. Who was flying the Spads?"

"Commander Bud Reynolds was leading the flight, and Lieutenant Bob Doane was his wingman."

"Well, I'm recommending the Air Medal for both of them," CAG said as he tried to scratch the itch inside the cast with a long Q-tip.

The radio speaker blared, "War Chief, this is Sea Devil Seven-Five on your three-two-zero radial at sixty-two."

Barber reached to lower the volume and said, "Roger, Seven-Five, my head is two-seven-zero. Your signal is Charlie on arrival."

"Roger, Charlie," Tom said.

"That's Tom and Ensign Arnold," Barber said to CAG. "They'll be aboard in about thirty minutes."

"Tom reminds me so much of his dad," CAG said remembering the days when he and Red Barber had flown the F-2 Banshee jets in Admiral Thomas Colby's squadron. "I should send the Admiral a message and brief him on my rescue. Have you heard if the flag ship will be in Subic Bay for Christmas?"

"No sir, I haven't," Barber answered. "Operations probably has their schedule for the next thirty days."

CAG reached for a pad of paper and began to draft a message. "Are you and Beth staying at the Army-Navy Club while we're at Cubi?"

"Yes, sir, Lieutenant Commander Jack Rand's flying me across Manila Bay in the H-two-charlie."

"Red, I wish you wouldn't fly in that damn hukie-two. The ship's COD will be on the beach at Cubi Point. I'll fly you to Manila International airport in the C-one."

"God, you're beginning to sound like Tom Colby. I've been riding shotgun with Rand for three months. I can even fly the helicopter. If something goes wrong, you just have to remember to bottom the collective pitch control and autorotate to a nice, soft landing."

"Well, I can see that Jack Rand has you brainwashed about his helicopters," CAG said as he tore off a sheet of paper and climbed out of the high chair.

I enjoyed your visit, CAG," Barber said, "Be very careful and don't fall down one of the ladders and break your other arm."

"See you at dinner, Red," CAG said as he walked out of Pri-Fly and down the nine ladders to his office. He was looking forward to six days of rest on the beach in the Philippines. *It will be great to see Beth Barber again*, he thought.

241

Seventh Fleet Flag Office
USS Providence, CLG-6
Tonkin Gulf

Vice Admiral Thomas Colby looked up from his desk when the communications messenger opened the door and walked inside. He stopped in front of the large wood desk and stood at attention. "Excuse me, Admiral," the messenger said, "I have a message for you from the *USS Concord*, sir."

Colby stopped writing and looked up at the tall, black sailor. He read the name 'JONES' stenciled above the left pocket of his shirt. "Is it good news or bad news, Jones?"

"Oh, it's great news, Admiral," Seaman Jones answered. "It's all about your son's rescue of the Carrier Air Wing Commander."

"Well, that does sound like good news," Colby said and reached for the folder. "Thanks, Jones, you're dismissed." Jones did an about-face, marched from the room and softly closed the door behind him. Colby opened the folder and read:

SECRET
ROUTINE 192246Z DEC 65

FM: USS CONCORD
TO: COMMANDER SEVENTH FLEET

BT
SUBJ: PERSONAL FROM CAG DICK BROWN
1. CONGRATS ON YOUR THIRD STAR, BOSS. WHEN IS THE WETTING DOWN PARTY?
2. STORY OF MY RESCUE: CAG BROWN TANGLED WITH A SAM (AND LOST) DURING THE ALPHA STRIKE. EJECTION FROM SKYHAWK WAS ROUTINE. MARTIN-BAKER SEAT WORKED AS ADVERTISED. FIVE MINUTES AFTER PARACHUTING INTO HAIPHONG HARBOR, I WAS RESCUED BY AN AIR FORCE HELICOPTER (HH-3) FLOWN BY THE ELITE U. S. NAVY COMBAT RESCUE TEAM:
    CDR. TOM COLBY - PILOT IN COMMAND
    ENS. TIM ARNOLD - COPILOT
    PO3 STEVE JACKMAN - FIRST CREWMAN
    AN ROY LEWIS - SECOND CREWMAN

HELO MADE A FAST APPROACH TO SURVIVOR. PETTY OFFICER JACKMAN (WEARING FACE MASK AND SWIM FINS) JUMPED FROM THE HELO TO CHECK FOR INJURIES AND TO ENSURE THAT FIGHTER PILOT WAS CLEAR OF HIS PARACHUTE.

MEANWHILE HELO LEFT THE AREA TO AVOID THE ENEMY ARTILLERY FIRE FROM THE BEACH. HELO APPROACHED AGAIN AND DROPPED THE RESCUE CABLE. PO3 JACKMAN CONNECTED HIMSELF AND ME TO THE CABLE WHILE INTENSE ENEMY ARTILLERY FIRE RINGED THE HELO. TOM JERKED US OUT OF THE WATER AND LEFT THE AREA IN EXCESS OF 100 KNOTS. WHAT A RIDE! WHAT A RIDE!

3. THE FLIGHT CREW IS RECOMMENDED FOR THE FOLLOWING AWARDS:

CDR. TOM COLBY - NAVY CROSS
ENS. TIM ARNOLD - NAVY CROSS
PO3 STEVE JACKMAN - SILVER STAR
AN ROY LEWIS - SILVER STAR

4. CAG BROWN IS BUYING DRINKS AT THE ARMY-NAVY CLUB, 22 TO 25 DEC. HOPE YOU CAN MAKE IT.

WARM REGARDS, COMMANDER DICK BROWN

ET

SECRET

Admiral Colby pressed a button that connected him with the Chief of Staff, and said, "John, come in for a minute."

"Yes, Admiral, right away," Captain John Roy Lester said as he grabbed the notebook and walked into the Flag Office.

"Have a seat, John," Admiral Colby said and handed him a folder.

"Thank you, Admiral," Lester said as he sat in the chair beside the desk and opened the folder. He skimmed the message and then read it again in detail. "Commander Colby has certainly distinguished himself and the SAR crew in the combat zone. This brings their rescue total to forty-three, without a combat loss to the SAR detachment."

"That's right," Colby said amazed that Captain Lester was keeping such an accurate tally of the Sea Devil rescues. "Please re-address the message to USS Shiloh, CINCPACFLT, CNO and the White House."

"Aye, aye, sir," Lester said as he rose to leave the office.

"John, is Shiloh still playing with the Russian submarines in the Sea of Japan?"

"Yes, Admiral," Lester said.

"I'm getting damn tired of our our SAR pilots having to beg a helicopter from the Air Force when we have three SAR helicopters on the *Shiloh*. Send the carrier a message that I want those helicopters delivered to Cubi Point by the 25th of December."

"Will do, sir. Anything else Admiral?"

"What's on our schedule for Christmas?"

"Nothing special," Lester said and glanced at his notebook. "We'll be cruising around Yankee Station."

"That's what I thought. Schedule us for a port call at Subic Bay on the 24th of December. You and I might as well go over to the Army-Navy Club and drink some of CAG Dick Brown's scotch."

"Yes, sir," Lester said and walked from the Flag Office to inform the Commanding Officer. Christmas in the Philippines would be welcomed by the Flag Ship crew.

The Oval Office
The White House
Washington, D.C.

The President was alone in the Oval Office when he read CAG Brown's message to Seventh Fleet. *It was damn nice of Thomas to forward this message to me*, he thought as he reached for the telephone and dialed Margaret Colby's number. When she answered, he said, "Good afternoon, Margaret. I just received a message from Thomas, and thought I'd give you a call and let you know that he and Tom are fine."

"Thank you, Lyndon," Margaret said. "Did the message say where they would be for Christmas?"

"Tom's on the *USS Concord*. The carrier will be at Cubi Point in the Philippines. Thomas will probably take the Flag Ship to Subic Bay for Christmas."

"I thought Tom was on the *USS Shiloh*," Margaret said.

"Well, apparently Tom's flying SAR missions from the *Concord*. In fact, he just rescued the Air Wing Commander and was nominated for the Navy Cross. You're not supposed to know that. Can you keep a secret?"

"Don't try to bullshit me, Lyndon!" Margaret said with alarm. "The United States Navy does not recommend a pilot for the Navy Cross unless there was a lot of combat involved. Was Tom wounded?"

"No, darling," the President said. "He flew into Haiphong Harbor and picked-up CAG Brown after he had ejected from his jet. Thomas doesn't say anything about the helicopter being hit by enemy fire. I'm sorry that I upset you so much. I will make some calls about Tom, if you'd like."

"No thanks, Lyndon. I've just been so worried about Tom since he was wounded in Da Nang. I didn't mean to snap at you."

"Well, Tom saved the life of an Air Force pilot during that attack, and General Curtis has recommended him for the Air Force Cross?"

"Is that General Steve Curtis?" She asked.

"Yes, darling, do you know him?"

"Louise and Steve Curtis were our next door neighbors when we were stationed in Hawaii. Steve is Tom's godfather, and their daughter, Ann, was Tom's first girlfriend."

"It's a small world," the President said. "How're you feeling today?

"Much better, thanks. Dr. Woods assigned Lieutenant Commander Paul Thompson as my doctor. He feels that we can get my leukemia back in remission."

"Thank God, I've been praying for you, Margaret."

"You're so nice, Mr. President. I almost forgot to tell you that Tommy is flying his mother, Judy and Jackie Anderson out to the Flying C for Christmas. Tommy said that they would be here before dark on Saturday. Can you come by for a drink?"

"I'll sure try to work it into my schedule," he said and remembered the vivacious Jackie Anderson. "We're flying to the ranch in Texas for Christmas. I'll give you a call if I can make it out Saturday night."

"Good-bye, Lyndon. Thank you for calling and God bless you."

"Good-bye, Margaret," he said and hung up the telephone. Then he remembered he had promised to show Jackie Anderson around Camp David when she came to Washington. That was a promise he planned to keep.

THIRTY-THREE

Crash of H-Two-Charlie Angel

500 feet above Manila Bay
Republic of the Philippines

It was a beautiful tropical morning with unlimited visibility. Tom Colby could see Manila International Airport out the right cockpit window at their two o'clock position. Ann Curtis would land there this afternoon, Tom reminded himself. His overnight bag was stowed in the aftercabin. Ensign Bull Walker sat in the second crewman seat. He and Ensign Tim Arnold would return the HH-3 to the *Concord* and continue to ferry the ship's officers to various locations on the island. Tom had finally convinced CAG Brown to ride in the HH-3. Beside CAG sat the ship's operation officer, Commander George Parker.

Tom flew wing on the H-2C helicopter as they crossed Manila Bay from NAS Cubi Point to the Army-Navy Club. The H-2C, commonly called the Two-Charlie, was a major engineering change from the single engine H-2A/B helicopters. Kaman Aircraft Corporation had added another jet engine, beefed up the main transmission, added a four-bladed tail rotor, and installed an automatic blade fold system. Lieutenant Commander Jack Rand was pilot of the H-2C. Commander Red Barber sat in the copilot's seat. He flew the helicopter. Three of the ship's officers sat in the aftercabin.

Beneath the floor of the cockpit was the electronics compartment. Here the battery was located along with the major electronic components of the aircraft. Miles of electrical wire started in the compartment and ran throughout the fuselage of the helicopter. The screw holding the automatic rotor brake wire to the terminal began to vibrate loose. With each vibration of the helicopter, the screw slowly turned in a counter-clockwise direction. The screw made one last wobble and fell out of its socket. The wires touched, and the automatic rotor brake tried to stop the main rotor from turning.

In the cockpit, Rand notice the red warning light of the automatic rotor brake, and saw the rotor tachometer began to slow down. "**I HAVE THE AIRCRAFT, BOSS**," he yelled into the intercom. He grabbed the controls and applied full throttle to both engines. The tachometer stabilized at 190 revolutions per minute. The rotor brake disk began to glow red, and smoke was blown away in the rotor wash. Rand turned and flew toward the beach. He pressed the mike switch and said, "Seven-Five, this is Four-Two. We have a problem with the automatic rotor brake system. The warning light is on, and RPM is decaying. Do you see any fire or smoke?"

Tom had notice the abrupt heading change toward the beach and turned to maintain wing position. He flew closer to the H-2C and saw smoke coming from the transmission area under the rotor head. "Four-Two, smoke is coming from the transmission area," Tom said into the microphone. "Are you declaring an emergency?"

"Hell yes, Tom," Rand said. "I'm gonna try to get this bird to the beach before the blades cone. Something has happened to the automatic rotor brake system. I have both throttles stop-cocked, and I can only get one hundred and ninety rotor RPM. The blades will cone if the RPM falls below a hundred and fifty."

"Do you have parachutes onboard?" Tom asked.

"Negative parachutes," Rand answered.

The air controller in Pri-Fly listened to the conversation between the two pilots. He pressed the mike switch and said, "Four-Two, this is War Chief Tower, say the nature of your emergency, over."

Tom pressed his mike and said, "War Chief, this is Seven-Five. Four-Two has an emergency with the rotor brake system. He's attempting

247

to land on the beach. Stand by, please." He estimated that they were two miles from the beach. At this speed they would cross the shoreline in less than a minute.

Tim pressed the intercom switch and said, "Commander, tell Mr. Rand to pull the circuit breaker."

Jesus Christ, Tom thought. *That's the first thing Rand should have done.* He pressed the radio switch and said, "Jack, pull the rotor brake circuit breaker."

In the cockpit of the H-2C, Red Barber was staring hypnotically at the red warning light. When he heard Tom's voice on the radio, he reached up to the overhead panel and pulled the circuit breaker. The red light went out. The rotor tachometer climbed back to 207 revolutions per minute. He looked across at Rand and smiled.

"Jesus Christ! Thanks, Tom," Rand yelled into the radio. "The warning light's out and rotor tach is back to normal. I think we're gonna make it. Are we still smoking?"

"It's getting more dense," Tom said as they flew across the beach. "Recommend you make a precautionary landing."

"Don't get too close, Tom," Rand said. "This bird might still come apart. God, I hate to land and get sand into the jets. We are about ten miles from the Army-Navy Club. I'm gonna try to make it to the club heliport unless the smoke gets worse."

"Roger that, Four-Two," Tom said and flew behind the H-2C. "That was quick thinking, Tim," Tom said into the intercom. "You may have saved their butts. I wish the damn fire would go out."

The rotor disk of the automatic rotor brake had heated to a red-hot glow. As it cooled it began to crack along one side. When the crack reached the center of the disk, it broke apart. Centrifugal force hurled the shattered disk outward like a rifle bullet. One section of the disk struck the spar of the number two rotor blade and sliced through it like cutting butter.

Tom watched as the rotor blade was thrown away in a long arc toward the beach and heard Rand yell, "**JESUS CHRIST!**" The helicopter began to vibrate and shake from side to side as the remaining three blades tried to assume an equal share of the load. Rand bottomed the collective to enter autorotation as the rotor head tore apart. Very quickly, the helicopter disintegrated into thousands of small pieces that rained on the beach.

Tom pressed the radio switch and said, "CRASH, CRASH, CRASH! War Chief, this is Seven-Five. Four-Two just crashed on the beach, seven miles north of the Army-Navy Club heliport. Recommend you launch the back-up helicopter with a security force and body bags. I'm going to land on the beach and try to keep the natives away until security arrives, out."

Tom had a sick feeling in the pit of his stomach as he circled the crash site. The body of the fuselage had plowed a deep trench in a green field across the blacktop road from the beach. Filipino natives began to converge on the crash site as Tom landed in the middle of the field near the smoking fuselage. "Jesus Christ, Tim, where did all those people come from so fast?"

"From their grass shacks in the banana groves," Tim answered.

"You have the aircraft," Tom said as he unbuckled this seat belt. "Keep her turning and stay in radio contact with the ship. I'm going to go out there and help CAG, Bull and Commander Parker keep the natives away from the wreckage."

"I have the aircraft, Commander," Tim said as he watched Tom remove his helmet and put on the Sea Devil baseball cap. Tom did not want to look at the bodies of his friends in the twisted fuselage. He walked away from the wreckage toward the road as he saw a police car approaching. The car came to a screeching halt beside Tom. Two very fat men dressed in dark blue uniforms sat in the front seat. The driver wore sergeant stripes on his shirt sleeve. The passenger wore Captain bars on his collar. The sergeant jumped out of the car and ran around to open the Captain's door.

Tom saluted as he addressed the Filipino police officer, "Good morning, Captain, my name's Tom Colby, and we sure do need your help."

Captain Oscar Paz returned Tom's salute and said, "Good morning, Commander. I'm Captain Paz, and this is Sergeant Almazan. How may we be of service?"

"We need guards to keep your people away from the crash site," Tom answered. "Inside that smoking fuselage are five bodies of our shipmates. We will have help arriving from the ship very soon."

Captain Paz spoke very rapidly to Sergeant Almazan in Tagalog. Sergeant Almazan returned to the police car and began to talk on the radio. "We'll have security guards very soon, Commander," Paz said. "Tell me, do you have American cigarette?"

"Yes, Captain," Tom said as he unzipped a pocket of his flight suit and produced a pack of Marlboro cigarettes. He didn't smoke, but he had heard that the Filipino people were very fond of American cigarettes. He had bought two cartons at the ship's store to give away as tips. He handed the pack of cigarettes to Paz and said, "You may keep those, Captain."

"Ah, thank you, Commander," Paz said as he ripped off the top and lit one of the cigarettes. He put the pack in his shirt pocket as Sergeant Almazan finished talking on the radio and walked back around the car.

"Four units will be here soon, Captain," Almazan said looking at the cigarette between Paz's lips.

"Good work, Sergeant," Paz said. "Now go keep those farmers away from the crashed helicopter."

"Yes, Captain," Almazan said as he turned to walk away.

"Sergeant, would you like a cigarette?" Tom asked.

"Oh yes, Commander," Almazan answered as he wheeled around. Tom handed him an unopened pack of Marlboro's. Almazan took the pack of cigarettes and put them in his shirt pocket. He saluted and said, "You are most generous, Commander Colby." Then he turned and ran across the field toward the Filipino's who were walking toward the crash. He blew his whistle and waved for them to stop.

In the distance, Tom heard the wail of sirens and saw four white police cars speeding toward the scene. Captain Paz continued to puff on the cigarette. "Those men in the crashed helicopter were your friends, Commander?"

"Yes, Captain," Tom answered. "One of them was very close to me." He felt a tear trickle down his cheek and turned to looked out across Manila Bay. He saw two dark blue H-2C helicopters flying toward them, then he thought of Beth Barber. She was flying in today to meet her husband at the Army-Navy Club. Tom shook hands with Captain Paz and said, "Thank's for your help, Captain. The Navy will pay for the damage to the farmer's land."

"Sorry about the death of your friends," Paz said and motioned for Almazan to start the car.

Tom watched the car drive away and walked back to the HH-3 with a heavy heart. He strapped into the cockpit as the two helicopters were landing behind him. He saw eight Marines jump from the helicopters and run toward the crash. They were dressed in their camouflage uniforms and were armed with .45 caliber pistols. "Tim, the Marines have landed," Tom said into the intercom. He looked at the clock on the instrument panel. It was 11:45. They had been on the ground for almost an hour. Tom pressed the intercom switch and said, "Jackman, go get Bull and our passengers. I'm ready to clear out of this damn place."

"Yes sir, Commander, I read you loud and clear," Jackman said as he unplugged his helmet cord and ran toward Ensign Walker.

"The ship called, Commander," Tim said. "Captain Streeper wants you to meet him at the Army-Navy Club in short sleeve whites."

"Damn," Tom groaned. "That bastard knows I'm on leave. He wants me to go with him when he notifies Beth Barber that her husband will not fly home anymore. God, I hate to do that."

"We're all strapped in the cabin and ready for takeoff, Commander," Jackman reported over the intercom.

"Thanks, Jackman," Tom said and turned to give Tim the lift signal. Arnold loved to fly the big helicopter. He pulled up the collective, and the HH-3 lifted into a smooth 10 foot hover. Then he lowered the nose and quickly accelerated toward the road. He passed over the police cars at 50 feet and 120 knots. Then he banked into a steep climbing left turn and flew toward the Army-Navy club heliport. The beautiful tropical morning had turned into a sour, rotten day.

Army-Navy Club
Manila
Republic of the Philippines

Tom walked into the Army-Navy Club beside CAG Brown and George Parker. "Gentlemen, I suggest we check these bags and get a cold San Miguel beer," Tom said.

"I second that," CAG Brown said as he motioned for the bell captain. "Will you please take care of our bags and direct us to the bar?" He asked and slipped the captain a five dollar tip.

The bell captain pocketed the money and said, "No sweat, Captain. Your bags will be delivered to your rooms. Please follow me, gentlemen." He whirled around and marched down a long corridor that led to the Warrior's Lounge.

They sat at the bar while CAG ordered three San Miguel beers. CAG sipped the cold beer and turned to Colby, "What happened to the helicopter, Tom?"

"It must have been the damn automatic rotor brake, CAG," Tom answered. "Somehow it malfunctioned and came on in-flight. They got a warning light on the warning panel and decay in rotor RPM. If I had insisted that Jack make a precautionary landing, they would still be alive."

"Tom, I don't want any of this Monday morning quarterback crap," CAG growled. "Jack Rand was the pilot in command of that aircraft, and it was his full responsibility."

"Thanks, CAG," Tom smiled. "I should've offered to let Red Barber fly copilot in the HH-3."

"Tom, it's done. I don't want to hear anymore about it. We must be very positive when we face Beth Barber. God, I hate that chore."

"Me too, CAG," Tom agreed as he took a long drink of the cold beer. "My copilot said that Captain Streeper wanted me to meet him here at the club. I know that he wants me to tag along when he notifies Beth."

Tom felt a pair of soft hands cover his eyes as a female voice said, "Hi, sailor boy. Guess who this is, and you'll win the grand prize."

Tom could smell the fragrant Opium perfume. *God, Ann smelled good*, he thought and decide to have some fun with CAG and George Parker. "Damn, I should have looked at the information board to see which USO show's in town," Tom said. "Is it Jane Fonda?"

"No," Ann said and shook his head from side to side.

"Are you Ann Margaret?" He guessed again.

"Half right," Ann said as she pressed her breasts into his back. "You have one more guess, sailor boy. If you miss this time, you're permanently grounded."

252

"Ann? Ann? Ann?" Tom groaned. "Who do I know that is named Ann? Are you the beautiful, Ann Curtis?"

"Yes, darling," Ann said and kissed his lips. "You're the last person in the world that I expected to see in the Philippines."

Tom turned to look at the startled expression on CAG and Parker's faces. "Gentlemen, this is Ann Curtis. Her father is Commander of the Seventh Air Force. Ann, the gray haired one is Dick Brown, carrier air wing commander. The bald-headed one is George Parker, our operations officer."

Ann turned and offered her hand to CAG and said, "CAG Brown! You must be the pilot that Tom pulled out of Haiphong Harbor."

"That's me, pretty lady," CAG said and squeezed her hand. "It's down right sinful for a fighter pilot to be beholden to a rotorhead, but I love the guy."

"Me, too," Ann whispered in his ear and kissed CAG's cheek. Then she took George Parker's hand and said, "George, I'm so very pleased to meet you. Don't ever let Tom and CAG know that we girls have a weakness for bald men." She kissed him softly on the lips.

Parker was startled with the sensuous kiss, but recovered quickly and said, "May I buy you a drink, Ann?"

"No thanks, George," Ann purred. "I don't have time, but I'll take a rain check."

"Anytime, Ann," George said as he released her soft hand.

"Gentlemen, I haven't seen Tom Colby for almost twenty years," she lied. "May I borrow him for a few minutes?"

"By all means, Ann," CAG said. He turned to Tom, and said, "Go with the lady, Tom. I'll take care of Captain Sam Streeper."

"Good-bye, gentlemen," Ann said as she took Tom's arm and let him out of the bar. They walked to the elevator, and she punched the 6th floor button. When the door closed, she wrapped her arms around Tom's neck. "Are you in trouble with Captain Sam Streeper, sailor boy?" Ann asked as the elevator stopped at floor 6.

"No, sweetheart," Tom laughed. "Captain Streeper is Commanding Officer of the *Concord*. We lost one of the ship's helicopter's this morning. The Air Boss, Commander Red Barber, was killed. Captain Streeper wants me to go with him when he notifies the widow. Beth Barber is flying in this afternoon to celebrate Christmas with her husband.

"How sad," Ann said. "Was Red Barber you friend?"

"Yes darling. He flew with Dad when he was a young ensign. Red has been a life-long friend."

Ann led him to Room 612. "Come in, I know just what you need."

"I wish this was our Hong Kong trip," Tom said as he caressed her breasts.

"Well, I can call down and have room service send up a Filipino girl," Ann said. "Would you settle for that, sailor boy?"

"Hell, no! I want you and Kim,"Tom said, "not some Filipino."

"Darling, you need a bath," she said and filled the large tub.

Tom sat on the commode and removed his flight boots. Then he took off his flight suit and jockey shorts. "Please get in the tub with me, Ann," he begged.

"No, darling," she said. "I just took a bath thirty minutes ago. Lay back, relax and enjoy your bath. I'll turn down the bed and open the champagne," she said as she left the bathroom and softly closed the door. Quickly, she opened the door connecting the adjacent suite. Kim Ellis stood on the other side of the door dressed in a white teddy.

"Oh, Ann, I'm so nervous," Kim whispered.

In whispered tones, Ann explained that Tom's friend had just been killed in a helicopter crash. She added the part where Tom wished this was their Hong Kong trip.

"Then he really does want to make love to me," Kim said and hugged Ann.

"Yes, darling, he does," Ann answered. "Now help me get undressed and into my teddy before Tom gets out of the bath." Kim helped Ann into the black teddy. They walked over and turned down the covers of the king-size bed.

When Tom walked out of the bathroom, he saw Ann Curtis and Kim Ellis propped on the large pillows holding glasses of champagne. "Jesus Christ, there is a Santa Claus," Tom murmured and walked toward the bed. He crawled on his hands and knees between the two beautiful women. He lowered his head and sipped champagne from Ann's glass. Then he turned and drank from Kim's. The ladies sat the champagne

254

glasses on their night stands. Then all three collapsed on the large bed in a tangle of arms, legs, caresses and kisses. Tom Colby would remember this day for the rest of his life.

11,000 feet above
Fairfax, Virginia

Judy Anderson flew the Cessna 310 while Tommy checked the airways chart for the third time. The nine hour flight from San Diego, California had been a beautiful experience. He enjoyed flying with Judy. Behind them in the passenger seats, Jackie Anderson and his mother were sleeping. They should be getting close to the Flying C Ranch. Tommy spotted the rotating beacon that Samuel Watson had turned on two hours ago. He pointed out the left window at the green rotating beacon. He keyed the microphone and said, "Washington Center, Cessna Five-One-Three, over."

"Cessna Five-One-Three, Washington Center, go ahead."

"Roger, Center, Five-One-Three over Fairfax, Virginia. Have private airport in sight for landing. Will cancel flight plan via telephone, over."

"Five-One-Three, you're cleared to land at your discretion. Surface winds are one-nine-two at sixteen."

"Roger wind, out," Tommy said as he took the controls, pulled the throttles to idle and dived toward the ranch. "We'll buzz the ranch house to let Grandmother know that we're here," he smiled at Judy.

"Tommy, they've already spotted us," Judy said. "See that beautiful, black Rolls parked near the hangar?"

Tommy saw the Rolls-Royce, then he saw his grandmother and Samuel Watson standing beside the automobile, waving. He rocked the wings and dropped the gear. "Landing check-off list, please Judy," he said.

Judy read the landing check list and Tommy acknowledged each item. "Landing check-off list complete, turning final," Tommy said. He touched down fifty feet from the end of the runway. After the landing roll out, he turned around and taxied back down the runway. Samuel directed him toward the large hangar with an open door. He taxied inside the hangar and stopped the engines. He opened the cabin door and helped his mother and Jackie Anderson down the steps.

"Welcome to Virginia," Lieutenant Commander Paul Thompson said as Linda walked down the steps.

Linda rushed into his arms and kissed him as she asked, "What are you doing in Virginia, Paul?"

"I'm stationed out at Bethesda. Margaret invited me out for Christmas."

Linda recovered her composure and said, "Paul Thompson, this is Jackie Anderson. Jackie, this is Dr. Thompson who saved my father's life." Jackie Anderson shook his hand and kissed his cheek. Then she introduced her daughter, Judy. Tommy Colby was hugging his grandmother when he saw the white Lear jet parked in the back of the hangar.

"Did you buy a Lear jet, Grandma?" Tommy asked.

"Yes, darling. That's Grandfather's Christmas present."

"May I look inside, please?"

"Yes, darling," she laughed. "The cabin door is unlocked. You and Judy may look inside."

Tommy grabbed Judy's hand and they ran toward the jet. He opened the door and lowered the steps for Judy, then followed her inside. He sat in the pilot's seat and looked at the rows of gauges and instruments while Judy sat in the copilot's seat beside him. "How'd you like to fly this baby, Judy?"

"I bet you that I could get it off the ground," Judy answered then said, "We must go Tommy." They closed the door of the jet and walked to the Rolls. Watson drove toward the ranch house.

"The factory representative promised to come out Christmas Eve and take you and Judy for a ride," Margaret said to Tommy.

"Thank you, Grandma. That's the only Christmas present that I want," he said and kissed her cheek.

"The weatherman's predicting snow tonight, Mr. Tommy," Watson said. "So maybe we'll have a white Christmas for you folks."

"Do you have a snow plow to clear the runway?" Tommy asked.

"Yas sir, Mr. Tommy," Watson laughed as he answered. "We have three or four snow plows around the ranch. We always keep the runway clear of snow."

THIRTY-FOUR

Gold Wings For Kim

Room 612
Army-Navy Club Hotel
Republic of the Philippines

Tom unzipped the bag and removed the short sleeve white uniform. He dressed and sat on the sofa waiting for the ladies and tried not to think about the death of Commander Red Barber. Instead, he concentrated on the fragrant scent that lingered in the room. The suite door opened, and Ann and Kim walked toward him. "God, you two are so beautiful," he said as he bent to kiss Ann.

She turned her cheek for his kiss and said, "Tom, please don't smear our lipstick." He noticed that she was wearing the pair of miniature Navy gold wings that he had given her in Hawaii. "Tom, don't you think Kim has earned her wings?" Ann asked. "I hope you have an extra pair."

"I carry an extra pair for just such an emergency," Tom laughed as he walked to the closet and opened the bag. He pinned the miniature gold wings to Kim's white blouse, above her left breast. He saw her nipple harden as his hand brushed against her silk blouse. He kissed her cheek, and said, "Kim, you're now a life-time member of the Colby sex club."

Kim looked down at the small pair of gold wings resting on her left breast. She put her arms around Tom's neck and kissed him. She broke the kiss and said, "Thank you Tom, I will always wear them proudly."

257

"Damn, Kim," Ann said as she reached for a kleenex and wiped Tom's lips. "Now, you've smeared your lipstick." She reached inside her purse for the lipstick and quickly repaired the damage to Kim's lips. Then she took Tom's left arm, "Now listen, you two, no more kissing until we've had some lunch."

"I'll drink to that," Tom said and offered Kim his arm. He could hardly wait to see the expression on CAG's face when he walked into the restaurant with a gorgeous blonde and brunette clinging to his arms.

Warrior's Lounge
Army-Navy Club

CAG Dick Brown sat at the bar nursing a cold San Miguel beer. He thought about the beautiful blonde lady who had taken Tom up to her room. *Tom Colby should've been a fighter pilot,* CAG thought, *rotorheads just aren't suppose to make out like that.* "Son-of-a-bitch!" CAG said as Tom walked into the lounge with two stunning ladies on his arms. They walked toward CAG.

Ann was the first to speak as CAG stood beside the bar stool. "CAG Dick Brown, I'd like you to meet Kim Ellis. Kim, this is CAG."

Kim offered her hand to the tall, white hair Commander. *God, he's so handsome,* she thought. CAG reached for Kim's hand and raised it to his lips. She felt weak in the knees as CAG kissed her fingers. "Is CAG a Navy title?" she asked.

"No, it's a Navy acronym for Carrier Air Wing Commander," Tom said. "He's the chief hancho in charge of all the aircraft on the carrier."

"Well, I'm impressed," Kim said and reclaimed her hand.

"CAG, we'd be honored to have you join us for lunch," Tom said.

"Yes, please have lunch with us," Kim said.

"Okay, I'll have lunch with you, if you'll will knock off the CAG crap," he said. "Just call me Dick."

"Dick, it is," Kim said.

"Where's George?" Ann asked looking around the empty lounge.

"He's having lunch with Captain Streeper and Beth Barber," CAG answered. "Come on Tom, I'll buy you and these pretty ladies the biggest steak in the joint," he said and led Kim toward the restaurant.

Flying C Ranch
Fairfax, Virginia

"I hear the White House helicopter coming, Miss Jackie," Watson said as he grabbed her bag and started toward the door. "Would you like to ride shotgun down to the airport and back, Mr. Tommy?"

"Yes, Sam," Tommy answered as he put on his heavy coat and followed Watson out to the Rolls.

Jackie Anderson slipped on the full length mink coat and kissed Margaret's cheek. "Thanks for the loan of this beautiful coat, Margaret."

"Enjoy your dinner at Camp David, dear," Margaret said. "Now, you'd better hurry out to the Rolls before Watson explodes."

Jackie said, "Bye Linda, I hate to rush off like this. I'll probably be home sometime in the morning."

"Have a good time," Linda said. She walked her to the door and watched as Tommy held the door open for Jackie. Then he jumped in the front seat, and Watson was speeding toward the airport.

"We'll have dinner when they return from the airport," Margaret said as she walked to couch and sat beside Admiral Woods.

*   *   *

It was nine o'clock when Watson served chocolate cake and coffee to the dinner guests in the living room. Linda ate the last morsel of chocolate cake on her plate. "I have to walk off some of this food," she said. "Paul, do you feel like walking down to the corral and back?"

"Yes, Linda" Thompson said and grabbed his parka.

"Samuel, will you get Linda a warm coat?" Margaret asked.

"Yes ma'am, I've already got it," Watson said as he held the coat for Linda. Then he reached into the closet and came out with a fur hat. "This'll keep your head warm, Miss Linda," he said and gently placed it over her red hair.

"Thanks, Sam," Linda said and buttoned the coat.

"You all watch out for patches of ice," Watson warned as he closed the large front door behind them.

Linda gasped as the cold air hit her lungs. She reached for Thompson's arm and said, "I've been in California too long. How do you stand this cold weather?"

259

"It helps if you have a warm woman to snuggle with," Paul laughed as they walked bristly toward the barn. He opened the door and they slipped inside.

Linda could smell the hay and the aroma from the horses as Paul kissed her. "Do you have a girlfriend to snuggle?"

"No darling, I've been too busy to start a relationship. You're the last woman that I made love to."

"I want you again," she said, "but not here in the barn. Will you come to my room tonight?"

"Oh, God yes," Paul moaned. "We'd better get back to the house."

They walked out into the night air. "Oh, it's freezing," Linda said. "Let's run." She jogged toward the ranch house. Paul jogged behind her and thought about the pleasures the night would bring them.

Dining Room
Army-Navy Hotel

Tom ate the last piece of steak and felt strength flow back into his tired bones. He glanced at Ann and saw that she was finishing her lobster tail. Kim had hardly touched the seafood plate as she talked to CAG. He invited Kim to go flying in one of the small private airplanes that one could rent at Manila International Airport. Kim looked at Ann. She saw Ann nod her head, and accepted his invitation. CAG glanced at his watch. It was almost 2 o'clock. He grabbed the check and said, "Tom, you and Ann sit here and have coffee and dessert. Kim and I are taking a taxi out to the airport and go flying. Please, excuse us."

"Have a nice flight," Tom said as CAG and Kim walked toward the cashier. He turned to Ann and said, "They were mooning over each other like teenagers."

"Are you jealous that CAG's taking one of your women, darling?"

"Heck no," I appreciate you arranging the special love treat for me, but now I realize that I would rather have you on a one-on-one basis."

"Thanks Tom, I was hoping you'd say that," Ann said. "Come now, we must go back and have coffee with Beth Barber and your Captain."

Tom reached for her hand. "Sure you feel up to that?"

"Yes darling, I lost a husband in this war. I know what Beth is going through. Sometimes the best therapy is just having a friend to talk to." She rose from the chair and walked toward the table where Beth Barber and Captain Streeper were sitting. Tom strolled along behind her.

Flying C Ranch
Fairfax, Virginia

Linda soaked in the tub. The hot water felt great after flying in the airplane all day. Then she remembered that Paul would be coming to her room soon. She got out of the tub and grabbed a large bath towel. She had a lot of primping to do before Paul got to the room. She lit a candle and placed in on the nightstand. The candle cast a soft glow to the room. She pulled the covers up to her chin. She would rest for just a few minutes. Her eyes closed and she drifted into a light sleep.

*   *   *

Tommy stared at the clock as the hands crept toward 11 o'clock. Judy had asked him to wait until everyone was asleep before he came to her room. He turned out the lights and eased the door open. He peered out the small crack in the door and saw Dr. Thompson enter his mother's bedroom. He eased the door shut and decided to wait another 10 minutes. When the clock read 11:10, he open the door. The hallway was clear. He walked to Judy's door and entered the room.

Judy was laying in bed waiting for him. "What kept you so long?" She asked. "I thought maybe you'd gone to sleep."

"Darling, I saw Dr. Thompson go into Mother's room," he said as he got in bed beside her. "So I thought I'd better wait awhile."

"You're upset because he might be making love to her, right?"

"Yeah, I guess so. Do you think it's okay?"

"Sure do," Judy whispered.

"Are you going to be this opened-minded after we are married?"

"No way, you big lug. You're all mine for at least the first ten years," Judy answered as she rolled on top of him.

"I won't be tired of you in ten years, Judy. Sometimes I don't think I can ever get enough of you." She stopped his talking with a kiss. Then her hands were making love to him. Tommy Colby was ready for a lifetime of loving from this beautiful lady.

261

THIRTY-FIVE

Ann Lands On The Carrier

Army-Navy Club Hotel
Republic of the Philippines

Tom Colby and Ann Curtis walked into the hotel restaurant at 11 o'clock for the Sunday brunch. He slipped the hostess a tip and asked for a window table. She picked up two menus and said, "Please follow me, Commander." She led them to a table that overlooked the water and the heliport. Tom held the chair for Ann, then sat in a chair next to her. "Would you like a cocktail?" The hostess asked.

"I'd like a glass of champagne," Ann said.

"Make that a bottle of champagne and a Bloody Mary, please," Tom said.

"You may go through the buffet line anytime you'd like," the hostess said and walked away to get their drinks.

Ann wore a white blouse and blue slacks. Tom noticed that she wore the gold wings above her left breast. He wore the short sleeve dress white uniform with gold wings and ribbons. The hostess returned with a tall bottle of champagne and a large Bloody Mary. She popped the cork and poured a glass of champagne for Ann. Then returned to the front of the restaurant. "I don't see CAG or Kim," Tom said as he sipped his drink.

"They're probably still upstairs in bed," Ann laughed, "or maybe they're in that helicopter."

Tom looked out the window and saw the Navy H-2 Sea Sprite helicopter approaching the heliport. Then he saw the three gold stars on the front of the helicopter. "That's Dad's helicopter," he said as two Naval officers dressed in short sleeve white uniforms got out of the helicopter and walked toward a blue sedan. The crewman walked behind them carrying two bags. "That's Dad and his aide. Looks like they plan to stay here at the Club. Want to invite them to join us for brunch?"

"Yes, darling, I insist. I haven't seen Father Colby in twenty years. Think he'll be surprised to see me?"

"Oh, I'm sure he'll be surprised. Okay, I'll invite them over if you promise to be good and not embarrass me."

"I promise to be a good girl," she winked and sipped the champagne. Tom walked outside as the sedan pulled up to the curb. The Lieutenant jumped out of the front seat and opened the door for Vice Admiral Thomas Colby.

"Good morning, Dad," Tom said and saluted his father.

"Good morning, Tom," the Admiral said as he returned Tom's salute. He grabbed Tom's hand and then pulled him into a bear hug. "I've been reading a lot of message traffic about your rescue escapades."

"Did you hear that Red Barber died in a crash, yesterday?"

"Yes, I heard about Red's accident," the Admiral answered. "I also heard that you were flying wing on him when the helicopter came apart."

"It was like living through a horrible nightmare."

"Well, those things happen, Tom." He turned to his aide, "John, this is my son, Commander Colby. Tom, this is my aide, John Turner."

"Pleased to meet you," Tom said as he shook Turner's hand. He noticed the gold wings above the two rows of ribbons on his uniform. "Well, let's get you checked in," Tom said and waved to the bell captain. "Raul, please take care of the bags for Admiral Colby's party. We'll be in the restaurant." He slipped him a tip.

"Okay, Commander," the bell captain said. "The bags will be in your room, Admiral." Raul gathered the bags and walked inside the hotel.

"Ann Curtis and I were just sitting down to brunch when we saw you land. We'd love to have you join us."

"The cute little blonde, Ann Curtis, that lived next door to us in Hawaii," Admiral Colby asked.

"Yes Dad, and she's still blonde and cute."

"John and I would enjoy having brunch with you and Ann. Come along, John. I want you to meet my goddaughter," Admiral Colby said as he walked toward the restaurant.

*   *   *

Ann stood as the three Naval officers walked to the table. "Good morning, Dad," she said and hugged him. Then she kissed his lips. *He tastes like Tom*, she thought. She grabbed her napkin and wiped the lipstick from his lips "Sorry about the lipstick."

"Don't worry about it, Ann. I'd like you to meet my aide, John Turner. John, this is my goddaughter, Ann Curtis."

"I'm so pleased to meet you, John," Ann said and offered her hand.

"The pleasure's mine, Miss Curtis," Turner replied.

"Please call me Ann," she said to Turner. Then turning to Admiral Colby she said, "Dad, sit over here beside me. Would you like some champagne?"

"Yes, please," Colby said.

Ann poured a glass of champagne. She looked across the table at Turner and said, "Do you want some champagne, John?"

"I'd rather have a Bloody Mary, Ann."

Ann raised her hand and waved at their waiter. "There's Kim and CAG," Ann said as she stood and waved to them. CAG wore the short sleeve white uniform. Kim was dressed a white blouse and white shorts. CAG spotted Ann's wave and escorted Kim to their table. Admiral Colby and CAG greeted each other like long-lost brothers. Tom introduced Kim to his father and Lieutenant Turner.

"We need a larger table," Ann said to the waiter.

"You may have the one behind you," the waiter pointed.

"Thank you," Ann smiled at the waiter and led the group to the larger table. CAG and Turner ordered Bloody Mary's while Kim asked for a glass of champagne. The waiter hurried away to get the drinks.

"Ann, Dick's been teaching me to fly," Kim said.

"How did she do, Dick?" Ann asked.

"Kim's gonna make a fine pilot," CAG bragged. "I should've started her in the one-seventy-two, but all they had left was a three-ten. I rented it for the weekend. You and Tom are welcome to use it."

"Thanks Dick," Ann said. "I know that Tom and I would argue about who was going to be the pilot in command."

"Now wait just a minute," Tom said as he looked at Ann.

Admiral Colby raised his hands to stop the argument. He removed a photograph from his pocket. "I want to show you my Christmas present, but first I must swear you all to secrecy. It's supposed to be a surprise."

"We all swear," Ann said and reached for the photograph. "It's beautiful!" She exclaimed as she stared at the picture of the gleaming white Lear jet and passed it to Tom.

"Where did you get this photograph if it's supposed to be a surprise?" Tom asked and passed the photograph around the table.

"Watson sent it to me. Margaret would skin him alive if she knew."

"It's a beautiful jet, Admiral," CAG said and gazed at the jet. "You're one lucky man to have a wife like Margaret." He returned the photograph and said, "Come on, folks. Let's hit the buffet line. Flying all morning has made me hungry."

*   *   *

The waiter cleared away their plates and refilled the coffee cups as Admiral Colby said, "*Shiloh* anchored in the middle of Subic Bay this morning, Tom. Now, you'll have access to your SAR helicopters."

"Thanks, Dad," Tom said. "I was just getting comfortable in the Jolly Green HH-3. I'd sure like to keep her, but I promised General Curtis we'd return her when our helicopters got on station."

"Two aircraft carriers in port at the same time," CAG said. "I suggest that we all get in the three-ten and fly over and take a look."

"I must stay here and work on that report, Admiral," Turner said.

"Sure, John," Colby said.

"We've been flying all morning, Dick," Kim said. "I'd like to stay and play some tennis after John finishes the report."

"Okay Kim," CAG said as he remembered making love to her in the airplane that morning. "Oh, doggone it. I promised Beth that I would meet her at Cubi Point this afternoon. She wants to make arrangements to have Red Barber buried at sea. You can drop me off at Cubi Point, and Tom can fly the plane back to Manila. I'll try to get back over early tomorrow afternoon, Kim."

"I understand, Dick. I'll go to dinner with Ann and these gentlemen," Kim said as they stood and walked out of the restaurant. Turner waved for the Admiral's driver. Ann sat in the back seat between Tom and Admiral Colby. CAG sat in front next to the driver.

"Have a nice flight," Turner said and saluted as the sedan pulled away from the curb. "May I escort you to your room?" Turner asked and offered Kim his arm.

"Yes, John." Kim felt a tingling sensation as she took his arm. They were alone in the elevator. "May I have a kiss, please?" She asked and pushed the six floor button. She licked his lips and quickly darted her tongue inside his mouth. Kim broke the kiss when the elevator stopped. Turner followed her from the elevator. She removed the key from her purse and handed it to Turner. He unlocked the door and pushed it open.

"Please come in for a few minutes, John."

"Just a few minutes," Turner said and followed Kim inside the room. "I really do have a report to work on this afternoon."

Kim shut the door and put her arms around his neck. "I must have another one of your delicious kisses. You taste so good." Turner lowered his head to kiss her. This time his tongue was quick and exploring. Kim began to purr in her throat as she pressed her pelvis against him. She broke the kiss and began to unbutton his white shirt. His broad chest was almost hairless. His nipples were erect. She lowered her head and kissed his right nipple.

"Oh, my God, you're making me so horny," Turner moaned and began to unbutton her blouse. "Are you CAG's girlfriend?"

"No way," Kim laughed. "I just met CAG yesterday. He took me to dinner last night and flying this morning."

"Thank God," Turner groaned as he removed her blouse and stared at her large breasts. He reached behind her and unhooked the clasp. He removed the bra and tossed it toward the sofa. Then his hands were on her breasts. He kissed her again. *God, he felt great. This was the first woman he'd made love to in three months. This was definitely better than working on the report or playing tennis. Maybe he would play tennis with Kim later, if he had the strength.*

266

4,000 feet above Manila Bay
Republic of the Philippines

CAG flew the Cessna 310 across Manila Bay toward the Naval Air Station at Cubi Point. Tom sat in the copilot's seat. Admiral Colby and Ann Curtis sat behind them in the plush, leather passenger seats. CAG cruised the airplane at 200 miles per hour. He turned to look at Tom and said, "I got her down to 50 miles per hour this morning in slow flight. Think you can beat that?"

"I'd sure like to try," Tom said and reached for the controls. He pulled the throttles toward idle and lowered the landing gear. As the airspeed slowed to 90 miles per hour, he lowered 20 degrees of flaps. When the speed had slowed to 70 miles per hour, he began to push forward slowly on the throttles and held the 4,000 feet of altitude as the airspeed slowed to 45 miles per hour. *Well, at least I've have beaten CAG's 50 mph*, Tom thought as he continued to slow the airplane. When the airspeed read 40, the Cessna began a light shake, and the nose mushed forward. Tom realized that he was approaching the stall point of the aircraft. He pushed the yoke forward, and the airspeed began to climb.

"Pretty good for a rotorhead," CAG said. "I have the aircraft, Tom." He raised the flaps and landing gear and accelerated to 200 miles per hour. "That's Corregidor Island, Ann," CAG said as he pointed to the lush green island below at the entrance to Manila Bay. "Some of the old Japanese barracks are still visible."

Ann looked out the window at Corregidor. She remembered the story from history lessons in school.

CAG pointed through the windshield and said, "That's the *Shiloh* anchored in the bay, and the *Concord's* docked at the carrier pier." He looked over at Tom and said, "Switch to Cubi Point frequency." Tom dialed in the frequency and gave CAG a thumbs-up. CAG pushed the mike switch and said, "Cubi Tower, this is Cessna Five-Five-One, over."

"Go ahead, Five-Five-One," the tower operator said.

"Roger tower, Five-Five-One is a Cessna three-ten with Navy flight crew aboard. Entering your control zone for a survey of the bay, over."

"You're cleared into the control zone. Negative traffic this time, over."

267

"Thank you, tower," CAG dived the Cessna down to five hundred feet and flew along side the *Shiloh*. "There's our SAR helicopters, Tom."

"I sure will be glad to get them aboard the *Concord*," Tom said. He smiled as he remember that CAG did not want anything to do with the helicopters until he had been pulled out of Haiphong Harbor by the big HH-3. Now the SAR helicopter and pilots belonged to CAG. *That's the way it should have been, all along,* Tom thought.

CAG pressed the mike switch and said, "Cubi Tower, Five-Five-One, request frequency change to *USS Concord*, over."

"Change approved, Five-Five-One," the tower operator said.

Tom switched the radio to the *Concord* frequency. "War Chief Tower, Cessna Five-One, over," CAG said into the mike.

"Five-One, this is War Chief Tower, go ahead," the controller said.

"Roger tower, this is CAG Brown in a Cessna three-ten. Have Seventh Fleet aboard. Request photo pass along your port side."

"Wait one, sir," the controller said as he reached for the red telephone and dialed the bridge. CDR Chadwick Crowe, the Executive Officer of the carrier, was sitting in the Captain's chair reading the Bible. Crowe was a Southern Baptist lay minister. He enjoyed the peace and solitude of the deserted bridge. The Officer of the Day was stationed on the Quarterdeck while the carrier was in port. He reached for the red telephone.

"Sorry to bother you, Commander," the controller said, "CAG's flying a Cessna in our area with Seventh Fleet aboard. He's requesting a photo pass along our port side."

"If Seventh Fleet wants to make a photo pass, clear him," Crowe growled. He looked out the window of the bridge and saw the twin engine, red and white airplane. *What in the hell is CAG pulling, now?* He wondered.

"Five-One, you're cleared for a photo pass," the controller said.

"Thank's tower," CAG banked the aircraft toward the carrier and handed a small camera to Tom. "Take some pictures as we pass by."

"Do I have to focus?"

"No, just aim and shoot," CAG said as he lowered the altitude to 200 feet and slowed to 70 miles per hour. "The angle deck looks pretty clear, doesn't it?"

"The flight deck's clear, CAG," Tom said as he pushed the shutter of the camera.

"Would you like to make a touch-and-go on the carrier, Tom?"

"**JESUS CHRIST, CAG**! Have you lost your mind?" Tom yelled. "There's no way in hell the carrier's gonna clear us for a touch-and-go landing."

"Wanna make a bet?"

"I'll bet you a six-pack of Coors the carrier will not clear you to land, CAG," Admiral Colby said from the cabin.

"I'll take that bet, Boss, if you'll make it a six-pack of San Miguel," CAG said.

"We have a bet, CAG," Colby said and smiled at Ann.

CDR Crowe left the bridge and walked back to Pri-Fly as the Cessna continued to circle the carrier. He had just stepped into Pri-Fly when he heard CAG call again.

"Tower, Five-One, request touch-and-go landing, over," CAG said.

The controller reached for the red telephone, then stopped when he saw the Executive Officer walk in. "You want to talk to CAG, sir?" The controller asked and handed to microphone to Crowe.

"Yes, Jones, I'll talk to the crazy bastard," Crowe said as he reached for the microphone and climbed into Red Barber's high chair. He pressed the mike and said, "Five-One, is Seventh Fleet in that airplane?"

"Roger that, tower," CAG said as he recognized Chadwick Crowe's voice.

"Does he approve your touch-and-go?"

"Roger, that," CAG said.

"**THAT'S CHEATING, DICK**!" Admiral Colby yelled. "Our bet is null and void."

"Like hell, Boss. There was no pre-conditions in our bet."

CAG Brown smiled as he heard Crowe say, "Stand-by, Five-One. "We're manning the flight quarter stations. Will you need the mirror?"

"Roger that. Thanks Chad," CAG said.

Commander Crowe reached for the mike and announced over the ships public address system. "**NOW HEAR THIS. MAN FLIGHT STATION FOR TOUCH-AND-GO LANDING ON THE ANGLE**

DECK. LSO MAN THE PLATFORM." The carrier's duty section rushed to man their flight quarter stations.

LCDR James Stark was a mustang Landing Signal Officer. He put on his flight gear and ran to man the LSO platform. He grabbed the telephone and dialed Pri-Fly. "LSO stationed manned and ready," he reported, "What in the hell is going on?"

"Take it easy, Jim," Crowe said. "CAG Brown has Seventh Fleet in that little white airplane. He wants to do a touch-and-go landing on the angel deck. Do you have the paddles?"

"Roger that," Stark answered. "We're ready for CAG, if he wants to break his fool neck."

Crowe pushed the radio mike and said, "Five-One, your signal Charlie. Wind is down the angle at twelve knots."

"Roger, Charlie," CAG said as he flew 200 feet above the carrier. "Breaking now." CAG rolled the Cessna into a 45 degree left bank, and said, "You have the aircraft, Tom."

"I have the aircraft, CAG," Tom said as he took the controls and performed the slow flight routine. *So that is why CAG wanted me to do that slow flight*, he thought. Well, he'd show CAG that he still remembered how to make a carrier landing. The carrier was off the tip of his left wing. When he passed the stern of the ship, he started his approach. The airspeed was steady at 70 mph. At the 45 degree position, he saw the LSO with his red paddles spread wide. He glanced at the mirror behind the LSO and saw the green meatball. He reduced the airspeed to 60 mph as he followed the meatball down the glide slope. He flew a Roger Pass all the way. When the meatball disappeared from the mirror, the LSO gave the cut signal with his paddles.

Tom quickly pushed the yoke forward and jerked the throttles to idle. He counted one-thousand-and-one and flared the aircraft. The landing gear touched the flight deck near the number three cable. As soon as the gear touched the flight deck, Tom pushed both throttles to the firewall. The Cessna was airborne before the nose wheel reached the round down of the angle flight deck.

"Nice landing for a rotorhead," CAG smiled at Tom. He turned to look at Admiral Colby. "Boss, you owe me a six-pack of San Miguel."

"You lied and cheated," Colby said, "but I'll buy you a damn six-pack of beer."

Ann Curtis unsnapped her seat belt. She stood and leaned into the cockpit. "I'd like to land on the carrier, Dick. May I, please?" She kissed his cheek.

"**NO CAG! NO WAY**!" Tom screamed.

"Settle down, Tom," CAG said and turned the aircraft to fly down wind. "Admiral, do you mind if Ann makes a carrier landing?"

"It's okay with me, Dick," Colby said. "If CINCPAC Fleet or CNO hears about this, I'll be busted lower that an Airman Apprentice."

"Tom, please give Ann your seat," CAG said.

Tom unsnapped his seat belt and got out of the copilot's seat. Ann sat in the seat. Tom placed the straps over her shoulders and connected her seat belt then sat in the seat beside his father.

"Tower, Five-One, request one more touch-and-go," CAG said.

Crowe was surprised that the landing had gone so well. He was looking through the binoculars and saw Tom Colby make the landing. He reached for the mike and said, "Your signal is Charlie, Five-One. The wind remains down the angle at twelve knots."

"Roger, Charlie," CAG said. He trimmed the aircraft for slow flight. "You have the aircraft, Ann. I'll talk you through it."

Ann's hands were sweating as she held the steering wheel. She held the airspeed at a steady 60 miles per hour. When she reached the 45 degree position, she saw the man standing by the mirror with two large paddles in his hands. They were fluttering in the wind like flags.

"See the green ball in the mirror?"

"Yes, CAG," Ann said.

"Keep it right in the center. If you get too low, it turns red. If you are too high, it turns amber."

Ann nodded her head and concentrated on keeping the meatball in the center of the mirror. Her lineup with the center line of the flight deck was perfect. She could feel CAG's hands as he gently nudged the controls. His right hand was resting over her left hand where she held the throttles.

When CAG saw Jim Stark give him the cut with the paddles, he quickly pulled the throttles to idle. He felt Ann level the airplane. He waited one second as the Cessna dropped and was getting ready to pull

271

back on the yoke when Ann flared. She touched down on the number two wire and shoved the throttles to the firewall. The little Cessna leaped into the air.

"**I DID IT! I DID IT!**" Ann yelled. "Thank you, CAG. God, I knew I could do it." Sweat was pouring down her face.

"That was truly a beautiful landing, Ann," CAG bragged and handed her his handkerchief. He took the controls as Ann laughed and wiped her face. CAG pushed the mike switch and said, "Thanks for the landings, Chad. Switching to Cubi Tower."

"You're cleared, Five-One. Nice landings," Crowe said as he watched the Cessna fly toward Cubi Point. A beautiful woman with short blonde hair had made the last landing. *Maybe Pensacola would soon be training female aviators*, Crowe thought, but he had not heard of such a program. He reached for the mike and said, "**SECURE FROM FLIGHT QUARTERS**."

THIRTY-SIX

Liberty In Alongapo City

NAS Cubi Point
Republic of the Philippines

Captain Samuel Streeper and Beth Barber sat in the backseat as the Navy sedan entered Alongapo City. The driver dodged around the Filipino jeepneys, ancient American jeeps with canvas tops. Everywhere Beth looked, she saw groups of sailors walking arm in arm with young Filipino women. Beth asked, "Are they prostitutes?"

"I'd guess about ninety percent are," Streeper answered. "Most of them are peasants from the farms. They sell their bodies to support their families. The sad part is a lot of them have VD."

"I feel sorry for the young sailors."

"Beth, those men have been at sea, in the combat zone, for over three months, working twelve- and fourteen-hour days. When they get liberty, they want to drink and make love."

"I still feel sorry for them," Beth said. "They're some mother's son. What do you do when they come back to the ship with VD?"

"Dr. Davenport cures them with penicillin shots," he laughed. "I understand he has some very dull needles for repeat offenders." It was one o'clock in the afternoon when they crossed the Alongapo River leading to Subic Bay Naval Station. The Air Station was three miles around the bay at Cubi Point. The *Concord* was moored at the carrier pier.

273

Beth saw a sign that read CHUCK WAGON RESTAURANT. "Could we please stop, Sam?" She asked and pointed toward the sign.

"Certainly, driver stop at the Chuck Wagon."

"Aye, aye, Captain," the driver said and turned the sedan into the parking lot. The Chuck Wagon was a fast food restaurant similar to Burger King back in the states. Beth rushed to the restroom.

"We'll have lunch here, driver," Streeper said. "Be ready to roll in twenty minutes."

"Yes, sir," the driver said and walked toward the men's room.

Streeper ordered two barbecue sandwiches, french fries and coffee. He was sitting at one of the tables sipping coffee when Beth came out of the ladies room. She walked toward the table. "The barbecue's delicious, Beth," he said as she sat in a chair next to him. "I ordered coffee for you. Would you rather have a coke?"

"No, coffee's fine," she answered and picked up the sandwich. She munched the fries and tried not to think about Red. They had planned this trip for a year. Now he was gone. It was difficult to hold back the tears.

Streeper finished lunch and sipped the coffee. "Take your time, Beth. I didn't realize that I was so hungry. I'm going to the restroom, and I'll meet you at the car."

"Okay, Sam," she said and hurried to finish lunch. He had been so nice to her. She knew that he was anxious to get back to his ship. She finished her lunch and walked to the car. The driver opened the door. Captain Streeper sat in the back seat. "Thanks for the lunch," she said. The driver started the sedan and drove toward the Naval Air Station.

"There's the *Concord*," Streeper said as the sedan went around the hill. Then he saw a civilian airplane approaching the fantail of the carrier. *Looks like the sonofabitch is going to land on my ship,* he thought. **"Jesus Christ**!" Streeper yelled. "I don't believe what I'm seeing. That civilian airplane just landed on my aircraft carrier. Step on it driver, looks like he's turning downwind for another approach."

The driver was cruising at the 30 mph speed limit. He increased the speed to 50 as Streeper yelled again, **"I said step on it, driver**!"

"Captain, I'm doing fifty," the driver said.

"Okay, hold her at fifty," Streeper said and watched the airplane land a second time. "They even have the LSO waving him aboard. There

274

had better be a damn good explanation for this." He sat back in the seat and watched the twin-engine airplane fly toward Cubi Point. "You may as well slow down, driver," he said. Looks like he's gonna land at Cubi Point. Did you get his wing number?"

"No sir, I couldn't make it out," the driver said as he slowed the sedan. He turned on the road that led to the carrier pier and parked by the Officer's gangplank. He opened the rear door for Captain Streeper then ran around the car to open the door for Beth. The Petty Officer of the Watch struck the bell four times and announced on the ship's public address system, "**USS CONCORD ARRIVING**."

Streeper took Beth's arm and escorted her up the steep gangplank. He stopped at the Quarterdeck and saluted toward the rear of the ship. Then he turned to salute the Officer of the Day. He turned to the Duty Petty Officer and said, "Chief, please have a sentry escort Mrs. Barber to my cabin."

"Aye, aye, Captain," the chief said. "Please come this way, Mrs. Barber." He led her to the side of the Quarterdeck.

"Do you know who's in that airplane that just landed on my ship, Mr. Moses?" Streeper asked.

"Yes, sir, that was CAG Brown and Seventh Fleet," LT Charles Moses answered.

"Thanks, Charlie," Streeper said and regained his composure. "Do you know if Admiral Colby's visiting the carrier today?"

"He's not on our schedule of VIP visitors, Captain," Moses said. "His plane just landed at Cubi. Want me to call base operations?"

"Yes, please. Let me know as soon as possible," he said as he turned and walked toward his cabin.

Moses was reaching for the telephone when he saw the dark blue, Navy sedan drive down the carrier pier. "Let me know who's in that sedan, chief!" He yelled.

The chief looked through his long field glass. He saw the three stars on the shoulder boards of the Admiral sitting in the back seat. "He has three stars, Lieutenant. Looks like Seventh Fleet. Shall I announce him, sir?"

"Roger, go ahead chief," Moses said as he grabbed the telephone to call the Captain's Cabin. The Petty Officer of the Watch struck the bell six times and announced, "**SEVENTH FLEET ARRIVING**."

Captain Streeper was halfway across the hangar bay when he heard the six bells. He turned and ran back to the Quarterdeck. He stood beside Lieutenant Moses as Admiral Colby escorted a beautiful, blonde woman up the gangplank. CAG Dick Brown and Commander Tom Colby followed along behind.

Admiral Colby paused at the quarterdeck and turned to salute the fantail. Then he turned and saluted Captain Streeper and said, "Permission to come aboard, Sam."

Streeper returned the salute and said, "Welcome aboard the *Concord*, Admiral." He stepped forward to shake hands with Admiral Colby.

"Sam, this is my goddaughter, Ann Curtis," Colby said.

"Admiral, I met Ann at the Army-Navy Club yesterday. She was most helpful with Beth Barber," Streeper said and turned to take Ann's hand. "Welcome aboard the *Concord*, Ann."

"It's so big!" Ann exclaimed, "but it looks so little from the air."

"Were you in that airplane?" Streeper asked as he noticed the minature gold wings pinned above her left breast.

"Yes, I just made my first carrier landing on your ship. God, it was such a thrill!"

"Please follow me to the Cabin," Streeper said in a small voice. He took Ann's arm and escorted her across the hangar deck. "Watch out for those tie-down chains," he cautioned. "They can make a nasty bruise on your shin."

CAG turned to wink at Tom and whispered, "Ann really beat you, she got a number-two wire, where you floated and hit number-three."

"That'll be our little secret," Tom said. "If you tell Ann, I'll leave your ass floating in the Gulf the next time you eject from your little Skyhawk."

"I was just kidding, Tom. I can keep a secret," CAG said and followed after the group. *The rotorhead was a damn good aviator, and he also had a temper. Gotta remember not to piss him off,* CAG decided as his shin hit the tie-down cable. "**SON-OF-A-BITCH**!" CAG yelled as he hopped around on one foot and rubbed his shin. Then he hurried after the group as they walked into the Captain's Cabin.

*   *   *

"Sam, we have to be going," Admiral Colby said when heard the ship's bell clang four times, announcing that it was 2 o'clock in the afternoon. "I have a dinner engagement at the Embassy in Manila at six. Please tell CAG that we enjoyed the flight."

CAG Brown had asked to be excused earlier to check the Air Wing message traffic. The carrier landings had not entered the conversation as Captain Streeper and Beth Barber discussed the funeral arrangements for CDR Red Barber. "Sorry you have to leave so early, Admiral," Steeper said. "You're welcome aboard anytime for dinner."

Colby stood and turned to Beth Barber, "We have room for you in the Cessna," he said. "It'll save you a long car ride back to Manila."

"Oh, thank you, Admiral. I accept," she said and grabbed her purse. Streeper escorted them back to the Quarterdeck and saluted as Admiral Colby left the ship.

The Petty Officer hit the bell six times and announced, "**SEVENTH FLEET DEPARTING**." Admiral Colby held Ann's arm as they walked down the steep gangplank.

"Dad, does the ship make that announcement everytime you enter or leave the carrier?" Ann asked as she sat in the back seat of the sedan.

"Yes, darling," he answered. "It makes it awfully difficult to try to sneak home after you have been out drinking with your buddies." The driver started the sedan and drove up the carrier pier toward the airfield. He drove out on the ramp and parked near the Cessna.

"Dad, do you want to ride copilot,?" Ann asked.

"No, darling, you fly copilot, and I'll sit in back with Beth."

"Thanks," she kissed his cheek and sat in the copilot's seat. Tom was reading through the check-off list and started the number one engine. Then he started number two and taxied toward the duty runway. The tower cleared him for takeoff.

"Do you want to make the takeoff or landing?" Tom asked.

"I want to make the takeoff," Ann said as she grabbed the controls and smoothly added full power. She held the Cessna on the runway until

277

the airspeed reached 100 mph. Then she lifted the nose wheel and zoomed into the sky.

* * *

CAG Brown sat in Pri-Fly reading the stack of messages. He was hiding from Captain Streeper. He watched the Cessna turn left and fly toward the carrier pier. Ann rocked the wings from side to side and waved. "I'm surprised she didn't do a victory roll," CAG said to the duty controller.

"Is that the lady who landed the Cessna on the carrier, CAG?"

"Yes, that's her. She's one damn fine pilot," CAG said as the telephone rang. "If that's the Captain, I'm not here."

The controller answered the telephone, "No sir, Captain. I haven't seen CAG." He hung up the telephone and said, "You owe me one, CAG."

"Thanks, Jones," CAG said as he turned to the messages. *Maybe the Navy should consider opening flight school to female candidates. Maybe one day, but it won't happen in my lifetime,* he thought.

Army-Navy Club Hotel
Republic of the Philippines

Ann saw Kim sitting at the bar when she walked into the Warrior's Lounge with Tom and Admiral Colby. Kim climbed off the bar stool and walked to meet them. "Let's get a table," Ann said. "I just made my first carrier landing, and I'm buying the drinks."

"You did what?" Kim asked, astonished.

"Oh, she has the big head, Kim," Tom said. "She lucks out and makes one landing on the carrier."

"I'm proud of my goddaughter," Admiral Colby said. "The drinks are on me, folks." He waived for the hostess. "What happened to my aide?" He asked and looked around the lounge.

"It's my fault, Admiral," Kim said. "I talked John into playing a set of tennis. Now, he's up in the room working on the report."

"Did you beat him?" Admiral Colby asked as the hostess served the champagne.

"Sure did," Kim lied as she remembered making love to Lieutenant John Turner over and over in her room.

278

Admiral Colby raised his glass and said, "A toast to Ann. As far as I know she's the first female to land a civilian airplane on an aircraft carrier." He did not add, "while the aircraft carrier was in port, tied to the pier."

"Thanks, Dad," Ann said. "Was my landing as good as Tom's?"

"There's no way you're going to get me involved in that argument," Admiral Colby said. Then he turned to Kim and said, "I'm going to dinner at the Embassy in Manila tonight. Will you please go with me?"

"I'd love too, Admiral," Kim answered. "What time do we leave?"

"Cocktails are at six, so we should leave the hotel by five-thirty."

Kim looked at her watch. It was almost 3:30. She picked up her glass and drank the champagne. "Gentlemen, please excuse me, I must go upstairs and get ready. Ann, will you please help me do something with this hair?"

"Yes, Kim," Ann answered. "Dad, thanks for the drink. I must help your date get ready for the big bash at the Embassy." She turned to Tom, "I'll meet you later for dinner." She walked with Kim to the elevator. After the elevator door closed, she asked, "Did you seduce John?"

"Oh, yes, John's really a great lover."

"Well, you're probably the first woman the poor man has made love to in over three months," Ann said. "How does he compare to Tom?"

"Ann, I never compare my lovers. You know, in the past two days I've made love with Tom Colby, CAG Brown and John Turner. Tonight, I'm gonna make love to Admiral Colby. Do you think I'm a nympho-maniac?"

"You and I are both nympho's, darling," Ann said and kissed Kim's cheek. "Come, we must fix your hair. You want to look good tonight for your handsome date."

Thirty-Seven

The Lear Jet

Flying C Ranch
Fairfax, Virginia

Tommy awoke at seven o'clock and ran to the window. He pushed back the thick curtain and looked outside. The sky was overcast but no snow. Today he would fly the Lear jet. He put on a pair of jeans and a heavy sweatshirt and walked downstairs. "Good morning, Grandma," he said as he hugged Margaret Colby and kissed her cheek. "Did you sleep well?"

"Yes, darling. Did you?"

"No, all I could think about was flying the jet, today."

Watson walked into the kitchen. "Morning, Mr. Tommy. How many eggs you want for breakfast? We also have pancakes and waffles."

"I'll have three, scrambled please," Tommy said as he poured a cup of coffee and sat beside Margaret.

Linda was the last to come down for breakfast. "The wonderful aroma of that coffee woke me," Linda said and hugged Margaret.

"Did you sleep well, dear?" Margaret asked.

"Oh yes, I love that feather bed." Linda said.

Dr. Thompson stood and held a chair, "Sit here beside me, and I'll get you a cup of Margaret's delicious coffee."

"Thanks, Paul," Linda said as she sat in the chair. Watson walked into the room. "Good morning, Sam," she said.

"Morning, Miss Linda, how many eggs do you want for breakfast?"

"Just some wheat toast, please," Linda said.

"Miss Linda, this is a ranch," Watson said, "and you have to eat a good breakfast to get through the day."

"Okay, Sam," Linda smiled at the old Negro. "One egg, over easy, and wheat toast."

"Yes ma'am," Watson hurried to prepare her order. He glanced at the clock. It read 8:40. He sure wanted to go flying in the jet with Mr. Tommy and Miss Judy when the company pilot came at nine o'clock.

Linda finished her breakfast as the doorbell rang. "I'll get it," Watson said and hurried to the front door. He opened the door and saw the company pilot. "Come in, Mr. Barney," Watson said. "Join us in the kitchen for a cup of coffee before you go flying."

"Thanks, Watson," Steve Barney said and followed Watson to the kitchen. He saw Margaret Colby and walked over to take her hand. "Good morning, Margaret, are you flying with us today?"

"No, Steve," Margaret said. "Today you're taking up my grandson and his fiancée." She led him to the table and said, "This is Tommy and Judy, and that's my daughter-in-law, Linda. You met Dr. Woods and Dr. Thompson the other day."

Watson rushed over and sat a cup of coffee in front of the pilot. "Thanks, Watson," Barney said. "Would you like to fly with us today?"

"I shore would, if it's okay with Mrs. Colby," Watson answered.

"Quit sniffling, Samuel. You may go with them, "Margaret said.

"Thank you, ma'am," Watson smiled. "I'll fix us a thermos of coffee. Is that okay, Mr. Barney?"

"Yes," Barney said. "It'll be nice to have some coffee on the flight."

Margaret walked to the hall closet and returned with two brown leather flight jackets. They had a black fur collar similar to the Naval aviator flight jacket. She handed them to Judy and Tommy.

"Thank you, Grandma," Tommy said as he held the jacket for Judy. Then quickly put his on and pulled up the zipper.

"Thank you, Mrs. Colby," Judy said as she hugged Margaret and kissed her cheek. "These will keep us warm."

"Those are mighty fine coats, ma'am," Watson said as he placed the coffee thermos inside the picnic basket.

"Your coat's in the closet, Samuel," Margaret said.

Watson rushed to the closet and pulled out the flight jacket. He put on the jacket and pulled up the zipper as he walked back to the kitchen. "I shore do thank you, ma'am," Watson said. Then he turned to Judy and Tommy, "Let's go flying in that Lear jet before the snow starts." He grabbed the picnic basket and led the group to the Rolls-Royce.

"We'll be back in about an hour, Margaret," Barney said.

"Steve, I want you to teach both Judy and Tommy to fly the jet."

"I understand, Margaret," he said. "It'll be my pleasure to teach those kids. I might even teach Watson how to fly it," he laughed and walked out the door.

"Oh God," Margaret groaned. "There'll be no way to live with that old Negro if Steve lets him fly that jet." She and Linda looked out the kitchen window as Barney started the engines and taxied to the end of the runway. They heard the engines scream as the Lear accelerated down the runway and climbed into the Virginia sky.

Room 614
Army-Navy Club Hotel

Admiral Thomas Colby opened his eyes and looked at the nearly nude body of Kim Ellis. She lay on her back, snoring softly. She wore a black french garter belt and hose. Colby recalled how they had entered the side door of the club last night and rode the service elevator to the sixth floor. When they entered the room, Kim unbuttoned his shirt and removed his Navy uniform. Then she led him to the king-size bed. Kim removed all of her clothes except the black garter belt and hose. She turned on the radio and crawled across the bed toward him. They were slow and gentle with each other. It was midnight before they slept, entwined in each other's arms. *It must have been the black garter belt*, Colby thought. *I must remember to buy one for Margaret.*

Colby was jolted from his daydream as the telephone rang on the nightstand. He grabbed the phone before it woke Kim. He placed the receiver to his ear and heard John Turner, say, "Hello Kim, may I please come up for a few minutes? I need to make love to you again, so very much." Colby pushed the button to break the connection and left the phone off the hook. *Kim had been one busy lady if she made love to both*

CAG Brown and John Turner, he thought. He wondered if she had also made love to Tom.

"Was that Ann?" Kim asked in a sleepy voice.

"No, darling, it was a wrong number," Colby said and turned to see Kim stretching on the bed. "Are you hungry?"

"I'm starved," Kim smiled and looked at the clock. It was nine o'clock.

"Let me go down first," Colby said after he finished dressing. "You come down in about five minutes."

"Thanks for the loving, Thomas," Kim said and kissed his cheek. "It'll be hard to keep my hands off you at breakfast." She watched him walk from the room and close the door. Then she got out of bed and dressed. Walking from the bathroom, she looked at the clock. Twelve minutes had passed, and it was time to go to breakfast. She walked to the elevator and pushed the LOBBY button. Kim was going to enjoy this breakfast.

*   *   *

When Admiral Colby walked into the dining room, he saw LT John Turner sitting at a table drinking coffee. "Good morning, John," he said, "have you seen Tom or the ladies?"

"No, Admiral," Turner said.

"Let's move to that larger table," Colby said, "I'm sure they'll be along soon."

Kim walked into the dining room and waved at them. Colby stood and held the chair for Kim. "Let's order," she said. "Ann and Tom may not be down for hours." The waitress appeared and took their orders. They were just finishing breakfast when Ann and Tom walked into the room. "Sorry we couldn't wait," Kim said. "I was starved."

Ann wore white shorts and a white pullover tennis shirt. The white clothes were a sharp contrast to her golden Hawaiian tan. "We went to Pauline's night club last night and danced until midnight," Ann said. "I just couldn't wake up this morning."

The waiter appeared to take their orders. "I'm going to start with a Bloody Mary," Ann said. "Tom would you like one?"

"Yes, waiter, bring two Bloody Mary's," Tom said.

"Okay, Commander," the waiter said. "The kitchen's closing soon, do you want to order breakfast?"

"Sure, we'll go ahead and order," Tom said and ordered ham and eggs, hash browns, toast and coffee. Ann ordered wheat toast and coffee.

Ann said, "Tom and I are playing tennis later. Would you and John like to join us, Kim?"

"Sorry Ann, we can't," Admiral Colby said. "John and I must get back to the ship. We're leaving port this afternoon."

"I wish you could stay for Christmas, Dad," Ann said and kissed him. "I wanted you to have a nice Christmas."

"This has been a most wonderful Christmas for me, darling," he said and turned to kiss Kim's cheek. "Well, I must get my gear together. My helicopter is due soon. Have a nice Christmas," he said and shook hands with Tom.

Kim grabbed Turner and kissed his cheek. "Thanks for the tennis game, John," she said and winked at him. "I enjoyed playing with you."

"I'd like a rematch the next time we're in port, Kim," Turner said and turned to shake Tom's hand. He waved to Ann and followed Admiral Colby toward the elevator.

"You have a nice godfather, Ann," Kim said.

"Yeah, I like him," Ann said. "I think I'll keep him. Maybe he'll let me fly his jet."

"There comes the flag helicopter," Kim said as a Navy helicopter landed at the heliport. She saw a tall, black Naval officer jump from the helicopter and grab his bag. He turned and saluted as Admiral Colby and Lieutenant Turner climbed into the helicopter. "Look at that handsome Navy officer, Ann," Kim said. "I hope he plays tennis."

Tom Colby looked out the window and saw Ensign Tim Arnold walking toward the club. Arnold had played varsity tennis at the University of Southern California. "Ladies, that officer is my copilot, Tim Arnold. He will be your tennis partner, Kim."

"Oh, I'm looking forward to playing with Tim," Kim said and licked her lips. She had never made love to a black man. *This is truly gonna be a beautiful Christmas,* she thought and began to plan the seduction of Ensign Tim Arnold.

Flying C Ranch
Fairfax, Virginia

Tommy Colby flew the Lear jet in a touch-and-go pattern around the Flying C airport. Steve Barney sat in the pilot's seat and watched the black clouds moving toward the airport from the west. "We'd better make this our final landing before that front moves in," he said.

"Roger," Tommy said and concentrated on maintaining airspeed and rate of descent. He was surprised to find the Lear so easy to fly. It felt like driving the Jaguar with power steering. He touched down on the runway and pulled both throttles to the idle position. Back pressure on the control stick kept the nose wheel off the runway until the jet had slowed to 50 mph. As lift was lost on the horizontal stabilizer, the nose gently dropped, and the nose wheel touched the runway. Tommy tapped the brakes and turned toward the hangar. He taxied the jet inside the hangar and shut off the engines.

"Those shore were mighty good landings, Mr. Tommy," Watson said. He collected the coffee cups and packed them in the picnic basket.

"Thanks for the coffee, Sam," Barney said. "Next time we go up, I'll let you fly the Lear."

"Oh thank you, Mr. Barney," Watson said as they left the jet and walked toward the Rolls. "Do me a great favor and please don't say anything to Mrs. Colby until after I learn to fly. I just love to fly, and I want to be able to fly the Lear just as good as I drive the Rolls."

"Okay, I promise Sam, it'll be our little secret," Barney said as he climbed into the Rolls.

Snow began to fall as Watson drove the Rolls-Royce toward the ranch house. "We shore gonna have a mighty fine Christmas, Mr. Tommy," Watson chuckled as the snow struck the windshield. "Yes sir, it's shore gonna be a beautiful white Christmas."

THIRTY-EIGHT

Big Mother Call Sign

Army-Navy Club Hotel
Republic of the Philippines

Ann Curtis and Kim Ellis were in Room 612 dressing for dinner. "Tim Arnold's an excellent tennis player," Ann said. "How's he in bed, darling?"

"Oh Ann, everything I've heard about the black man's loving abilities are true," Kim answered. "God, he's so big. Want to swap partners tonight?"

"It's a very tempting offer," Ann smiled, "but I'll stick with Tom. Hurry and get dressed. Tim said that Joe Blackwell might come over to the club tonight."

"I want to be gone before Joe gets here," Kim said as she put on a red cocktail dress and brushed her hair. "I'll dance with Tim until midnight, then bring him back to my room and make love until dawn."

"My, you're sure energetic tonight," Ann laughed and put on a black cocktail dress. "Zip me up, darling. Think Tom will like this?"

"Oh yes, Tom's gonna love this dress. Hurry, we shouldn't keep our dates waiting."

*   *   *

Tom Colby and Tim Arnold sat in the Warrior's Lounge drinking beer. "What do you think about Kim Ellis?" Tom asked.

"Commander, she's fantastic," Tim grinned. "We made love all afternoon. Have you made love to her, sir?"

286

"No, I haven't," Tom lied. "Ann's kept me too busy to think about another woman."

"Ann's a very beautiful lady, sir." Then he remembered the message from the Skipper. "Commander Blackwell flew to the *Concord* this morning. They flew the SAR helicopters over from the *Shiloh*. I told the Skipper that I was the Maintenance Officer and accepted the birds."

"I'm glad you did. Are they in good shape?"

"Seven-One and Seven-Two are in great shape," Tim answered. "Seven-Three had some corrosion on the tail rotor that I pointed out to the Skipper. He reamed out the Maintenance Chief."

"I sure hate to take the Jolly Green helicopter back to the Air Force. We've been through a lot in that green giant."

"The Air Force chopper pilots sure picked an appropriate nickname when they called that monster the Jolly Green Giant," Tim said. "We need a nickname for our H-3 SAR birds. Remember when we first landed on the *Concord*, and the Air Boss wondered where he'd park the big mother-fucker's? In honor of Commander Red Streeper, I think we should call ourselves Big Mother."

"Big Mother," Tom repeated the name. "I like it Tim. Big Mother will be our call sign until Skipper Blackwell changes it."

"Oh, that reminds me, Bull's flying the Jolly Green over tomorrow morning and parking it here at the heliport for us to fly back to the ship. CAG wants us aboard the *Concord* by three o'clock. The carrier's getting underway for the Gulf of Tonkin before dark."

"I'm getting tired of this damn war, Tim. Aren't you?"

"Yes, sir. Oh yes, one more message. Skipper Blackwell said he was flying over to the club to have dinner with you tonight."

"Oh God, we gotta get out of here before the Skipper arrives," Tom said as he saw Ann Curtis and Kim Ellis step out of the elevator. "Let's go, Tim." Tom dropped some bills on the table and they walked to the elevator. Tom saw the bell captain. "We need a taxi, Raul," he said. "A Commander Blackwell may come by looking for me. Will you please tell him that I had to attend a dinner at the Embassy?"

"Yes, Commander," Raul said and blew his whistle to summon a taxi. They climbed into the taxi and drove away as a helicopter landed at the heliport.

"There's another one of your helicopters, Tom," Linda said.

Tom turned to the driver, "Take us to Pauline's." The taxi sped away toward Manila as CDR Joe Blackwell walked toward the club lugging his bag.

Joe walked to the registration desk and sat his bag on the floor. "What room's Commander Colby in?" He asked.

Raul Almazan walked to the desk and stopped beside Joe. "Are you Commander Blackwell?" He asked.

"Yes, I am," Joe said and turned to look at the bell captain.

"You just missed Commander Colby, sir," Raul said. "He asked me to tell you that he was going to a formal dinner at the Embassy, tonight."

"Damn," Joe said. "Did Commander Colby have a blonde or brunette lady with him?"

"No brunette, Commander," Raul lied. "Commander Colby's date for the evening is Ann Curtis. She has beautiful blonde hair."

"Yes, she does," Joe agreed. "I was kinda hoping that her friend, Kim Ellis, was with her."

"I'll take your bag to your room, Commander," Raul said. "The Warrior's Lounge is down that hallway if you'd like a cold beer."

"Thanks, a beer sounds good," Joe said and reached for his billfold. The smallest bill in his wallet was a five dollar bill. He handed the bill to Raul as they walked away from the desk.

"My name's Raul, if you want a girl tonight, just call this number and ask for me," he handed his card to Joe.

"Thanks, Raul," Joe said and took the card. He felt a stirring in his loins. It had been three months since he made love to Kim Ellis, and he needed a woman. "How much does she charge?"

"Ten dollars for a quickie, or fifty dollars for all night," Raul said as he continued to walk toward the elevator.

"Is she pretty?"

"Please step inside the elevator, Commander," Raul said as he took a package of photographs from his shirt pocket. When the doors closed, he pushed button 4 and handed three photographs to Joe. "They're all young and pretty, Commander. You may have your pick."

Joe stared at the photographs of the three Filipino women. They were nude except for a pair of bikini panties. He selected the tall girl with the large breasts. "That's Horny Connie," Raul said as the elevator stopped at the fourth floor. They walked down the hotel corridor to Room 416. Raul unlocked the door and carried the bag inside. "You pay me, Commander. Then Horny Connie will be up here in a few minutes with your beer."

Joe handed him a $50 bill. "You guarantee that Connie is clean?"

"Oh yes, Commander. My girls get a medical check every week. Business has been so slow that Horny Connie has not made love in over a week," Raul lied. "She'll accompany you to dinner at the club here or go dancing with you at any of the nightclubs in Manila."

"Thanks Raul, does the club have dance music after dinner?"

"Yes, a three piece combo starts playing at nine."

"That sounds good. Tell Connie that we'll have dinner here at the club tonight."

"Okay, Commander," Raul said as he pocketed the $50 bill and walked from the room. "Horny Connie will be right up." He walked toward the elevator smiling. Connie was his best prostitute. All the sailors liked her big breasts.

Room 612
Army-Navy Club

Tom opened his eyes and looked at the clock radio near his pillow. It was seven o'clock, Christmas morning. *That would make it 9 p.m., Christmas Eve in Virginia,* Tom thought. Ann was snoring softly on the other side of the large bed. He slipped out of the bed and put on his white uniform in the bathroom. He padded across the plush carpet in his stocking feet and paused at the door to slip on his white shoes. He closed the door softly and rode the elevator to the lobby. It was 10 minutes before the overseas operator got through to Fairfax, Virginia.

"Colby residence," Watson answered the telephone.

"Merry Christmas, Samuel," he said. "This is Tom, calling from the Philippines."

"**Merry Christmas, Mr. Tom**!" Watson yelled into the telephone. "Hold on a minute, and I'll get your momma." Tom talked to his mother for five minutes, telling her that he had dinner with Admiral Colby.

289

Tommy came on the telephone and told about flying the Lear jet. Then he was talking to Linda.

"Oh, Tom, we're having a beautiful white Christmas. We got two inches of snow today. How's your Christmas in the Philippines?"

"Too hot," he laughed. "It sure doesn't feel like Christmas out here. We're leaving this afternoon to get back on the little pleasure cruise."

"Please be careful," Linda begged.

"I will, darling," he promised. "It's really unofficial, but I think that we're going to Hong Kong in April. Will you meet me there?"

"Yes, darling," she answered. "I can hardly wait."

"That's all the news for now," Tom said and looked at his watch. He had been talking for 22 minutes. This phone call was going to cost a fortune. "Gotta run, love you. Have a safe flight back to San Diego." He clicked the receiver, then called room service and ordered coffee delivered to Room 612. He rode the elevator upstairs and slipped quitely into the room. He removed his uniform and put on the grey silk kimono Ann had given him in Hawaii.

Ann's eyes opened when she heard the soft knock at the door. "Lay still, lover," Tom said and opened the door for room service. He tipped the Filipino girl and rolled the cart to the bedside. "Merry Christmas, darling," he said and handed Ann a cup of the steaming black coffee. Then he removed a small box from the kimono and placed it on her stomach.

Ann opened the box and stared at the three carat diamond, solitaire ring. "It's so beautiful," she gasped and placed in on her finger. Then she jumped from the bed and walked to the dresser. She opened the bottom drawer and removed a package. She handed it to Tom and said, "Merry Christmas, lover."

Tom removed the red Christmas paper and found a gold Rolex wrist watch. "Thanks, Ann," he said and snapped it on his left arm. He noticed that diamonds marked the 3, 6, 9 and 12 o'clock positions on the face of the watch. "It's a beautiful watch, Ann," he said as he held the white silk kimono robe for her. "Bring your coffee over to the sofa."

"How do you wake up so early?" Ann asked and sipped the coffee.

"I got up this morning and called Mother. They're having a white Christmas with two inches of snow."

"Did you talk to Tommy?"

290

"Yes, the company pilot gave Tommy and Judy flight instructions in the jet this morning. Come on, let's go down to brunch. I'm hungry."

"I want to make love to you one more time, please," she said and led him toward the bed. She removed the white kimono. "This is the best Christmas present of all."

It was 9 o'clock when Tom and Ann walked into the restaurant. Tom saw Joe Blackwell sitting at the table with the Filipino woman. "Morning, Skipper," Tom said and gripped Joe's hand. "You remember Ann?"

"Morning, Ann," Joe said, "This is Connie."

"Hi Connie," Ann said. "I'm Ann, and this is Tom."

"Good morning," Connie smiled, displaying three gold teeth.

Tim Arnold entered the restaurant and walked to the table. Kim had insisted that he come down first. She promised to follow within minutes. He sat in the chair beside Ann as Joe introduced Connie. "Good morning, Connie," Tim said and reached across the table to touch her hand. *Man, she has to be a hooker*, he thought and stared at her large breasts.

"Has anyone seen Kim Ellis?" Joe asked.

"I haven't seen her since she left with her date last night, Joe," Ann said as Kim entered the restaurant. "Oh, here she comes, now."

Kim wore a dark blue mini-skirt with a white blouse. "Good morning all," Kim said and sat beside Tim. She looked across the table, "Good morning, Joe."

"Morning, Kim," Joe stammered forgetting to introduce Connie. He looked at the miniature pair of Navy gold wings pinned above Kim's left breast. *Who in the hell gave her those golden leg-spreaders,* he wondered.

"Come on everyone," Kim said as she stood and led them toward the buffet line. "Let's have breakfast. I'm famished."

*   *   *

Tom started the engines of the Jolly Green helicopter. Tim sat in the copilot's seat. Joe sat in the cabin in the first crewman seat. Tom quickly engaged the rotors while Tim completed the check-off list. Ann and Kim sat at a window table in the Warrior's Lounge. "There go our warrior's back to their war," Kim said and waved as Tom lifted the big helicopter into a 20 foot hover.

Tom saw Kim and Ann waving and rocked the helicopter from side to side. Then he saw two Navy jet pilots watching from the patio. "Hang on, Skipper," Tom said and turned the helicopter around until the tail rotor was pointing into the wind. "We're gonna show those jet jockeys what it's like to make a backward takeoff."

"Take it easy, Tom," Joe said over the intercom. "This baby is a hell of a lot bigger than the Bell helicopters we used to practice backward takeoffs at Ellyson Field." Tom eased up the collective lever and pulled back on the cyclic stick. The helicopter began a climbing, backward takeoff. At approximately 30 knots of backward speed, he eased off the pressure of the left rudder. The torque of the rotorhead spun the helicopter around to the right and forward flight.

"Little boys and their toys," Ann laughed as she watched the backward takeoff. "God, I wish I was married to Tom Colby."

"Not me, darling," Kim said. "Do you realize I made love to four handsome, virile men this weekend. I don't ever want to get married again."

Tom said, "You have the aircraft, Tim. Take us back to the ship."

"Yes sir," Tim said. He took the controls and flew across Manila Bay toward the *Concord*. Tom was lost in his thoughts. So much had happened, so fast. Tomorrow morning he would bury his best friend at sea. *War is hell*, he thought, *but Red Barber was not killed in combat. He was killed in a senseless, routine helicopter crash.*

THIRTY-NINE

Burial At Sea

USS Concord
South China Sea

The *USS Concord* (CVA-51) was as long as three football fields. She was an eighty-six thousand ton aircraft carrier named after the Battle of Concord. The eight, oil-burning boilers delivered steam to four engines, which could move her through the ocean at 36 knots. Now she had slowed to 16 knots as the carrier prepared to bury her dead in a sunrise service. Captain Samuel Streeper sat in the tall, swivel chair on the bridge. *God, I'm going to miss Red,* he thought and looked at the calm ocean through the windshield.

"Skipper, it's five minutes till seven," the OOD, said.

"Thanks, Charlie," Streeper said and stepped down from the chair. "You have the conn. At O-seven-hundred reduce speed to fourteen-hundred rpm."

"Aye, aye, skipper, I have the conn," LT Charlie Moses said and watched Captain Streeper walk down the ladder toward the hangar deck.

*   *   *

Streeper sat behind the podium in the chairs reserved for ship's company and looked at the flag draped casket. He felt the ship slow as the OOD's voice came over the speaker, "**NOW HEAR THIS. BURIAL AT SEA IN PROGRESS ON THE HANGAR DECK. MAINTAIN QUIET THROUGHOUT THE SHIP.**"

293

After the Chaplain's brief eulogy, the honor guard went through its rifle drill. Three nerve-jarring volleys of rifle fire echoed through the hangar bay. As the last mournful notes of taps ended, the pallbearers slowly pushed the casket toward the edge of the elevator. Two pallbearers held the American flag while the other four raised the end of the carriage. CDR Red Barber's casket slid down the carriage and plunged into the ocean. The honor guard folded the flag and gave it to Captain Streeper. He would mail it to Beth Barber on the next COD flight. Streeper stood to walk back to the bridge when CAG Brown and Tom Colby walked by.

"Nice service, Captain," CAG said. "What's our ETA for Yankee Station?"

"Around nineteen-hundred hours," Streeper answered. "Are you and Tom anxious to get back to the war?"

"Yes sir, Captain," CAG said. "Tom and I are anxious to get this damn war over so we can get back to our girlfriends in the PI, right Tom?"

"You're so right, CAG," Colby smiled.

"Tom, I understand that congratulations are in order," Streeper said. "Chad Crowe told me that you had carrier-qualified while we were in port. Do you want to fly in the A-4 strike with CAG ?"

"No, Captain," Tom said. "I'll stick with helicopters."

"Well, let me know if you change your mind," Streeper said and walked toward the bridge.

"I think he's halfway serious, CAG," Tom said.

"Naw, Tom," CAG replied. "Carrier captains get paranoid when they are invested with so much power. Some of them think they're God Almighty sitting in that high chair on the bridge. It's a shame. I remember when Sam Streeper was a damn fine CAG."

The *Concord* arrived back on Yankee station at nineteen-hundred-hours. The first strike mission was scheduled for twenty-one-hundred hours against the barracks at Vinh. Various strike missions would continue throughout the night. LCDR Craig Thomas, the new Air Boss, was surprised when he heard CDR Colby say, "Big Mother Seven-Five ready for takeoff." He had cleared the Big Mother helicopter for immediate takeoff. The helo would fly to the *USS Waddell* and stand by in condition-one SAR status.

*   *   *

The weeks rolled by and turned into months. The Sea Devil squadron continued to rescue Naval aviators and Air Force pilots as the MiG's and SAM's took their toll. At the end of February, the Sea Devil rescue record was 35 Naval aviators, 32 Air Force pilots and 8 ARVN pilots. The monsoons covered North Vietnam during the month of March and most of the missions were scrubbed. Then it was time to return the leased Jolly Green helicopter to the Air Force at Da Nang. Tom answered the summons to CAG's office and read the message from Seventh Air Force.

SECRET
ROUTINE, 120622Z MAR 66

FM: COMMANDER, SEVENTH AIR FORCE
TO: USS CONCORD (CVA-51)

PERSONAL FOR COMMANDER TOM COLBY, USN
SUBJECT: RETURN OF USAF HELICOPTER, SIDE NUMBER 775
1. PLEASE RETURN USAF JOLLY GREEN HELO, NUMBER 775, TO DA NANG ON 15 MARCH 1966. UNDERSTAND YOUR HELICOPTERS WERE DELIVERED TO CONCORD DURING PORT CALL AT SUBIC BAY.
2. THANK YOU FOR RESCUING 32 AIR FORCE PILOTS. YOUR ETA DA NANG NLT 1300 HOURS. REQUEST YOU, ENSIGN ARNOLD, CREWMAN STEVEN JACKMAN AND CREWMAN ROY LEWIS PLAN REMAIN-OVER-NIGHT AT DA NANG. INFORMAL AWARD CEREMONY AND DINNER WITH SEVERAL OF THE PILOTS YOUR CREW RESCUED.
3. AGAIN, THANK YOU FOR A JOB WELL DONE.

LIEUTENANT GENERAL STEVE CURTIS, USAF
COMMANDER, SEVENTH AIR FORCE
SECRET

"Uncle Steve got his third star, CAG!" Tom exclaimed, "and he's boss of Seventh Air Force, too."

"I'm not a damn bit surprised," CAG said. "Is General Curtis your uncle?"

"No, CAG," Tom said. "He's really my godfather. All the time we were in Manila I was committing incest with my godsister, Ann."

"Bullcrap!" CAG exclaimed. "Your sea stories are getting worse than mine. Go tell Ensign Arnold to pack his overnight bag for some liberty in Da Nang this Friday."

"Thanks, CAG. I wish you could pull some liberty with us."

"I'd love to, Tom," CAG said, "but us fighter pilots gotta stay here and be ready to fight the war when this rotten weather improves.

Da Nang Air Base
Republic of Vietnam

Tom flew the Jolly Green helicopter toward the Air Force Base at Da Nang. Tim was copilot. Petty Office Steve Jackman and Airman Roy Lewis sat in the cabin in the crew seats. Tom turned left to fly through a rain squall. "Might as well wash off all the salt spray that we can before we land," he said into the intercom.

"There's no salt spray on this bird," Arnold said. "I promised Jackman and Lewis a six-pack of San Miguel to keep the corrosion off this bird."

"Sounds like you made a very wise deal with the crew, Mr. Arnold," Tom laughed as he remembered promising Tim he could make love to Anah Thong if he kept the big Jolly Green helicopter free of corrosion. "You did a mighty fine job as Maintenance Officer. I'm proud of you."

"Thanks, Commander, we'd better call Da Nang," Arnold said when he saw the TACAN indicate that they were four miles from the Air Base.

Tom nodded as he pressed the mike switch and said, "Da Nang tower, Air Force helo Seven-Seven-Five, four miles west for landing, over."

"Seven-Five, say altitude," the tower said.

"Five hundred feet," Tom said.

"Roger, Seven-Five. Descend immediately to three hundred feet. You're cleared to the heliport behind base ops, over."

"Roger, tower," Tom said as he pushed the nose of the helicopter forward and descended to 300 feet. He flew down the wide taxiway and landed on the heliport marked on the large concrete parking ramp. "There's Captain Jasper," Tom said as he saw the white Air Force staff car speed toward the helicopter. A blue pickup truck followed the car. He stopped the rotor and shut off the jet engines. Tom walked down the cabin steps and returned Captain John Jasper's salute.

"Good afternoon, Commander Colby," Jasper said. "Please bring your bags to the staff car. The crewman will go with First Sergeant Jones."

"Thanks, John," Tom said and placed his overnight bag in the trunk of the staff car. He got in the back seat, and Ensign Arnold sat beside him.

"I have orders from General Curtis to take you and Ensign Arnold to his quarters," Jasper said as he started the staff car and backed away from the helicopter. You may take a shower if you'd like. Please change into your white uniform. I'll return for you at thirteen-thirty."

Anah Thong was waiting for them when the car pulled into the driveway. She kissed Tom and led him into the General's quarters as Tim was getting their bags out of the trunk. Tom whispered into Anah's ear, "Ensign Arnold's my copilot. He saved my life last month, and I'd appreciate it very much if you'd make love to him."

"Okay, Commander Tom, I'll do it for you," she said as she led him toward one of the rooms. "Take off your flight suit and take a shower."

Anah turned and motioned for Tim to follow her. She led him inside one of the rooms and softly closed the door. "Tim, my name's Anah," she said and kissed his cheek.

"I remember you, Anah," Tim said and looked into her eyes. "Your blue eyes are so beautiful."

"Thank you, Tim," she said and pulled down the long zipper to his flight suit. She looked at his broad, black chest, then she lowered her mouth to his right nipple and sucked.

"Oh God, Anah, that really makes me horny," Tim groaned and lowered his head to kiss her. She tasted like garlic.

"I'm glad you are horny," Anah giggled. "Sit on the bed."

Tim sat on the bed as Anah knelt to remove his flight boots. Then she pushed the flight suit from his shoulders. Tim stood and pushed it down his hips as he reached for the buttons on Anah's blouse. He saw that she was not wearing a bra and lowered his mouth to her small breasts.

*   *   *

Tom removed his flight suit and put on the robe that Anah had placed on the bed. He walked down the hallway toward the bathroom. He heard Anah giggle as he passed her room. He smiled as he stepped into the

297

shower and turned the water to full cold. *Tim earned this piece of tail,* Tom thought. He started singing as the cold water washed the sweat from his body. He realized how much he hated the brief Navy shower's on the carrier. He stood under the cold water for 10 minutes before he shut off the tap and grabbed the large, fluffy towel.

*   *   *

Tom sat in the dining room eating a chicken sandwich that the cook, Tuie Ky, had prepared for him. He sipped a cold Coke as Tim walked into the room. Tim was wearing the short sleeve, white uniform with gold wings and two ribbons, the Purple Heart and the National Defense ribbons. "I don't know what General Curtis has planned for us Tim, but soon you're gonna have more ribbons on your chest."

Tim sat in the chair across the table from Tom. "Commander, I just made love to Anah," he said. "Man, it was better than the nookie I got from Kim Ellis in the PI."

"You did what, you dumb bastard!" Tom exclaimed. "You mean to tell me that you balled the General's hootch girl, right here in his quarters. If the General finds out, he'll bust you back to Aviation Cadet."

Tim looked bewildered as Tuie Ky placed a sandwich and Coke on the table in front of him. When Tuie walked from the room, Tim said, "I thought you said you were going to arrange for me to make love to Anah."

"I was, Tim," Tom said, "but not here in the General's quarters. God, I hope that none of the servants saw you."

"No, sir," Tim whispered. "We were real quiet. No one saw us."

Anah Thong walked into the dining room dressed in a white silk pants suit. She looked at Tim and said, "Hurry, Mr. Timmy and eat your sandwich. We're all flying to Tan Son Nhut on General Curtis' big jet at two o'clock."

"You are one lucky Ensign," Tom said. "You cuckold the General's hootch girl and get awarded a medal all in the same day. Pretty damn lucky."

"What is meant by cuckold, Commander Tom?" Anah asked as Tim began to wolf down the chicken sandwich.

"It's a very seldom used American word meaning to make friends with the General's girlfriend," Tom lied.

298

"Mr. Timmy and I are very good friends," Anah said and bent to kiss Arnold's cheek. "Hurry and finish your sandwich," she said. "Captain John will be here in ten minutes. He gets mad as hell if all is not ready."

"Well, well," Tom said. "Looks like we are flying to Tan Son Nhut to get our medals and have dinner. Wonder why General Curtis is keeping us in the dark?"

"It's big surprise for you, Commander Tom. You must act surprised," Anah giggled.

"We will, Anah," Tom promised as he heard the beep of the car horn. "That must be Captain John. Let's go get our medals, Mr. Timmy."

Tim smiled as he drank the last of the Coke and followed Tom and Anah toward the waiting sedan.

*　　*　　*

Tom sat in the plush leather seats of the VIP KC-135 talking with Lieutenant General Steve Curtis as they approached Tan Son Nhut. Tim sat by Anah as she looked through a copy of *Sunset* magazine. Petty Officer Steve Jackman and Airman Roy Lewis sat in the rear section of the lounge sipping a beer.

"Ann called and told me that she had landed a plane on your ship while it was at the pier in Cubi Point," General Curtis said. "She said it was the most thrilling thing that she had ever done in her life."

"I apologize for that, General," Tom said. "CAG Brown is one crazy bastard. I would never intentionally risk Ann's life like that."

"I'm looking forward to meeting your CAG Brown," Curtis said.

"MAY I HAVE YOUR ATTENTION PLEASE," the pilot's voice came over the lounge speaker. "WE'LL LAND AT TAN SON NHUT IN FIVE MINUTES."

Tom looked out the window as the KC-135 swooped down and made a circling approach to the air base. It flew lower and lower over the thousands of wood-and-thatch shacks outside the airfield boundary and touched down with a squeal of tires.

*　　*　　*

"Mister President," the aide to Commander MACV said, "General Curtis' plane is taxiing in."

"Have all the arrangements been made?" The President asked.

"Yes, sir. Public affairs has arranged for civilian journalists and TV coverage. The MACV band is ready. General Scott and Vice President Ky will meet us at the operations building." The aide opened a box that was lined with medals. "Here's the Navy Cross, Air Force Cross, Navy Distinguished Flying Cross and Air Force Distinguished Flying Cross for Commander Colby and the citations that go with them. Vice President Ky will present the Vietnamese Air Gallantry Cross to Commander Colby and Ensign Arnold. These other boxes contain the medals for Ensign Arnold and the two enlisted crewmen."

"I hate to do this to my nephew," the President said. "Here's what we're gonna do, son. We start with Airman Lewis, then present medals to Petty Officer Jackman. Next is Ensign Arnold, and we keep Commander Colby for the grand finale."

*　　*　　*

Tom looked through the window of the KC-135 and saw the crowd in front of the base operations building. Ann Curtis stood between his father and the President of the United States. He glanced at General Curtis as the big jet taxied toward the group. "I didn't know that the Commander-in-Chief flew all the way to the war zone to present the Air Force Distinguish Flying Cross, General," Tom said.

"Who said you're getting the DFC?" Curtis asked. "It might be, as you squids say, just a Gedunk Medal."

"Thanks Dad Curtis," Tom said and shook the General's hand.

"You deserve it," Curtis said as the big jet stopped and the whine of the engines died away. "You gentlemen follow me and act surprised when the President pins the medals on you." He led the group down the steep stairs and across the red carpet toward the raised platform. The clouds parted and the afternoon sun shined through as the band played "Anchors Aweigh." *Thank God, the weather is good,* Curtis thought as he stopped in front of the podium and saluted the President of the United States.

FORTY

Death On The San Diego Freeway

Officer's Club
Tan Son Nhut Air Base
Republic of Vietnam

Tom Colby and Ann Curtis sat in the deserted lounge of the Officer's Club sipping Irish Coffee. Ann's feet were tired. She had danced with her father, the President, General Scott and Vice President Ky. She slipped off her shoes and gently rubbed Tom's leg with her foot. At nine p.m., President Johnson, Vice President Ky and the Flag Officers had left for a party at the American Embassy in Saigon. Tom and Ann declined the President's invitation to join them.

"Did you enjoy dancing with Vice President Ky?" Tom asked.

"Yes, he's an excellent dancer, but he smelled like garlic."

"Jesus, I still can't believe all these medals," Tom said.

"You didn't know about the medals?"

"Hell no, I thought that General Curtis had put me in for the Air Force DFC. The other medals were a complete surprise. CAG Brown must've recommended me for the Navy Cross when I pulled his tail out of Haiphong Harbor."

"You deserve them," Ann said. "I didn't realize that your flying was so dangerous."

"It's not half as dangerous as being a war correspondent in South Vietnam."

"Darling, it'll only be for six months," Ann said and changed the subject as she asked, "Where's Tim Arnold?"

"I think he sneaked Anah Thong up to his room," Tom said. "They're probably making love by now."

"I have some champagne in my room," Ann said as she slipped her feet into her shoes. "Would you like to come up for a glass?"

"Yes, darling," Tom said and stood. They walked to the lobby and rode the elevator to the third floor. "I want to take off this uniform with all these heavy medals and soak in a tub of cool water."

"Yes, master," Ann smiled as she unlocked the door and led him into the room. She kicked her shoes in the direction of the closet and walked to the bathroom to start his bath.

Tom removed his shoes and uniform and stepped into the bathtub. "God, this feels good," he said and sat in the cool water. "I don't think that I'll ever get acclimated to this heat and humidity." He leaned back in the tub and watched Ann slowly perform a striptease as she removed her clothes.

Ann popped the cork of the champagne bottle and poured two glasses. She handed a glass to Tom and stepped into the tub. "A toast to my hero," she said as she touched the rim of her glass to his and drank deeply.

Tom sipped the champagne and said, "I have a confession to make. I'm very proud of your landing on the *Concord*. Your landing was better than mine."

"Thanks, Tom," Ann smiled and sipped the champagne.

She sat the champagne glass on the side of the tub. "I enjoyed playing aviator with you in the Philippines. Now, I want to play submarine."

"I like your parlor games, beautiful lady," he said. He gathered her in his arms and tried to concentrate on Ann's submarine game, but his thoughts strayed. *God, I hope Linda's gonna be okay*, he worried as he remembered Michael's warning about the time being short for Linda.

Suite 1016
El Cortez Hotel
San Diego, California

Linda Colby retouched her makeup in the bathroom. She glanced at the clock. It was 6:10 p.m., and darkness had descended upon the city. She walked into the bedroom where Glenn Carson lay sprawled on the bed with his eyes closed. He moaned as Linda leaned down and kissed him, "Oh, that feels good, please spend the night with me."

"Wish I could, Glenn. I promise that after Tommy graduates we'll enjoy a weekend together, maybe San Francisco."

"It's a date," Glenn said and kissed her hand.

"I must run," Linda said. "I told Tommy I'd be home by six-thirty, and it's already after six."

Glenn got off the bed and opened his brief case. He handed her a package that contained one hundred $100 bills. "This is your bonus."

"Thanks, Glenn," she said and placed the package inside her purse. "I'll call you tomorrow or Wednesday, good-bye."

Glenn reached for the telephone as Linda closed the door. He dialed the valet number and said, "Bobby, have the Jaguar parked out front. Dr. Colby's on her way down." He closed his eyes and began to make plans for San Francisco.

32nd Street Officer's Club
Naval Station
San Diego, California

Captain David Freeman, USN, sat at the bar drinking his sixth martini. He was the Operations Officer on Commander, Cruiser-Destroyer Force staff. Freeman was an alcoholic. He finished the drink and climbed unsteadily off the bar stool. He collected his pack of Lucky Strikes and lighter as the bartender walked toward him.

"Can I call a taxi for you, Captain?" The bartender asked.

"Hell no, Sam," Freeman said and walked toward the door. "I only have about five miles to drive. I'll be fine."

"Drive carefully," the bartender said as Freeman weave toward the door. He started the Lincoln Continental and drove toward Interstate 5. He was oblivious to the honking horns as he entered the freeway exit ramp and drove north in the southbound lanes. Cars swerved to avoid the speeding Continental.

*   *   *

Linda followed a white Cadillac as she drove the Jaguar in the number 3 lane of the San Diego freeway. The Cadillac suddenly swerved to the right and crashed into a pickup truck. Linda watched in shock as the truck began to roll over and over. Then she saw the headlights of the car coming head-on in her lane. She wrenched the steering wheel to the right and kicked at the brake as the two automobiles crashed together. She felt the sledgehammer crash and was thrown into the steering wheel. All of the breath rushed out of her, and there was only darkness. She did not feel the station wagon crash into the rear of the Jaguar. Cars continued to pile into the wreckage until the freeway screeched to a stop. People wept and screamed as they crawled from their mangled cars. A traffic helicopter flying above the freeway called the California Highway Patrol.

*   *   *

Linda stood on the sidewalk of the deserted street above the freeway and stared at the tangled mess of wreckage. Suddenly a yellow airplane landed on the street and stopped near her. Michael Colby waved from the open cockpit. She laughed and ran to the airplane. She climbed up the side of the airplane and sat in the rear cockpit. Michael stood in his seat and leaned over to kiss her cheek. He fastened her shoulder harness to the seat belt and wrapped a white scarf around her neck.

"Hang on, beautiful lady," Michael said and pushed the throttle to the firewall. The little bi-plane leaped into the sky and zoomed toward the heavens. Linda had heard Tom talk about seeing Michael's yellow airplane. Wouldn't he be surprised to learn that she was flying with Michael.

Flying C Ranch
Fairfax, Virginia

Samuel Watson answered the telephone on the first ring. "Yes suh, Mr. Tommy, hold on just a minute." He placed the receiver on the table

304

and walked into the den. "Your grandson is calling from San Diego, ma'am."

"Thank you, Samuel," Margaret said as he reached for the telephone and said, "Hello, Tommy."

"Grandma, are you sitting down?" Tommy asked.

"Yes, darling," Margaret answered. "I'm feeling much better."

"Please listen, Grandma," Tommy pleaded, "Mother was killed in the Jaguar this evening."

"OH, GOD NO!" Margaret screamed and struggled to composed herself. "Are you there alone, honey?"

"No, ma'am. Judy and Mrs. Anderson are here."

"Please let me speak to Jackie."

"Okay Grandma, hold on a minute," he said and motioned for Jackie Anderson. "Grandmother wants to talk to you." He handed the telephone to Jackie.

"Hello, Margaret," Jackie said.

"Hello, Jackie. How's Tommy holding up?"

"I'm afraid he's in a state of shock," Jackie whispered. "The Highway Patrol notified us about ten minutes ago that Linda was killed in a freeway accident. Some drunk driver entered the exit ramp of the freeway and crashed head-on into the Jaguar. It's a real mess. Three people were killed and many were seriously injured."

"Oh God, this is such a shock," Margaret sobbed. "Take Tommy to your home tonight. Samuel and I will fly out just as soon as we can."

"We'll take care of Tommy," Jackie assured her.

"Thanks Jackie, Let me speak to Tommy again, please."

"Wait a minute, Margaret," Jackie said and waved at Tommy.

"I'm back on the line, Grandma," Tommy said.

"Tommy, have you called your mother's parents, Admiral and Mrs. Bush?"

"No, Grandma, I was gonna call them next."

"I'll call them, Tommy. Samuel and I will fly out just as soon as I can located the charter pilot. Please spend the evening at Mrs. Anderson's. Give Judy a kiss for me."

"I will, Grandma, good-bye," Tommy said and hung up the phone.

Margaret sat beside the telephone and cried. Watson walked in with a tall glass of bourbon and water. "This'll help some, ma'am," he said and handed her the glass.

"Thanks, Samuel," Margaret smiled and sipped the drink. She glanced at the clock. It was 11:32 p.m. "I must call the White House," she said and reached for the telephone. "Hello operator, this is an emergency," Margaret told the White House operator. "Please tell the President that this is Margaret Colby, and there has been a tragic death in the family."

She sipped the drink and heard the President say, "Hello Margaret, what happened?"

"Oh, thank God that I got through to you, Lyndon. Linda was killed in an automobile accident tonight in San Diego. Will you please notify Tom and Thomas?"

"Certainly, darling. Do you want me to call Admiral Bush?"

"No, thank you, Lyndon. I'm going to call them next. Samuel and I are flying to Pensacola tomorrow. We'll pick up Eileen and Raymond and fly to San Diego."

"Margaret, it may take two or three days for Tom and Admiral Colby to get home," the President said. "I'll fly out Wednesday or Thursday. We should plan Linda's funeral for Thursday. Does that sound okay?"

"Yes," Margaret said. "Thanks for your help. We'll see you in San Diego, good night." Margaret hung up the receiver as Watson walked back into the den. "Samuel, please call the charter service and hire Steve Barney to fly the jet for us. Then I'll call Eileen and Raymond Bush and let them know when to meet us at the Pensacola airport."

"Yas ma'am," Watson said. "If you had let me learn how to fly the jet, we could leave right now for Pensacola."

Margaret wiped the tears from her eyes and smiled at Watson as she said, "Well, you've finally convinced me, Samuel. Mr. Barney may teach you to fly the jet. You may fly it all the way to California."

"**THANK YOU, MA'AM**!" Watson yelled and picked up the telephone. "I'll call Mr. Steve right now. He gave me his home telephone number just in case we needed him. This shore is one big emergency."

306

Pensacola Municipal Airport
Pensacola, Florida

Watson flew the jet most of the way from Virginia to Florida. Steve Barney had control of the radio. He taught Watson how to fly the VOR and follow the roads in the sky, called airways. The sun was rising as Watson flew the jet across Pensacola Bay and lined up with runway 22. "Nice landing, Sam," Barney said as the main gear kissed the runway. *Damn, Watson was a natural pilot*, Barney thought as they taxied toward the terminal.

"Thank you, suh, I shore enjoyed that," Watson grinned as he parked the jet and pulled the throttles to the shut-off position.

"I'll have the aircraft serviced while you and Mrs. Colby meet Admiral and Mrs. Bush. Then we'll have breakfast," Barney said as he opened the cabin door and lowered the steps. Watson held Margaret's arm as she walked down the steps and across the ramp. She hugged Eileen Bush.

"Did you see my landing, Admiral?" Watson asked as he shook hands with Raymond Bush.

"I didn't know you were a pilot, Watson," Admiral Bush said as he released Watson's hand and embraced him in a bear hug. "That was a very nice landing. Thank you for taking such good care of Margaret."

"Yes suh, Admiral. This ole nigger is one mighty fine pilot," Watson said. "I'm gonna fly you folks all the way to San Diego in my beautiful jet, and we's gonna say good-bye to Miss Linda all nice and proper. Now, let's get some breakfast. Flying shore makes a person powerful hungry."

FORTY-ONE

Death Of Angel 22

USS Concord
Yankee Station

CAG Dick Brown sat at his desk reviewing the targets the Secretary of Defense had selected for the *Concord* to attack when the telephone rang. Chief Wallace answered and placed his hand over the mouthpiece, "The Captain's on the line for you, CAG."

CAG nodded and picked up the phone, "Good morning, Captain."

"CAG, please come to the bridge. We just received a personal message from the White House that I want you to handle for me," Streeper said.

"On my way, Captain," CAG said as he hung up the telephone and grabbed his blue baseball cap. "I'll be on the bridge, chief."

"Roger, CAG," Chief Wallace said as he watched CAG rush out of the office.

CAG walked onto the bridge and saw that Captain Streeper's chair was empty. "The Captain's in his sea cabin, CAG," the OOD said.

"Thanks, Charlie," CAG said and walked to the door leading to the sea cabin. He knocked twice and entered. Captain Streeper was sitting behind his desk.

"Come in and pull up a chair," Streeper said as he handed CAG the message folder. CAG sat in a chair beside the desk and read the message from the White House.

PASS TO: COMMANDER, SEVENTH FLEET
              COMMANDER, 7TH AIR FORCE
PERSONAL FOR CDR TOM COLBY, USN
     TOM, I DEEPLY REGRET TO INFORM YOU THAT LINDA WAS
KILLED IN AN ACCIDENT IN SAN DIEGO AT EIGHTEEN TWENTY-TWO
PACIFIC STANDARD TIME. TOMMY WAS NOT IN THE AUTOMOBILE.
LADY BIRD AND I SHARE IN YOUR GRIEF. SEE YOU IN SAN DIEGO ON
4 APRIL.
     7TH AIR FORCE WILL ARRANGE TRANSPORTATION FOR CDR
COLBY AND COMMANDER, SEVENTH FLEET. GENERAL CURTIS, I
SUGGEST YOU LAND AT NAVAL AIR STATION, REAM FIELD. FUNERAL
PLANNED FOR 4 APRIL.

LYNDON B. JOHNSON
PRESIDENT OF THE UNITED STATES

"JESUS H. CHRIST!" CAG groaned. "Have you told Tom?"

"No CAG, that's your job," Streeper said.

"Damn, this is really gonna break his heart, Sam. May we use your office?"

"Yes CAG, my sentry is trying to find Commander Colby."

The Marine sentry knocked on the door and entered. He stood at attention and said, "Excuse me, Captain, Commander Colby's here."

Tom walked into the sea cabin as the Marine sentry left and softly closed the door behind him. *Jesus, this must be a bad one*, Tom thought as he saw the sober looks on the faces of CAG and Captain Streeper. "Please have a seat, Tom," Captain Streeper said. Tom walked forward and sat in a chair beside CAG.

"Tom, there's just no way to make this any easier," CAG said and handed him the message from the White House.

"Oh, God," Tom said after reading the message. Tears were streaming down his face.

"I'm sorry about Linda's tragic accident, Tom," Streeper said.

Tom wiped tears from his eyes and said, "I'm not going home for the funeral, Captain Streeper."

"BULLCRAP, Tom!" CAG roared. "That message is a direct order from the President of the United States to meet him in San Diego on the fourth of April. Commanders just don't say no to the Commander-in-Chief."

"Take it easy, CAG," Streeper cautioned as the messenger knocked on the door again and entered.

"Excuse me, Captain, we just received an operation immediate message from the Seventh Air Force," he said as he handed the message to Captain Streeper and walked from the room.

Captain Streeper read the message and passed it to CAG Brown. CAG read the message. "This is your ticket home, Tom," he said and handed the message to Tom. He stared at the message, then smiled as he read the message from his godfather, General Curtis.

TOP SECRET
OPERATION IMMEDIATE, 022234Z APR 66

FROM: COMMANDER SEVENTH AIR FORCE
TO: COMMANDER SEVENTH FLEET
      USS CONCORD (CVA-51)
SUBJ: AIR TRANS FOR COMMANDER COLBY AND 7TH FLEET.
1. TOM, PLEASE ACCEPT MY CONDOLENCES. ALL FACILITIES OF 7TH AIR FORCE ARE AT YOUR DISPOSAL IN THIS PERSONAL TRAGEDY.
2.   AS DIRECTED, KC-135 WILL DEPART DA NANG AIR BASE ON 3 APRIL, NOT LATER THAN TEN-HUNDRED-HOURS, FOR SAN DIEGO, CALIFORNIA.
3. REQUEST YOUR ETA AT DA NANG VIA MESSAGE.

LT.GEN. STEVEN CURTIS
COMMANDER, 7TH AIR FORCE
TOP SECRET

"Uncle Steve has a real plush VIP jet, CAG," Tom said and handed the message to Captain Streeper. "I wonder if he'll let his hootch girl act as our hostess again, like he did on the flight to Tan Son Nhut."

"Does that mean you'll go?" CAG asked.

"Yes," Tom said. "Captain Streeper's messenger's gonna walk through that door within the next five minutes with a message from Admiral Dad, ordering my butt on that jet liner."

Captain Streeper said, "Go pack your bag, Tom. The COD will take you to Da Nang at O-nine-hundred."

"Thanks Captain, I really appreciate your help," Tom said. He walked out of the sea cabin and softly closed the door behind him.

"Young Colby's gonna be an Admiral someday, CAG," Streeper said, "Maybe even CNO. Now, get back to the Air Wing business. I have a lot of work to do before O-nine-hundred."

*   *   *

Tom sat in the passenger seat of the C-1A COD aircraft. Some human factors engineer had decided to install the passenger seats facing to the rear in military aircraft. This enhanced survivability during crash landings, but it was rough on passengers during catapult shots from an aircraft carrier. Tom hated CAT shots. The COD taxied forward toward the catapult. He felt the jolt as the aircraft mated with the catapult shuttle. The COD crewman walked to Tom's seat and yelled, "**ARE YOUR STRAPS TIGHT, COMMANDER?**"

Tom pulled hard on the shoulder straps. They were biting into his shoulders. The seat belt was locked around his hips. He locked his hands around the shoulder straps. The crewman sat in the seat across the aisle from Tom and pulled his straps tight. The aircraft began to shake and bounce as the pilot advanced the throttles to takeoff power. When the catapult fired, all of the air rushed from Tom's lungs. His hands lost their grip on the straps and snapped back, trying to pull his arms from their sockets. He hung in the straps for three seconds while the COD was hurled down the catapult, then they were flying.

"**JESUS**!" Tom yelled. "How can you take that everyday?"

"It gets to be routine after the first dozen or so, Commander," the crewman smiled as he opened the cooler and brought out two Cokes. He handed one to Tom.

"Thanks," Tom said as he pulled the tab and took a long drink. The COD would take him to Da Nang Air Base where he would board General Curtis's KC-135. *It's going to be a long, sad flight to California*, he thought as he drank the Coke.

*   *   *

Tom was sleeping when the KC-135 crossed the International Date Line. He regained the day that he had lost, and it was April 3, 1966

311

once again. The jet liner cruised at 41,000 feet. Their estimated time of arrival at Hickam Air Force Base in Hawaii was 8 a.m., where they would clear customs. The jet would be serviced and readied for a 10 a.m. departure for California. Louise Curtis would join them for the last leg of the flight. General Steve Curtis and Admiral Thomas Colby sat in the forward lounge drinking coffee and smoking cigars. Anah Thong refilled their cups and said, "I'm going to check on Commander Tom."

"Don't wake him if he's sleeping, Anah," Curtis said and sipped the hot coffee.

"Okay, General Steve," Anah said and walked to the rear lounge. Tom was snoring. She lowered her head and kissed his cheek. Smiling, she walked back to the forward lounge. "Commander Tom's sleeping. We'll let him sleep for another hour before I wake him for breakfast."

"I hope that I didn't make a mistake bringing Anah to the States," Curtis said. "She's like a daughter and wants to go to Disneyland."

"Well, you should stay over an extra day and take her, Steve," Admiral Colby said. "I'm sure that Louise would enjoy it too."

"Yes, Louise might enjoy Disneyland. I just hope that she likes Anah. You never know how wives will feel about another woman."

"So true, so true," Colby said and waved at Anah. "May I have another cup of that delicious coffee?"

"Yes, Admiral," Anah said and filled his cup.

"Thank you, Anah," he said and watched her walk back to the kitchenette. *It is going to be very interesting to find out what Louise's reaction will be to this beautiful oriental lady,* he thought and sipped the coffee.

USS Belknap
PIRAZ Station
Gulf of Tonkin

LT Terry Fox started the engine of the H-2 Sea Sprite helicopter and quickly engaged the rotors. He went through the takeoff check list as LCDR Bob Wilson left the Combat Information Center (CIC) and ran to the helicopter. The crewman helped Bob with the shoulder harness and seat belt. He gave the pull chocks and tiedown sign as Terry called for takeoff clearance. As LT Fox lifted from the deck, Bob wrote the takeoff time on his knee pad, 4:22 p.m. Bob pressed the intercom switch and said, "We have an Air Force F-4 Phantom down behind Vinh. The Sandys will escort us across the beach to the pickup site. Sure wish Tom Colby was here to back us up."

"We'll get them, Commander," Terry said with confidence as he accelerated the helicopter to 130 knots and climbed to 2,000 feet.

"CIC said the Sandys would be on Two-Fifty-Five point Seven," Bob said and set the frequency into the UHF radio.

"Navy Angel, this is Sandy One, over."

"Sandy One, Angel Two-Two at two-thousand-feet, five miles from the beach," Bob said into the mike.

"Tallyho Two-Two, climb to angels-five, will join on you."

Bob saw the two A-1 Skyraiders fly toward them and join on his left wing. The Skyraider was a piston-engined aircraft with a large four-bladed propeller. Each plane had four twenty-millimeter guns in the wings. They carried two external fuel tanks and a variety of ordnance that included two 500 pound bombs under each wing, sixteen 2.75-inch rockets, and white phosphorus smoke rockets. Sandy One pulled ahead of the helicopter and led them toward the beach.

"Angel Two-Two, Sandy One. We have a positive ID on the flight crew. They're in a clearing about ten miles inland. Pilot's okay, but the BN has a broken leg. I want to make a low pass before you start your approach."

"Roger, One," Bob said. He watched as the Skyraider dived toward a clearing in the jungle.

"Looks all clear Two-Two," Sandy One said as he climbed out of the dive.

"Roger, One," Bob said as he took the flight controls and started a spiral approach toward the clearing. He saw one man laying on the ground and another holding a smoke flare. He planned to land near the injured BN. That would be a lot faster than hoisting them aboard. When he was 10 feet above the ground, fifty-two North Vietnamese soldiers stepped out of the jungle and sprayed the helicopter with automatic rifle fire.

"**SWEET JESUS! IT'S A DAMN TRAP, SANDY ONE!**" Bob screamed into the mike. He pulled up on the collective and accelerated out of the clearing. He felt a hard blow to his chest as a bullet hit his flak vest. Several bullets had struck LT Fox in left arm and neck. His lifeless body was slumped in the shoulder harness.

"Can you make it to the water, Two-Two?" Sandy One asked.

"Don't think so, Sandy," Bob answered. "Copilot's dead, and my crewman is seriously wounded or dead. The bad news is my fuel tank in the bottom of the helicopter is shot to hell. This helo may flame out any minute." Bob knew that he was flying in the dead-man's curve and climbed to 300 feet. At least 200 feet of altitude was required to enter autorotation if the engine failed from fuel starvation.

The beach was two miles away when the engine quit, and the H-2 dropped like a rock. **"MAYDAY! MAYDAY! TWO-TWO GOING IN!"** Bob screamed into the mike and flared the helicopter above the trees. The rotor blades chopped through the trees and lost their momentum. The helicopter bounced through the branches and fell to the ground. Bob was slammed violently forward, then his world went black. Sandy One flew over the wrecked helicopter. The pilot saw no sign of life on the ground. He turned and flew back toward the clearing where Sandy Two was strafing and bombing the Vietnamese soldiers. The Air Force Jolly Green rescue helicopter was fifteen minutes away from the crash site.

*　　*　　*

Bob struggled to regain consciousness. He felt comfortable and safe in the shattered cockpit. Then he saw a double-wing, yellow airplane dive toward the clearing. He recognized the airplane as a Jenny, the World War II Navy flight trainer. The plane came to a hover like the Harrier jet, and slowly settled to the ground beside the wrecked helicopter. This Jenny had three open-cockpits. The pilot climbed from the front cockpit and walked toward Bob. He saluted and said, "My name's Ensign Michael Colby, Commander." He removed the white scarf from around his neck and tossed it to Bob. "This scarf will keep you safe until brother Tom comes for you. Now, I gotta collect my passengers and run. I'm behind schedule. May the Force be with you."

Bob was even more startled to see Lieutenant Terry Fox and Petty Officer Smith walk from the wreckage dressed in white flight suits. They climbed into the two rear cockpits of the Jenny while Ensign Colby climbed into the pilots seat. Colby pushed the throttle forward. The little Jenny leaped into the air and zoomed into the sky.

Bob opened his eyes and looked at the shattered instrument panel and broken windshield. He looked at Terry Fox and saw all the blood. He flexed his hands and moved his feet. He hurt all over, but nothing seemed to be broken. He wondered why the helicopter didn't burn. Then he remembered all the fuel was gone. Slowly he unbuckled his seat belt and climbed out. Tears rolled down his cheeks when he looked in the cabin and saw the twisted body of Petty Officer Third Class Wayne Smith.

Jesus, I must be hallucinating, Bob thought as he remembered the emergency radio. He wrapped the white scarf around his neck and reached into his survival vest for the radio. As he raised the radio to his lips an oriental man stepped from the jungle and pointed a rifle at him. Bob slipped the radio back into his vest and raised both hands above his head. The man walking toward him did not look like a soldier. He looked more like a farmer and was extremely nervous.

Bob lowered his hands and gave the recognition "sign" of a Master Mason. His grandfather had told him this worked during the Civil War. A rebel soldier lay wounded on the ground when a Yankee soldier lowered his rifle to plunge the bayonet into his body. The rebel flashed the sign of a Master Mason. The Yankee then raised the rebel soldier from the ground and treated his wounds. *What the hell did he have to loose?*

Bob broke into a big smile when the man lowered the rifle and propped it against his leg. He responded with the "penalty sign" of a Master Mason. The Vietnamese pointed toward the helicopter and gave the "sign" again. Bob shook his head. The man grabbed Bob's arm and urged him toward the jungle. They disappeared under the trees as Bob heard the roar of the big radial engine of the Skyraider. He knew that Sandy One would be taking photographs of the wrecked angel. Air Intelligence would attempt to make the decision whether to list the helicopter crew as missing or killed in action. *Well, by the grace of God I'm alive, and I'm damn glad that Linda Colby is taking care of my million bucks.*

FORTY-TWO

Long Flight Home

KC-135 at 41,000 feet,
Enroute to Hickam Air Base,
Honolulu, Hawaii

Anah Thong sat the cup of coffee on a small stand beside the bed. She kissed Tom Colby gently on the lips and watched his eyes flutter open. "Good morning, Commander Tom. Breakfast in fifteen minutes."

"Thanks, Anah," Tom said as stood and put on his jockey shorts.

"Hurry, Commander Tom, breakfast will be cold," Anah smiled and closed the door behind her.

Anah is cute and sexy, Tom thought as he shaved and dressed in a fresh white uniform that Anah had hung at the foot of the bed. She even had the gold wings and ribbons placed correctly.

* * *

In the forward lounge of the KC-135, General Curtis read through a stack of Air Force messages. He handed a message to Admiral Colby and said, "The *Belknap* SAR helicopter was shot down yesterday during a rescue attempt of an Air Force F-4 crew. The Sandy pilot circled the area and saw no signs of survivors."

"Damn, Steve," Admiral Colby swore and read the message. "Tom's friend, Lieutenant Commander Bob Wilson, was pilot of that crew. Wait until after breakfast before we brief Tom."

"Sure, Thomas, Tom has had enough bad news to last a lifetime."

Tom opened the door and walked into the lounge. "Good morning gentlemen, sorry I slept so late."

"Breakfast is ready," Anah said. "Come to the table before the eggs get cold."

They sat at the small table while Anah served broiled sirloin steaks, scrambled eggs, hash brown potatoes, toast and orange juice. Tom ate with relish. *I would love to have a hootch girl who can cook and screw like Anah,* he thought. *Uncle Steve is one lucky General.*

"Tom, I'm afraid we have some bad news," Admiral Colby said.

"Dad, I just can't take more fucking bad news."

Anah walked over and whacked Tom on the back. She said, "Officers and gentleman do not say the fucking word, Commander Tom."

"Touche, my cute friend," Tom said and stood to kiss her cheek. "I will try my best never to say that word again."

Tom sat in the chair and said, "I'm ready, Dad."

"We just received a message that the *Belknap* helicopter was shot down yesterday near Vinh during a rescue mission," Admiral Colby said and handed the message to Tom.

Tom read the message and said, "Son-of-a-bitch, I hope Bob got out of that bird." He glanced at Anah.

"That is okay to say, Commander Tom," Anah smiled. "General Curtis say it all the time."

"Anah, you're precious in your innocence," Tom smiled at her. He turned to General Curtis and said, "The message states the crew were killed in action, but my money's on Bob. I have a gut feeling that he's alive."

7th Air Force KC-135 at 33,000 feet
Enroute to NAS Ream Field

Louise Curtis fell in love with the jet liner. General Curtis was pleasantly surprised that his wife liked Anah Thong. They became friends while Anah combed her hair and told how Commander Tom had saved

317

Major King's life during the Viet Cong raid on Da Nang. She opened her purse and showed Louise the Purple Heart Medal that General Curtis had given her. "I'm so happy to fly to America to see Commander Tom's ranch," Anah said, "but most of all I want to see Disneyland."

"Well dear, we'll ask General Curtis to stay an extra day and take us to Disneyland," Louise said.

"Oh, you are so kind and beautiful," Anah squealed. "Okay, if Commander Tom comes to Disneyland with us?"

"You ask him nicely, Anah, and I'm positive that Tom will go to Disneyland with us," Louise said and looked into the mirror to check her hair. Steve had told her that the President was flying out to California for the funeral. *Yes*, she decided, *her hair was perfect for meeting the President and Lady Bird.*

The KC-135 landed at NAS Ream Field at 4:10 p.m. The pilot taxied to the ramp and parked beside Air Force One. Watson and Tommy were waiting in a rented limousine to drive the party to the Colby ranch in Bonita. "Welcome home, Admiral," Watson said.

"When did you and Margaret get here?" Admiral Colby asked.

"We flew out in the jet yesterday, suh," Watson answered. "You're just gonna love the jet. I flew most of the way from Florida. Mister Steve let me make the landing at the Pensacola Airport and at Brown Field. I'm shore getting to be one fine pilot, suh."

"Well, I'm glad Margaret is letting you fly it," Admiral Colby laughed as he introduced Watson to Louise and Steve Curtis and Anah Thong. They gathered the baggage and climbed into the limousine for the short drive to the ranch. Tommy sat in the front seat beside Watson and listened to the stories about the Lear jet.

The Colby Residence
Bonita, California

Tom Colby kissed his mother, then Eileen Bush. He shook hands with Admiral Bush then led Anah toward the bar where the President sat beside Jackie Anderson. "Uncle Lyndon, this beautiful lady is Anah Thong," he said. "Anah, this is the President of the United States."

"I agree with you, Tom," the President said and kissed Anah's hand. "She sure is pretty."

"Thank you, Uncle Lyndon," Anah said and kissed his cheek. "I am so happy to be in America. Mrs. Curtis is taking me to Disneyland."

Tom kissed Jackie Anderson and introduced her to Anah. Admiral Colby walked over and introduced Louise and Steve Curtis to the President. "I'm sorry you didn't get to meet Lady Bird, Louise," the President said as he shook her hand. "She and the girls flew down to the ranch yesterday." He turned to shake hands with Curtis, "Thanks for flying the Colby boys home Steve, I'll make it up to you."

"It was my pleasure Mr. President," Curtis said.

"Knock of the Mr. President crap, Steve. Call me, Chief."

"Yes, sir, Chief," Curtis smiled.

"Let me buy you a drink, Uncle Lyndon," Tom said as he walked behind the bar and picked up a bottle of Jack Daniels and two glasses. "I need to walk and talk." They went outside and walked toward the corral. Two secret service agents strolled along behind them. He poured two glasses of whiskey and handed one to the President.

"The last time I was out here, you were admiring my little ole Wu-Wu-Two DFC, Tom," the President said. "It sure looks mighty good to see you wearing both the Navy and the Air Force Cross."

"Uncle Lyndon, this war sucks," Tom said. "While I was gone to war, my wife was killed by a drunk Navy officer who was driving the wrong way on the freeway. This morning I learned that my best friend, Lieutenant Commander Bob Wilson, was shot down in North Vietnam while trying to rescue two Air Force pilots. He's probably being tortured right now in some stinking POW camp. I've had just about all the grief I can stand."

"Sorry Tom, sure do wish I could hurt for you," the President said. He took the bottle from Tom's hand and poured two small shots in their empty glasses. He raised his glass and said, "A toast, to Linda and Bob Wilson. May the good Lord watch over their spirits and bodies, amen."

"Thanks," Tom said and drank the whiskey. A tear rolled down his cheek. "I just don't think if I ever want to come back to this ranch since Linda won't be here."

"You don't have to go back to Vietnam, Tom. You're qualified to fill a variety of jobs in the Pentagon. I would love to have you at the White House."

"Thank you," Tom said. "I may take you up on that offer when we get back from this little pleasure cruise, but I have to go back and try to find Bob."

"Well, we've had enough to drink tonight, Tom. Your mother's taking us to dinner at the Hotel Del Coronado tonight, so we need to get back up to the bunkhouse and wash up."

*　　*　　*

Margaret Colby could not sleep. She lay in bed and listened to Admiral Colby snore and relived the events of her busy day. She had gone to the morgue to identify Linda's broken body and sign for the possessions that was in the Jaguar. Linda's purse contained $5,000 in cash and an envelope that was addressed to "Tom Colby, Personal." Margaret had opened the envelope and read the letter.

Dearest Tom,

This is my "what if" letter. So much has happened that I must explain it to you in case Tommy and I are involved in an accident before you come home. The $10,000 cash is the bonus on my last real estate transaction. The key is to my safe deposit box at California First Bank. The money is Bob Wilson's. I knew it was stupid to let a million dollars remain in the safe deposit box when it could be earning interest. I have deposited $800,000 in several banks. The pass books are in my safe deposit box.

The 22 trust deeds are properties I bought with my real estate earnings. I love my job with American Financial Services. I'm Vice President of Real Estate. Mr. Glenn Carson is President and General Manager. I hope you never read this letter, and I will be able to explain all this when you get home from the war.

Love ya lots,

Linda

Margaret had gone to the bank and opened the safe deposit box with Linda's key. She removed everything from the box and placed it in a large shopping bag. Watson drove her back to the ranch. Next, she called

American Financial Services and asked to speak to Glenn Carson. She told Carson about Linda's tragic death.

"OH GOD, NO! IT CAN'T BE TRUE!" Carson screamed and struggled to regain his composure.

Margaret said, "Linda was my daughter-in-law. I identified her body and collected her possessions from the coroner. She had five thousand dollars in her purse?"

"Are you sure it was only five thousand?" He asked.

"Yes, there was five thousand dollars in her purse."

"That was the bonus on Linda's last real estate transaction, Mrs. Colby," Carson replied, "but it should have been ten thousand dollars. Please don't worry about it though. I have connections, and I'll check into it. When's the funeral? Some of our staff will want to come, if it's okay with the family."

"Please come, Mr. Carson," Margaret said. "The funeral is scheduled at ten o'clock Thursday morning at Glen Abbey cemetery."

I'm looking forward to meeting Glenn Carson and finding out more about this mystery, she sighed as she closed her eyes and drifted into a troubled sleep.

FORTY-THREE

Burial At Glen Abbey

The Colby Residence
Bonita, California

Samuel Watson watched Anah Thong drink coffee. He liked the cute Vietnamese lady. She had bounced down the stairs at 7 a.m. announcing she would help prepare the breakfast. Admiral Colby and General Curtis came downstairs at 7:30 for breakfast. The presidential limousine picked them up at eight. They rode to Ream Field with the President for the morning briefing. "How long have you been a servant to the Colby family, Sam?" Anah asked.

"I'm an employee, Miss Anah, not a servant," Watson corrected. "My black people have been free for over a hundred years."

"Well, it seems like my people have been fighting for freedom for a hundred years," Anah said. "All I've known is fighting and war."

"Was you father a soldier?"

"Yes, Daddy was a Colonel in the French Foreign Legion."

"So you get those beautiful, sexy blue eyes from your father," Watson laughed.

"If you like sex, I'll make love to you," Anah said and kissed his cheek. "I made love to Mr. Timmy. He's a black Navy pilot, and he's a good lover." She licked her lips. "I'll slip in your room tonight, Mr. Sam."

322

Watson felt a stirring in his loin, but before he could answer, Tom entered the kitchen. He wore jeans, an old Naval Academy sweatshirt, and cowboy boots. "Good morning, pretty lady," he said.

"Mr. Sam and I will fix special breakfast for you, Commander Tom," Anah said as she ran to the stove to cook an omelet.

"Morning, Mr. Tom," Watson said and poured a cup of coffee for Tom. "Did you sleep well, suh?"

"Yes, Sam. After breakfast I'm gonna take Anah horseback riding."

Anah placed the omelet in front of Tom and said, "Will you hold me on, so I won't fall off?"

"Yes, I promise you won't fall," Tom said and looked at Anah's tight silk skirt, "but you can't ride in that skirt. Run upstairs and ask Mother Colby to find you a pair of Linda's riding jeans."

Anah kissed his cheek and walked up the stairs like a lady.

"After the funeral, I want to fly the Lear jet with you, Sam."

"We shore will, Mr. Tom," Watson laughed and jumped up to pour Tom a fresh cup of coffee. "I want you to teach me how to do the victory roll, suh."

"I'll try, Sam, but I may have forgotten how. We don't fly acrobatics in helicopters."

The front door opened and Tommy Colby and Judy Anderson walked toward the kitchen. "Good morning," Watson said, "you all just gotta taste Miss Anah's omelets." Anah walked into the kitchen wearing jeans and a blue, high neck sweater. Tommy glanced at his father, when he saw Anah wearing a pair of his mother's jeans. His father was smiling.

"Turn around, Anah," Tom said and patted the baggy seat of the jeans. "I guess these will do." He turned to Watson and said, "Vietnamese women don't have fat asses like American women, right Samuel?"

"Miss Anah's posterior looks might cute to me," Watson answered truthfully.

"You're kind, Sammy," Anah said, "and you'll have a nice reward."

"Anah and I are going riding," Tom said. "See you all in about an hour." He and Anah walked out the door toward the stable.

"Dad seems to be in a good mood this morning," Tommy said.

"Lord yes, Mr. Tommy," Watson said and placed two plates in front of them. "Mr. Tom and me are flying the Lear jet after Miss Linda's funeral. He's gonna teach me the victory roll."

Little Chapel of the Roses
Glen Abbey Cemetery
Bonita, California

Tom sat in the pew and held his bridge cap as the Baptist minister preached Linda's sermon. He and Admiral Colby wore dress blue uniforms with large medals. General Steve Curtis wore Air Force dress blues. President Johnson work a dark blue suit with a red striped necktie. Tom wore aviator sunglasses. He noticed that his father and General Curtis were also wearing sunglasses. Several pews behind them Coach Sherman Wallace sat with the entire football squad. The minister ended the sermon with a prayer. The pallbearers carried the casket to the grave site. *This is gonna be the tough part,* Tom thought as the casket was lowered into the grave. He lowered his head and thought about Bob Wilson. *He willed Bob to live in his imagination. He could see Bob running from the wrecked helicopter toward the jungle.* Then it was over. Watson nudged his arm. He looked up and saw that Linda's grave had been filled with the fresh dirt. Beautiful flowers covered the grave.

"Is this cemetery for rich people, Commander Tom?" Anah asked.

"No, Anah," Tom said. "Rich and poor people are all buried here."

"I like America," Anah said and stood to stretched. Her legs were sore from horseback riding. She had held tightly to the saddle horn with her left hand and guided the mare with her right. She was like a kid on her first merry-go-round ride. Tom saw the President talking to a tall, white-haired man. He beckoned for Tom to join them.

"Tom, this is an old friend, Sam Salvatorie," the President said. "Sam, this is my nephew, Commander Tom Colby."

"Sorry to meet you under these circumstances, Tom," Salvatorie said and offered his hand.

"Thanks, Mr. Salvatorie," Tom said and shook hands.

"Call me Sam," Salvatorie said and turned to introduce Glenn Carson. Tom shook hands with Glenn, who was also wearing dark sunglasses. There were tear tracks on his cheeks.

324

"Linda worked for us, Commander," Glenn said. "I'd like to meet with you today, if possible, to go over some items."

"Certainly Glenn," Tom said. "I have an appointment to fly for the next hour. Can we meet for a late lunch?"

"Yes, please meet me in the Sky Room at the El Cortez Hotel."

"See you at one," Tom assured him and turned to say good-bye to other guests. *Thank God, this is finally over,* Tom thought and waved for Watson.

El Cortez Hotel
San Diego, California

Tom left the Mustang for the valet to park and walked to the elevator. He wore brown slacks and a brightly colored Hawaiian aloha shirt. Flying the Lear had been good therapy. He had taught Watson to perform barrel rolls and the victory roll. Watson was a natural pilot. He was smooth on the controls, and his landings were textbook perfect. Andre met him as he walked into the Sky Room. "Is Mr. Glenn Carson here?" Tom asked.

"Please follow me, sir," the maitre d' said and led Tom to the window table beside the piano.

Glenn stood and shook hands with Tom and asked, "Would you like a drink, Commander?"

"Yes, Jack Daniels on the rocks," Tom said and added, "I would prefer to be called, Tom."

"Tom, it is," Glenn said and sat in the plush chair. "This was Linda's favorite table. God, I've just gotta stop thinking about it. She was so energetic and full of life." He removed the glasses and wiped his eyes. He reached inside his coat pocket and withdrew an envelope and handed it to Tom. "Our company carries a two hundred thousand dollar life insurance policy on all employees and associates. They also have a double indemnity clause for accidental deaths."

Tom opened the envelope and removed the check. The payee was listed as, "Commander Tom Colby, USN." The amount was $400,000. He said, "Thanks Glenn, how did you meet Linda?"

"Commander Bob Wilson recommended Linda to us."

325

"Now, I remember. You were flying with Bob in his three-ten when the Border Patrol agent knocked Bob on his butt at Brown Field, right?"

"Correct," Glenn laughed. "Have you seen whales while you were flying off the San Diego coast?"

"Yes, we often see them out in the Ream Field practice area. Did you hear that Bob was shot down over North Vietnam?"

"No!" Glenn exclaimed. "Did he get out?"

"Bob and his crew are listed as killed in action, but I have a gut feeling that Bob's alive." The waiter took their order and hurried to the bar for another Jack Daniel's on the rocks. Tom didn't remember drinking the whiskey. *Damn, I've got to eat some lunch before I get plastered,* he thought as the waiter sat the fresh drink in front of him.

Lunch arrived and Glenn ordered a bottle of Chardonnay. "Sorry, Tom, that was an automatic response. Linda always enjoyed Chardonnay with her meal."

"I would also enjoy a glass of wine," Tom said. The waiter pulled the cork and poured two glasses of the sparkling wine. They ate lunch in silence, each lost in their thoughts.

"How much longer do you have to stay in the Navy?" Glenn asked.

"It's not a matter of having to stay in the Navy. I chose the Navy as a career because I love to fly. I can retire in three years on twenty. Since I made Commander, I can stay for twenty-six years. If I'm lucky enough to make Captain or Admiral, I can remain on active duty for thirty years or longer."

"If you decide to retire, we'd like for you to be our corporate pilot."

"How much does the job pay?"

"Around a hundred thousand a year," Glenn answered.

"That's a very attractive offer, Glenn, "but I must go back to Vietnam and try to find Bob."

"If you find Bob Wilson, I'll guarantee you a hundred thousand dollar reward," Glenn said.

"The United States Navy would court martial my butt if I accepted any reward, Glenn," Tom said, "but I might consider letting you pay me under-the-table."

"We have a deal," Glenn said as he reached across the table to shake Tom's hand.

"Thanks for the lunch," Tom said as he stood and picked up the insurance check. "I hate to eat and run, but I promised a young lady that I'd take her to Disneyland."

FORTY-FOUR

R & R In Hong Kong

Hong Kong
British Crown Colony

Jack Warner sat in the back seat of the taxi and clutched the leather notebook in his lap as the driver dodged through the traffic. The driver turned right on Nathan road, a four-lane boulevard with wide sidewalks. Jack left the taxi four blocks short of his destination. It was a beautiful, clear day. A perfect day for walking as the sun hung low in the western sky. He walked at a fast pace with a spring in his step. A walk that he had learned during his short career in the Marine Corps.

He carried the notebook in his right hand and thought about the lunch disaster with Major Calvin Stillman, USMCR. They had become friends at Flight School in Pensacola. Cal flew the C-130 Hercules, Marine transport plane out of Chu Lai. He was certain that he would not survive his twelve month tour in Vietnam. Cal had flown 127 Marines from Chu Lai to Hong Kong for seven days of rest and recuperation, commonly referred to as R and R. They would leave Kai Tak Airport at 6:00 p.m. for the return flight to Chu Lai and the combat zone. Jack glanced at his watch, he was right on time. He left the sidewalk and walked into the Yacht Club Park.

"Daddee!" Jack glanced to his left to see his four-year-old daughter, Sherry, running toward him from behind a tree. Kathy Warner was walking toward him. Beside Kathy was Ann Curtis and Tom Colby.

Sherry grabbed his leg, and he bent down to kiss her. "Hi, Daddy," Sherry said and kissed his cheek. "We saw Uncle Tom's big boat this afternoon."

Jack kissed his wife and shook hands with Tom. "Who's the beautiful blonde?"

"Jack, this is Ann Curtis, my college roomie," Kathy said. "Ann, this is my husband, Jack."

"Kathy tells me that you've published two novels," Ann said and offered her hand. A Nikon was slung over her shoulder.

"Yes, and I'm about finished with my third," he said and took her warm, soft hand in his, "but this consulting business keeps interfering with my writing time."

"Ann's a war correspondent for the *Washington Post*, " Kathy said.

"Well, I'm impressed," Jack said and released her hand. He glanced at his watch and grabbed Sherry's hand. "Come along guys, the boat will be waiting for us." He walked briskly down the pier while Sherry ran to match his pace.

Kai Tak Airport
Hong Kong

Victor Chang supervised the crew as they swarmed over the giant C-130 Hercules, cleaning and polishing the aluminum skin. Staff Sergeant George King, USMC, was the plane captain. He was responsible for everything that happened to the airplane while it was on the ground. "What time's your takeoff, Sergeant King?" Chang asked.

"It's supposed to be classified, Vic," King answered. "Don't say anything to the workers, but Major Stillman said that he wants the wheels in the well by eighteen-hundred-hours. That's six p.m. civilian time."

"My crew will be done with the wax job by seventeen-hundred," Chang said and looked at his wrist watch. "I'll watch the plane for you if you want to go to the bar for a beer." He blew a whistle and motioned for his driver.

"Thanks a lot, Vic," King said as the Rolls-Royce pulled up by the side of the plane. "I'll have two quick beers and be back in thirty minutes. Sure wished I had time for one more piece of poontang." Nobody was going to blow up his airplane while Vic's people were working on it.

Chang smiled as the Rolls carried Sergeant King toward the terminal. Maybe he should open a house of prostitution to service the young Marines. He would have a ready market since the big airplanes flew in a fresh group of 120 Marines each week. He reached for the tool box and climbed the scaffold under the number three engine. He attached a small bomb to the combustion chamber of the turbo-jet engine. The bomb was designed to look like an engine accessory. He set the trigger to explode when the airplane climbed to 100 feet of altitude. Then he went inside the airplane and opened the electronic panel. He located the wires leading to the feather button of the number 3 and number 4 propellers. He switched the wires and closed the panel.

Victor Chang was a Hong Kong businessman, not a murderer. The Vietnamese cartel had paid him $50,000 in gold and promised another $50,000 when the American airplane was destroyed. His plan was to disable the plane on takeoff and force it to land in the shallow bay. The young Marines were taught to evacuated an airplane that ditched in the water. They would be out of the airplane before it sank to the shallow bottom of the bay.

Chang closed the tool kit and left the airplane. He walked around the airplane and yelled at the crew. The coolie had missed waxing a spot on the side of the fuselage under the gold letters, UNITED STATES MARINE CORPS. The coolie rushed to obey his orders and rubbed the gold letters until they glistened in the sunlight. Chang smiled as he watched the crew work. Victor Chang always did a number-one job to keep his customer's happy.

CIA Yacht
Hong Kong Harbor

Jack and Tom sipped cold beers on the fantail of the CIA yacht. The yacht was taking them to the famous floating restaurant for dinner. "I was truly sorry to hear about Linda's tragic death," Jack said. "I would've flown back for the funeral, but it was all over when I got back from a field operation."

"Thanks, Jack," Tom said and sipped the cold beer. "General Curtis flew Dad and me home in his KC-135 jetliner. On the way back to the States, we got a message that my friend, Bob Wilson, was shot down on a rescue attempt near Vinh, and declared killed in action. Uncle Lyndon flew out for the funeral on Air Force One. Mother is staying at my home in Bonita until Tommy graduates from high school. The only fun part of the whole ordeal was taking Watson for a flight in Dad's Lear jet. I taught him how to do victory rolls. The other fun part was taking General Curtis's hootch girl, Anah Thong, to Disneyland."

Jack placed the notebook on the small table. The name Anah Thong had triggered an alarm in his mind, but he could not recall the details. He would look into it later. "This is my brains, Tom," he said and opened the thin lap-top computer revealing a typewriter-style keyboard and a green LCD display.

Tom still did not trust Jack since the foul up with Operation Get Even, where the wounded gook had tried to grenade the Jolly Green helicopter. "Does it have James Bond gadgets inside it?" He asked.

"No Tom, this doesn't belong to the Agency. It's a genuine portable computer. I did a favor for a friend, and he made this one especially for me. It has a 68000 microprocessor and eighty megabytes of memory. This baby has enough storage for a whole book." Jack typed in a code and gained access to the directory. He typed in LCDR. ROBERT WILSON, USNR. A message appeared on the display. "You never saw this," he said as he turned the screen toward Tom.

TOP SECRET
26 APR 66, CODE 601-235568-26-4
FOR: AGENT JOHN WARNER-EYES ONLY
SITUATION: LCDR. ROBERT WILSON, USNR, MISSING-IN-ACTION 2 APR 66, DURING RESCUE ATTEMPT NEAR VINH, DEMOCRATIC REPUBLIC OF VIETNAM.
1. INTEL HAS POSITIVE AUTHENTICATOR SUBJECT IS ALIVE AND IN GOOD STATE OF HEALTH. AIR INTEL PHOTOS REVEAL THAT LT. TERRY FOX AND PETTY OFFICER WAYNE SMITH WERE KILLED-IN-ACTION. RECOVERY OF BODIES NOT ATTEMPTED.
2. WILSON IN HANDS OF UNKNOWN FRIENDLY FORCE.
3. AGENTS BRIEF, 1300 HOURS, 3 MAY 66, TAN SON NHUT.
TOP SECRET

"Jesus Christ," Tom whispered. "Thanks a lot, Jack. I had a gut feeling that Bob got out of the helo. How in the hell are we gonna rescue him out of North Vietnam?"

"You want in on this after you almost got your ass blown off in our last operation?" Jack asked.

"Just try to keep me out," Tom said and thought about the reward that Glenn Carson had offered for the rescue of Bob Wilson. He looked toward Kai Tak Airport where a C-130 transport was taking off. He could read the lettering on the fuselage, UNITED STATES MARINE CORPS. "Some of the leather-necks are returning to the war zone after R and R in Hong Kong."

"That's probably Major Stillman's plane," Jack said as they watch the airplane slowly gain altitude. "I had lunch with him today at the club. He sure has a morbid outlook on his tour in Vietnam."

BOOM

Tom jumped up at the sound of the explosion from the C-130. He walked to the rail and watched as pieces of the number-3 engine fell into the bay. Fire streamed from the engine as the ruptured fuel lines spewed jet fuel on the hot engine. Then he saw the number-4 engine go to the full feather position. "The pilot feathered the wrong engine, Jack," he said as the airplane nosed over and glided toward the water. "There's no way in hell that he can keep her airborne with both engines out on his right wing. God, I hope he doesn't hit those boats."

Ann aimed her Nikon and clicked the shutter.

Jack ran forward and directed the coxswain to steer toward the distressed aircraft. The pilot was making a valiant effort to dodge the numerous boats and yachts as he glided toward the bay. A large yacht turned and tried to flee from the crippled airplane. The C-130 skimmed across the bay and struck the water. The left wing tip hit the fleeing yacht and knocked off the rear end. The yacht turned over and began to sink. The big C-130 quickly sank to the bottom of the bay. The top 10 feet of the vertical stabilizer stuck out of the water. Heads of the survivors began to pop out of the water with agonizing slowness. "Do you know how many Marines are aboard the plane, Jack?" Tom asked.

"Cal said around a hundred and twenty," Jack answered as the coxswain neared the sinking yacht. "My God, that's Prince Charles' boat!"

Tom kicked off his shoes and dove into the water. He swam toward a man who was struggling to swim in the water. Jack grabbed a life bouy and threw it toward Tom. Within minutes, the crew pulled Tom and Prince Charles aboard the yacht.

"Easy with his arm, Tom," Kathy Warner said as she reached into her black bag for a syringe. She plunged a needle into the fleshy part of Prince Charles' shoulder. The morphine would ease his pain after the adrenaline shock subsided. She applied a soft splint to his left arm while Ann draped a blanket over him and propped a pillow under his head.

Prince Charles opened his eyes and smiled as he looked at Ann's blonde hair glistening in the sunlight. "I must be in heaven. Are you an angel, luv?"

"Yes, your Royal Highness," Ann teased. "My name's Angel Ann, and that's Angel Kathy treating your broken arm."

He glanced at Kathy's red hair and said, "Thank you Dr. Kathy for making the pain go away."

"You're quite welcome your Highness," Kathy said and strapped his left arm in a sling. "Would you like a cup of tea or a beer?"

"A beer, please. If Angel Ann will hold it for me."

Ann reached inside the cooler for a beer and removed the top. She sat on the deck and cradled his head in her lap. She held the bottle to his lips and he took several long swallows. Two large crash-fire rescue boats left the pier at Kai Tak Airport and sped toward the crash site with sirens wailing.

Tom knelt beside Ann, "How's Prince Charles feeling?"

"I feel great, mate," Prince Charles said as the morphine reached his central nervous system. He felt like he was floating on a cushion of air. The beautiful angel was holding him to the boat.

"Damn, I probably ruined my Rolex," Tom said as he removed the gold wrist watch Ann had given him for Christmas. He shook the watch and put it to his ear. It was still ticking.

"Not to worry, mate," Prince Charles said. "I'll buy you a dozen gold watches for fishing my tail out of the bay." He raised his head and sucked on the bottle of beer.

Jack maneuvered the yacht toward the seven Marines who were standing on top of the fuselage. They strained to hold their heads above water. One-by-one they grabbed the Jacobs ladder Tom threw over the side. Silently they climbed aboard the boat and glanced anxiously at the submerged airplane, hoping their buddies would find the exits. Tom draped blankets around their shoulders and gave each man a bottle of beer.

*   *   *

As the C-130 began to sink, Staff Sergeant George King had popped the overhead escape hatch. He pulled Major Stillman through the opening. The copilot, Captain John Leach, was the third man out of the aircraft. Four more Marines got out before the airplane filled with water. The remaining 116 Marines drown as they frantically tried to kick out the windows. Finally, all was quite, except for the wail of the sirens as the two rescue boats arrived on the scene.

Vung Yen Village
Democratic Republic of Vietnam

Bob Wilson sat in the small bedroom of the thatched hut and looked at his precious survival radio. A bullet had struck the voice section rendering it useless, but the emergency beeper still worked. He would have to be very careful to conserve the battery. It had been six weeks since his H-2 Sea Sprite helicopter was riddled with bullets, killing his copilot and crewman. A North Vietnamese fisherman had led him away from the wreck minutes before the NVA soldiers arrived at the crash site.

The door opened and a tall, beautiful Vietnamese lady walked into the room with a tray of food. She placed the tray on his lap and washed his face and hands with a warm cloth. "Hurry Bobby, and eat food. Friday is lodge night. You're honored guest," she said as she sat on the floor beside him. Her name was Quyen Toon. She was the second miracle that Bob had experienced after his Masonic signal was recognized by Ben Toon. He had followed the fisherman ten miles through the dark jungle to the fishing village of Vung Yen. Quyen spoke English.

On the tray was a large bowl of boiled rice and three small fish. The fish had been cooked whole. *Why are their eyes always open?* Bob wondered. He had spent the day working on Toon's boat. His muscles ached from pulling on the long, heavy net. They caught 72 small fish. He finished the meal and smiled as Quyen wiped his mouth. "Thank you, Quyen, for that delicious dinner," he said to her in Vietnamese. Quyen had been teaching him the language. At first, she was too frightened to look at him. Now, she wanted to spend every minute with him.

She kissed him softly on his lips and said, "Hurry Bobby, and put on clean clothes. Daddy Toon will leave soon for the lodge." She picked up the tray and left the room. Bob looked at the tan cotton trousers and white shirt that Quyen had left for him. He took off the smelly work clothes and put on the clean trousers and shirt. He walked across the path and entered Ben Toon's house. Ben had taken him to the lodge the two previous Friday night's. They walked to the lodge in silence. Bob tied the masonic apron around his waist and shook hands with the Tyler. A Third Degree ceremony was scheduled tonight. He was looking forward to it.

FORTY-FIVE

Knighthood

Hong Kong
British Crown Colony

The CIA yacht rushed Prince Charles and the seven Marines to the airport pier. They were loaded in ambulances and rushed to King Edward Hospital. Dinner at the floating restaurant was momentarily forgotten as Tom Colby, Ann Curtis and the Warner's rode to the hospital in the police car. Jack was talking to the police while Tom searched for refreshments. He walked into the private waiting room with five Cokes and a bag of cookies for Sherry.

"Thank you, Uncle Tom," Sherry said as she opened the cookies and offered one to Ann.

"No thank you, darling," Ann said.

Tom handed Cokes to Kathy and Ann. Then he sat beside Ann and sipped his Coke. On the way to the pier, he had removed his wet clothes and changed into a pair of Jack's trousers and shirt. He thought about the 116 young Marines. *They had fought bravely in Vietnam, only to die in the plane crash while returning from rest and recuperation in Hong Kong.*

In a room across the hall Jack talked to the two policemen. George Goodridge appeared to have seniority. Inspector William Albrecht was forty-five. His red hair and smiling eyes contrasted with Goodridge's bald-head and solemn eyes. Both detectives wore gray wool suits. Inspector Goodridge took a tape recorder from his briefcase and set it on the table.

He plugged in the microphone and punched the record button. The cassette began to rotate as he announced the place, time and date.

"Dr. Warner, do you know this conversation is being recorded?" He asked.

"Yes, Inspector," Jack answered.

"Do you have any objection to being recorded?"

"No, sir."

"Give us your name and address, please."

"John Paul Warner. Our home address is Arlington, Virginia."

"Your occupation?" Goodridge looked his note pad.

"I'm a writer and computer consultant."

"What was the purpose of your visit to Hong Kong?"

"My wife, Kathy, needed time off from the hospital. We made this a vacation and business trip. I'm doing research for my next novel."

"I understand you are acquainted with the pilot of the aircraft."

"Yes, that's correct. Major Stillman and I became good friends while we were attending Navy Flight School in Pensacola, Florida. We had lunch today at the Town House Club."

"You're a flier, doctor?"

"Yes, I had a very short career in the Marine Corps. I was flying a H-46 helicopter when the engine failed. We landed on top of some big trees, and it was a long fall to the ground. My back was injured, and the Corps gave me a disability discharge."

"Did Major Stillman seem distraught or depressed?"

"Oh, God yes! He was downright morbid all through lunch, talking about how he was not going to live through his Vietnam tour."

"Did the pilot feather the wrong engine?"

"Yes, Inspector. In fact, Commander Colby brought that to my attention."

"Do you think that the airplane was sabotaged?"

"I have no way to draw a conclusion on that, Inspector. We heard an explosion as the airplane was taking-off from Kai Tak Airport. The number-three engine began to burn, and the pilot feathered the number-four engine."

"Did you know that Prince Charles' boat was in the Bay, doctor?" Albrecht asked.

"No, sir."

"Did the pilot make every effort to avoid Prince Charles' boat?" Goodridge asked.

"Yes, sir, but you must realize that with two engines out, on the same side, the pilot could not keep the heavily loaded airplane in the sky. He had to try to land in the middle of all those boats."

"Well, I think we have covered everything," Goodridge said.

"Good day, gentlemen," Jack said. He walked across the hall and entered the private waiting room. He saw the group talking to Queen Elizabeth and Prince Philip.

"Your Majesty, this is my husband, Dr. Jack Warner," Kathy said.

"Good evening, Dr. Warner," the Queen said. "I'm sorry that Charles spoiled your dinner plans." The Queen was dressed in light green suit. The Prince wore a dark blue, double-breasted suit. He stood to shake Jack's hand.

"Good evening, your Majesty," Jack smiled.

"Dr. Warner," the Queen said formally, "We wish to express our most profound gratitude for your action this afternoon in saving Prince Charles' life."

"You're welcome, your Majesty. I was glad to be of service, but Commander Colby deserves the praise. He had the foresight to see that Prince Charles was injured. He dove into the water and saved the Prince's life."

"I think you're both hero's," the Duke of Edinburgh said. "How shall we reward these gentlemen, darling?"

"With all due respect, Prince Philip, I'm a United States Naval officer and cannot accept any reward," Tom said. "Please give the reward to Jack."

"Commander Colby, must I remind you that you are half-British by birth? Margaret would be ashamed of you not acknowledgeing your birthright," the Queen chastised.

"I apologize, your Majesty," Tom said. "I'm very proud to be half-British."

"Your apology is accepted, Tom. One of the wonderful things about being Queen is that I am permitted to recognize meritorious actions and reward them properly. Accordingly, I have decided to invest you and

Dr. Warner as Knights of the Chesterfield Order. You will henceforth be known as Sir Thomas Edward Colby and Sir John Paul Warner."

"Since we spoiled your dinner plans, we'd be most happy to have you dine with us at the Hilton," Prince Philip said.

The Queen stood and said, "Come ladies, the Hilton has the most marvelous leg of lamb." She led them toward the elevator.

Vung Yen Village
Democratic Republic of Vietnam

Bob Wilson sat on the south side of the Masonic Lodge as Dan Toon was raised to the sublime degree of a Master Mason. He rehearsed the few phrases of the Vietnamese language that Quyen had taught him so patiently. The Senior Warden gave the charge to brother Toon, then it was time to present the apron. Bob stood and faced the East and saluted the Worshipful Master. He spoke the Vietnamese words that Quyen had taught him, "Most Worshipful Master, I'd be most honored to present the apron to Brother Toon." The Worshipful Master smiled and nodded his approval.

Bob walked to the alter and picked up the Masonic apron. He stood before Toon and said, "My brother, it's my great honor to present you with this lambskin, or white leather apron. It's an emblem of innocence and the badge of a Mason - more ancient than the Golden Fleece or Roman Eagle; more honorable than the Star and Garter, or any other Order that can be conferred upon you at this time or any future period by king, prince, potentate, or any other person, except he be a Mason." Bob ended the presentation by saying, "I hope you'll always wear it with pride to yourself and honor to our fraternity." He stepped forward and tied the apron around Toon's waist. He adjusted the apron flap then shook hands with the smiling Toon.

Bob and Ben Toon walked back to the thatched huts in silence. "Good thing you do for cousin Dan," the elder Toon said as he stopped by Bob's door. "Good night."

"Good night, Ben." Bob watched the old fisherman walk across the road to his small house. Then he walked into the tiny room and saw that Quyen had turned down his bed. She lay in the bed under the light sheet.

"How was your speech, Bobby?" Quyen asked.

"It went great," Tom said and sat on the bed to removed his shoes.

"Come to bed and tell me about it," she said and pushed back the cover. She was nude beneath the sheet.

"Quyen, I've tried to explain why I cannot make love to you," he groaned as he removed his shirt and trousers. "I can't make love to a Master Mason's daughter."

"Daddy Toon is not my father, Bobby! My father was a Sergeant in the French Foreign Legion. He was not a mason."

"Ben Toon's not your father?"

"No, Bobby," she laughed. "Daddy Toon is my uncle. I come to live with him as a small girl when my momma die."

"Why in the hell didn't you tell me," Bob groaned as he lowered his head to kiss her. "God, I've wanted to make love to you for so long." Quyen pulled Bob under the cover and blew out the candle. The room was filled with darkness and her purring sounds as they made love. A long time later, Bob arose and put on his trousers. He must write his message in the sand again. Maybe one night a recon plane would take a picture of his message. He walked to the beach and drew large letters in the sand.

SOS   LCDR WILSON   SN 667679 USN
RADIO BROKE   MSG FOR CDR COLBY
USS CONCORD SOS

He walked back to the thatched hut and wiped the sand from his feet before crawling in bed with Quyen. She smiled and rolled into his arms. *This sure is a crazy mixed-up war,* Bob thought and caressed her sensuous body. He fell asleep as he listened for a plane to fly over his beach.

Dining Room
Hong Kong Hilton Hotel

CAG Dick Brown could not believe his eyes when he walked into the dining room and saw Tom Colby sitting at the table with Queen Elizabeth and Prince Philip. CAG was wearing his Navy short sleeve, white uniform with gold wings and ribbons. He saw Ann Curtis' beautiful blonde hair as she raised a hand and waved to him. *Damn, this has to be good,* CAG thought and strode toward the table. "Pardon the intrusion, your Majesty," CAG address the Queen. "I wanted to say hello to Tom and Ann."

"Good evening, Commander," the Queen's eyes smiled at him. "Sir Thomas, please introduce your brother officer."

Sir Thomas, CAG thought. *Is young Colby some sort of knight?*

"I'd be most happy to, your Majesty," Tom said as he stood and shook hands with CAG. "This is CAG Dick Brown. He's the Carrier Air Wing Commander on the *Concord.* CAG, this is Queen Elizabeth and Prince Philip. You remember Ann Curtis. This couple is Sir John and Lady Kathy Warner, and this young lady is Princess Sherry."

"I no princess, Uncle Tom," Sherry said. "I'm your beautiful niece."

"That's quite correct, Sherry," Prince Philip said and stood to shake CAG's hand.

CAG walked to the head of the table and said, "I'm so please to meet your Majesty." The Queen offered her hand. CAG shook it gently.

"Would you prefer to be addressed as CAG or Dick?" She asked.

"Please call me Dick," CAG said and released her hand.

"Dick, we'd love to have you join us for a brandy," the Queen said. "I want to tell you about Sir Thomas and Sir John rescuing the Prince of Wales from the bay this evening, after the Marine airplane crashed into his boat."

"Was Prince Charles injured?" CAG asked as he sat in the chair beside Ann Curtis.

"His left arm was broken," the Queen answered. "Lady Kathy is an excellent surgeon. She administered medication and immobilized his arm. Charles will not let anyone but Lady Kathy touch his arm."

"I can vouch that Tom is a hero, your Majesty," CAG said. "He flew his helicopter through intense enemy fire and saved me from almost certain death when my jet was shot down near Haiphong Harbor before Christmas. I recommended him for the Navy Cross Medal. He has also been awarded the Navy Distinguished Flying Cross."

"I want to hear all the details, Dick," the Queen said as the waiter served CAG a brandy. "Margaret and I are good friends, and I want to write her a long letter about Sir Thomas' heroic exploits in Vietnam."

"Your Majesty, I'm a correspondent for the Washington Post. May I please take a photograph of you and these two heroes?" Ann asked.

"Certainly, Ann, I would be delighted. Come, gentlemen," she beckoned to Tom and Jack. Ann smiled as she focused the Nikon. This was an unexpected scoop. After Queen Elizabeth and Prince Philip said good night, Tom excused himself and walked to the front desk. He drafted a telegram to Glenn Carson in San Diego.

GLENN

HAVE POSITIVE PROOF THAT LCDR BOB WILSON SURVIVED THE CRASH STOP WILL ATTEND AN INTELLIGENCE BRIEFING ON 3 MAY STOP PROMISE TO FORWARD DETAILS AS SOON AS POSSIBLE. BEST REGARDS

SIR THOMAS COLBY
HONG KONG HILTON HOTEL

Tom smiled and walked back to the lounge. CAG sat in the lounge beside Ann and sipped his drink. "To Sir Tom and Ann," CAG said as he raised his glass of scotch. "Jesus, you kids are so lucky to have each other and be so much in love. I wish that Kim Ellis had flown out with you, Ann. That lady has really gotten under my skin. This is the first time I've been in love since I lost Charlene, four years ago."

Ann reached for her purse and wrote Kim's telephone number on a piece of paper. "Give Kim a call, Dick," Ann said as she place the paper in his hand. "I promise you that she'll be in Hong Kong by sunrise."

"Thank you so very, very much, Ann," CAG said. He stood and kissed her cheek and walked toward the lobby to call Hawaii.

"Did you tell CAG we're staying here at the Hilton?" Tom asked.

"No, darling."

Tom drained his drink and said, "Let's go, Ann. I want to make mad, passionate love to you all night long."

"I've heard you make promises like that before, Sir Tom," Ann laughed and took his arm. They hurried toward the elevator. "I've never made love to a knight before," Ann said and raised her head to kiss him. The door closed as the elevator rose toward the twentieth floor. "Do you love me, Sir Tom?"

"God yes, darling," Tom answered as he held her in his arms. "I have always loved you, beautiful lady."

"I would love to have your baby, Sir Thomas."

"Jesus Christ, Ann!" Tom exclaimed. "Don't talk like that. Tommy and Judy will probably make me a grandfather one day soon. I'm too old to be starting another family."

"You're only as old as you feel, sailor boy, and tonight I feel like a college girl." The elevator stopped at the 20th floor. Ann took his hand and led him toward the suite.

FORTY-SIX

Message In The Sand

Navy Recon Flight
40,000 feet above Vinh
Democratic Republic of Vietnam

The RA-5C Vigilante flew over Vung Yen Village at 3 a.m. The big twin-engine jet was built by North American Aviation. Lieutenant Charles Oaks loved to fly the big bird. She was supersonic with a service ceiling of 60,000 feet. This made her an ideal platform for photo recon. His mission was to photograph the beach from Vinh to Da Nang. Then he would land at Tan Son Nhut Air Force Base near Saigon where the film would be delivered to the Defense Intelligence Agency (DIA). He had no idea he was taking photographs of a message scrawled in the sand by a Naval aviator.

Charles cruised at Mach 1.2 - faster than the speed of sound or a rifle bullet. He didn't worry about the MiG's or Surface to Air Missiles. He would be over South Vietnam before they could scramble a MiG or get the SAM site operating. He concentrated on flying the route prescribed by DIA and thought about the day of liberty that he would enjoy at the Air Force Base.

*   *   *

The sonic boom from the Vigilante rippled through the fishing village of Vung Yen. Bob Wilson heard the boom and thought it was a distant bomb dropped by the A-6 Intruder. He rolled over on the small bed and pulled Quyen into his arms then drifted back into a peaceful sleep. He dreamed of the golden hills of southern California. He awoke before sunrise and walked to the beach. He was raking out his message when a small girl fell from a fishing boat into the water. The boat was tied to the short pier that jutted out into the bay. The mother was cooking over a charcoal fire, and did not see her daughter's frantic struggles. Bob yelled a warning as the girl sank beneath the surface. He ran out on the pier and jumped into the water. His hand clutched the girl's clothing brought her to the surface. She lay lifeless in his arms as he climbed onto the pier.

Her frantic parents huddled around Bob as he held the girl upside-down by her feet. The mother began to scream as water drained out of her daughter's mouth and nose. Bob placed her on the pier and gently pinched her nostrils with his left hand. He lowered his head and blew into her mouth. His right hand, resting on her rib cage could feel a tiny heart beat. He continued to administer mouth-to-mouth resuscitation to the child. The village was quickly awakened by the mother's frantic screams. They began to gather on the beach near the pier and watched as the American pilot blew into the girl's mouth. Quyen knelt beside him and said, "She's dead, Bobby. Give her to family."

Bob shook his head and continued to breath for the small girl. He had counted twenty-two breaths when the child sputtered. She spit out water and started to cry. Bob handed her to the sobbing mother. Then he took Quyen's hand and walked down the pier toward their shack. The people on the beach parted for them and quietly bowed. He wanted to change out of the wet clothes and get back to the pier before Toon's boat set sail for the fishing lanes. Quyen grabbed a towel and rubbed his back, "Hurry and put on dry clothes. I go with you on the boat today."

Bob stepped into the trousers and quickly buttoned the cotton shirt. He placed an old straw hat on his head and said, "Let's go, Quyen-san."

Quyen grabbed a basket and dashed out the door ahead of him. "Today, we have a picnic, Bobby, and then I teach you more Vietnamese talk." The crowd of villagers were still clustered on the beach as Bob and Quyen walked down the pier to Toon's boat.

Ben Toon was smiling. He kissed Quyen's cheek and shook hands with Bob. "Today, you be Captain," he said and placed Bob's hand on the tiller. The crew cast off the lines and pushed the boat away from the pier. The sail filled with air, and the boat began to move out of the harbor. *It's just like driving an airplane,* Bob thought as he cautiously moved the rudder and tacked the boat into the quartering wind. Quyen appeared at his side with a bowl of steaming rice and fish. She fed him breakfast with chopsticks. *It's nice being the Captain,* he thought, *but I'm getting damn tired of eating rice and fish three times a day.*

Hong Kong Hilton
British Crown Colony

Tom Colby checked for messages at the front desk while Ann went to the newsstand for a copy of the *Washington Post* and the *New York Times.* The clerk handed him a telegram from Glenn Carson and Ann's package of photographs. Kim Ellis ran across the lobby to meet them. She hugged Ann and kissed Tom. "Dick told me all about your heroic deeds, Sir Tom," Kim said.

"I see you've met the Warners," Tom said when they reached the table.

"Good morning, Tom, Ann," CAG Brown said.

"Morning, CAG," Tom said and handed Ann the photographs. As she passed them around the table and explained the scenes to Kim and CAG, Tom opened the telegram from Glenn Carson.

SIR THOMAS COLBY, HONG KONG HILTON
CODE: HK-7727

THANK YOU FOR THE BRIEF ON LCDR ROBERT WILSON STOP OUR AGENT IN HONG KONG IS VICTOR CHANG STOP CHANG INDUSTRIES 700 KOWLOON ROAD STOP VIC WILL PROVIDE ANY ASSISTANCE YOU NEED DAY OR NIGHT TO NEGOTIATE WITH VIETNAMESE STOP

MOST SINCERELY
GLENN CARSON
SAN DIEGO, CALIFORNIA

Tom folded the telegram and passed it to Jack Warner as Ann ordered breakfast. He ordered steak and scrambled eggs, hash brown potatoes, and a double order of wheat toast. Sipping the hot coffee, he watched Jack read the telegram. Warner's expression never changed as he folded the telegram and put it in his shirt pocket. Victor Chang's name had triggered an alarm in his memory bank. He was anxious to get to his computer and run a check.

"Kim and I are going flying later in the morning if anyone would care to join us," CAG Brown said.

"I'd love too, CAG," Ann said, "but I have to go down to the Associated Press office and file my story to the *Washington Post*."

Kathy Warner explained that she was expected at the hospital to see Prince Charles.

Tom said, "Jack and I meeting with the accident board investigators about the crash of the Marine C-130 Hercules."

The group finished breakfast in silence and mentally planned their busy day. Tom and Jack were the first to leave in search of Victor Chang Industries. Ann was next, followed closely by Kathy Warner.

CAG lingered over a second cup of coffee and talked with Kim Ellis. "I want you to stay with me, here at the Hilton, Kim," he said.

"I'd love to, Dick. I want to soak in a warm bath, and then make love to you all morning," she purred. CAG stood and placed some bills on the table to cover the check. They were walking toward the elevator when they met Ensign Tim Arnold.

"Hi, Tim," Kim said and kissed his cheek. Her knees almost buckled as she remembered making love to this well-endowed black Ensign at the Army-Navy Club in the Philippines.

"I have an operational immediate message for Commander Colby, CAG," Tim said and handed CAG the message. "Have you seen him?"

"You missed him by five minutes, Tim," CAG said and read the message. "You can probably catch up with him at Kai Tak International Airport." They watched as Tim walk back outside and hailed a taxi, then held hands and walked inside the elevator. CAG pushed the number-18 button and pulled the beautiful brunette into his arms. He kissed her deeply. He was going to make this morning last a lifetime.

Associated Press Office
Hong Kong

The taxi dropped Ann at the Associated Press office on Nathan Road. She flashed her press pass to the receptionist and asked to borrow a typewriter. She sat for a few minutes to collect her thoughts and started to type on the old, manual Royal typewriter. Her headline read:

DECORATED NAVY PILOT AND CIVILIAN AUTHOR RESCUES PRINCE CHARLES FROM HONG KONG BAY AFTER CRASH OF U.S. MARINE C-130 TRANSPORT.

Ann typed the story in short, descriptive sentences. She explained how Major Cal Stillman, USMC, from Dothan, Alabama, had tried to land the crippled airplane in the bay. She briefly mentioned that 116 Marines were killed in the crash. The boat on which she was a passenger had rescued Prince Charles and the seven surviving Marines. Then she switched to King Edward Hospital where Queen Elizabeth had knighted Sir Thomas Edward Colby and Sir John Paul Warner for their heroic rescue of Prince Charles. She patiently proofread the story and made a few corrections. Then she took the two typed pages and two photographs to the receptionist. "I need to get his story on the wire to the *Washington Post* as soon as possible."

"That will be expensive, Miss Curtis," the receptionist said and looked at a coded sheet. "It'll cost one hundred and twenty-six dollars."

"Do you take American Express?" Ann asked as she took the Gold Card from her purse.

"Yes, of course," the receptionist answered. "Have a seat and fill out this form." Ann filled in the information and gave the form to the receptionist. She picked up the receipt for $126 and walked to the telephone booth in the lobby. Ed Brown, the *Washington Post* overseas editor, answered on the first ring. It was 9 p.m. in Washington, D. C.

"Sounds like a front page story, Ann," Ed teased. "You did a great job. Hopefully, this will sell some papers. All we have going now is anti-war protestors. When are you flying back to Vietnam?"

"Next Thursday, on the second of May," she answered.

"Well, have a good flight," Ed said, "please be careful and don't get your cute ass blown off in one of those exotic French restaurants in Saigon."

"Right Boss, give my love to Edith, good night," she broke the connection. What she needed was a good tennis workout. She thought about going back to the hotel and asking Kim Ellis to play, then realized that Kim and CAG Brown would probably spend the day in bed. She hailed a taxi and asked the driver to take her to the Hong Kong Racquet Club. She could always find some tennis buff eager for a game.

Chang Industries
Kowloon, Hong Kong

Jack sat beside Tom in the back seat of the taxi and typed on the keyboard of his portable computer. He moved the display panel to the right for Tom to read the screen.

```
SUBJECT: VICTOR CHANG
COMPANY NUMBER: HK268294
NATIONALITY: CHINESE
SEX: MALE
EYES: BROWN
HAIR: BLACK
HEIGHT: 58 IN
WEIGHT: 162 LB
DOB: 4-30-20
NICKNAME: VIC
COMMENTS: SUBJECT CONDUCTS BUSINESS WITH DEMOCRATIC
REPUBLIC OF VIETNAM, VIET CONG, COMMUNIST CHINA, AND
INTER-NATIONAL MAFIA. NO DISCLOSURE AUTHORIZED.
```

"This may explain why the Marine airplane fell out of the sky," Tom said as the taxi pulled into the parking lot of 700 Kowloon Road. Jack asked the driver to wait as he and Tom walked into the office. The driver lit a cigarette and leaned back in the seat as the meter continued to run. The secretary told them that Mr. Chang was at his Kai Tak Airport office. They walked back to the taxi. Jack asked the driver to take them to the Kai Tak Airport. He snubbed the cigarette and pulled out into the busy traffic.

*   *   *

As Victor Chang expected, the C-130 Hercules was not extensively damaged from the crash into the bay. His salvage crew had lowered rubber pontoons under the wings and fuselage and floated the airplane to the surface. The tugs gently towed the airplane to the seaplane ramp. The landing gear was lowered and the airplane towed to the parking ramp near his hangar. The Hong Kong harbor police and coroner were busy removing the 116 bodies as Jack and Tom stepped from the taxi. Tom looked at the gold letters on the side of the fuselage, UNITED STATES MARINE CORPS.

"We're looking for Mr. Victor Chang," Tom said to the Chinese man.

"I'm Victor Chang," the man said and extended his hand to Tom. "Please call me, Vic."

"I'm Tom Colby, and this is Jack Warner," Tom said as he shook Chang's hand.

"Good morning, Jack," Victor said and shook Warner's hand. He led them into a large office that contained a desk and a leather couch. "Please be seated, gentlemen. May I offer you coffee or tea?"

"Nothing thanks, Vic," Tom said and handed Chang the telegram from Glenn Carson. "Our friend, Commander Bob Wilson, is apparently a prisoner of war in a village near Vinh in North Vietnam. Mr. Carson feels that you might be of assistance to us in obtaining his release."

Victor sat in the large chair behind the desk and typed a message into his computer. "Ah, yes, the optimistic, Mr. Glenn Carson," he said and read the message on the screen:

CODE HK-7727
ASSIST COMMANDER TOM COLBY, USN, TO OBTAIN RELEASE OF
LCDR BOB WILSON FROM NORTH VIETNAM. $50K AVAILABLE FOR
EXPENSES.
G. CARSON, SD-5525

Tom noticed that Victor wore a large, gold Masonic ring on his left hand. "I see that you are a fellow traveling man, Vic," Tom said as he admired the ring.

"Yes, Tom," Victor said. "I've traveled through three degrees. Is Jack a Mason?"

"No Vic," Tom said. "Jack is content being a fiction writer."

"Gentlemen, I'll make some inquires about Bob Wilson through my business associates and get back to you," Victor said as he stood. "Where are you staying?"

"We're at the Hilton, Vic," Tom said as he stood and shook hands. A white Rolls-Royce was waiting as Chang escorted Tom and Warner from his office. "My driver will take you anywhere you want to go, gentlemen," Victor said as a taxi pulled into the parking lot. Tim paid the fare and hurried toward Tom.

"I have a message for you, Commander," Tim said.

"Thanks," Tom said and put the message in his shirt pocket. He turned and said, "Vic, this is Tim Arnold, the best copilot in the United States Navy. Tim, this is Vic Chang."

"I'm very pleased to meet you, Tim," Victor said as he gripped the black officer's hand.

"Nice to meet you, Vic," Tim said. "Is there a tennis court near here where Navy men can play?"

"Yes," Victor said. "Get in the Rolls with Tom and Jack. My driver will drop you at the Hong Kong Racquet Club. Tell Mr. Goodman that you're my guest. Good day, gentlemen." He waved as they climbed in the Rolls and drove toward the city. He wondered about the telegram that Commander Colby had received and walked back to his office. This was going to be a very profitable day for Chang Industries.

FORTY-SEVEN

The Caves Of Vung Yen

Hong Kong Racquet Club
British Crown Colony

Ann Curtis was lobbying tennis balls against the practice wall when she saw Tim Arnold walk into the club. She ran over and kissed his cheek. "Are you looking for a game, sailor boy?" She asked.

"Yes," Tim said. "Is there someplace to change into my shorts?"

Howard Goodman had assigned Ann one of the VIP locker rooms. "I'll share my locker with you," Ann said. She took his arm and walked toward the small bungalow.

"God, this is a nice club," Tim said as they walked into the room. He glanced at the double bed against one wall.

"That bed is to be used only for massages," Ann laughed and kissed his lips. "Go ahead and change, I'll wait for you outside."

She was practicing her serve when Tim walked onto the court wearing a red University of Southern California T- shirt and white shorts. *God, he's handsome,* Ann thought as she remembered the remarks Kim had made about his large manhood. She gathered the tennis balls and walked to meet him. "I know you played varsity tennis at Southern Cal," Ann said. "How many points are you gonna give me?"

"Let's play the first set even, then we'll negotiate points, pretty lady," Tim said.

Ann won the first set, 7 to 5, and was leading in the second set, 3 to 2 when she missed a backhand shot. Her short, blonde hair was held back by a white sweat band. "Damn!" Ann yelled when her backhand was low. The ball struck the top of the net, and fell back on her side of the court.

"That was game, pretty lady. Set all tied at three-three," Tim said and walked toward the net. "Let's take a five minute breather." He walked to the vending machine and returned with two cans of cold Coke.

Ann looked at the *USS Concord*, anchored in the bay. "Thanks, Tim," she took a long drink. "Do you like living on an aircraft carrier?"

"Not really," he answered truthfully. "I love to fly, but sea duty can be a drag. The ship is always rolling and moving. You can always hear noise and feel vibrations."

"Did you know that I landed a Cessna 310 on the *Concord*?"

"Yes, pretty lady," he laughed. "One of the sailors snapped a picture just as you touched the deck. CAG Brown had it enlarged and framed. It's mounted in the wardroom, so you're immortalized forever in the *Concord*."

"That was sweet of Dick," Ann smiled and sipped the Coke. "He's so in love with Kim Ellis. You may not get to make love to her again."

"No sweat," Tim said as he looked into her blue eyes and felt a stirring in his groin. "Making love to Kim in the Philippines was a great experience for me. I'm just surprised that she told you."

"We girls talk and brag about our conquests, just like you men," Ann smiled. "Kim said that you were a wonderful lover."

"I have a proposition for you, Ann," he said as he gently took her hand. "I'll forfeit the set, if you'll let me take you back to the room and make love to you."

Ann stood and pulled him to his feet. "Tim, this must be our special secret. I intend to marry Tom Colby. He must never know that we made love. Do you agree?"

"Oh God, yes, Ann, I swear that I'll never tell anyone." As they walked toward the room, he said, "Did you know that Commander Colby's being ordered to Tan Son Nhut Air Base for a special operational briefing this Friday?"

"Oh, that's perfect," Ann said and opened the door to her room. "Tom's probably saving it for a special surprise for me. God, I can hardly wait to tell all the correspondents in Saigon that I beat the great All-American Tim Arnold in tennis," Ann laughed as she closed the door and raised her lips for his kiss.

Town Club
Hong Kong

After dropping Tim Arnold at the Racquet Club, the limousine took Tom Colby and Jack Warner to the Town Club. They thanked the driver and walked inside to the coffee shop. The pretty Eurasian waitress brought two cups of steaming coffee. Tom handed the message to Jack. "Did you arrange for this?"

"Yes," Jack sipped the coffee. "I know that you and Bob Wilson are close friends, and you'd want to be in on the rescue operation. But mainly, I picked you because you're the most qualified man I know for this job."

"Thanks, Jack. Can I take some of the SAR crew with us?"

"No, not to Tan Son Nhut. Later we'll make decisions about the rescue unit, and you'll be able to pick the crew."

"Sounds fair," Tom said and finished the coffee. Jack paid the check and motioned for Tom to follow him out the rear door. They walked down the alley and hailed a taxi.

"The limo driver was watching the front door," Jack said. "Wonder why Mr. Chang is so interested in tailing two tourists?"

"I don't know," Tom said. "You're the expert in this cloak and dagger business."

"Tom, my friend, you'd make an excellent agent for our company," Jack said as he gave directions to the driver. He planned to stop at the agency's office on Nathan Road and check the message traffic from Saigon. Also, he wanted to run a data search on Anah Thong. If she was an enemy agent, there should be some data on her. He opened the lap-top computer and typed in the access code.

"I'd like to have one of those toys," Tom said as the display screen came to life and listed the menu. "How much do they cost?"

"A lap-top like this will probably cost five grand, but this is one of a kind. Alan Casebolt has a small computer company in Santa Barbara, California. I think it's called Caseware, Incorporated. They're developing software for the new, F-fourteen fighter. I checked it out for the Navy a few months ago, really good stuff, cuts processing time in half and generates real-time fighter intercept and SAM solutions. The Navy's gonna award them a contract soon."

"Dad's last job was at NavAir. He didn't say anything about this," Tom said. "Probably thought it would be insider trading and a conflict of interest."

"Thinking about buying some Caseware stock?" Jack asked as he typed on the keyboard.

"Well, it sounds like good investment to me. Who knows about the pending contract award?"

Jack shut down the computer and closed the keyboard. "No one, Caseware doesn't even know yet. After they get the contract, Alan is gonna need some capital to expand. They're listed on the New York Exchange. You should check it out?"

"Okay," Tom said. "What about you?"

The CIA agent shook his head. "I don't play the market, Tom. The Company would be all over my ass if I made money on inside information."

"Yeah, you're right," Tom agreed. "I might invest one-hundred-thousand if Alan will build me one of those toy computers."

"Alan will build a gold-plated one for a one-hundred-thousand stockholder," Jack said. The taxi dropped them at the Chang Bank Building. Entering the elevator, Jack punched the top button, number-21. The Agency leased the top two floors of the building.

"Good morning, Mr. Warner," the blonde receptionist welcomed Jack with a bright smile and checked his pass. He waved at Tom and entered an unmarked door. The receptionist ushered Tom to a large lounge with comfortable chairs. He picked up a copy of the *New York Times* and turned to the financial section. Caseware, Inc. was listed at ten and one-quarter. When Caseware got the Navy contract, the stock would increase in value tenfold. He remembered Linda's life insurance money. *It will be a very wise investment.*

355

Vung Yen Village
Democratic Republic of Vietnam

The sun was setting when Ben Toon piloted the boat toward the pier. They had made a record catch in the nets. The elder Toon divided the catch between his neighbors as Bob Wilson and Quyen Toon walked toward the village. He bathed in a tub of water and dressed in clean clothes as Quyen cooked their supper of fish and rice. Bob ate the food in silence. He knew his presence was a danger to every person in the village. If the North Vietnamese Army found him, they would burn the village and slaughter the people. He was tempted to steal one of the fishing boats and sail to South Vietnam. He explained his fears to Quyen.

"I need a place to hide until I can contact the Navy rescue unit."

"Bobby, I know safe place," Quyen said. She told him about caves in the hills behind the village. She gathered blankets and food, and Bob grabbed his radio. He followed her out the back door and into the trees. It was a mile to the caves. He was breathing heavy as Quyen led him up the hill to a large cave. She spread blankets and lit a small candle. "You'll be safe here, Bobby."

"Thank you, Quyen," Bob said and bent to kiss her lips. "Don't tell anyone where I'm hiding, not even Daddy Toon, okay? I'm afraid the soldiers will come looking for me and torture your people."

"I understand, Bobby," Quyen said and pulled him down to the blankets. He kissed her lips as she reached up to unbutton his shirt. They made love and lay on the blankets to rest. Afterwards, they walked to the beach where Bob dug large letters in the sand.

SOS WILSON IN CAVE BEHIND VUNG YEN SOS

He walked Quyen back to her small hut in the village and kissed her good night. She promised to cover the message before sunrise. While walking back to the cave, he heard distant rumblings as jets bombed Vinh. *What a crazy, screwed-up world*, he thought and realized that he was in love with Quyen Toon. He heard the sonic boom as a jet flew over the beach at 1:16 a.m. *I sure hope that was a photo-recon bird*, he thought as he lay on the thin blankets and slept.

The Colby Residence
Bonita, California

Margaret Colby was reading the *San Diego Union* newspaper when Samuel Watson walked into the room with an arm load of newspapers. "Did you find a copy of the *Washington Post*?" She asked.

"Yes ma'am," Watson answered and placed the newspapers on the coffee table. "There's a story about Commander Tom in the Post."

"Has he been hurt?" Margaret grabbed the paper. "I thought he was in Hong Kong for rest and recuperation." Then she saw the headline.

NAVY PILOT RESCUES PRINCE CHARLES FROM HONG KONG BAY AFTER U. S. MARINE TRANSPORT CRASHES INTO YACHT

She read the article and noted Ann Curtis' byline. "Samuel, the Queen knighted Tom after he saved Prince Charles's life! Have you read this?"

"Yes ma'am, it shore will be nice to address him as Sir Tom."

"Oh, it is so sad that all those young Marines lost their lives in the crash," Margaret said and read the article again. "Samuel, I want to sent a clipping to Thomas. Will you please run back down and buy an extra copy?"

"They only had five copies of the *Post,* ma'am," Watson said. "I bought all of them."

"Thank you, Samuel. Make us a cup of tea, and I'll read the article to you."

"Yes ma'am," Watson said and hurried toward the kitchen. A cup of tea would be the perfect setting for Miss Ann's story. The doorbell rang, and Watson hurried to the door.

"Telegram for Mrs. Colby," the Western Union man said.

"This is Mrs. Colby's residence. I'll sign for it," Watson said as he scribbled his name on the clipboard and handed the man a dollar. He closed the door and walked back into the living room. "Now, don't get all upset until we knows what it's all about, ma'am," he tore open the envelop. "It's a telegram from Sir Tom in Hong Kong," he laughed and handed the paper to Margaret. She took the telegram with trembling hands and read.

DEAR MOTHER,

IN HONG KONG FOR FIVE DAYS OF REST STOP HAD DINNER WITH QUEEN ELIZABETH AND PRINCE PHILIP STOP BUY FORTY THOUSAND SHARES OF CASEWARE, INC FOR ME STOP REPEAT BUY FORTY THOUSAND SHARES OF CASEWARE, INC STOP CASEWARE STOCK IS SURE THING STOP MY LOVE TO TOMMY, JUDY AND JACKIE STOP I LOVE YOU MOTHER STOP TELL WATSON TO TAKE CARE OF THE JET FOR DAD AND ME STOP CASEWARE STOCK IS A TENFOLD INVESTMENT STOP BUY SOME CASEWARE STOCK FOR DAD.
LOVE
SIR THOMAS EDWARD COLBY

Margaret stood and walked to the telephone. She dialed her broker in Washington, D. C., and said, "Good morning, George, this is Margaret Colby calling from San Diego."

"Hello, Mrs. Colby. What can we do for you?"

"Please check out Caseware, Incorporated for me. I think it's listed on the New York Exchange."

"Yes, ma'am," George said as he typed on the computer. "I found it, Margaret. It's listed at ten and one-quater."

"Purchase forty-thousand shares, George. It's for my son, Tom, who's serving in Vietnam."

"I didn't know Tom was in Vietnam. Is he flying combat missions?"

"Yes, he's flying the combat rescue helicopters. His squadron has rescued over seventy-five pilots who were shot down," Margaret answered proudly.

"Well, that's marvelous news, Margaret. Is there anything else the agency can do for you today?"

"Yes, George, please check and see if more Caseware stock is available. I might want another forty-thousand shares in a few days."

"Yes ma'am, have a nice vacation." They both hung up.

George Levin looked at Caseware stock again. It was not a very impressive stock. Margaret Colby must have a hot tip to risk that much money. He decided to buy two thousand shares for his portfolio. He had been Margaret's broker for 20 years, and she very seldom picked a loser.

FORTY-EIGHT

The Murder Of Ben Toon

Tan Son Nhut Air Base
Republic of Vietnam

World Airways, flight W-106, began descending from cruise altitude fifteen minutes out of Tan Son Nhut. The sprawling Air Base sat on the northwest side of Saigon. World Airways was one of a half dozen commercial airlines flying Military Airlift Command (MAC) contract flights to and from Vietnam and R and R flights from Vietnam to Hawaii and Hong Kong. Tom Colby sat in the window seat. He was dressed in green walking shorts and a tan cotton knit shirt. Ann Curtis sat between Tom and Jack Warner. *Damn the plane is awful high, at least 5,000 feet,* he thought as the pilot banked left to line up with the runway. He felt the plane vibrate as the pilot lowered the landing gear and flaps. Then the pilot dove the Boeing 707 toward the touchdown point of the runway.

"Hang on Jack, this is gonna be a steep approach," Tom warned. "God, I hate to ride back here. I'd much rather be flying this baby."

"He has to be at least five thousand feet to avoid ground fire from our so-called allies," Jack said as he closed the lap-top computer and slid it under the seat in front of him. The pilot expertly flared the big jet, and the main gear kissed the runway. Tom breathed a sigh of relief as the jet liner rumbled down the runway.

"Welcome to Vietnam, ladies and gentlemen," the stewardess said over the PA system. "Please remained seated until we reach the terminal and the plane has come to a complete stop. The weather's clear with a temperature of ninety-four degrees." The ground crew drove a truck with the aluminum steps to the front left side of the jet liner. The stewardess unlocked and pushed open the large exit door. The cabin filled with hot, humid air that smelled like rotten cabbage and burnt jet fuel. The G.I.'s gathered their carry-on baggage and stood in the aisle. They began to file off the airplane and walk down the steep steps.

"Gentlemen, I'm buying steaks at the Officer's Club," Ann said.

"Thanks, Ann," Tom said and turned to Jack. "Do you have any plans for the evening, Jack?"

"Nothing special, Tom," Jack said. "My assistant is meeting us at the terminal. We'll have dinner at the club and drive into Saigon."

"Tom, I have a two-bedroom suite at the Le Meridien in Saigon. You're welcome to use the extra room," Ann said.

"Is it air-conditioned?" Tom asked.

"Yes, it's air-conditioned."

"Okay, I'll take it," Tom said. "That will sure beat sleeping on Jack's couch." They followed the G.I.'s down the steps and across the ramp to the terminal.

Jack flashed his CIA badge at the Vietnamese custom's agent, and said, "Miss Curtis and Mr. Colby are with me."

"Yes sir, please follow me," the custom's agent said and led them across the lobby to a small waiting room. A tall woman with short red hair ran across the room and embraced Jack Warner. She wore white walking shorts and a white cotton blouse. A brown purse was slung over her right shoulder. She kissed his lips and asked, "How was the vacation in Hong Kong?"

"Very nice, Sharon," Jack said as he turned to introduce Ann and Tom.

"Pleased to meet you, Ann," Sharon said. "I enjoy your articles in the *Post.*" She turned and offered her hand to Tom. "It's so special to meet you, Sir Tom." He saw the twinkle in her soft blue eyes.

"Damn!" Jack exclaimed. "I see you've learned of our exploits in Hong Kong."

"Yes Jack, Ann's article gave an excellent account of your heroic deeds along with a photograph of you two with the Queen."

Jack tried to shift the conversation away from the rescue of Prince Charles. "Is our schedule clear for the evening, Sharon?"

"Yes, sir," Sharon said.

"Ann's treating us to dinner at the Officer's Club. Please join us, and then we can drive into Saigon after dinner."

"Love to, Jack," Sharon said. "The sedan is parked out on the south forty." She picked up his lap-top computer and led the way to the exit.

"I sure hope the sedan's air-conditioned," Tom groaned as he lifted his bag and followed them.

"You're a wimp, Tom Colby," Ann teased as she slung the bag over her shoulder and followed Sharon. "What you need is a hike in this nice, warm weather to make you feel good."

They ate dinner at the crowded Officer's Club restaurant. Tom and Jack ordered a steak while Ann and Sharon were more adventurous, ordering a variety of seafood. After they had wine and dessert, Ann paid the bill and left a generous tip for the waiter.

They left the club and walked to the sedan. Sharon stopped at the front gate of Tan Son Nhut. The bored sentry was dressed in green camouflage fatigues, a blue beret, a flak jacket and held a M-16 rifle. He glanced at Sharon's ID and looked the Americans in the back-seat, then waved them through.

"Air Force has nice security, Jack," Tom said from the back seat.

"Hell, it's the standard joke that more Viet Cong agents live on the base than in Saigon or the jungle," Jack said.

They rode in silence as Sharon maneuvered the sedan through the maze of traffic. She stopped in front of the Le Meridien Hotel, and smiled at Ann, "Thanks for that delicious dinner, Ann. Good night,Tom. I'll pick you up at this spot at exactly seven a.m." The sedan disappeared into the traffic as Tom picked up the bags and followed Ann toward the double glass doors. He felt a blast of cold air from inside as the doorman opened the door.

"Thank God, for air-conditioning," Tom said as they walked across the marble lobby of the hotel. Six large marble pillars held up the blue-and-gold ceiling. Across the lobby from the front doors was the registration desk with three clerks working behind it. Four Vietnamese soldiers sat at their stations, armed with M-16 rifles. In the rear of the lobby was a tiny elevator. They entered the elevator and rode upwards. The elevator was a glass cage that offered a spectaculor view of the elegant lobby.

When the elevator stopped, Ann held the door open while Tom grabbed the bags and followed her down the hallway. She unlocked the door and pushed it open. The air in the room was hot and stale. She turned on the air-conditioner while Tom dropped the bags and looked at the room. "It's not the Sheraton Moana, but I like your snake ranch, pretty lady."

"Thanks," Ann laughed. She turned and kissed him quickly and felt the damp shirt stuck to his back and pulled away. "Please run a cold bath for us while I get out of these sticky clothes."

"Okay, darling," Tom said as he walked into the bathroom and turned the cold faucet to full force. He peeled off his clothes and sat in the cool water and waited for Ann to join him.

Vung Yen Caves

Bob Wilson sat in the mouth of the cave and gazed at the stars. In the old days, aviators and seafaring Navy men had navigated by the stars. Now, most navigation was accomplished by electronics. Soon, more precise navigation will be possible using orbiting satellites. Quyen would arrive soon with his evening meal. He had been in the cave six days. *It is like being confined to a prison, but nothing like the Hanoi Hilton prison,* Bob shuddered. He knew that eventually someone in the village would talk about the American pilot and the North Vietnamese Army would come searching for him. He would talk to Quyen about stealing a boat and sailing down the Gulf toward Da Nang.

*   *   *

Captain Huey Toon led the company of North Vietnamese soldiers toward the village of Vung Yen. Colonel Nuguyen Than was commander of the soldiers. "You are certain the Yankee pilot is in the village?" He asked.

"Yes, Comrade Colonel," Huey answered. "My cousin reports that Commander Wilson has been living in the village for a month. He saved a village girl from drowning, and everyone thinks he's a hero."

"Well, we have a special room reserved for their American hero in the Hanoi prison," Colonel Than said. He motioned for the radio and issued orders to the soldiers who were circling around the village to prevent any avenue of escape.

"Now, Captain Toon, let's pay our respects to the Mayor of Vung Yen. What's his name?"

"Ben Toon, Comrade Colonel," Huey answered as they walked toward the mayor's house house.

"A relative of yours, Captain?"

"A distant cousin, Comrade Colonel."

Colonel Than motioned to the platoon leader. Two soldiers ran forward and knocked on the door. They stood on either side of the door as Ben Toon walked out to the porch. There was deep fear in his heart as he looked at Captain Huey Toon and the Colonel.

"Greetings Captain Toon and Comrade Colonel," Ben said as he struggled to control his voice. "Welcome to our humble village. Will you please come in for a cup of tea?"

"No, thank you," Than answered. "Please accompany us to the village square and call a town meeting."

"As you wish, Comrade Colonel," Ben said. He calmly led them toward the square. When they reached the square, Colonel Than signaled to the platoon leader. He pointed an AK-47 toward the sky and pulled the trigger. The booming noise of the AK-47 alarmed the village. People ran to the square. Soon, all of the villagers were gathered around the Mayor and group of army officers.

Colonel Than stepped forward and said, "Good people of Vung Yen, it has come to our attention that a Yankee pilot is hiding in your village. The People's Army has come to take the Yankee pig to prison." He turned to looked at Ben Toon. "Mayor Ben, have you seen this Yankee pilot?"

Ben knew that lying to Colonel Than would be futile. "Yes, Comrade Colonel, Commander Bob has been our guest for several weeks."

"**YOUR GUEST**!" Colonel Than thundered. "You do not invite the Yankee pigs who drop bombs on your women and children into your homes to be your guest! Where's this Yankee pig?"

"He's been gone for over a week," Ben answered truthfully.

"Search the village!" Than ordered. The soldiers rushed to obey his orders. They searched every hut and reported back to the platoon leader. The American pilot was not in the village.

Colonel Than turned toward Ben Toon and said, "You have one last chance to tell me where the Yankee pig is hiding before I burn the village to the ground. Where is he?"

"I don't know, Comrade Colonel," Ben said. "He probably went south toward Da Nang."

"**SEIZE HIM**!" Than ordered pointing toward the mayor. Two soldiers ran forward and tied Toon's arms together behind his back. Then they tied him to one of the poles that surrounded the platform.

Captain Toon felt bile rise in his throat as Than pull a short dagger from its sheath. Few men had lived through Colonel Than's interrogation. "Comrade Colonel, please let me talk to Mayor Toon," he said.

"Very well, Captain," Than said and stepped aside. "See if you can get the fool to talk."

Captain Toon stood in front of the Mayor and pleaded, "Ben, please tell us where the pilot is hiding. Is it worth your life to protect him?"

"Cousin Huey, we helped Commander Bob because he is a Master Mason in distress. Have you forgotten your Masonic vows so quickly? I honestly don't know where he's hiding. I think he left the village to protect us. He's probably sneaking south toward Da Nang."

Captain Toon turned in defeat toward Colonel Than. "Cousin Ben says that the Yankee pig is trying to get to Da Nang, Comrade Colonel."

Quyen stood at the rear of the crowd beside her cousin, Dan Toon. She watched in horror as Than raised the knife and slit the Mayor's shirt from top to bottom. The women of the village began to cry and beg for mercy for Ben Toon.

"**BE QUIET**! Colonel Than roared at the women. The wailing stopped and silence settled over the group, except for an occasional sob. Than turned back to face Ben and drew the knife swiftly across the Mayor's lower abdomen. Ben screamed as the knife ripped through his entrils. He lowered his head and watched his intestines spill out of the gaping hole and fall into a bucket the soldiers were holding. He knew that death was here. He prayed that Dan and Quyen would escape this torture. The soldiers walked to the fire near the bottom of the platform and poured the Mayor's intestines into the fire.

Dan Toon lowered his head and whispered into Quyen's ear, "Go get Commander Bob and meet me on my boat at midnight. Be very careful, the soldiers must be watching from the forest."

"I will be careful, cousin Dan," Quyen promised. She turned and walked away.

"WE WILL BE BACK TOMORROW NIGHT!" Colonel Than yelled at the villagers. "A man will die every night until you tell us where the Yankee pig is hiding." The soldiers marched away from the village. The elders cut the ropes holding Ben Toon to the pole. They eased his body to the ground. One of the women place a cushion under his head. Ben closed his eyes and prayed for his soul.

Quyen walked to her hut. Once inside, she raised a secret trapdoor and grabbed a small nylon bag. Then she gathered the supper that she had prepared for Bob Wilson. She climbed down the ladder into the tunnel and closed the trapdoor. The tunnel would take her safely under any soldiers lurking in the forest. The tunnels were dug during the French-Vietnam War. She knew these old tunnels well. She had played in them when she was a child.

*   *   *

Bob Wilson was alarmed when he heard the automatic rifle fire coming from the village. He knew the soldiers must be searching for him. Eventually, they would search the caves. He must make plans for an escape tonight after Quyen brought his food. Thirty minutes later, Quyen slipped quietly into the cave. She grabbed Bob and hugged him tightly and sobbed, "Oh Bobby, the damn soldiers killed Daddy Toon."

"Oh, my God, no," Bob said as he held the trembling Quyen in his arms. "I know I should've left the village long ago and headed south. It's my fault that Ben Toon is dead."

"Not your fault, Bobby," Quyen said and wiped her eyes. "Crazy damn colonel killed Daddy Toon with a knife. Sit and eat, we must make plans." She opened the small basket and placed the food in his lap.

"You know what, I'm beginning to like fish and rice," Bob said as he ate the food. "When we get back to the States, I'm gonna take you to the Sky Room restaurant in San Diego and buy you the best food in the place."

"You are taking me to America, Bobby?" Quyen asked.

"You damn right I'm going to take you with me, Quyen," Bob said as he pulled her into his arms and kissed her lips. "When we get to California, we're going to be married."

"Oh Bobby, I'm so happy," Quyen said as she sat beside him and told him about Colonel Than and Captain Huey Toon. "Dan said for us to meet him on his boat at midnight."

"Thank God," he whispered. "Now I won't have to steal a boat. If we just had a radio that worked, I could contact the rescue helicopters."

Quyen jumped from his arms, as she remembered the nylon package. She handed it to him and said, "When I was sweeping out your message this morning, I found this package that the airplane must have dropped last night."

"Thank you, Jesus," Bob said as he opened the package and removed a survival radio wrapped in an American flag. Now, he would be able to talk to the pilots as they flew their attack mission toward Vinh and Hanoi. He pulled Quyen down to the blankets and unbuttoned her blouse. The war could wait while he gave thanks and made love to this beautiful angel.

FORTY-NINE

Escape From Vung Yen

Vung Yen Village
Democratic Republic of Vietnam

It was five minutes passed midnight when Bob Wilson and Quyen Toon slipped aboard Dan Toon's boat. "Be very quiet," Dan cautioned as he led them down the steps into the cabin. "The soldiers may be watching the village. We must get away before the moon rises." He released the mooring lines and poled the boat away from the pier. Then he raised the jibsail, and the Junk slowly sailed away into the darkness. Quyen lit a small candle that cast a dim glow over the cabin. The cabin contained a small kitchen and four bunk beds. Quyen lay on one of the beds and was soon asleep. Bob removed the radio from the bag and climbed the ladder to the deck. He took the tiller while Toon raised the mainsail.

Dan secured the sail and walked aft to take the tiller. "Thanks for helping us get away," Bob said. "I'm so sorry about Ben's death."

"Colonel Than is an animal," Dan said. "He will torture and kill until he's certain that you have escaped. Please take Quyen with you. Colonel Than will kill her next."

"I'll take care of Quyen," Bob said and heard the jets fly overhead. "Dan, I must use the radio, okay?"

"Go ahead, Bob. The soldiers cannot hear us now."

Bob turned on the radio and said, "Mayday! Mayday! Mayday!"

367

CAG Dick Brown lead the flight of eight A-4 Skyhawks. He pressed the mike and said, "Mayday, this is Red Strike Leader, identify yourself."

"You're directly overhead me at this time!" Bob yelled into the radio. "This is Commander Robert Wilson, Navy helo number Two-Two from the *Belknap*. I was shot down on the second of April."

"Are you injured, Two-Two?" CAG asked as he passed the lead to his wingman and began to circle the area.

"No, I'm okay. I'm on a fishing junk, headed toward Da Nang."

"Roger, Two-Two," CAG said, "Stand by." He switched the frequency and passed the information to *Concord* strike operations. He pressed the mike and called Bob, "Two-Two, this is Red Strike Leader. War Chief advises you to continue present course. Rescue helo will be overhead at first light, over."

"Thanks, Red Leader," Bob said and turned off the radio to save the battery. The sea became choppy as the wind started to gust. Dan gave the tiller to Bob and went forward to lower the mainsail.

"Go below and get some rest," Dan ordered as he returned to take the tiller. Bob climbed down the steps into the cabin and lay in the bunk next to Quyen. He was smiling as he drifted into the first peaceful nights sleep he'd had in weeks.

Le Meridien Hotel, Saigon
Republic of Vietnam

Tom Colby stood on the sidewalk in front of the Le Meridien Hotel. A white sedan pulled to the curb at 6:59 a.m. The back door opened and he climbed inside. "Good morning, Tom," Sharon greeted him from the driver seat, then gave her full attention to the morning traffic.

"Tom, Bob Wilson was almost captured by the North Vietnamese Army last night. Somehow he got away and is sailing south on a fishing junk," Jack Warner said.

"God, don't you ever sleep?" Tom asked.

"The situation agent called and briefed me this morning," Jack said. "We've never had a POW escape from North Vietnam. We want Bob Wilson real bad, Tom."

"Are we going after Bob today?"

"No, I don't think we'll be able to get to him today. A monsoon just moved into that area and reduced the visibility. Your SAR pilots are flying the helo's from the *Concord* to Da Nang this morning. After the briefing, you and I will fly to Da Nang. We'll coordinate the rescue effort with the 366th Air Force Helicopter Rescue Squadron."

"Bob's a Naval aviator, Jack," Tom said. "My Sea Devil detachment should get the first crack at his rescue."

"I'll give your helicopters a fifteen-minute head start before I launch the Jolly Green Giants," Jack laughed. Sharon stopped at the gate of Tan Son Nhut. The sentry glanced at her pass, smiled and waved the car through the gate. Tom was looking forward to the CIA briefing. He wanted so much to rescue Bob Wilson. *The poor bastard has probably been through hell*, he thought.

Vung Ho Bay
Democratic Republic of Vietnam

Vung Ho Bay, nestled in a azure blue cove, was almost completely surrounded by a rocky reef. The reef offered some protection from the large waves driven by the monsoon winds. Dan Toon had found the bay during the night. He and Bob anchored the boat between a reef and the narrow stretch of beach. Through the driving rain, he could see the outlines of other boats anchored in the bay. Then he heard the sounds that chilled his heart, sounds of trucks on the road above the beach. He opened the cabin door and stepped in out of the rain.

Quyen Toon had slept until noon. Now, she was cooking their lunch over the small charcoal stove. "Good morning, Dan," she said as he removed his raincoat and sat at the small table. "Is the storm bad?"

"The wind has reduced some, Quyen," he said, "but it'll probably rain all day. We should stay here until dark. Then maybe we can slip out of the bay and sail south."

"Dan, as soon as the weather breaks the helicopters will come," Bob said. "Quyen and I will hide in a cave above the road until the weather clears."

"Not a good idea, Bob," Dan said. "I heard trucks on the road. That means the army is nearby."

369

"Jesus, of all the rotten luck," Bob moaned. "If the damn weather had just stayed clear, we could have sailed all the way to Da Nang."

"Not nice to swear, Bobby," Quyen said and placed two steaming bowls of rice in front of them. "Eat lunch, and all will be well."

"Wish I had your faith, Quyen," Bob said and ate the rice. When he got back to California, he vowed never eat another bowl of rice as long as he lived.

Da Nang Air Base
Republic of Vietnam

The KC-135 landed at Da Nang at 12:05 noon. Tom Colby, Jack Warner and Sharon Quinn were the only passengers in the big jet liner. Tom had been impressed when Jack called the operations officer at MACV and said the agency needed air transportation to Da Nang, code one-tripple-A. The Air Force Colonel had called back within ten minutes and said the KC-135 was available for immediate takeoff.

Lieutenant General Steve Curtis stood at the bottom of the stairs. Beside him was Steve Smith, the Commanding Officer of the 366th Helicopter Rescue Squadron. Tom saw the new major leaves on Smith's collar. "Congratulations on the promotion, Steve," Tom said and gripped his hand.

Jack introduced Sharon to the Air Force officers. General Curtis welcomed Sharon to Da Nang and led the group to his staff car. Tom sat in the backseat between Smith and Curtis. Sharon sat in front between Jack and Captain Jasper, the General's aide. "Ann told me about your heroic exploits in Hong Kong, Tom," Curtis said. "Did the Queen really knight you and Jack as members of her Royal Court?"

"It was all Jack's fault, Uncle Steve," Tom answered. "He insisted that we take a boat ride across the bay to some famous floating restaurant. A Marine C-130 airplane fell out of the sky and hit Prince Charles' boat. Jack and I fished the Prince out of the bay, and Queen Elizabeth insisted that we accept some Order of Knighthood. I'm not sure that it's legal for a Naval officer to accept such an award."

"Well, I'm positive that your mother will find some way to make it legal," Curtis said. "Even if she has to go all the way to the President."

"I was afraid you would say that, sir," Tom said. "Any day now, I expect to get orders from BUPERS shipping me to Adak, Alaska or the South Pole."

"I wouldn't worry about it, Tom," Curtis said and changed the subject. "Jack, I asked the club to send cold cuts over to the Command Action Center. We can have a working lunch while we're updating the SAR status."

"Excellent idea, General," Jack said as the sedan stopped in front of Seventh Air Force Headquarters. Captain Jasper jumped out of the car and ran around to open the door for General Curtis. He was disappointed when the General did not invite him inside for lunch.

The SAR update revealed that weather in the rescue area was clearing. Tom wanted to get airborne before dark. He suggested the two Navy H-3 helicopters get airborne and refuel at the Marine Air Field at Hue. A Jolly Green helicopter could fly to Hue and be on stand-by as a backup SAR. Curtis approved the plan.

Tom rode to the 366th Squadron with Major Smith where he changed into his flight gear and briefed his SAR crew. They tookoff at 5:10 p.m. Tom and Tim Arnold flew the lead helicopter. Ensign Bull Walker and Lieutenant (j.g.) Rick Jackson piloted the second helicopter.

Vung Ho Bay
Democratic Republic of Vietnam

Bob Wilson smiled as the monsoon winds subsided. The rain stopped as dusk fell. He turned on the radio and waited for the rescue aircraft to call him. He heard the C-130 fly over and soon the radio came to life, "Clem Two-Two, this is Red Crown. Do you read, over?"

"Roger, Red Crown," Bob answered, "Read you five-by-five, over."

"Two-Two, status please."

"Two-Two aboard junk in Vung Ho Bay. What's the ETA on the angel?"

"Three-zero minutes. We'll orbit south of Vinh and vector the angel to your position."

"Thanks, Red Crown. Two-Two leaving junk. Overland rescue will be quicker and safer."

"Good luck, Two-Two, call if you need help. Red Crown standing by this frequency."

Bob turned off the radio and looked at Toon. "Dan, we must go. The helicopter will be here in thirty minutes. Can you get us to those rocks?"

Dan lowered a long pole in the water and touched the bottom. He nodded his head and pulled up the anchor. He pushed the boat toward the rocks. Quyen stood beside Bob as he looped the rope around a big rock. He shook hands with Toon and handed him the rope.

"Thanks, brother Dan. I hope someday to be able to repay you for all your kindness." He stepped from the boat to the rocks and reached for Quyen's hand.

"Good-bye, cousin," Quyen said. She kissed his cheek and jumped to the rocks beside Bob.

"Good-bye, little cousin," Dan said as tears rolled down his cheeks. "Have a happy life in America." He poled his boat away from the rocks and raised the sail. Bob and Quyen sat on the rocks and watched as the boat sailed from the bay and entered the Gulf. Then they cautiously walked toward the beach and vanished into the night.

FIFTY

Wedding Bells

2,000 Feet Above the Tonkin Gulf
Off-Shore Quang Khe

The two Navy H-3 helicopters flew up the Gulf at 120 knots. "Damn, it's gonna be a black night, Tim," Tom Colby said as he looked toward the beach. "Sure hope Commander Bob picks a nice level spot for his rescue. We'll have much less exposure time to enemy fire if we can find a clear space to land." In the cabin, Petty Officer Steve Jackman and Airman Lewis checked the rescue hoist and their M-16 rifles. Dr. Jim Davenport clutched his leather bag and prayed that no one got shot. He was now a permanent member of the Sea Devil rescue team. Tom insisted the five-man crew wear white silk scarfs around their necks. *May the Force protect us, brother Michael,* Tom prayed.

*   *   *

Bob Wilson sat beside Quyen Toon under a small tree and held his radio. Then he heard the sound he'd been waiting for, the wail of jet engines pulsated by the beating rotor blades. He pushed the emergency beeper and counted to five, then switched it to voice.

"Have a beeper at nine o'clock, Commander," Tim Arnold said as Tom banked the helicopter into a left turn and flew toward the beach.

"Red Crown, this is Sea Devil helo Seven-One. Inbound on emergency beeper. Sea Devil Seven-Two will orbit present position."

373

"Roger, Seven-One. Your pigeon is one mile inland, near a rice paddy. He will signal with flashlight. Good hunting, out."

Tom crossed the beach at 2,000 feet and 140 knots. He pressed the mike switch and said, "Seven-One, feet dry."

"Roger feet dry."

Bob listen to the exchange between Tom and Red Crown. He pressed his radio switch and whispered, "Sea Devil Leader, this is Two-Two. This place is swarming with soldiers. I'll give you four, quick flashes. Suggest a spiral approach and land in rice paddy. Quyen and I will jump in the helo, over."

"Wait one," Tom said. "Understand we have a party of two for pick up, over."

"Affirmative," Bob said and aimed the flashlight toward the helicopter and flashed it four times. "Estimate surface winds two-seven-zero at ten knots."

"**Tallyho**!" Tom yelled into the mike when he saw the four flashes of light. "Starting approach."

*   *   *

Captain Dan Than and two soldiers waited in a cave that over-looked the meadow where Bob Wilson and Quyen Toon hid under a small tree. The soldiers cleaned their AK-47 rifles in the dark and waited for orders from their captain. "Are they still under the tree, Captain?" one of the soldiers whispered.

Captain Than pulled a short dagger from his belt and knelt beside the soldier. He placed his mouth close to the soldiers ear and said, "You speak one more time, and I will cut your throat. I told you not to talk or make any noise. Understand?"

The soldier felt the sharp edge of the knife pressing against his throat. He was afraid to move his head against the sharp dagger. He began to sweat and slowly nodded his head.

"Good," Than whispered and returned the dagger to his belt. He knelt beside the other soldier and whispered in his ear, "Is your rocket launcher ready, comrade?"

The soldier was afraid to speak. He quickly nodded his head and reached for the rocket launcher.

"Excellent, comrade. When the Yankee helicopter starts to hover, I want you to shoot him out of the sky." The soldier vigorously nodded his head again.

Captain Than stood in the mouth of a cave and smiled. He knew that the soldiers would instantly obey his commands. He looked through his binoculars and saw the form of two people sitting under the tree. Then he heard the distant noise of a helicopter coming from the beach. He was shocked to see flashes of light below in the rice paddy. He pointed toward the tree and whispered to the soldiers, "Wait for my order to fire, then shoot the helicopter out of the sky." They aimed their AK-47 rifles at the tree. *Father will be proud of me when I shoot down the Yankee helicopter,* he thought, *I must take him a piece of the wreckage.*

*   *   *

Ensign Tim Arnold lowered the landing gear handle and pressed the intercom switch. "Troops we're gonna land in a rice paddy and pick up Commander Wilson and a Vietnamese girl. Please don't shoot them."

"Roger, Mr. Arnold," Jackman said. "All secure back here for landing."

Tom bottomed the collective and started a spiral dive toward the rice paddy. He saw Bob blink the flashlight twice then shine a steady beam toward the cockpit. He cushioned the landing with up collective and landed twenty-feet from where Bob Wilson sat in the rice paddy clutching Quyen Toon.

Quyen was frightened as the hurricane wind from the rotor blades whipped at her. "**Close your eyes**!" Bob yelled and held her in his arms. Then he picked her up and ran to the helicopter. He tossed Quyen inside the door and jumped in behind her. He heard bullets strike the helicopter as the soldiers fired toward the jet noise.

"**READY FOR TAKEOFF**!" Jackman yelled into the mike as he fired the M-16 out the cabin door. He yelled into his mike again, "**They's shooting from a cave up the hill**. Dr. Davenport grabbed a M-16 rifle and fired toward the cave. Unknown to him, five of his bullets plowed into Captain Than's body. He was dying as he fell across the soldier who was aiming the rocket launcher. The other soldier continued to fire at the helicopter. The rocket screamed out of the cave trailing a tail of fire. It exploded in a ball of fire in the tree beside the helicopter.

"**Good, God!**" Tom yelled when he saw the tree explode. He yanked up the collective and accelerated across the rice paddy. The windshield exploded into the cockpit. Tom was showered with fragments of glass, then felt two hard blows to his chest as the AK-47 bullets hit his survival vest.

"You have the aircraft, Tim. I think I'm wounded," Tom said as he released the controls.

"Oh, please God, no! Please protect us," Tim prayed as he climbed to 2,000 feet and saw the white ribbon of sand far below. He pressed the mike switch and said, "Red Crown, Sea Devil Seven-One, feet wet. Pigeon aboard, over."

Roger, feet wet. Any combat damage?"

"We're checking," Tim said. "We took heavy small-arm fire from the hillside. A rocket just missed and exploded beside us. Our windshield's gone. We have a lot of bullet holes in this bird, and I think my pilot's wounded. Please stand by."

"I'm okay, Tim," Tom said over the intercom, "Not bleeding anywhere, but I may have a broken rib. This fantastic flak vest saved my life."

"Thank, God," Tim breathed into the mike. "Okay troops, check for battle damage. I know we took some rounds back there. Was anyone hit?"

Dr. Davenport had immediately checked Jackman and Lewis, then Commander Wilson and the pretty Vietnamese woman. He pressed the mike and said, "This is Dr. Jim. We're all, okay back here. We have a few new holes in the skin of the bird, but none of us were hit."

"Thanks, doc," Tom said then press the radio mike, "Red Crown, this is Seven-One. We have extensive battle damage, but we can make it to home-base. Negative injuries."

"Great news, Seven-One," Red Crown said. "Well done, Sea Devil rescue. We'll trail along behind the helo's. Drink's at the club on us."

"Thanks Red Crown, break, Seven-Two join on me," Tom said as he blinked the outside lights, on and off.

"Tallyho, right behind you," Bull Walker said and slid into a right echelon formation.

"I'm gonna check on Commander Bob and the troops, Tim," Tom said as he unstrapped and walked back to the cabin. He hugged Bob Wilson and yelled in his ear, "**You're one lucky man, Commander Bob**."

"**Thanks Tom**," Bob yelled. "**This is Quyen Toon**! **She saved my life**!"

Tom looked at Quyen in the dim cabin light. She was beautiful. He was reaching for her hand when Quyen hugged him and kissed his lips. He heard her say, "Thank you for saving Bobby and me."

Tom walked back to the cockpit and strapped into the seat. *Damn, it is good to have Commander Bob back,* he thought. He wondered what General Curtis and the CIA would do with the North Vietnamese woman.

*   *   *

Ensign Arnold landed the H-3 on the VIP Heliport in front of Seventh Air Force Headquarters. General Curtis and Jack Warner walked toward the helicopter as Tim stopped the rotor blades and secured the jet engines. Bob helped Quyen from the helicopter and turned to salute Curtis. "Good evening, General. I'm Lieutenant Commander Bob Wilson and this is Quyen Toon."

"Welcome to Da Nang, Bob," Curtis said as he returned Bob's salute and shook his hand. Then he turned to Quyen Toon and said "Welcome to Da Nang, Miss Toon." He shook her soft hand. *Damn, she is almost as beautiful as Anah Thong,* he thought. Then he introduced Jack Warner to Bob and Quyen.

"Commander Wilson, we have an ambulance waiting to take you and Miss Toon to the hospital for a check up," Curtis said.

"Certainly, sir," Bob said as he took Quyen's hand and walked toward the ambulance. He turned and waved as Tom climbed down from the pilot's seat. "Thanks again Tom, see you later."

Tom watched as Bob escorted Quyen to the waiting ambulance. Then he turned to General Curtis, "Uncle Steve, the Red Crown rescue unit is buying drinks for the Sea Devils. Could Captain Jasper drive us to the club?"

Curtis motioned for Captain Jasper to join them. "John, please take these gentlemen to the Officer's Club." Then he turned to Tom and said, "I'll be over later to buy you a drink."

"Thanks, General," Tom said and turned to his crew. They were busy counting bullet holes in the big helicopter. "Come on guys, this is an all-hands muster."

"Be right there, Commander," Jackman yelled and threw his flight gear inside the helicopter. "Come on, Roy and Dr. Jim, the Red Crown guys are treating us at the club."

General Curtis watched as the helo crew climbed into his staff car. He walked up to the helicopter and looked at the bullet holes. "What award do we recommend for Commander Colby and the Sea Devil crew, Jack?"

"We go for the big one, General," Jack said. "The Medal of Honor for the pilots, and the Navy Cross for Dr. Davenport and the crewmen. If your staff will initiate the paper work, we'll support you, sir."

"Thanks Jack, what're we going to do about Miss Toon?"

"No problem there, General. The agency will take care of it," Jack assured him. He knew that Langley would be delighted with a North Vietnamese refugee who could also speak French and English.

Base Hospital
Da Nang Air Base

Jack Warner and Sharon Quinn conducted the debrief of Bob and Quyen in the Senior Conference Room of the Base Hospital. Both agents were recording the conversation. Jack had a small tape recorder in the inside pocket of his gray suit. Sharon's recorder was inside her purse. They had reviewed the doctor's report prior to the debrief. Both subjects were in excellent health. The female was pregnant.

"That about wraps it up, Bob," Jack said as he closed the notebook. "Do you have any questions?"

"Yes," Bob said and looked at Quyen. "Miss Toon stays with me. She's half-French. Can you get her back to the states for me?"

"Well, it would be helpful if we had a passport," Jack said.

Bob removed Quyen's French passport from the pocket of his blue robe and slid it across the table. "This'll make things a whole lot easier,

Bob," Jack said as he looked at the passport and gave it to Sharon. "We'd like to transfer you to the Navy Balboa Hospital in San Diego. I can arrange for Miss Toon to accompany you to California."

"We're going to get married when we get to San Diego," Bob said.

"Bob, it would simplify things a lot if you two were married here in Vietnam. Then Quyen could accompany you as your dependent," Jack suggested.

"That's a great idea," Bob said, "but I know there must be tons of red tape involved."

"Sharon and I will take care of everything," Jack assured him. "When would you two like to get married?"

"This afternoon in the Base Chapel," Bob said. "Can you arrange that?"

"Certainly," Jack assured him. "I'll take care of the red tape while Sharon takes Quyen to the Base Exchange to shop for a wedding dress. I suggest that you two get out of those hospital clothes and get dressed. We have a wedding to plan." He took Sharon's arm and ushered her to the door.

Base Chapel
Da Nang Air Base

The chapel was packed for the wedding. Ann Curtis had flown to Da Nang on the afternoon courier flight. She stood beside Quyen as matron of honor. Tom stood beside the groom as best man, while Bob and Quyen exchanged wedding vows. The Chaplain said, "I now pronounce you man and wife. You may kiss the bride."

Quyen wore a white, silk dress. Bob and Tom were dressed in their short sleeve, white uniforms with shoulder boards, ribbons and gold wings. Bob lifted the veil from Quyen's face and kissed her lips. Then they turned and walked down the isle toward the front door where Captain Jasper waited with the staff car. Bob laughed when he saw the car. The Sea Devil flight crew had decorated the car with shoe polish, balloons, and long streamers of crepe paper. The couple waved to the crowd then got in the car for the short ride to the Officer's Club for the reception.

"I'm so glad that you rescued Commander Bob and Quyen," Ann said and took Tom's hand. "Now, I have my story. I'm going back to Washington in June and start writing my novel."

"What's your story about, pretty lady?" Tom asked.

"The title of my novel is *Escape From Vietnam*. It may not be a best seller, but it's a book that must be written."

"I understand, Ann," Tom said as they walked toward the parking lot. "The *Concord's* going back to San Diego next month. I'm tired of this ugly war. Uncle Lyndon said I could pick my next assignment. I want to work the Helo Desk in NavAir."

"That's fantastic, Tom," Ann squealed and hugged him tightly. "It's going to be so nice having you as my neighbor."

FIFTY-ONE

The Medal Of Honor

Rose Garden
The White House

Tom Colby sat in the back seat of the Rolls-Royce beside his mother as Samuel Watson turned into the White House driveway. Ensign Tim Arnold sat in front beside Watson. He had listened to Watson's stories about flying the Lear jet during the long ride from the Flying C ranch in Fairfax, Virginia. Tom felt uncomfortable wearing the sash of knighthood. The Knight Order of Chesterfield medal felt awkward around his neck. "Do I have this thing on right, Mother?" he asked. The green sash was a sharp contrast to his white Navy uniform.

"Yes, darling," Margaret said. "I called the English Embassy this morning. The sash goes from right to left across your chest."

"Well, it doesn't feel right to me. I hope none of the Navy brass is there to see this outfit."

"Thomas Edward, you should be ashamed," Margaret scolded. "I'm very proud that you were knighted by the Queen."

"Sorry, Mother," Tom said. "I'll get use to it. What do you think LBJ is gonna say when he sees it?"

"Something appropriate, I assure you," Margaret said.

"You look mighty good, Sir Tom," Watson said. Then he turned and looked at Arnold, "I'm mighty proud of you winning the Navy Cross, Mr. Timmy."

"Dammit to hell, Sam!" Tom yelled. "Tim deserves the Medal of Honor just as much as I do. I tell you, it's a racial thing. I'm very tempted not to accept the medal." Tim's recommendation for the Medal of Honor had been reduced to the Navy Cross. The Navy Cross recommendations for Dr. Davenport, Petty Officer Jackman and Airman Lewis had been lowered to the Silver Star.

"Tom, please don't get upset again," Margaret said as Watson stopped at the gate.

The Marine sentry saluted and said, "Captain Schmidt is waiting for you all at the Rose Garden. Please drive around to the west parking lot."

"Yes, suh. Thank you, suh." Watson said and returned the salute.

"You stop that, Samuel," Margaret said and turned to Tom, "I've told him and told him that he must not salute the Marines on the gate."

"It's no big thing, Mother," Tom said and felt the tension began to ease out of him. "Sam would have made a great Navy officer."

"Why, thank you kindly, Commander Tom," Watson said and smiled at him in the rearview mirror.

"Thanks for having me out at the Flying C, Mrs. Colby," Tim said as he tried to change the subject away from the award ceremony. "I have really enjoyed the ranch very much."

"You must come by and see us anytime you're in Washington, Timmy," Margaret said as Watson pulled into the parking lot.

Captain John Schmidt, USN, waited for the Rolls-Royce. He was dressed in his short sleeve, white uniform with shoulder boards, ribbons and gold wings. He opened the back door for Margaret, saluted and said, "Welcome to the White House, Mrs. Colby." He stared at the green sash around Colby's neck and quickly regained his composure as he returned the salutes of Tom and Tim. Then offering his arm to Margaret, he said, "Please follow us to the Rose Garden, gentlemen." Watson got out of the car, adjusted his chauffeurs cap and followed along behind Tom and Tim. He was sure proud of these two brave Navy pilots.

Tom saw Dr. Davenport, Petty Officer Steve Jackman and Airman Roy Lewis. They stood and saluted as Captain Schmidt led Margaret to

382

the front row of seats. "Afternoon, troops," Tom said and returned their salute. He introduced the Sea Devil aircrew to Margaret and Watson then saw Ann Curtis sitting on the left side of the garden in the reporters section. He beckoned for her.

Ann wore a light green suit with a white blouse. He hugged her tightly and kissed her cheek. "Please sit with us, Ann," Tom said as they all took seats on the front row. The Marine Corps band began to play. It was a beautiful day in the Nation's Capital, and the war seemed so far away.

Everyone stood as the President walked out of the White House and entered the Rose Garden. He walked to the front row and kissed Margaret Colby on the cheek then shook hands with Tom, Tim, Dr. Davenport, Jackman and Lewis. He turned and walked to the podium and asked the group to be seated. He told the group about awarding medals to this aircrew at Tan Son Nhut Air Base the previous March. *Captain Schmidt has done his homework,* Tom thought as the President read his short speech, praising the Sea Devils for rescuing 96 pilots that were shot down by the North Vietnam missiles.

The President ended his speech with an announcement. "Today, we are gathered to honor these Navy men for rescuing the first prisoner of war from Vietnam, Lieutenant Commander Robert Wilson. Captain Schmidt, proceed with the award ceremony."

Schmidt stood and said, "Commander Davenport, Petty Officer Jackman and Airman Lewis, front and center." The crew stood and walked toward the podium. They stood at attention in front of the President while Captain Schmidt read the citation. The President pinned the Silver Star medals to their uniforms.

"Ensign Timothy Arnold, front and center," Schmidt ordered.

Tim stood and walked to the podium. The president pinned the Navy Cross Medal to his uniform while Schmidt read the citation.

Schmidt then turned and said, "Commander Colby, please come forward."

Tom squeezed Ann's hand, then stood and walked to the podium. He smiled at the President as Captain Schmidt read the citation that Lieutenant General Steve Curtis had written in Da Nang. The President held the Congressional Medal of Honor in front of him. He opened the long blue ribbon and slipped it over Tom's head. He whispered in Tom's ear, "This is the big medal, Tom. Keep your nose clean, and you'll make Admiral." Then he stepped back and saluted Tom and shook his hand.

Schmidt spoke into the PA mike, "This concludes the awards ceremony. The recipients and guests are invited into the White House for a reception." The President offered Margaret his arm and walked toward the White House.

A yellow bi-plane buzzed across the Rose Garden at 90 knots and 100 feet of altitude. **NAVY-ONE** was painted on the side of the fuselage in large black letters. Linda Colby sat in the front cockpit beside the pilot. She was not wearing a helmet. Her short red curls and the white silk scarf around her neck blew in the wind. No passengers sat in the rear cockpit. Ensign Michael Colby waved then pulled back on the stick and performed a series of victory rolls as the Jenny gained speed and zoomed out of sight like a commet.

Tom felt goose bumps as Ann clutched his arm. "I saw the yellow airplane, Tom," she whispered. "Is Linda the beautiful red head?"

"Yes darling, that was Mike and Linda," Tom whispered. "I never know when brother Mike's gonna show up. This may be a Heavenly pickup or they just wanted to see the show." He glanced at the spectators and press. No one was looking up at the sky, except he, Ann and Samuel Watson. The old black man watched as Michael performed the victory rolls then he turned and smiled at Tom and Ann. Tom waved at Watson then turned to Ann. "Please join us for a glass of champagne."

"I would be honored, Sir Tom," Ann smiled as she squeezed his hand. "When do you start your new job?"

"Monday morning," Tom said and thought about his new job at the Pentagon. Then remembering the crewmen, he turned and said, "Come on, troops. Let's go drink the President's booze."

"We're behind you all the way, Commander," the Sea Devil crew said as they marched toward the White House.

FROM THE AUTHOR

The Sea Devils were the most decorated Navy squadron in the Vietnam War, acing out the world-famous Topgun Tailhookers. CDR Clyde E. Lassen, USN, was awarded the Congressional Medal of Honor for a heroic night helicopter rescue of two downed F-4 Phantom pilots in 1968 (similar to the rescue of LCDR Bob Wilson in Chapter 49). U. S. Congressman Randy (Duke) Cunningham and his backseater, Willie Driscoll, became the Sea Devils 98th and 99th rescue on May 10, 1972 off the coast of North Vietnam near Haipong. The Sea Devil flight crew wore green flight suits, and for years, Ace Cunningham told everyone that he had been rescued by the United States Marines. After 'Sea-Devil-One' enlightened Duke that the Sea Devil squadron had rescued him, he became a staunch supporter and comes to our reunions.

My first combat SAR missions were with the HS-4 Black Knights on the *USS Yorktown (CVS 10)*. My thanks to Captain Bud Reynolds (CO of HS-4) for the assignment. After HS-4, I was ordered to HC-1 at NAS Imperial Beach, California. Thanks to Captain Bill Quarg, I received a SAR Det on the *USS Hancock (CVA-19)*. This is where I rescued CAG Dick Brown. Two months later, I lost a great friend when CAG Brown lost his second battle with a SAM. It was at HC-1 where Captain Dave McCracken (then a LCDR) started the Combat Aircrew Rescue school. Dave flew the H-2 in combat SAR and later became CO of the Sea Devils. Finally, my thanks to a very special friend, CDR Lloyd Parthemer (first Commanding Officer of the Sea Devils). Lloyd and I had to do things to support our troops in combat that I would not dare put in print.

385

Sea Devil aviators and crewmen are scattered to the four winds. Ensign Bull Walker (my good friend, Bill Terry) rose to the rank of Admiral. The first NavCad - helo type to reach flag rank, but that's another story. . .

Also, a special thank you to my brother, Dr. Will Jowers (USAF type, retired), who also flew numerous combat missions in Vietnam. His steed was the F-105G Wild Weasel jet. His combat experience and air stories are greatly appreciated and used quite liberally in this book.

As we were going to press, I received an email from Sea-Devil-One (CDR Pathermer) that our shipmate, LCDR Michael White (USN retired), had died of a massive heart attack. Several months ago, I was developing the Death Angel character to fly the death plane (the yellow, bi-wing Jenny). Michael's name immediately came to mind. So in this book, Mike fills the role of Ensign Michael Colby, USN (deceased), who flies all over the world, ferrying Naval aviators to their celestial resting place. Mike also made fantastic modifications (Engineering Orders) to the yellow bi-plane. Course, his side number is **NAVY-ONE**. His Jenny can hover like a helo, sprout pontoons for water landings, and quickly accelerate to the speed of light (if necessary to pick up a brother aviator). The jet jocks cannot hope to keep up with Mike, not even the space shuttle. Besides me, very few people have seen **NAVY-ONE**. Fellow Sea Devils, don't become alarmed if you see a yellow, double-wing Jenny fly-over one day or land in your backyard. It's only Mike coming by for a visit or to show-off his victory roll.

We'll miss you, Mike White, at our reunions, but you will always be immoralized in our hearts and my book. Would love to see you anytime, but please postpone my pick up for another 25 to 30 years. I have a lot more books to write.

The Force be with you'all,

Jim Jowers

AUTHOR JIM JOWERS' NOVEL
MAY BE ORDERED
BY MAIL OR TELEPHONE

TO ORDER:

Mailing Address: DRS II ENTERPRISES
6301 Wisteria Drive
Milton, Florida 32570

Telephone: (850) 623-2876

email: drsii@aol.com

Yes, please send the title and number of books indicated below:

Title	Unit Price	Quantity	Subtotal
THE SEA DEVILS*	$12.95		

TOTAL:_____
+ Postage & Handling @ $3.00 each:_____
+ Sales Tax (FL 6.5%) @ $0.85 each:_____
GRAND TOTAL:_____

* - Any <u>squadron mate of HC-7</u> may have this book for a total of $10.00, plus "postage and sales tax (shown above)." Please pass the word that my novel is finally available. They make great gifts (JWJ).

Make checks payable to: <u>DRS II Enterprises</u>

Ship to:
Your Name _____
Address   _____
City _____ State _____ Zip code _____